DEAD MAN'S DEBT

DEAD MAN'S DEBT

Elliott Kay

© Copyright 2016 Elliott Kay

Cover Illustration Copyright 2016 Lee Moyer
Cover Design Copyright 2016 Lee Moyer
Leemoyer.com

All rights reserved.

ISBN: 1530028485
ISBN 13: 9781530028481

To Erica,
who kept me going on all this from start to finish.

Cast of Characters

Archangel
President Gabriel Aguirre
David Kiribati, Minister of Intelligence
Robert Kilpatrick, Minister of Defense
Theresa Cotton, Foreign Minister
Andrea Bennett, Press Secretary
Victor Hickman, President's Chief of Staff
Sofia Rojas, Union Assembly Ambassador
Admiral Meiling Yeoh, Chief of Naval Operations

Ministry of Intelligence:
Agent Vanessa Rios
Agent Ezekiel Jones
Madinah, Captain of the freighter *Muattal* (reserve asset)

On the *SS Argent*:
Casey, Commanding Officer
Paul Santos, Executive Officer
Aaron Hawkins, previous Executive Officer (deceased)
Jidenna Okeke, Chief Engineer
Claudia Renaldo, duty communications specialist
Nicholas Schlensker, duty helmsman

Archangel Navy:
Admiral Meiling Yeoh, Chief of Naval Operations
Cmdr. James Beacham, Chief of Staff to Admiral Yeoh

On the battleship *ANS Beowulf*:
Rear Admiral Todd Branch, Commanding Officer
Lieutenant Commander Trevor Jacobson, Security Officer
Lieutenant Zach Corleissen, Chaplain
Master-at-Arms 1st Class Phil Lewis
Master-at-Arms 2nd Class Jessica "Jesse" Baldwin
Master-at-Arms 2nd Class Tanner Malone
Ensign Perez (Communications Watch Officer)
Signalman 3rd Class Avery Sinclair
Storekeeper 2nd Class Pedro Guzman
Boatswain's Mate 3rd Class Sanjay Bhatia
Corpsman 3rd Class Ed Matuskey
Electrician's Mate 3rd Class Rob Sullivan

Marines of Bravo Company:
Lieutenant Adam Breckenridge (deceased)
Gunnery Sergeant Michelle Janeka
Sergeant Brent Collins
Sergeant Alicia Wong
Corporal Martin Ravenell
Private Gavin Foster
Private Joseph Fitz (deceased)

Temporary Assignment Personnel:
Chief Boatswain's Mate Bill Everett
Boatswain's Mate 3rd Class Abdul Mohammed
Damage Controlman 3rd Class Cassandra Fuller
Survivalman 3rd Class Chris Baljashanpreet

On the corvette *ANS Joan of Arc*:
Lieutenant Lynette Kelly, Commanding Officer
Lieutenant Darrell Booker, Executive Officer
Gunner's Mate 3rd Class Sol Ordoñez
Operations Specialist 3rd Class Renata Montes

Others:
Lt. Miguel Duran, Commanding Officer, Corvette *ANS St. George*
Ensign Nathan Spencer

Union of Humanity:
Assembly Chairman Bindar Dhawan
Assembly Vice-Chairman Terrence Jackson
2nd Lieutenant Madelyn (Allison) Carter, Union Fleet Marines*

NorthStar Corporation:
Anton Brekhov, Chairman and CEO
Maria Pedroso, Vice President of Risk Management
Jon Weir, Chief Administrative Officer
Terry Donaldson, Chief Financial Officer
Maria Pedroso, Vice President of Risk Management
Christina Walters, Vice President of Public Relations
Jeff O'Neal, Chief of Security to the CEO
Commodore Jean Prescott, Commanding Officer, NorthStar Security Fleet
General Carruthers, Commanding Officer, Michael Occupation Forces
Garrett Masters, Risk Management
Lori Smith, Risk Management

Lai Wa Corporation:
Ji Xue, President and Senior Director
Lung Wei, Director of Operations

Kingdom of Hashem:
Prince Murtada
Colonel Husam Basara
Prince Kaseem
Prince Khalil
Halima Al Farran, Union Assembly Ambassador
Usman Mansour

On board the pirate vessel *Vengeance* (defunct):
Casey, captain
Lauren Williams, quartermaster
Wilson, engineer (deceased)
Joey Chang, ship's surgeon (deceased)
Jerry

*Note: Readers from first editions of Poor Man's Fight and Rich Man's War will remember Madelyn Carter as Allison Carter. As part of the re-release of PMF and RMW under the Skyscape imprint, Allison's name was changed to Madelyn to avoid confusion caused by similar-sounding names. No other content or story-based changes were made during the transition.

Prologue: The Deal

> *"Primarily, Archangel faces dangers from alien incursions, interstellar piracy, and historical antagonism with the Kingdom of Hashem. The first is the most remote threat, and any such attack would attract defense support from the entire Union. The latter two threats, then, must be addressed in any plans for a change in our relationship with corporate security providers. Recommendations follow."*
>
> --Defense Intelligence Briefing, January 2271

EIGHT YEARS AGO

"I'd love to go back to my old unit and show my last sergeant how much money I've earned on the outside," Chang muttered. "Right before I stab him to death."

He took a pull from his bottle of whiskey, then handed it off to Lauren. Dust and bright light kept him squinting despite his photoreactive contacts. The pirates stood under *Vengeance's* looming hull, watching the small swarm of activity around the grounded freighter across the dry prairie.

"The recruiters tell you military experience makes you more competitive in the job market. Once it's time to get out, everyone tells you the exact opposite. 'Being a veteran doesn't make you special,' they say. 'Nobody owes you anything. Civilian companies might not respect your skills. Medals don't mean shit on a job application.' And that's all true, of course. As if it should scare you.

"They also tell you that you'll never make enough money on the outside to support yourself," Chang continued. "Never mind how many dumber and lazier people than you manage it. They remind you that the military takes care of your housing and your food and medical and all that bullshit. As if you'll never swing that on your own like everyone else does."

Lauren drank down the last couple of gulps from the bottle, then tossed it aside in the dirt. Her eyes drifted over to her right. "Guess they didn't feed you that shit, huh, Casey?" asked the blonde.

The captain stared off at the other ship, his unshaven face set in a pensive frown and his long black hair billowing in the wind. "Oh, they tried to scare me with all the same bullshit," he said, his voice scratchy as always. "Just weren't trying to keep me. More like they wanted to rub it in."

"Stupid assholes," Chang agreed.

"The fuck's taking so long with this, anyway?" Casey grumbled.

Lauren watched him thoughtfully. "Hey, Casey, I didn't mean to poke," she said. "I'm standin' around drinking in the sun. The booze is talking more than I am."

"Didn't think anything of it." He gave her a small shrug. "Ancient history. Not like I'm ever gonna thank all the fuckers who screwed me, but I'm better off now. And in better company."

Then he looked back at the scarred, captured freighter up ahead. "Still. I'd like to get this wrapped before I grow a beard. This shit is starting to feel like having an actual job again."

Casey strode out from under the destroyer's protective shade, kicking up dust with every step. The walk, like virtually everything else about New Bangkok, wasn't terribly pleasant. Gravity was a touch too heavy for comfort. The ozone terraformers once introduced into the upper atmosphere never set in quite right, leading to scorched plains like this one—and, of course, skyrocketing medical problems and failing agriculture.

One hundred and sixty years after its founding, New Bangkok supported only a handful of settlements along narrow bands of its continents. Anyone who could afford to escape had long since done so. Those that remained lived in a trap of debt created by the Lai Wa Corporation, the very people who had bungled New Bangkok's terraforming in the first place. Lai Wa could fix it, too, if they could be bothered to invest the money.

If not for "failed" worlds such as New Bangkok, *Vengeance* and ships like her would have a much tougher time finding places to port and conduct business. Convenient as the world was for Casey, though, even he couldn't approve of this sort of waste. Lai Wa allowed a viable, habitable world to rot over unpaid bills—an entire God damned *world*. And that same corp refused to sell off its stake and let someone else take over, screwing everyone they left behind.

No one could make Lai Wa sell, or forgive any of that debt, or admit to their screw-ups. Only two other corporations could check Lai Wa's power, but the Big Three rarely stood in one another's way. Why spoil that party when they could all enjoy it together?

One had to wonder when the whole racket might end—if ever.

Casey refused to play along. He didn't matter much at all in the big scheme of things, but he would not bow. He would take. The freighter that now loomed over him and the laser-scarred NorthStar logo on its side attested to that. All he had to do now was sell it off… which usually amounted to the most tedious part of capturing a ship.

"Jerry, how are we doing?" Casey asked as he came upon his tall, balding comrade. The other pirate stood near the freighter's lowered main gangway. Beyond him, men and a few women in grubby but ordinary clothes checked over every bit of *NSF Fair Winds*, captured five weeks earlier by *Vengeance* under Casey's elected command. Any buyer would naturally want the ship looked over. This whole fiasco seemed a bit over the top, though. The buyer brought in two dozen techs to test everything from the magnetics on the landing struts to the tensile strength of the cargo netting.

"I saw one of them pull some fluid out of the gangway hydraulic system a couple minutes ago," Jerry said, and then nodded when Casey blinked. "Yeah. The hydraulics. The old-fashioned shit you use for back-ups in case the main system goes—"

"Aw, for fuck's sake," Casey grumbled. He stomped up the gangway, flicking open a channel on his holocom. "Wilson, you still in engineering?"

"Yes, indeed," came the reply. "They're buttoning things up here. Took an awful lot of the engines apart checking things over, but it's finally wrapping up."

"Thanks." That was at least something. *Fair Winds* flew just fine. Wilson and his snipes had to repair a few things after the freighter's capture, sure, and she was still a little beaten up on the outside, but the ship was sound. The buyer had to know that. At this point, the "inspectors" probably hoped to shave down the price based on wear and tear on the upholstery or how long it'd been since someone defrosted the freezer in the galley. Casey didn't get into this business out a love for spreadsheets and checklists. He wanted to cut his deal and head out.

"Hey! Grease monkey!" he snapped. "Yeah, you, with the socket driver! Where the hell is your boss? We could've been out of here an hour ago!"

"Pardon me, er, Captain Casey?" asked a voice off to his side. Another "inspector" approached, this one with short, dark hair and a goatee over features from Earth's Pacific Islands. He appeared to be pushing middle age, implying he couldn't afford longevity treatments—or that he was quite old. Either way, he must have stumbled pretty hard in life to end up among a black market crew.

Casey knew how that could happen. Much of *Vengeance's* crew had stumbled pretty hard in life, too.

"Mr. Lee is in the captain's office," said the man. "I'd be happy to walk you over."

"I can find it myself," Casey replied. "Ain't like we didn't have the run of this ship for five weeks."

With a deferential nod, the other man said, "Be that as it may, we've been asked to escort all visitors. I'll have to accompany you."

"Oh, so it's Lee's ship now? He makes the rules?" Casey gestured for his guide to lead the way. "Might want to actually pony up before he gets to that point."

"I quite understand, captain."

Casey keyed up his holocom as they walked. Screens blossomed in mid-air to reveal Lauren, Chang, Jerry and a couple of others. "Hey, I'm headin' up to talk to our buyer," he advised. "I'll find out how much longer this is gonna take. Speak up if anyone wants to come along."

"Long as the price doesn't come down, I think we're all good," said Lauren. A general consensus of agreement followed from the others on the channel. "That changes, let us know and we'll join you."

"Right. Talk to you when I know something." Casey killed the screens.

"The captain of the ship doesn't do the negotiating?" the guide wondered. "If Mr. Lee is used to dealing with another representative, should we fetch him?"

"Just a matter of keeping everything honest," Casey answered, surprised that the guy would speak up. Perhaps he wasn't a simple grunt after all. Maybe he was whatever passed for middle management. His skin and clothes weren't as dirty as everyone else's. His diction was better, too. "Tougher to skim off the top when you've got other people watching."

The guide came to a stop at the captain's office, brow high with curiosity. "And yet you will be the only pirate in the room."

"Sure. Tell you what—get Mister Lee to try undercutting my crew by offering me cash on the side." Casey's lip curled back in a partial sneer. "See how well that works out for him."

His guide opened the door and walked inside. Casey doubted this was any sort of ambush, but he took nothing for granted. Looking inside, he found no Mr. Lee, nor anyone else in the cabin. When his guide walked around to the other side of the captain's desk and settled into the comfortable chair with a pleasant smile, Casey understood the implications perfectly.

"Thank you for the warning," said his guide. He gestured welcomingly to one of the seats in front of the desk. "I'll be sure not to include any money with my offer."

Casey glanced over his shoulder into the passageway, both directions, expecting to see bodyguards but finding none. Nobody came out to take his weapons or restrain him. "So is Mister Lee a subordinate?" he asked. "Or did you hire an actor to play him?"

The other man's smile brightened. "He's a senior agent. Doesn't go into the field much anymore, but he was born for this sort of cover. It gives him an opportunity to get out of the office. Now, I'm not here to arrest or assassinate you, Captain. You arranged a terrible tactical situation for such things."

"Yeah, I'm not worried about that," said Casey, still in the doorway.

"Then you must be worried about what I intend to offer. That's understandable. Captain, I admire your honest and egalitarian approach to running your crew, but I think you'll soon understand why I'd prefer we keep this conversation private. If you decline, we'll still purchase the ship as agreed, but that will be the end for us. I know you were happy to find a more forthcoming fence than the Tongs. It's nice to have another competitor in the mix, isn't it?"

"The Tongs aren't the only show in town."

"No, but we both know they're only the best of bad options. Everyone else is either too cheap, too jumpy, too focused on only a few systems, or too easily compromised. But that's neither here nor there. Would you like a seat?"

Frown still in place, Casey entered and sat down. The door closed behind him, but he expected that. "What do I call you?"

"I half expected you to recognize me by now. Then again, I suppose I'm not in the public eye all that often. Normally I wear a suit, too. And it's a big galaxy." He leaned forward on the desk. "My name is David Kiribati. I'm the Intelligence Minister for the system of Archangel, which you'll no doubt verify on your own once this is over. I'm a public official, so it won't be that hard. Naturally, I've already arranged an airtight alibi for myself," he assured his guest. "Tell anyone you want that you met me. I've got all the deniability I need. Still, I would prefer you not discuss this meeting with anyone."

"What do you want?"

"More ships, for starters," Kiribati answered. "I'm happy to keep buying. This is a good arrangement for me. You provide the ships, I'll gladly pay in fuel, munitions, supplies, or cash, as I've done with these last couple of catches."

"Doesn't work like that," Casey shook his head. "I don't call all these shots. We vote on it. We don't focus on any one type of target, and we don't follow anyone's schedule but our own."

"Sure. You've got to look out for you and yours. I won't ask you to give up hitting independent settlements and mining colonies and all that. But I think we both know how influential you're becoming. You're a successful pirate. You're also a damn good captain. I know about your service with the Union Fleet, and how it ended. Nasty business."

Casey's expression grew dark. "How much do you know about that?"

"I know you took on three Krokinthian raiders with one destroyer and came out on top. You lost a good number of people along the way, but you saved a mining colony in that fight—an illegal mining colony. They shouldn't have been out there in Krok territory in the first place. And I know NorthStar made sure you lost your command and your career over the whole incident. They weren't grateful for the lives you saved. They were angry at you for exposing their operation. You embarrassed them.

"All those shipmates dead. All those risks taken. Seven hours playing cat-and-mouse with alien warships, three-to-one odds when even one of them was probably more than a match for most destroyers. That had to be an awful day. I don't care if you're on a ship or in a trench, seven hours is a long fight."

"Been in a lot of fights there, Dave?" Casey sneered.

"Would you believe me if I said I had?"

"Nope."

"Then credit my honesty, at least," Kiribati chuckled. "But back to you. To go through all of that, only to be court martialed and dishonorably discharged on petty charges? They made sure you'd never work a respectable ship again, let alone hold a command. Can't even get a loan or a business license with something like that on your record in most systems. That's enough to turn a good man bad.

"Except you were never exactly a 'good' man, were you, Captain?"

Casey's stony expression held. "What's that word even mean, anyway?"

"Hell if I know," Kiribati admitted, "but the fact that you don't care says something. Regardless, I think we can agree that you did a good thing that day, and nobody cared. Quite the opposite, in fact. And after all that, what's the point, hm? If you can't even get along by playing along, well, fuck the whole system, right?"

"Is telling me all this supposed to intimidate me?" Casey asked. "Should I be surprised that you did your homework?"

"I wanted to establish credibility, Captain. I'm a man with an agenda. You asked what I want from you. I want you to keep doing what you're doing, but I'd like you to do it in certain directions. I'll be happy to continue buying any ships you capture, and certain other forms of loot, at rates competitive with your other potential fences."

"What do we get in exchange?" Casey asked. Kiribati's smile broadened. "What?"

"Oh, just that no one's ever truly 'good' or truly 'bad,' as we were saying," Kiribati explained. "You didn't ask, 'What's in it for *me?*' You asked, 'What do *we* get?' You're a pirate and a murderer and yet you understand loyalty. Those other pirates in your crew—they're your *friends*, aren't they?" Kiribati held up his hands. "Nothing meant by that. Merely another observation.

"In exchange, you get intelligence. Astronavigation protocols for ships worth hitting. Naval patrol route data. Recon reports. We both know how much guesswork goes into piracy and how often you can float around hunting for viable and profitable prey. I can help. I'll make sure to dress it all up so it doesn't look like it's coming from my people. If you follow up on it, great. If not, it's your call, but I'm not inclined to send you into any traps. I need someone like you to work with me for the foreseeable future."

"So you pick the targets?"

"I'll offer suggestions and help. It's up to you to make the most of it."

"Who would we be hitting? And where?"

"Exactly the people you want to hurt, for the most part. Maybe a couple of shoreside raids down the line, depending on how things go. Mostly within or near Archangel space."

"What else?"

"I'll need you to avoid certain targets. Archangel Independent Shipping Guild ships, for one. Nothing too big, either, at least of our own assets."

Casey frowned. "Shipping Guild? What about the rest of your people?"

"Operating near Archangel while completely exempting Archangel as a target would look awfully strange, don't you think? The system should be a lower priority, but I understand that an opportunity may arise now and again. Just don't let it get out of hand."

"And when you've got what you want, we conveniently get caught?" mused Casey. "No, not caught. You wouldn't want me to talk afterwards. We're not gonna survive capture, are we?"

Kiribati's smile faded. "No, Captain. No capture. No assassinations. Sure, the capture of a pirate band like yours would make my organization look good, but that sort of PR gets forgotten all too quickly. I have much more to gain from a long-term alliance.

"If all goes according to plan, I'm going to need you for what comes next. I think you'll want to be a part of it, but that's in the future. Let's take things one step at a time."

CHAPTER ONE

Enemies on all Sides

"We're two years into this mess and nothing has improved. The CDC collapsed six months ago and the entire Union is still suffering from the fallout. NorthStar is still stuck in Archangel. Michael is still occupied. And right next door, Hashem's king and his finest son are dead and the two eldest princes are still tearing the kingdom apart.

"None of the Union's other systems have benefitted from any of this, either. We've got more piracy, more arms traffic, more unemployment, more debt, destabilization everywhere, and we know the Kroks are watching on the borders! Now a lot of people would rather not face up to this, but at some point, someone has to ask: do we even have a Union anymore?"

--MARS GOVERNOR REVEREND HARRY TIDEWATER, FEBRUARY 2279

Colonel Husam Basara longed for the battlefield so much it hurt. He missed the thrill of danger and the rush of triumph over his enemies. He'd been born and raised to lead men in combat, not hide out on a space station in the middle of nowhere. Yet that was exactly where fate had landed him. Fate, and the irritating limitations of modern medicine.

Station 46 wasn't even a military outpost by design. Its builders intended only to study the properties of the world below, but the researchers abandoned it two years ago. No one wanted to be stuck so far from civilized space after the Kingdom of Hashem fell into civil war. Indeed, the only vessel to enter the whole system for a week now lay off the station's starboard annex, illuminated on the command center's status screens.

"Freighter *Muattal*, you are cleared for shuttle launch," announced the bridge watch commander at his desk. Colonel Basara observed mostly out of boredom. The colonel worked to maintain a high standard of discipline, but in the end there was little activity. They simply needed to be present, watchful, and ready.

Command of Station 46 represented Prince Murtada's deepest trust. The site held one of the keys to his final victory. Yet one could stand guard for only so long before monotony set in.

"Acknowledged, control," replied the freighter captain. "Shuttle launch in two minutes."

"Commander," spoke up Colonel Basara, "is Lieutenant Farooq on watch in the shuttle bay?"

"He is, sir."

"Notify him that I am on my way. A casual visit. No inspections. I don't want to startle him on my arrival." Basara headed below decks, wishing for something more exciting than the sight of a tramp freighter's crew unloading plastic crates and barrels from a shuttle.

He would give almost anything for a good battle right about now.

Basara understood the horrors of war, of course. He carried memories of lost friends and comrades, and he knew firsthand the pain of wartime injury. Two years and several corrective procedures after that first day of the Scheherazade campaign, Basara's knee still wasn't quite right.

The medics on the scene had claimed his knee would be fine. The doctors on NorthStar's assault carrier told him after his surgery that it would fully realign within the week. He limped back into the field to find the heaviest fighting already over. Basara turned to quelling any further resistance to Prince Murtada's rule, much as he'd done on Qal'at Khalil after the pirate raid there, but unarmed demonstrators and amateurish insurgents offered little challenge. The limp remained until royal doctors performed even more corrections—invasive ones, requiring cloned tissue and long physical therapy.

So many chances for glory stolen with a single punch to the knee and a fall from his tank.

And then, for the last three months, this. Custodian of a treasure chest far from the front lines. Hand-picked for top-priority ennui. Promotion as a consolation prize.

The shuttle had already settled by the time Basara arrived in the spacious landing bay. Technicians, inspectors, and security personnel worked diligently around the shuttle's crew. The latter did the grunt work of offloading cargo pallets and other containers. Unlike the tan vac suits worn by Basara's people, the shuttle crew wore civilian garb, rugged and dirty and hardly military. Filtration masks covered their mouths and noses.

Frowning curiously, Basara joined the watch officer. He noticed as his stride picked up that his knee hardly bothered him today. That, at least, was a good sign. "Lieutenant Farooq," he said, pulling the man's attention away from the opened cargo container and the enlisted crewman training a chem sniffer on its contents.

"Sir," answered Farooq, offering a salute.

Basara returned the motion. "As you were. Do not let me distract you."

"No distraction, sir," Farooq replied, nodding to his aides. Everyone except the crewman operating the sniffer unit moved off to other duties. "Everything seems to be in order."

"Why the masks?" gestured Basara.

"A ventilation problem on the shuttle, sir. My people have verified it. Their circulation system blew a filter upon launch, but they continued ferrying cargo rather than pausing for repair. The masks are for the stench on the shuttle."

"I see," Basara murmured. Now that he considered it, a stale odor lingered even after the passing shuttle crewman moved on with his cargo. Basara watched disdainfully as the next crewman approached with his anti-grav pallet for inspection. The masked man bowed his head as he pushed his load. "Rough living, apparently."

"Yes, sir. I'm sure they wish their freighter could dock with us directly."

"They may wish all they want," said Basara. "We accept no more than one shuttle at a time. Good station security requires limited access."

"As you say, sir. Come on, over here!" Farooq snapped at the freighter crewman. "We haven't got all day!"

"That's not entirely true, is it?" Basara murmured. "The war is light years away. We've nothing better to do here…"

His voice trailed off as the shuttle crewman came within reach. The filtration mask covered the crewman's jaw, mouth, and nose, but the top half of his head remained perfectly visible. Basara saw short, dark hair, green eyes that tended to look away, deeply tanned skin…and a small, simple golden ball earring on the young man's left earlobe.

He never forgot a face.

"You!" Basara blurted with instant rage. His hand went to the sidearm on his hip. Lieutenant Farooq and his assistant froze in surprise.

The crewman's shoulders sagged. "Aw, Christ," he groaned.

His heavy boot delivered a shockingly fast roundhouse kick to Basara's jaw. A popping sound filled the colonel's ears as he fell to the deck, his weapon clattering away.

The colonel didn't black out, but it was a near thing as he struggled to rise. The pain and disorientation were overwhelming. He saw Farooq draw a pistol. The freighter crewman wrapped his arm around the lieutenant's wrist and pulled him off-balance, turning the fine young officer into a human shield.

Farooq jerked forward. The tip of a knife poked out through his back.

Basara tried to yell out a warning to the rest of his troops, but his mouth refused to form words. He scrambled backwards, taking cover behind the nearest machinery. Born and bred to command men in combat, Basara's broken and dislocated jaw allowed him only to scream in wordless, impotent rage.

His knee, though, worked just fine.

• • •

Tanner jerked his knife free, but didn't release his victim willingly. The station crewman pulled the lieutenant from Tanner's grasp, having dropped the chem sniffer to come to his superior's rescue. The crewman also landed a solid right hook that knocked the filtration mask clean off Tanner's all-too-recognizable face.

Only then did the crewman go for his sidearm, but that left him open. Tanner slashed low with his blade, tearing wickedly across the man's thigh, then came right back up to put a fatal cut through the crewman's neck.

With all three immediate threats down, Tanner saw what he feared: every security trooper and armed crewman in the shuttle bay had their guns drawn. Some focused on the other "shuttle crewmen," forcing them to raise their hands in surrender. Most focused on Tanner, who no longer had any human cover complicating their lines of fire.

Obviously, the only way to salvage this mess was to make a distracting spectacle of himself.

Tanner dove to the right for cover as the shooting began. He almost made it to the open doors of some tall, empty containers before a slug hit him in the side. Though his coat and jumpsuit were all made of the same high-grade protective materials found in combat jackets, the impact still took him off his feet. He spun halfway around before collapsing into the open containers, wondering if the bullet broke any ribs.

The firing ceased, replaced by shouting in Arabic that Tanner was too distracted to translate. A burly security trooper moved in, seizing Tanner's right wrist and twisting hard enough to force the knife from his hand. Tanner threw all his weight backward into the container, pulling the man after him. He delivered a brutal punch with his left hand, then another. The blows helped him pull free, but they didn't get rid of the trooper.

More guards would be behind this one, probably ready to light Tanner up rather than take him prisoner. He punched again, wondering what he could possibly do about that, and then saw the answer on the trooper's belt. Tanner grabbed for the grenade with both hands, twisting the detonator but leaving the weapon on its clip. The move opened him to a couple of hits from his opponent, but he endured those to get the job done. Then he fell back onto his butt, raised both feet and kicked the trooper in the chest as hard as he could.

Two more foes stood ready to catch the trooper as he fell back. Tanner grabbed for the door of the open container to pull it shut behind him, but a rifle butt slamming into his shoulder prevented that. Suddenly two more men loomed over him, hammering Tanner with their rifles. He curled up to protect his head.

One rifle butt came down on his upper back. Another hit his shoulder again. Tanner's clothing mitigated some of the impact, but it still hurt, especially when one of them tagged him in the same spot where he'd taken the bullet.

The grenade detonated only a couple of meters away, instantly killing its bearer, the two men beside him, and Tanner's rifle-wielding attackers.

His first glance through the haze revealed a sudden shift in priorities all around him. Most people dove for cover out of reflex and common sense, not knowing if more grenades were incoming. Tanner saw more enemies behind storage bins and machinery up ahead. Tumbling out of the cargo container, he snatched a rifle from one of the fallen security troopers and turned it on his new targets.

The weapon only offered a plaintive beep of refusal. *Naturally*, he thought. Much like the Archangel Navy, his enemies kept all their weapons keyed to magnetic signatures in their users' gloves. "Shit!" Tanner growled bitterly, throwing away the weapon as he scrambled from his now all-too-exposed position.

That left him running right back toward the shuttle. He heard and saw much more gunfire now, both the loud banging of bullets and the soft but distinct hum of lasers, along with the blaring of the station's alarms. Thankfully, some of the gunfire offered him protection. His violent, stumbling antics provided enough of a distraction for his comrades from the shuttle crew to retrieve their guns from the cargo crates.

Not all the bodies lying around the shuttle were Hashemite personnel. His side of the fight had already suffered some casualties.

From behind one of the cargo containers, his team leader—a big, burly man with dark stubble on his head and chin—blasted away with a laser carbine. "God *damn* it, Malone," snarled Ezekiel, "I knew it was a mistake to bring you!"

"Yeah? So did I!" Tanner snapped back, hiding behind the container beside the other man. "What did I say? What was the first thing I said? I said, 'Hi, I'm Tanner Malone and this is a terrible fucking idea!'"

"You couldn't even keep it together for two minutes?"

Tanner searched frantically for one of the secret latches on the container. "That guy recognized me with only half my face showing. What else did you want me to do?" He found the right spot: a panel popped open to reveal a handgun sealed inside large foil packet full of sniffer-defeating goo. Naturally, tearing open the packet turned out to be embarrassingly difficult.

"You might have drawn less attention to yourself if you hadn't kept ducking your head like you were trying to hide something. All that bullshit with the masks was just to cover for *your* stupid ass being here. You could've at least tried to sell it!"

By the time Ezekiel finished shouting, Tanner had his slime-covered weapon free and clear. He popped up over the top of the crate to join in the shooting.

He found fewer targets than he'd feared. Fighting still raged, but Ezekiel's team had done plenty of damage. Their foes didn't look all that well-coordinated, either, though by now Tanner had forgotten the role he had played in ensuring that.

Movement drew Tanner's attention to his left, past the nose of their shuttle and the one open landing spot beside it. The large bay doors were opening, with more security troopers already flooding inside.

"Aw, shit," Tanner blurted, turning his weapon on the new arrivals. "Flankers!" He fired off a sustained burst in the hopes of suppressing them. "We've got flankers on the left!" He tagged one trooper, sending others diving to the deck or scrambling for the nearest cover.

Noise and tension built around him, along with a sudden, large rush of motion in his peripheral vision as their shuttle lifted a single meter into the air. The grey craft lurched backward and turned, pivoting at the point of its nose so that the rest of its body could sweep around in an arc.

Bodies and boxes flew as the shuttle knocked aside everything in its path. Few of the enemy had time to cry out. Then the shuttle's magnetic landing struts slammed down onto the deck once more. Tanner cringed as the craft's afterburners fired. Even the lowest test level of power spat out enough flame and heat to incinerate anyone on the other side of the open bay doors.

The afterburners cut out as suddenly as they had activated. As if following a conductor's lead, the guns all seemed to fall silent with the shuttle. Tanner dared to stand upright. He saw no more weapons aimed at him or his allies. A trickle of broken pipes and overhead panels clattered to the deck, but otherwise the whole bay seemed shocked into silence.

The shuttle's odd twist had brought the cockpit around to face Tanner directly. Through the canopy, Tanner saw Boatswain's Mate 3rd Class Sanjay Bhatia stand up in his seat at the helm, point right at him, and then twirl his finger at his ear in the universal hand signal for insanity.

"*Me?*" Tanner pointed at the wreckage left by the shuttle's thrusters.

Movement in the corner of his eye drew his attention and his aim away from Sanjay once more. He found a pair of unarmed techs dragging a third man to the nearest exit. Tanner recognized the injured one as the officer he'd kicked at the start of the fight. He lowered his gun.

"What the hell are you doing?" Ezekiel growled, bringing up his carbine.

Tanner grabbed the weapon's barrel and shoved Ezekiel. "What the hell are *you* doing?"

Ezekiel threw an elbow in retaliation, tagging Tanner in the face and sending him stumbling back. Out of reflex if nothing else, Tanner spun around and delivered a kick to Ezekiel's hip, once again preventing the team leader from firing.

"Woah, stop! What's going on?" demanded several masked teammates, jumping between the two as the three Hashemites escaped through a hatch.

"That's a good question!" Ezekiel roared.

"You know the Rules of Engagement," Tanner fired back. "Which one of those guys looked like a legitimate target to you? The two unarmed janitors, or the one who couldn't even walk?"

"This is a covert op! You're not here to play master-at-arms!"

Tanner shook his head. "Guess everyone should've thought of that before they put me on the team, huh?" he asked. Then he waited. "Is this where we have our staredown now? 'Cause I don't care which one of us wins that. You step off the ROE and the Hashemites won't be your biggest problem."

Ezekiel looked ready to tear Tanner in half. He was older, larger, and at least as dangerous as anyone Tanner had ever tangled with. Moreover, Tanner was far out of his element. Other than Sanjay and a couple personnel loaned out by the navy for this op, everyone here was a veteran agent of the Ministry of Intelligence.

Still, Tanner refused to back down. He wasn't allowed. This was the job he'd signed up for.

"'Mission critical' my ass," Ezekiel fumed, turning away. "Alpha team, on me. We head to Deck Seven right now. Malone, you stay at the back and try to remember whose side you're on. Bravo, you and the shuttle boys secure this space and straighten the boat out so we can jet out of here right away. Move!"

Tanner glanced over his shoulder toward the shuttle. He saw Sanjay still there behind the canopy. Once again, the tall, young bo'sun gave him the "loco" hand motion.

• • •

Ezekiel and the other agents stacked up on either side of the heavy, sealed doors. Tanner stuck to the back of the group as ordered.

With everyone in place, Ezekiel gave a nod. An agent at the control panel tapped in a specific entry code. Nothing happened at first. "You'd better be in there," muttered Ezekiel. "Or this whole job is already a failure."

A couple more heartbeats passed before the doors snapped open. No gunfire erupted as the team moved in. Tanner heard people call out the all-clear before he came around the corner.

He found a set-up not all that different from the brigs on *Beowulf* or *Los Angeles*, though it didn't look like part of the station's original construction. A research facility like this wouldn't need sealed jail cells with opaque metal doors. Most research stations wouldn't have dead security troopers lying in one corner, either. Two nervous station technicians sat behind the main control desk, alongside a familiar face. Her presence instantly explained the dead guards.

She smiled brightly as Tanner entered, casually bracing the butt of her pulse rifle against her hip. Scavenged bits of body armor accessorized the same khaki jumpsuit worn by the technicians. Her long, black hair was pulled back in a ponytail, keeping it all out of her lovely, golden face.

"Tanner, hi!" Agent Vanessa Rios beamed as Tanner groaned.

"Oh, you gotta be kidding me."

She looked at him with big, innocent doe eyes. He might have fallen for them if he didn't know her better. "Aw, c'mon," she said, "I was looking forward to seeing you! I went to all this trouble!"

"Are you why I'm here?"

"Vanessa," grumbled Ezekiel.

"Yes, indeed," she answered Tanner, though her smile faded as she glanced at Ezekiel. "I'm on it. Relax. Gentlemen," she said to the technicians beside her, "this is Ezekiel, and this is Tanner. I don't know the others. Ezekiel, Tanner, this is Sergeant Ghalib, and this is Technical Specialist Hilel. They are men of good conscience who made all this possible. You can imagine the risks they've taken. They're coming with us."

"Understood," Ezekiel replied. He gestured to one of the women on his team. "Kimiko, you're with them. Get 'em armored up as best you can with whatever we can scrounge here. Vanessa, where's the primary?"

"In the back. I'll take Tanner. We can unlock the other cells from here."

"Then let's get on it, people."

Tanner followed Vanessa back around one corner of the compartment. Behind them, Ezekiel and the rest of the team set to opening up the cell doors. "You mind telling me what's going on?" Tanner asked. "Nobody would explain who we're here to pick up."

Vanessa threw an amused smirk over her shoulder as she walked. "Zeke gave you the 'need to know' bit, huh? I knew he would. Such a jackass. Hey, is Sanjay here?"

"Yeah." Tanner blinked. "You asked to have him on the mission, too?"

"Sure. I knew who'd they'd put in charge of this op. Figured you should have someone solid at your back. Also, I like Sanjay. Thought it'd be good to say hi."

"Vanessa—"

"You're here for a specific purpose. Yes, I'm the one who said you were needed. For a few reasons. Partly, I wanted to talk. But mostly it's for the primary objective."

"What objective?" Tanner pressed. "What the hell's going on?"

"It's right around this way. So, like I said, how've you been? I haven't read your mail in months."

That stopped Tanner in his tracks. "You read my mail?"

"Not regularly, no. But I know the guy who does. Are you still dead set on getting out of the navy when your enlistment is up?"

"Are you—is this really the time for small talk?"

Smiling proudly as if Tanner had overcome algebra for the first time, Vanessa said, "Yes. Yes, it is. How often do we get the chance? Everyone else in the world engages in small talk at their jobs, and this is who we are. You should get used to this. Are your parents still doing okay on Arcadia?"

"This is not who I am!" snapped Tanner. "This is what I do because I'm *stuck* with it! This is five years of my life, or until this stupid war is over—whichever happens *last*," he added sourly, "and then I'm gone. I'm *out*. No second term. No more uniforms, no more guns, no more hoping to God I can murder the other guy before he kills me first!"

Vanessa listened patiently. He realized then that he was shouting and dialed back his anger. "Yes," he said, "I want out. I'm gonna do my time and go to college and move on and be like all the other normal people out there."

"I can't argue about the uniforms," she conceded, "but I don't buy the rest of it. You're not normal people, Tanner. Normal people get caught up in events and try to ride them out. You see what's going wrong and you step up to fix it."

"Yeah, because I've been conditioned for that," he retorted. "And because I'm stuck with that as my job."

"Doesn't matter. You can go become a survey specialist or a laboratory scientist and you'll still see crises and chaos and fucked up situations all your life. You'll have to step in and fix things because you *know* that *you can*. And don't try to tell me I'm wrong, because it takes one to know one.

"This is who you are now," she said, poking his chest. "Learn to live with it. And learn to be happy with it, too. Humanity's a mess. Always has been, always will be, whether your home planet is free or not. Doesn't mean you have no right to be happy."

His mouth tried to form words and failed. Eventually: "You couldn't write me a letter?"

"Sure, and I could've gotten reprimanded for revealing that your mail gets watched by the Ministry. Here, we have nothing recording us. Besides, I needed you for this other thing. So…?" she prompted.

Tanner let out a sigh. "My parents are fine," he said. "Sharon almost got run out of her job because of her 'politically-charged' comments about the war in her classroom, but the school administration backed down. They're okay."

"Good." Vanessa smiled. "Dating anyone yet?"

"No. I wish."

"See? Is small talk that hard? You can do this."

"Okay, fine. Small talk." Tanner glanced over his shoulder to make sure no one was coming to join them. "Aaron Hawkins. Did you know him?"

"Aaron—? Oh. No." She frowned. "The Ministry of Intelligence is a big group, Tanner. We don't all know each other." To her credit, she only barely hesitated. MA school taught quite a bit about body language and other signs of lying. Vanessa did not blink, did not repeat the question to give herself time to think or any number of other tells Tanner learned about. Her attempt to put the question into context seemed legit.

Then again, she had much more experience than he did. He took for granted that she was a better liar than he was an interviewer.

"See, I figured you both had Ministry assignments on starships," Tanner explained. "And unless all the public info on how the Ministry is organized is a big façade, you're in the same category and likely had a lot of the same training, and—"

"—and I'm covert while he was public?"

"Posthumously," Tanner pointed out. "After *Argent* made such a splash at Raphael, they had to give something to the media. By then Hawkins was dead. He had ten years as a navy officer and no command experience before joining the Ministry. There's no way in hell he was the captain of a ship that large. They cooked that up for the media, didn't they?"

"You'd know more about hero narratives than I would."

"Was she really scrapped after the battle like they say?"

The agent shrugged. "I wouldn't know. Not my department. Why are you asking me this? That fight was almost two years ago." She tilted her head then as a memory seemed to click into place. "Are you still on about *Argent* almost killing us on Scheherazade?"

"Only if I can prove a motive," Tanner replied gravely.

Vanessa made a face, but stepped in closer. "Hawkins was one of Kiribati's loyalists," she hissed. "Like Ezekiel out there. I'm not in that club. I'm busy with this whole war going on. What's on your mind?"

"Vanessa," came a voice from back down the hallway. "How are we doing?"

"Almost good to go," she called in response.

"No time to explain now," Tanner said, jerking his thumb over his shoulder toward Ezekiel's voice. "Curiosity, mostly."

"Uh-huh. Well, if something's up, let me know. Quietly."

Getting back to business, Vanessa turned to one of the all-metal cell doors to input a couple of codes. "Our primary here got captured by Murtada's people a couple months ago. And by Murtada's people, I mean Murtada's and not NorthStar's, or he wouldn't be here. I wanted him to see someone he could trust. You're the closest thing I could come up with. You've never met," she added, "but he wrote you a couple letters once."

The cell door beeped and slid upward. Vanessa stepped aside.

No furniture graced the small compartment other than a simple toilet, sink and a flat slab attached to one wall as a bed. The prisoner lay huddled in the cold cell, long unshaven and unwashed. His torn slacks and dress shirt bore old blood stains. He neither moved nor spoke as they entered, but his eyes tracked them.

Tanner moved closer, studying a man repeatedly confirmed by multiple sources to have been killed two months ago. "Prince Khalil," Tanner breathed.

The prisoner blinked. "*Meen*," he croaked out. "*Hadah meen?*"

Though he'd tried to brush up during the trip here, Tanner's Arabic came up short. He opted for English: "I'm Tanner Malone, Your Highness."

The name meant nothing to the prisoner at first—and then it did. His head tilted. His shoulders rose as he struggled to sit up on the bed.

"Sir, this is Agent Rios. She fought with me on Scheherazade. She got me here. You can trust her, and you can trust me. We're here to get you out. You and all the other prisoners."

Though his hand shook, it found Tanner's. His eyes held Tanner's with a strength that didn't match his malnourished and beaten body. His grip grew stronger with another breath, and then Prince Khalil said, "They tell me my brother, Murtada has won, and that I must acknowledge him to end the war."

Tanner shook his head. "No, sir. We've both still got wars to win."

Footsteps outside the cell drew their attention. Tanner looked over his shoulder to see Ezekiel, gun in hand and a stern expression on his face. "Station security is getting itself together again," he warned. "We have to move."

"I think we're about ready to go," Vanessa answered, glancing back to the prince.

"Your Highness?" Ezekiel asked.

Khalil looked to Tanner. "This is Ezekiel," he explained. "He's the leader of the mission."

The prince gave Ezekiel a nod. "Thank you. I am weak, but I can move. How many others are with us?"

"We've recovered eight other prisoners, sir."

Khalil winced. "Only eight? We are not leaving anyone behind?"

"I can't verify any other survivors of the group Murtada captured," answered Vanessa. "I'm sorry, but the rest either didn't make it or they aren't here."

"Then I am ready to go. With help."

"I've got this," said Tanner, moving in to take one of Khalil's arms over his shoulder.

Khalil waited until Ezekiel disappeared once more. "I can't help but notice what you did not say about your leader."

"I'm sorry?"

"You said that I could trust Agent Rios."

"You can trust Ezekiel to get you out of here safely," explained Tanner. "I can't imagine any reason he would hurt you or your people."

"But…?"

Tanner caught sight of the grin on Vanessa's face before she slipped out of the cell. "I don't pretend to know his priorities."

• • •

Tanner all but carried Khalil to the shuttle, and later to sick bay on the freighter. He stuck by the prince's side while the doctor examined him. The prince demanded to he see his fellow prisoners before anything else. With every new face, the prince looked warily to Tanner for cues.

That look floored the younger man. Khalil was a *prince*. He'd governed worlds and led armies. Tanner dreaded even having to manage a handful of non-rates on a cleaning detail or a watch section. Khalil's eyes spoke as much to his suffering as his strength.

Tanner introduced Sanjay as someone Khalil could trust. Beyond that, he chose his words carefully.

"I have some questions for you, Your Highness," put in Ezekiel as he stood at the foot of the bed. "The sooner, the better."

"He needs rest," repeated the doctor.

"We'll be in FTL for over a week," Tanner pointed out. "There's nothing you can do with any of the prince's intel before we get back to Archangel."

"I would not be of much use to you now, anyway, Agent," agreed Khalil. "I am sorry."

Ezekiel nodded. "Fair enough, Your Highness. My apologies. Malone, we should speak outside."

Tanner looked to Khalil. "I am sure I will be fine now," said the prince.

Vanessa followed the men outside to Ezekiel's obvious annoyance, but he said nothing to her. "Malone, did someone put you in charge when I wasn't looking?" Ezekiel asked.

"I'm not sure what you mean," Tanner replied. "I'm here to look out for him, right? The doctor said he needs rest."

"You're here to back up your superiors, too, or didn't they teach you anything about the chain of command in basic?"

"Well, you're free to write up a bad performance eval—oh, wait, except you can't document any of this with the navy, can you? Covert op and all. Gosh. Not sure what to tell you. Hey, you don't think this will mess up my chances at getting promoted, do you?"

Ezekiel glared, lingering briefly to give Vanessa a similarly dirty look before stalking down the passageway.

Tanner felt Vanessa's hand on his shoulder. "You know you're only proving my earlier points, right?"

"I don't know what you're talking about," said Tanner, though not angrily. "I'm just another good little soldier. Shut up and keep my head down and all that. This is above my pay grade."

"Bullshit. You can operate on any level you choose. Sooner or later, even you have to accept that."

"Says you."

"Like I said, it takes one to know one." With that, Vanessa slipped away.

Looking through the sick bay window, Tanner saw Khalil sleeping as the doctor entered notes on his holocom. Nothing more needed doing here now.

Tanner wandered to the galley. He'd already missed the evening meal thanks to the last few hours sitting in sick bay, but the freighter's cooks allowed for a small degree of self-service.

Alone in front of a heating unit, waiting for a simple box of dinner to warm up, Tanner had plenty of space to think. Vanessa's advice rolled around in his head. He wasn't sure what to make of it.

The clunking sound of the old-fashioned coffee maker nearby drew his attention. "Evening, Captain Madinah," Tanner said.

The bearded man smiled. He seemed at once hard-bitten and gentle. Tanner suspected Madinah had seen enough rough times that he no longer had anything to prove to anyone. "You know," said the captain, "I've forgotten whatever false name I am supposed to call you."

Tanner shrugged. "I'm told I shouldn't speak to you at all. Or the crew."

The captain nodded. "It is the way of these things." He glanced over his shoulder. "One might almost forget what it means to be the captain of one's own ship. Almost."

"You don't strike me as the type to forget, sir."

"I am not." He pulled his cup from the machine. "You came back with casualties, but things seemed to go well, otherwise."

"Yes, sir. We did a good thing today."

"I am aware. It is why I agree to do these things in the first place. They pay me, of course, but only a fool puts his life on the line merely for money. A fool, or a criminal. I believe you have dealt with more than your share of the latter." He watched Tanner thoughtfully. "You have done good things, too, Mr. Malone. It may seem like long ago, given all that has happened since then. I remember what it was like to be your age. But I think you will find a great many people in my business who will not forget *Yaomo*, or *Vengeance*. Or the one who brought them low. NorthStar's propaganda machine may try to make you out to be a vicious killer, but it is hard to cast those deeds as crimes."

"Thank you, sir," Tanner said, feeling humbled.

The captain reached out. "I am honored to have you aboard."

Shaking the captain's strong hand, Tanner found himself glancing around the galley. As before, the two men were still alone. "Sir," he ventured, "do you have a minute?"

"Things seem quiet. I believe I can spare a few."

Tanner hesitated. He wondered if he might not be going too far already.

He wondered if he might prove Vanessa right, or if that would even be a bad thing.

"This ship was at the Battle of Raphael, correct?"

"Yes. Under a different registry and identification, of course. We are not an Archangel vessel, legally speaking. But we were there. All part of our peculiar line of work."

In truth, Tanner had another ship in mind entirely, but he asked, "Can you tell me how a civilian freighter captain comes into this peculiar line of work?"

CHAPTER TWO

The Status Quo

"Intelligence estimates that NorthStar forces control only Michael's five largest cities, with light forces distributed among other key areas. Despite Michael's relatively light population, the planet is too large for NorthStar to establish a widespread occupation given their commitments in Hashem and elsewhere. As has generally been the case in interstellar warfare, control is maintained through the occupation of major population centers backed up by the threat of orbital bombardment.

"However, NorthStar's control of the planet remains oppressive. Trade and communications are either closely monitored or cut off entirely. Peaceful protests are often violently crushed. NorthStar's occupation forces are entrenched and formidable."

--ARCHANGEL NAVAL INTELLIGENCE REPORT, MARCH, 2279

"Pull out! Pull out, people, we gotta go! They're blowing the base! Move!"
Tanner barely noticed the order. Baffles in his helmet selectively filtered through the din of combat in the small hallway, but noise wasn't his

problem. Matters at hand demanded his full attention. Crouched at the corner behind a fallen gear locker and firing away with his laser rifle at the opposition—which seemed endless—Tanner didn't track Lt. Breckenridge's voice as well as he should. The faceplate eye lenses created a sense of tunnel vision, too, even if the specs and manuals assured no obstruction of vision.

NorthStar troopers in full combat gear pushed up from the other end of the hallway. They moved in without panic or recklessness, leapfrogging from shelf to storage bin to open doorway and covering one another all the while. Tanner was out of grenades, low on ammo and holding the corner all by himself. At this point, his rifle ran on power cells stripped from Private Fitz, dead beside him.

Fitz was from Uriel, only two months out of basic. This was his first combat mission. Tanner tried to look out for him and in turn, Fitz stuck to Tanner. Now Fitz lay dead. Focused though he was on shooting, part of Tanner still wondered if Fitz would've been better off without his help.

Then again, an awful lot of others on this mission were already dead, too.

He felt a hand on his shoulder and heard a gun going off just over his head. "Malone, we're out!" shouted Breckenridge. "Let's go! They're blowing the base!"

Tanner looked back and saw everyone else clearing out of the control room. Baldwin kept hold of the handcuffed watch officer, shoving and dragging him along despite her smaller size. The rest of the team, most of them marines, either hustled out with her or lay dead. Numerous other NorthStar techs and troopers lay there, too, but some of them were only stunned.

Breckenridge's team had intended to take more prisoners. They hadn't expected all the techs and officers to be armed. Even that was a small problem compared to everything else that had gone wrong.

"The sappers got through to the dock?" Tanner asked, turning back to pop off a few shots. They'd need to keep their pursuers back if they hoped to get out of here. Tanner didn't plan on staying more than a few seconds to give the team a head start against any pursuit.

"No! Roland is bombarding!"

"What?" Tanner burst. He looked up at his superior, but the lieutenant's faceplate hid his expression. The younger man realized any protests were pointless. It wasn't as if his arguments would change the situation.

Tanner pushed himself away from his bit of cover. He glanced over his shoulder and saw Fitz looking back at him, no faceplate, not even a helmet, mumbling a single plea: "Don't leave me."

It carried through the gunfire. It carried through the passageways. As Tanner and the lieutenant made a hasty push through the emergency pressurization control doors at the end of the corridor, Tanner looked down and saw Fitz laying right there amid the debris, begging for help with wide blue eyes.

Except Fitz had died with his helmet on back in the other room.

"What the hell was the point to all this?" demanded Tanner as he and Breckenridge ran through a soundless hallway. Tanner heard only his own breath and the warnings in his helmet earpiece now. They had to haul ass. "If they were gonna bombard the site, why are we even here?"

"I don't know!" Breckenridge answered. "Something changed, or maybe they just gave up. I don't know!"

Up ahead they found Baldwin, her captive, and the handful of remaining marines collected in the command center's battered, airless lobby. Through the windows, most of them shot out already, Tanner could see other buildings and the flashes of other firefights and the grey moonscape beyond.

Fitz lay here, too. Still without a helmet. Still pleading. Still ignored.

"Move out!" ordered Breckenridge. "Western pick-up site! Go!"

The team hustled on his order. Tanner took up the rear with Breckenridge to provide covering fire. The sky held no atmosphere, revealing nothing but stars and void. Somewhere up there, far out of sight, one of Archangel's two battleships and her escorts waited to blast the moon with missiles and laser cannons.

Far out to the left, Tanner saw a team of Beowulf's marines crossing an open lane in much the same fighting withdrawal as his own team. Somewhere among them were Alicia and Ravenell, Tanner hoped, but he couldn't leave his team to check on them. Not with a voice in his headset warning of moments left to get clear. Not with landing shuttles waiting exposed for pick-up.

Breckenridge cried out on Tanner's right. The lieutenant stumbled and fell to the prefab street, blood flowing from a hole in his back just over the hip. Tanner dropped his rifle to seize Breckenridge by the collar of his combat jacket. He hauled the lieutenant to shelter at one of the sturdy, shoulder-high gravitic field projectors that made life on a moon more practical. Seconds dwindled to plug both the hole through Breckenridge and the two holes in the man's vac suit.

The suture cartridges on his belt fixed the first problem. Drawing one marker-sized tool in each hand, Tanner jabbed both the entry and exit holes through Breckenridge's flesh. Quick-sealing antiseptic gel covered the wounds. Breckenridge cried out louder; the instruments weren't gentle. Tanner could spare no time for the officer's pain, focused instead on slapping electrostatic tape pads over the vac suit punctures.

Laser blasts and bullets flew past, making no sound. The silence made it easier to ignore combat until he finished his first aid. His chosen cover would hold up for a few seconds, at least. Grav field projectors required dense, heavy machinery. What Tanner didn't expect was help in hoisting Breckenridge up to his feet.

"C'mon, let's go," Baldwin growled, getting one of the lieutenant's arms over her shoulders and heaving along with Tanner.

"The prisoner," Breckenridge groaned, trying to keep up, though in truth Tanner and Baldwin practically carried him.

"Already handled! Move!" she demanded.

They made it another ten steps, fifteen at most before Breckenridge jerked out of their grasp and Baldwin screamed and fell. Their collapse pulled Tanner to the ground, too. Lasers continued flashing overhead from behind them. Picking himself up, Tanner saw large, fatal holes up and down Breckenridge's back. Baldwin clutched her bloody left forearm. "Tape! I need tape!"

"Keep your hand on it!" Tanner urged. He ducked low, then rose up with Baldwin hanging over his shoulders, running without grace and nearly without balance. For all he knew, the awkward burden saved him. He couldn't move in a remotely straight line, but that probably made him and Baldwin harder to shoot.

He didn't have far to go. They were already on the outskirts of Port Astonaco. In a few dozen meters, the grav field would wane and running would get easier. He would worry about the problem of flying exposed through the air in long, vulnerable bounds when it happened. Better to get clear first.

They'd come to wreck the dockyards, gather intelligence and prisoners, and hopefully free some of the dockworkers and engineers. NorthStar had held the moon port as long as they'd occupied Michael, which loomed brightly over the southern horizon. The navy couldn't bombard the site, according to all the briefings, because of the risk—the inevitability, really—of killing Archangel citizens. No one was even so crass as to use a term like "collateral damage." The Archangel Navy was more honest than that.

Apparently that calculus had changed over the course of the raid. No one explained it over the comm net. Maybe someone panicked because of the high casualties, or the unexpected level of resistance, or some factor outside Tanner's grunt-level view. He'd been focused on raiding the control center for intel and captives with his team. The dockyards, the defense grid cannons, the fuel cell facilities, and the hangars were all for other teams.

So far, he hadn't seen any of the big explosions they'd expected from the sappers. Many of the defense cannons still fired energy blasts and missiles up into the stars.

Then the ground shook, knocking Tanner and Baldwin down again. An orange ball of fire erupted from Port Astonaco's dockyard. No more bullets or lasers came from the pursuers. Gravity evaporated as more of the port came under fire and the field generators lost power. NorthStar's troopers now sought shelter from the wrath raining down from Roland *and other ships too far above to see.*

Archangel's remaining raiders also needed shelter, but the landing shuttles seemed far away. Another terrifying explosion lit up the endless night. The ground heaved, sending Tanner and Baldwin sailing for long meters through weak gravity.

Tanner heard a man's clear, calm voice announce something about coming out of FTL; then he landed on his side against a bulkhead.

The lights in the corvette's galley shone only in a dim red hue to allow *St. George's* passengers—too many for her crew berths—a chance to sleep. Tanner awoke on a cot, not the rocky surface of a moon. His helmet sat within easy reach as always, not on his head. He wore no combat jacket, either. Only his regulation vac suit, loosened up a bit for sleeping.

The disastrous raid on Michael's moon lay months behind him. Even the last-ditch bombardment had failed in its goals. NorthStar still held Port Astonaco.

"Repeat," said the ship's skipper over the PA, "all hands, secure for FTL transition."

"Bad dreams?" asked the man sitting on the cot beside his.

Tanner grunted. "Yeah, pretty bad."

"I get them, too, now," admitted a weary Prince Khalil. "I didn't have them in the cell. Now that I am out…" He held up his hands to show his lack of tools to fix the problem. "As bad as the pirates were as captors, they only wanted money. Harming me did them no good. They were not merciful, but…their abuse was casual, not driven by purpose."

Though Khalil had over twenty years on Tanner, his longevity treatments should have kept his body looking at about the same age. The stresses of the last couple of years had worn him noticeably beyond that. For all Tanner's rough times, he knew his woes paled in comparison to Khalil's experiences.

The prince seemed inclined to address Tanner and the others as equals. He offered respect without distance or formality. Several of his aides, freed along with him from Station 46, shared the improvised sleeping space. Khalil had insisted that he be allowed to sleep there with them, leaving the more comfortable sleeping spaces for older or more infirm aides. All were awake now, given the announcement, slowly clearing the sleep from their eyes and rising.

"I've been in and out of therapy since my first real fight," Tanner said, rubbing his face.

"Has it helped?"

"Yeah." He grinned a little. "It's why I keep going back."

"Then why do you ever stop?"

"Because I think I'm done. And maybe I am. Only then some other stupid thing happens. I dunno. I'm getting better at all of this, but…" He looked around at the others. Most seemed like they were trying to politely ignore the conversation. Perhaps some actually managed it. "Sometimes you can put the bandage on yourself. Sometimes you need a doctor. Why should we treat the mental stuff like it's different?"

"I believe the English phrase is 'preaching to the choir,'" said the prince. "My father held outdated views on such matters."

"Your father doesn't have to live your life," Tanner replied a little too quickly, but immediately realized his transgression. He felt the glares from Khalil's companions even if he didn't see them, though the prince seemed neither shocked nor offended. "I'm sorry, Your Highness. I didn't mean—"

"I understand. My father was never a friend to your people. If he could see me here now…well. He might recognize your compassion, but he would also see Archangel's self-interest."

"I've been told that without the civil war, Hashem would probably have taken NorthStar's side when Archangel broke away."

Khalil nodded. "Undoubtedly. Even kings owe debts. NorthStar would surely have bid my father take action. Maybe political. Maybe military. Maybe both. Given a chance to satisfy debts by harming another state, one with whom he shared a rocky past? Yes, he would have done that." The weary prince looked away. "My father wanted me to be king. My mother as well. Enough to defy tradition to make it happen. Both of my brothers knew it."

"None of them ever asked what you wanted, did they?"

"No. I accept it as necessary for the good of my people, given the alternatives, but no." His eyes met Tanner's again. "Do you follow the path of your parents? Were they soldiers?"

"My mother served in the Union fleet," said Tanner. "She was an engineer. Damage Controlman 2nd Class Guadalupe Chavez. She met my father after she got out."

"Did she want you to serve?"

"No," Tanner huffed. "God, no. I asked, when I was a kid. A couple of times before she died. I asked if she wanted me to enlist. Asked if that would make her proud."

"What did she say?"

"The same thing my father said. They didn't want me to become one thing or another. They only wanted me to be happy."

"Then I believe, Mr. Malone, that you should obey your parents."

"All hands, all hands," broke in a calm, steady voice over the PA, "FTL transition in five minutes."

"Hey, Tanner," Sanjay beckoned from the other side of the galley. "Captain says we can go up on the bridge if we want."

Tanner nodded. "I should head up, Your Highness."

"Of course."

Tanner picked his way through the maze of cots and tables filling the corvette's small galley, grateful for space to walk freely once he joined Sanjay at the ladder well. Behind him, one of *St. George's* bo'suns stepped in to help their passengers secure the compartment for the possibility of trouble. No ship entering Archangel could count on safe passage these days, hence the transfer onto a military vessel for the last leg of the journey.

"Do you remember when the worst thing we had to worry about around here was pirates?" Sanjay asked as they entered the bridge. He nodded politely to Lt. Duran. "Skipper."

"Morning, Sanjay. Tanner," Duran said over his shoulder.

"Sir," Tanner replied, then looked back to Sanjay, lowering his voice to avoid interrupting any of the work on the bridge. "It was only three years ago."

"Seems like longer," said Sanjay. "Then again, I guess it all depends on how you define '*pirates*,' right? Either way, still a bunch of assholes waiting to kill or kidnap you and steal all your stuff."

The state of the bridge underscored Sanjay's point. The armored plating was up, eliminating the usual streaks of light visible through the canopy in FTL. Even though most of the crew stood ready for battle stations, none of the weapons were powered up, nor was the electrostatic reinforcement field running. The corvette was still safe.

No one had yet figured out how to threaten an object moving faster than light.

Tanner considered Sanjay's comparison, but shook his head. "It's not the same. Legally, I guess, but not in practice."

"What's the difference?"

"NorthStar's guys have rules. Might not always follow them, but you could say that for any military. There's still some level of order to hold the craziness in check. Plus corporate troops aren't typically drunk or drugged out of their minds. It's a roll of the dice either way if you lose a fight, but I'd take the corporate odds over the other option."

"And with that expert opinion," spoke up Lt. Duran, "it's showtime." He keyed the PA button at his station. "All hands, we are dropping out of FTL in five…four…three…"

As always, Tanner felt his stomach lurch along with the ship. He'd gotten better about light speed transitions over the years, but he still kept track of the nearest waste chute in case his stomach staged a revolt. *St. George* was a good ship, with a helmsman that knew how to ensure a smooth ride. Even so, the captain kept the vessel at a fast clip at sublight speeds, and the ship signaled ample stress and tension.

Duran's vac suit bore the bloodstripes of a combat veteran. Every other member of the crew wore them, too. *St. George* had seen more than her share of action. Tanner had been on *St. George* twice before—once during basic training and again just after the last serious incident of piracy in Archangel. Back then, no one on board had combat experience. Now it was all too common.

The holographic display over the ops table at the rear of the bridge shifted to its usual tactical projection, registering all the signals and light already present on St. George's arrival while building up its two-light-minute "bubble" of active sensor readings in every direction. Raphael and its moon Azarias showed up right where they belonged. So did Michael and Astonaco.

Tanner and Sanjay kept silent as the bridge crew worked. It seemed at first that *St. George* had approached Archangel at a clear and open point. Given the vastness of space, that wasn't a shock. Even so, nobody wanted to take a smooth ride for granted.

"Contact!" announced the junior ops specialist. "Ahead starboard high, five seconds out." Given the corvette's speed, more specific bearings would change too quickly to be announced.

The holographic overlay on the bridge canopy created an enhanced visual. "She's drifting in space, sir," said the ops specialist, relaying details from her sensors. It all fit with the image of the dark hull on the canopy screen. "Willow-class freighter. No signals, no power signs. That's why we didn't see lights right away. There aren't any."

"Helm, slow us down and swing around in a loop," instructed Duran. "We'll have to take a look, but I'm guessing she's been out here for a few days now. She's ice cold, plenty of hull damage, no beacons. Doesn't look like one of NorthStar's, either." He glanced back at Tanner and Sanjay. "Guys, I think we'd better clear the bridge just in case."

"Aye aye, sir," nodded Tanner. "Thanks for having us up."

"Thank you, sir," Sanjay chimed in. With that, the pair went on their way. "Doesn't look like it's a whole lot better being taken by NorthStar," Sanjay noted once the hatch was closed.

"Probably not, no."

The pair returned to the galley, where all the ship's passengers were now assembled. "How are we doing?" asked Vanessa.

"So far, so good," explained Tanner. "We came across a drifting freighter right as we dropped out of FTL. Regs say we have to go in for a look. I don't expect it'll be more than a couple of minutes. Seems like old news."

"They would delay with his highness on board?" asked one of Khalil's advisors.

"We'd do it if we had our own President on board, sir," Sanjay answered readily. "Besides, if anyone saw us come in and blow right past a wreck, we'd draw more attention for acting out of the ordinary."

"It is fine," Khalil conceded. "I would not want anyone in need abandoned on my account."

"Probably just a fly-by, anyway," said Tanner. "Long enough to get a good sensor sweep and then we'll be on our way to Raphael."

"And from there?" asked the advisor.

Tanner shrugged. "From there, Sanjay and I head back to our ship and Vanessa goes with you to wherever the Ministry plans to take you."

"And none of this ever happened, for either of you," Vanessa reminded the younger men.

"I owe you all much more than I can say. I've no doubt your president will have some idea of how I can repay the favor," Khalil added with a slight, sober grin. "Regardless, there are the orders of politicians and then there are the actions of men and women like yourselves. I don't take these things for granted. Thank you, all of you," he said, looking from Vanessa to Sanjay, and then to Tanner, "*again*. I will not forget this."

• • •

"NorthStar has regretted the entire situation from the beginning. We have reached out time and again to peacefully resolve Archangel's misunderstandings. Unfortunately, the government of

Archangel clings to violence, deception, and theft. Even the Aguirre Administration does not dispute that their forces fired the first shots and took the first lives. Aside from that, however, his government misrepresents the situation at every turn.

"Our Asset Recovery and Custody operations on the planet Michael are orderly, compassionate, and fair. Michael's hospitals provide better care than ever with abundant NorthStar aid. Michael's children are back in school, also with our support. Domestic civil authorities provide security without any interference from NorthStar personnel, and indeed we have provided aid at every request. Civilians offer testimonials to NorthStar's good stewardship daily—"

"So here's my thinking," Andrea Bennett broke in. Her voice halted the speech from NorthStar's public relations chief, Christina Walters, now frozen in mid-sentence in the middle of Andrea's office. The holographic image, offering complete fidelity to Walters's pert good looks and professional poise, held firm while Andrea turned to face her visitor. "She's an executive-level official, right? Doesn't that make her a military target?"

Admiral Yeoh's lips pursed with a hint of amusement. "Potentially," she conceded.

"So there's no reason you can't maybe drop a destroyer on her smug little face, right?"

"I'm not sure she constitutes quite that level of response, but I'll see if the opportunity arises."

"Completely justified if you ask me," grumbled Andrea. She folded her arms across her chest in frustration. "Every company has people like this. Governments, too. People who spend all their time in a cozy office coming up with ways to tell you that bad things are good. They say 'stress encourages innovation' and that you should 'do more with less.' They piss on your leg, tell you it's raining, and then offer to sell you an umbrella with a smile. This woman?" Andrea scowled, jerking her thumb over her shoulder at the hologram. "She's their *queen*."

"It is hard to believe her success at salvaging her company's image after all they've done. All they've been caught doing."

"That's because you're a rational person!" Andrea burst. "You don't just accept things at face value! She's not going after rational people. She's not even trying to win any arguments. All she has to do is muddy the waters, sow a little doubt, and then all the people out there who don't want to believe the truth can excuse themselves from making any judgments or confronting their own cognitive dissonance. *'Oh, well, both sides must be lying, so I guess I'll keep on buying my NorthStar-brand beer,'*" Andrea fumed.

Admiral Yeoh's serenity never wavered. Andrea expected the head of the Archangel Navy would be perfectly calm if she woke up in the middle of a house fire. Still, Yeoh's brow knit together curiously. "NorthStar makes a beer?"

"They make everything."

"Who would drink it?"

Andrea's eyes flared again, and she gestured back to the holographic brunette. "People who listen to her!" Then she caught Yeoh's faint grin. "You're poking at me, aren't you?"

"You look like you need the release."

"Sorry." Andrea waved her hand through the hologram—not quite with the force of a slap, but surely with some cathartic effect—to wipe the image out of her office. Then she stepped around to the other side of her desk to sink into her chair. "I'm going crazy waiting to actually do something. But I imagine you know what that's like."

"Only for the last year and a half, yes," agreed Yeoh.

Andrea tugged on a lock of her short, curly black hair. "I'm tired of being on defense."

"You think of what you do as defense? I rather envy your freedom to go on the attack."

"Sorry," Andrea corrected with a sympathetic smile. "I meant that I'm tired of seeing your people on defense. Not me."

A sharp knock on Andrea's open door drew the attention of both women. Andrea's aide leaned inside. "They're done," the aide reported.

Andrea stepped up beside Yeoh. "Window. Blinds," she said. One wall of her office faded from opaque grey to complete transparency. The view revealed the hallway beyond the public affairs center, not much to look at even with the lavish décor found throughout Ascension Hall. Admiral Snyder strode through with his head up. Both women could tell it required an act of will. His posture and dignity were a deliberate choice. Others in his position would have walked slower, perhaps even shuffled, and looked down at the ground.

"What'll happen to him?" asked Andrea.

"He will not face charges, no matter what some in the Senate or media might demand." Yeoh's voice carried neither bitterness nor compassion. "They could try to hold hearings on the Astonaco raid or even push for a court martial, but that would be a waste of time. By the letter of his orders and his authority, Admiral Snyder did nothing wrong. I know the president offered him a choice of new posts—all of them non-combat commands. Whether he accepted one of them or chose retirement is something we'll know soon enough. In the meantime, his exit would appear to be my cue."

"Yeah," Andrea exhaled. "I imagine I'll be in there as soon as you're done."

Yeoh's lips pursed into a faint smile once again. "Thank you for keeping me entertained while I waited. It's always good to talk to you."

"You, too. And Admiral?" she asked, giving pause to Yeoh's exit. "I've had your back. All along. Don't let them make you think otherwise."

The other woman's smile grew slightly. "I know. I am grateful. Thank you."

Admiral Yeoh knew how early to arrive at Ascension Hall for a meeting, how to keep herself occupied once there, and when to be outside the president's door so as not to waste any of her own time waiting on him. His schedule followed predictable patterns. Today, she waited for only a minute by his personal secretary's desk before Victor Hickman opened the door to the president's office. The chief of staff smiled politely and said, "Admiral. He'll see you now."

Yeoh found President Aguirre in his customary spot for morning briefings, seated on a couch beside his Minister of Intelligence. David Kiribati stood to greet Yeoh along with the President. Both men wore amicable expressions on their faces.

"Admiral, thank you for coming," said the President. "Please, have a seat."

"Thank you, sir." She took up a spot on the couch opposite the president's with a small table between them. Aguirre and Kiribati sat again.

"So, this is where I say it: you were right and we were wrong."

"Sir?"

"About the moon raid. Hell, about everything. I wanted to start off by coming clean. I benched you last year to escape some of the heat I felt from the Senate and the media over the course of the war. Everyone knows it, too. I've done the political thing and avoided actually saying so until now. I'm not going to say it publicly, but I'll say it to you in here. I overrode your decisions and put other people in charge of operations when it should have been you. That created confusion and doubt in the navy and outside of it, too, because things aren't supposed to work that way. I couldn't fire you because I knew it was wrong. But I couldn't change my mind on things that you knew were bad ideas from the start, like the moon raid. So here we are."

Yeoh noticed that Kiribati's expression hardly changed. The spymaster said nothing. Not long before the war began, he'd had a more collegial relationship with her, or at least made an effort to create that impression. As the war had approached, he became so guarded that Yeoh no longer considered him an ally.

"It's appreciated, sir, but I have not been waiting on such an explanation."

"No, it's an apology," Aguirre grumbled, "and it's completely deserved. You made a brilliant defense of Raphael. You built the navy up to the point where it could stand against an invasion, and when the time came, our people performed incredibly, thanks to you. The fact that we're still in this fight is largely because of you.

"But after the shock passed and we all adjusted to the reality of this war, people thought less about Raphael and the other remaining free worlds and more about what we'd lost. We saw the intelligence reports and the rogue broadcasts that got through NorthStar's barriers. We saw the suffering. Everyone wanted to rush to the rescue, and you said…what was it? Some pre-Expansion phrase?"

"Burn the village to save the village," said Kiribati.

"Yeah. You said you wouldn't do that. But people were impatient, and with a planet under occupation, that's understandable. We had the warships to take on their blockade, and we had the ground troops. You said we would do tremendous damage to Michael on our way in. No one wanted to hear that. You told the truth, anyway, and you were right."

"It would also leave us weak in the face of a counter-attack," Yeoh reminded him quietly.

He let out a sigh. "We didn't have the power to take on the Big Three and their fleets when we first started talking about breaking away. You found a way to change that equation. I wanted you work that kind of magic again. Everyone wanted you to do that again for Michael. That's not possible, though, is it?"

"No, Mr. President," Yeoh answered. "A liberation offensive would likely be even more destructive than the initial invasion."

"And we've seen that now with the moon raid."

Yeoh didn't reply. Admiral Snyder had his regrets. She saw no reason to rub salt in those wounds, whether he was present or not.

"So, again, here we are," said Aguirre. "Has your strategic outlook changed since we last spoke about it?"

"No, sir. We must go on the offensive, but we cannot do so here. We require a different battlefield."

Aguirre nodded. "And every other battlefield risks widening the war. If we attack NorthStar holdings in other systems, we risk drawing those systems into the conflict against us."

"That cannot be a military decision alone," said Yeoh. "This problem requires a political solution." She looked at the two men carefully. "Mr. President, Minister Kiribati…I am, of course, aware of covert operations involving navy personnel. This meeting coincides with the conclusion of one such operation. I am most curious."

Kiribati chuckled. "Can't keep any secrets from you, can we?"

"That depends on the secret," said Yeoh. She didn't look at him.

"Well, be that as it may, you're right," Aguirre confirmed. "We took your advice. Honestly, I wanted to follow that advice months ago, but we didn't have an opportunity until now." He looked to the slick gold holocom on his wrist to check his messages and smiled. "Good timing. Admiral, we're shifting from this discussion to that political solution you mentioned. Would you mind staying? Your input may be valuable."

"Of course, sir."

"Good. No more shutting you out. We play it your way from here."

Kiribati remained silent. Yeoh didn't mind. Nothing he could say would restore her trust in him, nor would it remove any unspoken caveats from Aguirre's words. "Thank you, Mr. President," she said.

The president rose. Yeoh and Kiribati stood in response. "The protocol people say we should all be on our feet when he arrives," Aguirre explained.

"Of whom are we speaking, Mr. President?" Yeoh asked.

"Prince Khalil. He's right outside." Aguirre tilted his head toward Kiribati. "David's people and the protective services snuck him into the building."

"Not that his enemies don't know who has him," Kiribati added. "I'm sure you've seen the Navy's portion of the report already, admiral."

"I have," Yeoh replied.

"A bit more complicated than we would've liked," said Kiribati. "Loose ends and all."

"I am satisfied with what I've read."

"Spilled milk either way," Aguirre pointed out. "No use crying about it now. At any rate, I had an irritating talk with some of the foreign ministry's people about etiquette and propriety for all of this. Monarchy's always such a pain in the ass. Too much deference gets you in trouble with people here in Archangel, too little respect tends to piss off the visitors. Apparently we can dodge all that if we focus on his terrible ordeal, though, so put on your quiet sympathy faces." With that, the president tapped the holocom on his cufflink to open one of the side entrances to his office.

Prince Khalil stepped inside, clean-shaven and dressed to his secular sensibilities. He looked healthy, but thinner than before the war. His entourage presented a familiar sight: men and women in business suits, along with a protection detail. Foreign Minister Theresa Cotton accompanied them, ushering the prince inside.

"Your Highness, I'm so sorry about your father." Aguirre shook hands with professional warmth. He guided Khalil to a pair of well-appointed chairs near the window. "Such a tragedy."

"Yes. Thank you." Khalil followed Aguirre's lead. If his advisors felt this was a breach of courtly etiquette, none of them spoke up. The seating arrangements came off as if they were improvised, but all knew it had been planned in advance. The group of advisors hovered as near as diplomacy permitted.

"We've sent word to your wife and children through our people in the Foreign Ministry. Our message includes an offer of safe transport if they want to come here, and for your associates' families. How are you holding up? I've read the reports."

Khalil nodded. "I am recovering. The doctors on the journey here did excellent work. You sent good people."

"We're glad you're safe, Your Highness."

"Of course, Mr. President. Your concern is greatly appreciated. We all owe you a great debt. But I would not want to waste your time with my personal concerns. I understand Archangel's stalemate has not changed since my capture, correct?"

The president's small, irritated sigh confirmed the statement. "No change at all. NorthStar keeps enough ships here to threaten the rest of the system. They hit our ship traffic and we hit theirs. Attrition hasn't had much strategic impact on either side."

"And any move to liberate Michael would likely be catastrophic for the population there?" Khalil guessed. "I've faced the same decision more than once in the last two years."

"Between you, me, and…well, everyone else in this room," grumbled Aguirre, "we've ruled out a liberation strike. The risks are unacceptable. Still, we've got to go on the offensive. The bright side is that NorthStar is so heavily invested in both their war with us and with supporting your brother in Hashem that they're spread thin everywhere else. Admiral Yeoh here wants to change the game by moving on NorthStar's holdings outside the system."

Both men looked to Yeoh. To her credit, she didn't miss a beat. "NorthStar cannot retreat without losing their greatest point of leverage, and with it the war," she said. "Nor can they advance without becoming the clear aggressor, causing much more of the Union to turn against them. Conversely, the president has already explained our own dilemma. We must change this dynamic."

"If I could, I would invite you to Hashem to fight NorthStar all you like," sighed Khalil. "Their support gives Murtada the advantage against both myself and my brother, Kaseem. However, military aid from Archangel would undercut my legitimacy. I am already too deeply in your debt. Such debts are often a political liability."

"We had hoped to give you some deniability regarding those debts, Your Highness," put in Kiribati. "Unfortunately, it seems likely that one of your rescuers was identified by the base commander, who was allowed to escape. That said, we believe Murtada never told NorthStar he had you in the first place. Given the effort he put into creating the impression that you're dead, he may keep quiet and continue that game as long as he can. Regardless, he knows you're free and who made it happen."

"I shall never complain about my freedom," Khalil noted. "However, were I to secure my kingdom with a borrowed army, many would wonder who truly rules."

"Our strategy is less about force than politics, Your Highness," spoke up Theresa. "Neither of your brothers have much credibility outside the Kingdom. They'll lose even more credibility after your survival becomes public, and the details of what was done to you."

Khalil shook his head. "Both of my brothers wield enough information control to block such news within their territories. The truth might sway more of Hashem to my side, but not if goes unheard. Even then, they will claim my survival is a myth and that any evidence is faked."

"Begging your pardon, Your Highness," Theresa replied, "I said outside the Kingdom."

"The Union Assembly has arranged for a special session in two months to focus on the conflict here in Archangel," explained Aguirre. "We've agreed to attend, and so have NorthStar and Lai Wa. Several proposed peace deals are floating around. Most are well-intentioned, but they're not going to fly."

"Hashem has Security Conference priority in the Assembly because it borders Krokinthian space," noted Theresa. "The whole point of the Union has always been a united defense and diplomatic front against alien states. *Nobody* trusts Murtada or Kaseem with the responsibility of guarding the borders, but currently Murtada has one of his people in Hashem's Assembly seat. He holds the largest portion of the Kingdom.

"However, the worlds that give Hashem its Security Conference priority are still loyal to you. Al-Farabi and Palmyra have publicly rejected both of your brothers' claims to the throne. You may not be able to take the Kingdom yet, but as you have Al-Farabi and Palmyra, you can take the Assembly seat."

"How does this matter?" Khalil asked with slightly more curiosity than skepticism. "When was the last time the Assembly managed to do anything?"

"We think we can change that," Aguirre answered. "Together. We've got other support in the works. Prince Khalil, our problems require military force, but neither of us can win through force alone. We have to change the dynamic, and we think we can do that in the

Assembly. Your Security Conference priority means you can bring motions forward in the Assembly while skipping the usual red tape, and Hashem's vote carries a lot of weight."

Again, Khalil shook his head. "Mr. President, what Assembly motion will make any difference in your conflict or mine?"

"One that levels the playing field, Your Highness."

• • •

Though *St. George's* flight path drew the corvette near *Beowulf* in orbit around Raphael, it was nearly another day before Tanner and Sanjay made it back to their ship. Delivery of Prince Khalil and the rescued Hashemites took priority. After that, the handful of navy personnel borrowed for the mission by the Ministry of Intelligence had to be debriefed, interviewed, debriefed again, and reminded *ad nauseam* not to talk about the mission to anyone under any circumstances.

They could not discuss it among themselves.

They could not discuss it with superiors, regardless of security clearance and regardless of direct orders.

They could not discuss it even if the entire story appeared in the media.

They could not journal it, nor allude to it in song or in graphic art—which of course left Tanner asking with great amusement what previous incident had led the Ministry to develop such specific instructions. Predictably, his questions were neither welcomed nor answered.

With uniforms and personal belongings returned, they were sent on their way. In Tanner and Sanjay's case, that meant a shuttle ride straight back to *Beowulf* along with a good number of other navy types, marines, and even a few civilians, all wearing vac suits per standard navy practice.

"Now docking with *Beowulf*," announced the pilot over the PA. "Ship's time is 0752 hours. We are in ready condition and alpha standby status with no drills currently underway."

"Fuck," Tanner groaned, his head thumping against the back of his seat. "Why is it that every time I leave the ship, I make it back too late for breakfast but in time for a full work day?"

"God hates you," snorted his companion. "Thought you'd have figured that out by now."

The passenger seated in front of them turned to glare over his shoulder. "The Lord doesn't hate anyone, kid," said the older man, "but I don't look kindly to people who speak of Him with that sort of disrespect. Archangel wasn't founded for people to spit on His name."

Sanjay almost cracked a grin. Tanner nudged him with an elbow. "Not a problem, chief," he spoke up before Sanjay could respond. A thump vibrated through the shuttle as the magnetic landing struts clamped down on the flight deck. "No disrespect meant."

With passengers rising from their seats, the chief had no time to invest in further dirty looks. Sanjay, however, shot one at Tanner. "Not worth the hassle," Tanner warned.

"Only 'cause he didn't say it to *you*."

"Hey, it's not about Catholic primacy." Tanner kept his voice low, glancing up toward the shuttle's exit to make sure the chief was already out of earshot. "I don't understand how people can be like that, either, but it doesn't really matter. A chief's a chief. He doesn't need a reason to tell either of us to shut up. I catch that shit sometimes, too. I don't like it any better than you do."

Sanjay rolled his eyes. "Yeah, I guess not, Heretic Second Class Malone."

"I'm actually baptized," Tanner muttered as the pair rose, scooped up their helmets, and shouldered their bags. "That's gotta at least get me to Heretic First Class."

They stepped off the shuttle into *Beowulf's* spacious landing bay and a swarm of activity. Built to berth small craft beyond its usual complement of four shuttles and a corvette, the battleship offered plenty of versatility—and plenty for its crew of thousands to do. Yet some departments ran with a little more accommodation than others.

"Hey, Sanjay, are you back?" called a voice from across the deck.

Sanjay looked up at the bo'sun with first class pips. "Just have to stow my stuff!"

"Long trip?"

"Long enough. Been up all night."

The bo'sun gave a dismissive wave. "You can go hit the rack until lunch if you want. Come by and see me after that and we'll find you something to do."

Sanjay smiled broadly, responded with an "Aye aye," and then turned back to see the shocked look he knew would await on Tanner's face.

"She just—that bo'sun gave you the morning off? That actually happened?"

"It's called karma, church boy." Sanjay slapped Tanner's shoulder before heading off.

"That's not even how karma works!" Tanner shouted after him. "Try reading a book!" Sanjay responded with an upturned middle finger over his shoulder. Tanner didn't respond. It was as much a friendly goodbye as anything else.

On a ship with thousands of crew serving in different jobs and different schedules, the two might not see one another for a week or more. Sanjay knew that when he requested *Beowulf* as his duty station out of rating school, but it seemed wise to shoot for a ship where he at least knew someone. Tanner arrived on *Los Angeles* through much the same thinking. He still felt grateful for the command decision to shift almost the entire crew of the badly damaged *Los Angeles* over to *Beowulf* after the Battle of Raphael. The move kept a well-trained crew together.

The year and change since then offered plenty of tough times and low moments. Tanner was deeply grateful for the presence of familiar faces and genuine friends.

Turning to his own business, Tanner headed to the exit. Much as he wanted to ditch the bag of clothes and other sundries slung over his shoulder, he knew it would be better to catch what he could of the morning briefing. Lt. Commander Jacobson expected that level of diligence from all of his people: ship's business first, personal matters second. Knowing Jacobson, Tanner's shoulder bag might well sit in the MA office for a full work shift before he had a chance to get back to his own berth.

He didn't quite make it to the exit. "Malone," came her voice, low and firm as always.

Tanner stopped in his tracks. "Morning, Gunny," he said.

"You've been away for a while."

"Yeah. Just, uh, got back."

Gunnery Sergeant Janeka nodded, staring at him silently.

"Training mission," he said. "Not much to tell about it."

"Mm-hm."

"You know. Routine. Kinda boring." It was almost the exact opposite of a staredown. Rather than trying to hold her gaze, Tanner found it impossible to look away.

"Long mission," said Janeka. "Been gone almost a month."

"You kept track?"

"I keep track of a lot of people."

He didn't know what to say.

"How are you?" she asked, still staring.

"Fine." He waited. She, too, waited. He swallowed. "How are you?"

"I've been on 'routine training missions,' too," she said, ignoring the question. She waited. Tanner nodded in cautious understanding.

She surely had someplace else to be. Yet here she was. "How are you?" she asked again.

"I'm okay," he said. "Thank you for asking."

"Good. I look out for my people. I won't pry, but if you need to talk to someone about how *boring* it all was, I'm around."

By that point, Tanner's mind had returned to regular speed. Janeka surely knew the rules of the Ministry and their covert ops. She'd been given all the same gag orders, probably many times over in her career. Much like the chief on the shuttle, she knew what she could get away with. "Thank you, Gunny," said Tanner.

"You need a haircut. Grappling classes are at 1900. I expect to see you there if you're not on watch. Good to have you back, Malone." Janeka turned to leave.

"Gunny," he spoke up. "You know how all the talking heads in the media keep saying we can't shoot our way out of all this?"

"Yes. I'm inclined to disagree, but I've heard it. Why?"

"I, uh…I think maybe someone's been listening. That's all."

Then it was the gunny's turn to nod in understanding. "I see. Back to work, Malone."

"Aye, aye, Gunny."

• • •

"…been at least a month since we've had to roust anyone out of their bunks, so I think we can drop the wake-up sweeps from our priorities," said Lt. Commander Jacobson from his small podium. The opening hatch at the other end of the ready room didn't throw him off, but as he finished his sentence he gave a nod to the newcomer. "Good to see you, Malone. Welcome back."

Thirty seats in neat rows filled the space between Tanner and his department head, with only half of them occupied. As usual, one shift's worth of MAs would be in their bunks by now, while another would be on-call but otherwise released from work.

"Didn't mean to interrupt, sir," Tanner said, setting his bag down behind the seats on the way to his usual chair. "Sorry about that."

"No problem," Jacobson replied. "We'll get you caught up. Moving on: today marks three weeks with nobody in the brig. I'd love to make it to a full month, and so would the XO and the skipper, but we all know that's not entirely up to us. Still, focus on de-escalation. Don't jump for the first chance to exercise your authority. Also, we officially have no captain's masts on the calendar…"

Tanner listened as he settled in, noting that Jacobson's news was all fairly routine. He set his helmet down in the empty seat to his right and glanced up to MA2 Baldwin on his left, who greeted him by way of a slight grin. He then quietly brought up the message program on his holocom and opened the daily department briefing. Barring amusing gossip, Tanner didn't look forward to catching up to the mountain of messages he'd missed over the last month.

"Okay, last thing," Jacobson said with a bit of a sigh. Tanner glanced up and saw the unmistakable "It's Not My Idea" look on the boss's face. "Some of you know we did, in fact, have an incident last night. I asked that it be kept quiet until I could deal with it, so here it is.

"At 0100 hours, passing through the engineering spaces between Thruster One and Thruster Three, Master Chief Floyd discovered what he described as 'lewd behavior' on the third level landing. Master Chief Floyd says the individuals, whom he believes were one male and one female, heard him coming and somehow managed to get their vac suits zipped up—folks, please, hold your questions—zipped up and fled. The master chief pursued, but slipped and sprained his ankle. And somehow, in spite of all the ship's security measures and all the personnel on watch, both suspects escaped and remain unidentified."

Tanner listened with his eyes wide. *This*, he thought. *This is what I come back to. You've got to be kidding me.*

"Now I want to make clear," said Jacobson with all the gravity he could muster, leaning forward on the podium and silently ordering the grins off of everyone's faces with his eyes, "the XO is taking this matter *very seriously*. This was inappropriate conduct, it was an inappropriate use of that space, and it led to a physical injury. Moreover, this is an increasingly common violation of shipboard discipline, and—okay, what, Baldwin?" he all but groaned. "You're sitting there like you're about to explode, so get on with it."

"No, sir," Baldwin managed, her face beet red and her eyes wide. "I'm sorry sir. I didn't want to interrupt. Go on." She held her tongue for another second before the words escaped. "But we're totally calling this one the Case of Floyd's Phantom Fuckers, right?"

"God damn it, Baldwin!" Jacobson groaned as his subordinates released the laughter built up throughout his monologue. "This isn't a cruise liner, and we're not the entertainment coordinators! It's our job to curtail this stuff, not treat it like it's a joke. We've gone easy until now, but times are changing. The XO is pissed. The ship's senior NCO is pissed. As of today, we don't give out friendly warnings. We break it up and we put people on report."

"Sir," Tanner asked, showing less amusement than his shipmates, "is there any reason to believe these weren't two consenting adults? Any reason at all?"

"No, Malone, there's not," answered Jacobson, "or we'd be having a very different discussion."

"I imagine so, sir. So this is what we do now? We've got a planet under occupation and it's our job to stop people from fooling around in private?"

"On this ship, when it's under inappropriate circumstances, yes. Yes, it is."

"And yet, sir, regulations specifically *don't* prohibit relationships. We're all adults."

"The regs do prohibit inappropriate relationships, and also inappropriate or lewd conduct and gross public displays of affection."

"Without ever defining what those are, sir."

"Malone," spoke up MA1 Lewis from the front row, "we'll talk about it later."

Tanner held his tongue. Any other officer probably would've bitten his head off by now. The moment had already testified to Jacobson's patience. Tanner also knew Jacobson couldn't be thrilled about this, either, but it was his job to back up officers and senior NCOs like Floyd. "I'll forward that concern on up, Malone," Jacobson grumbled. "In the meantime, no more breaks. No more turning a blind eye. We take this one seriously. Understood?"

"Yes, sir," came the response, united but unenthusiastic.

Tanner sank back into his chair. "Well, I can tell you it wasn't Sanjay this time, 'cause he was out with me."

Amid the laughter, Tanner heard Baldwin say, "Good." He sat up again to look at her, but she kept her eyes on their boss.

"Great. Three suspects down, counting Floyd." Jacobson rolled his eyes. "That leaves us with just under seven thousand to go. That'll be all, people. Dismissed."

"Tanner, hang around," Lewis said as the others rose. "I'll find you something to do."

"Aye, aye," Tanner sighed. He looked to Baldwin. "Has it been like this?"

"Pretty much. Last week it was litter in the lower passageways." Her eyes darted around quickly. "On the bright side, since you've been gone a month, nobody thinks that Floyd's Phantom Fuckers were you and me."

"Well, you know I'm not opposed to—ow!" Tanner laughed as Baldwin punched him in the arm.

"Shut up," Baldwin grumbled. "At this point it'd be like sleeping with my brother."

"So it's been quiet?" Tanner asked. "I came straight here from the landing bay. I haven't heard anything about what's gone on since I left."

"Two false alarms and one false start," she said. "Went into general quarters all three times, but two of 'em were non-emergencies and the other was a back-up call for a fight that was over before we got there. Nothing else has really changed, except for bored tightwads inventing problems like date nights in the ladder wells. Anyway, I'm on patrol with Sanchez. Find me at chowtime if you're not busy. I'll get you caught up on all the gossip."

"See you." Tanner looked forward to talking to her. The two were often inseparable, romantic inclinations or no. For now, though, he had other priorities. One of them was the hope of avoiding any serious work until he'd had a chance to sleep. The other involved a good deal of reading.

His electronic pile of messages beckoned. Naturally, routine shipboard traffic made up much of it. Even after trashing the outdated daily update stuff, he'd still have plenty to catch up on. Grimacing, Tanner scanned to see what he had in the way of personal messages.

His parents still wrote to him regularly, but he'd been able to tell them he'd be out of contact for a bit. He saw a letter from Madelyn, who only wrote to him after he wrote back. He saw something from Lt. Kelly, which immediately made him grin. Nothing in his file looked urgent.

Questions presented by his trip continued to nag at him. He wouldn't find answers in his personal mail. In truth, he doubted he'd find them at all on *Beowulf*. Still, the ship drew in men and women from all over Archangel. Someone might well know something. His conversations with Vanessa and Madinah at least gave him some hints as to where to start looking—or who to look for.

Most of *Beowulf*'s sensitive files required the use of secure desk terminals. The MA office held two such stations. Tanner had all the security clearance for full access, but he still needed a good reason to use it. He wasn't part of any active investigations. Hell, he'd been out of contact with the ship for weeks, with little interaction with anyone until this morning. That thought led to the excuse he needed.

Tanner moved over to one of the terminals. The computer accepted his user information without question. His queries would be simple enough, anyway. He didn't even need to put in anything genuinely sensitive. Simple background inquiries would be enough.

"Hey, Tanner, I haven't forgotten about you," said Lewis. He leaned on the other side of the desk with the screen in between them. "How was your trip?"

Immediately, Tanner wondered if Lewis knew he was over here abusing his security clearance. *Get a grip, Tanner. Be cool.* "It was a training mission."

"Yeah, I figured that. You okay?"

"Okay as I ever am."

"Figured that, too, what with the way you're talking to the boss." *Oh. Right. That.* Tanner sighed. "This is chickenshit, Phil."

"We all know that, and we'll handle it as best we can," Lewis explained. "Nobody's surrendering their own judgment or input here. Once we make a show of clamping down on this, people will be more careful about where and when they fool around. Jacobson's not going to let anyone's career get crushed over a little indiscretion."

"That doesn't make it any less petty. This is exactly the kind of thing that I hate the most about the military."

"I thought you hated the fighting most?"

Tanner opened his mouth to retort, but then closed it. "Yeah, that, too." He shook his head. "I don't have it in me to get worked up about things like this. Nobody's getting hurt. Nobody's gonna die. Give me any reason to believe either of those people weren't there willingly, I'll be all over it. Until then the only thing that makes me angry about this is that it's an issue at all."

"You ever have a job before coming into the military?"

"Sure." Tanner shrugged. "Nothing serious. I did some conservation work outside of town in the summers. Can't imagine what the desert looks like now," he mumbled.

"You never had any petty chickenshit to deal with in that job?" asked Lewis. He didn't wait for an answer, of course. He already knew it. "This isn't my first career. Don't let the longevity treatments fool you. I've had plenty of jobs, and there was chickenshit to go around in all of them. Don't let it get to you. Jacobson's not going to let anyone get strung up for blowing off a little steam.

"Anyway, we should probably find something useful for you to do, even if it's just patrolling for spring breakers hiding in the engine spaces."

"Yeah, about that." Tanner gestured to the computer screen. "So I've only got 467 messages to catch up on. Obviously half of that is going to be daily plan stuff and other things I can trash. I could use some time to flash through this."

"You can't do that on your holocom?"

"Sure. There's something else. More chickenshit, probably, but maybe I can head it off." Tanner hoped his frown was convincing. "A chief on the shuttle this morning blew up at a couple other enlisteds about religious stuff. I know it's not my place to stick my nose in a chief's business, but he was pretty intense. I wanted to cruise through the personnel files to see what he's all about. Maybe point the chaplain at him to settle him down."

Lewis scowled darkly. "You know damn well it's not your business worry about how some chief behaves."

"Hey, I'm not going near him," Tanner assured Lewis, holding up his hands. "The boss wants us to de-escalate, right? I'm just thinkin' about easing tensions. Tactfully."

"Who is it?"

"I didn't recognize him. He might be new. But he had a Uriel accent and I remember his face well enough. Don't worry, I'm not gonna get into a pissing match. Not even close."

The older man's frown lessened. Though the department's role was largely one of law enforcement and security, most of the MAs saw themselves as the ship's peacekeepers. Even so, rank and military courtesy mattered. "I guess we'll call this a learning experience if you manage to hang yourself," he decided. "I'll leave you to it, then. But keep your eye out for new messages. It's still early in the day. I might find something more useful for you to do."

"Aye, aye," Tanner replied as his supervisor walked away.

Assured of a few moments of privacy, Tanner input his search parameters. As he expected, the chief didn't come up at all. The man's accent tended more toward Gabriel than Uriel, anyway. Still, the premise gave him a chance to search the personnel files.

The chief's rant was hardly surprising, or even that troubling. Instead, Tanner's search followed the clues he'd garnered from talking with Captain Madinah about his ship and the refits provided at the Uriel Naval Shipyard.

He couldn't narrow his search too much. Queries left a trail. It might look odd if he asked the computer who among *Beowulf's* crew might have worked on any of the civilian ships that helped in the Battle of Raphael. He had to settle for looking over every enlisted engineer who'd served on a shore billet on Uriel. The wider parameters took time, but eventually he found someone on *Beowulf* who might fit the bill.

Tanner couldn't leave his ship. He would have to settle for finding someone on board who might have at least seen *Argent's* trail.

CHAPTER THREE

Fishing

"Most of the crew doesn't do any shooting at all. The helmsman steers, the gunners shoot and the captain leads. That's not the whole crew, though. Not even close. You need people who take care of supplies and nurses and cooks and secretaries. In a battle, a lot of those people might seem useless, right? Who cooks dinner during a fight?

"No, what those people do is they fix the ship. If you get in a battle, you're going to get hit. It's like a fight on the street. You plan on getting hurt. That's part of fighting. On a ship, you have to fix damage right away. So like I said, the captain leads and the helmsman drives and the gunners shoot. Pretty much everyone else takes care of the damage. Everybody's a firefighter. Everybody plugs the holes. That was my specialty. I had more training than most. But when a fight starts, it's pretty much everyone's job to keep the ship together."

--GUADALUPE CHAVEZ-MALONE
VIDEO RECORDING, "TAKE OUR PARENTS TO SCHOOL DAY," OCTOBER, 2262

> *"Did you see the recording? This is why we don't want Tanner's mom as a parent volunteer. She takes on every inappropriate question the kids ask. That's not the kind of talk we should have in school, especially with the kids at this age."*
>
> --Daniella Ramos
> Internal message, NorthStar Educational #712,
> October, 2262

"Dropping out of FTL in ten...nine..."

"Wait on my command, everyone. Don't jump the gun."

"...four...three...two...one."

No one ever enjoyed the transition out of FTL, but the bridge crew handled it well. No warning signals flashed, nor did anyone show disorientation or nausea. Granted, the helmets made that a little difficult to confirm, but at a glance, Casey saw everyone hold it together as expected.

He gave his bridge crew no more than that glance. Solid timing concerned him much more than anyone's health. From the captain's chair, Casey watched intently as the ship's sensor bubble grew. He heard call-outs from different stations reporting their readiness. As soon as he saw a nav point to confirm his ship's position, Casey gave the order. "We're go for Broken Wing. Do it, people."

Though no one could hear the explosion happen all the way back at the ship's aft end, Casey and the bridge crew still felt the sudden jolt. *Argent*—not that anyone was supposed to call her that anymore, nor did she look the same these days—lost her course as the blast knocked her off her trajectory and her thrusters cut out. "Helm, keep us out of a spin, but don't make it look easy."

"Aye, aye, sir," Schlensker called back. "Half-assed stabilization underway."

Casey smirked and glanced at the astrogation table again to confirm their position. *Argent* drifted off from her original Raphael-bound course at a rapid clip thanks to post-FTL velocity. Though she was only a few light minutes away from the system's capital, that distance would soon grow rather than shrink.

Now he only had to hope the right people would take the bait.

"I'd still feel better if we could confirm that our back-up is ready to go," grumbled Casey's XO. Paul Santos sat strapped into his station chair like everyone else. He lacked the nervousness of his dead predecessor. He was also considerably more eager for action against the enemy. Like Santos, a good number of *Argent's* crew were originally from Michael, and they were understandably eager to punish their homeworld's occupiers.

"No faith in your old navy buddies there, Santos?" Casey asked.

"I've got faith, sure, but it's been over a week since we've seen anybody or heard anything. A whole lot could've happened since then. If there was one good battle in the time that we were sitting around in deep space…ah, sorry," Santos said, waving his hand dismissively. "Same stuff I said in the planning sessions. Beating a dead horse."

Casey shrugged and cast his gaze toward his comms officer. "What about it Renaldo? Picked up any signals yet? Is the war over?"

"Only regular civilian band stuff, cap'n," came the answer. "Villalobos took a tumble in the second quarter of game two and wrecked his ankle. Might be out of the playoffs."

Curses, groans and a few mocking chuckles broke the tension for most of the bridge crew. Casey rolled his eyes. "Well, there you have it, people. Your daily dose of normalcy. The Union's not screwed up enough to stop professional sports, so things can't be all that bad." He pressed a button to open the direct line to his chief engineer. "Mr. Okeke, how are we?"

"Just reaching for the comm to report in, captain," came the response. "The charges went off clean and easy. The breach has us venting as planned. No damage to operating systems, no hull integrity problems. I'll have it sealed up as soon as you want it done."

"Alright, good work. We'll give it a minute or two to make the problem look good. Give 'em a trail of gas to look at. If you don't hear from me in three minutes, go ahead and seal it up."

"Aye, aye, captain."

Casey cut the channel and looked back at the astrogation table. By now, anyone on or near Michael or Raphael could see *Argent*. Her system entry and transition from FTL put her in a reasonable position for a ship approaching the capitol: far enough out to be safe from the stresses of gravity wells during transition, yet close enough that she wouldn't be exposed for long—except for her "engineering accident," of course.

Ordinarily, such a ruse might appropriately involve a distress call. Casey had certainly made such moves as captain of *Vengeance*, but that was piracy, back when he answered to no one. Now, though he was putting pirate tactics to good use, he still had to keep his jailers happy.

They were already touchy enough about the precedent this might set for ships in legitimate distress. It took some time for them to come around to using dirty tactics like this, but in the end, Casey didn't see the harm. This was a war zone. Every ship in distress would be treated with suspicion.

He stared at the tactical screens above him and waited. Contacts appeared here and there, most of them several light minutes out. Some orbited Michael, some Raphael. Virtually nothing occupied the vast space between the two worlds. All seemed quiet.

Schlensker straightened *Argent* out from her feigned loss of control. Okeke reported the deliberate breach in engineering was now sealed.

They waited.

Casey despised his captors, of course. He didn't care for doing their dirty work, either, though at least it broke up the monotony of life in his mobile prison. Admittedly, that life had improved after his performance at the Battle of Raphael and the "loss" of his previous minder. Casey couldn't be sure if Kiribati suspected the truth, but once Hawkins was replaced, things got better. At the very least, Santos had more shipboard experience. He led more and nagged less. No one got friendly, exactly, nor was anyone about to let Casey off the ship. Still, Santos and the other agents—those that Casey had identified, at least—treated Casey more like a captain and less like a hated convict.

Even that improvement chafed at Casey when he gave it too much thought. Accepting command of a ship rather than rotting in prison was a no-brainer. Past that, he resented the carrot-and-stick approach. He hated feeling like anyone's tool. The approval of his jailers was every bit as galling as their disapproval.

Casey cleared those thoughts from his head. Hopefully, they would not return anytime soon. He didn't know how long they'd be sitting here. "C'mon, you fuckers," he grumbled. "Take the bait. Send someone out here to—"

His wish was granted four times over. Ships suddenly dropped out of FTL around *Argent* in rapid succession, spread out at distant angles just beyond weapons range. This was a much bigger response than they'd expected: one cruiser and three of NorthStar's converted "starliners," which in reality were about as much of a threat as any dedicated destroyer in Union space—much like *Argent*.

Casey didn't wait for communications signals or scans. His people were all at battle stations already, but some few aspects of the ship had not yet turned to full readiness for the sake of baiting the hook. That game, he realized as the third ship winked into the vicinity—before the fourth arrived, even—was up before it began. He activated the electrostatic reinforcement system right away.

Lasers flashed from the lead cruiser to strike *Argent*'s aft quarter. The big warship opened up with missiles as well, sending them streaking out in curving lines to detonate ahead and behind its prey with sensor-blinding chaff explosions. Another missile blew up close enough to *Argent*'s hull to rattle everyone inside.

"Oh, son of a *bitch*," Santos snapped.

"NorthStar ships signaling," Renaldo announced. "Heave to, power down, demanding visuals comms with the captain—!"

"What, did they recognize us?" Santos asked.

"They're firing drag drones!" warned another bridge officer.

"Yeah, I see 'em," growled Casey. The new contacts spread out around *Argent*, creating a field of both comms-jamming static and artificial gravity waves that made the transition into FTL a dangerous prospect. The man-sized drones would chase *Argent* until they were shot down or recalled by their owners. Casey would have gladly used drag drones in his pirating days if they weren't so expensive and difficult to acquire. He hadn't expected NorthStar's interceptors to be so quick to employ them. He hadn't expected them to shoot before saying hello, either.

They would realize from the way *Argent* withstood the opening shots that her defenses were up. That meant there was no hope of playing for time by pretending to be a helpless civilian vessel, nor any point in holding back now. "Full defensive spread! Helm, turn us into that fucker to port and charge! Guns, target to port!"

Argent shuddered and lurched as she went from a steady drift to sudden acceleration. Schlensker put her into the course ordered by his captain. The stocky, bearded helmsman managed to catch Casey's eye with a glance over his shoulder. "If she moves—?"

"Let 'er move!" Casey waved his hand with exasperation. "We're breaking out, not ramming!"

"Right," Schlensker replied, turning back to his controls with wide eyes. *Like I'm supposed to read your mind*, the helmsman thought. *Psycho bastard.*

Argent turned in toward one of the combat-ready liners—*Cliona*, according to *Argent's* files—with most of her guns blazing away. Several other turrets let loose streams of explosive projectiles to catch any missiles that might come in from the other vessels, but *Argent's* aggressive pass at *Cliona* ate up much of her attention.

Despite Schlensker's need for clarification, the ranges involved in starship combat left plenty of space for *Argent* to pass over *Cliona* without any real danger of a collision. Weapons built to fire on fast-moving targets over a hundred thousand kilometers away now had only a tiny fraction of such distance to overcome. Both ships were rocked by some of the same explosions as missiles detonated between them. Lasers bore into their hulls with virtually no loss of power from distance.

Argent got in one good shot with her main guns before *Cliona* was no longer in the big cannons' field of fire. Her secondary turrets rained down on *Cliona* with lasers. Missiles flew from their tubes, immediately making hard turns to streak down at the enemy vessel.

The other three enemy vessels didn't need to split their attention between offense and defense. Though *Argent* pushed through her first exchanges with *Cliona* without major damage, the cruiser and the other two liners pounded the Archangel vessel mercilessly.

One of *Argent's* main thrusters dropped offline with a chilling warning alarm on the bridge. Multiple hull failures along three of her four sides left her trailing red-hot debris and burning gases. Two of the dorsal laser turrets exploded into space.

Only Casey's sudden order to turn and charge saved *Argent* from the cruiser's main cannons. The other ships would be deadly enough, but the cruiser could end everything with a couple of solid hits. "Helm, hard to starboard!" Casey barked out. He hit the emergency release on his harness and leapt from his chair to lean over Schlensker's shoulder. The captain traced out a course on Schlensker's main screen with his finger. "Turn in right there, hard and fast, and keep turning! Don't pull out of it until I tell you!"

The helmsman obeyed. Saved from a heartbeat or two of withering fire, *Argent's* ES system quickly recovered some of its strength. "Guns!" called Casey. "I want you to shift missiles from one target to the next with every salvo! Don't try for knock-outs, just keep them all off-balance!"

"Aye, aye," came the response. Casey barely noticed. He had already opened up a screen from his holocom mirroring the fire control readout.

"I'm pulling Batteries Five and Six from your control for a couple minutes," Casey warned. He keyed up direct comms lines to both. "Battery Five, Battery Six, this is the captain. Focus your fire on those two drag drones. Wide-area payloads. Throw the bastards off their game and we'll get a chance to get out of this!"

"Planning an FTL jump out, captain?" asked Santos.

Casey glanced up to the XO's position. The damage control screens at Santos's station didn't offer much good news. Main engineering had escaped serious damage thus far. Much of the mass *Argent* had lost came from non-essential structures meant to embellish her disguise as a mid-range starliner. Her cargo bays, now open to the void, were mostly empty to begin with. Yet the damage would only grow with each passing minute.

"They might launch more drones to pin us down even if we nail the ones out there already," Casey grumbled, "but we've got nothin' better to do." He looked over his shoulder toward the comms station. "Hey, Renaldo! Might want to put out a distress call if you haven't already. Right now it'd look even stranger if we *didn't* call for help."

• • •

Tanner reminded himself that he'd done far worse things than this.

He'd stalled his scheduled lunch for this opportunity despite a growling stomach. He collected his food on the chow line, shuffled into the galley's main dining area, and looked for his…target? Mark? Victim?

He couldn't quantify the amount of blood on his hands. Not after *Vengeance* and Scheherazade and what happened to the *Saratoga*—no, thought Tanner. *I'm what happened to* Saratoga. *I pulled that trigger.* All of that, he considered, and all the battles in between and since…and yet he knew full well the right and wrong of his less violent actions, too. His silence about *St. Jude's* crew may have been for the sake of their families, but it was still a lie of omission. He'd been part of a propaganda machine, even if only passively. He never shared his suspicions and his knowledge about *Argent* with Admiral Yeoh, despite several chances to tell her personally, and still couldn't shake the feeling that his silence there amounted to a personal betrayal.

From the entrance to the galley's dining hall, Tanner spotted a grey vac suit, short blond hair, and the rank insignia of a third class electrician's mate. He wondered if he was about to add false friendship to his list of personal sins.

Yet Tanner had questions that he needed answered. "Hey, are these seats taken?" he asked as he came over to the table.

The young electrician's mate looked up and blinked, then looked to his couple of companions before answering. "Uh, no, they're open. Help yourself."

"Thanks. Not my usual chow time. I'm Tanner," he said, offering his hand once he settled.

"Yeah, I'm pretty sure everyone knows who you are," the other man chuckled, accepting the handshake. "Rob Sullivan. Transferred on a few weeks ago."

Tanner knew that, of course. He'd already read the file. He knew Sullivan was new guard and only a year into his rating. More importantly, he knew where Sullivan had been stationed for his rating-mandated apprenticeship phase.

Sullivan introduced Tanner to the others with him—low-ranking engineers one and all. The group seemed friendly enough. Nothing in Tanner's experience matched the cold shoulders and surliness he'd gotten from *St. Jude*'s crew, but that first year left its mark. Even now, he half-expected strangers in uniform to treat him with that same wall of disdain.

"Ship treating you okay?" asked Tanner.

"Well enough. Berthing areas still take some getting used to. My non-rate time was on *Monaco*, so it isn't like I don't know how life is on a ship, but they had me at Uriel Shipyards for six months after rating school. I had a regular barracks room there with only one roommate. Guess I'm still a little spoiled."

"Yeah, I know what you mean," said Tanner. "My first year was all corvettes and groundside. I had a barracks room on base, too.

A bed with nothing on top of me but the ceiling, actual closet space, no deadlines for laundry."

"Ah, you get used to it," said one of Sullivan's companions.

"Really?" Tanner grinned. "When? I've been here almost two years."

"You came on board when they took the ship, right?" Sullivan asked. "Straight from *Los Angeles*? That must have been crazy. I was on the *Andromeda* drop during Raphael. Broke my leg in the jump. I was almost useless until the fight was over."

"Hey, you got all the way across, right?" Tanner pointed out. "I know people who couldn't connect when they jumped, and they wound up floating around in space until someone could recover 'em after the fight. That whole deal was more luck than skill for all of us." Tanner knew how some who'd missed the jump still felt bad for it. Even some of those who missed the jump onto *Ursa*, which exploded before the fight was over. He figured the ones who missed that jump were the luckiest people of all.

"I hear that," agreed Sullivan. "Poor guys. We go through all that training and weapons and tactics school and all that, and those folks missed the first beat right when it's time for the big show, huh? That has to chafe. I mean, I fought and did what I could on a bum leg, but…wow." He shook his head. "Been in a couple scrapes since then, but what with rating school and all, it's not like I've had the chance to see much action. Glad to be on a battleship now."

Tanner stomped on his urge to tell Sullivan that he didn't have to prove anything. *That's exactly how you want him to feel*, he told himself. *He wants to measure up. Let that play out.*

It wasn't the only time Tanner got this sort of reaction on a first meeting. New arrivals on *Beowulf* were often self-conscious in the presence of the people who'd seized the ship in battle. It wasn't strange for them to show how they'd paid their dues. They wanted to belong.

Sometimes being *the* Tanner Malone had its advantages, too. Lots of people wanted to impress him.

"So what's it like at Uriel Shipyards?"

• • •

"Contact, bearing three-one-six by three-two-one, out of FTL at seven point two light minutes. Computer classifies her as probable space liner, specific class not yet determined."

Signalman Third Class Avery Sinclair listened to the lookout's report from his post on the bridge with his blue eyes glued to his own screens. The timing and position fit with expectations. Sinclair watched for any comms traffic from the new arrival. If this went according to plan, he wouldn't find any. No one coming into Archangel wanted to draw any attention to themselves…except in this case. Still, the ruse meant that things had to hold to the usual patterns. Sinclair scratched the blond stubble on his scalp with a gloved hand and waited.

"*Belfast* has her spotted," reported an older signalman to Sinclair's right. "*Madrid* says she has her as well."

"Skipper," called out the ensign standing—or, to Sinclair's thinking, looming behind them both, "both destroyers have her on their sensors."

"Contact shift," announced the lookout from her sensor post. "Sharp change in course and speed. Looks like she's going into a slight spiral."

At that, Sinclair glanced over at the lookout station. It had much the same set-up as comms, weapons, and ops: a handful of enlisted ratings all doing the actual work, a non-rate or two on hand to assist or observe for training purposes, and an ensign to "supervise." Sinclair understood how *Beowulf's* sheer size and complexity demanded a large bridge crew, but surely the command officers and enlisted ratings didn't need junior officers to serve as middlemen between them.

Basic training demanded that recruits abandon reasonable speech in favor of shouting. It wasn't as if the enlisted guys on the bridge would have trouble making themselves heard.

Sinclair turned his eyes back to his station. He called up a tactical display on one of his secondary screens. *Belfast* and *Madrid* lay off to *Beowulf's* port, with both destroyers at general quarters and ready for a fight for the last half hour. *Beowulf* was not expected to take part, but her captain still held off on drills and kept a close eye on the operation.

Everything Sinclair saw from the liner's position was seven minutes old. Her current course—more of an uncontrolled drift, from the looks of things—didn't bring her all that much closer to Raphael. He watched and listened carefully for any comms from the limping vessel, but still had nothing to report.

It seemed strange to him that the skipper didn't have the whole ship at general quarters. *Beowulf* was certainly ready to go. The battleship had been on rapid-response duty plenty of times. Sinclair had to chalk it all up to one bit of politics or another. Captains and admirals didn't usually include him in their plans.

Other officers, however, paid him all too much attention. "Sinclair," spoke up Ensign Perez behind him, "do you need that tactical screen to see comms traffic?"

"Ma'am, the screen lets me keep track of what's going on," he said, trying to sound helpful. As the chief told him when Perez rotated into the post of comms watch officer, it was as much the enlisted section's job to train her as an officer as it was her job to lead them.

She was a little younger than Sinclair, less than a year out of the Academy, and months behind some of her fellow graduates because of specialist training after graduation. That made her the greenest officer on the bridge. Sinclair, by contrast, had nearly finished with college before his money ran out and he wound up in basic with Oscar Company. He'd been on *Beowulf* from the day of her capture, having literally shot his way onto this bridge.

He was fairly convinced their experience gap was the reason she felt the need to micro-manage him.

"We've got an ops section to keep track of what's going on, and the lookouts," she said. "Keeping tabs on them while you should be focused on your own job will distract you."

"Well, ma'am, right now I don't have all that much else to keep track of, so it's not a distraction or…yes, ma'am," he said, managing not to sigh at the frown on her face. Green or not, she outranked him by a mile. Sinclair turned back to his station. "Turning it off—"

He saw the new contacts on the screen at about the same time the lookouts announced them. He also recognized the icons.

"New contacts!" the lookout shouted. "Two—*three* probable destroyers, one cruiser!"

Ensign Perez wasn't looking at her section when the announcement came out. Instead, she looked to the man in the captain's chair with something of a gasp. *Belfast* and *Madrid* would definitely be outclassed in a fight like that.

Sitting in the captain's chair, Rear Admiral Branch frowned and said only, "Balls."

"Ma'am," grunted Sinclair. Perez found him holding out her helmet from his seat. He already had his on. "You might want to strap in. This could get crazy."

Perez hardly had time to open her mouth in response before the admiral threw the general quarters alarm. She'd expected him to call for someone else to do it. Sinclair knew the admiral better than that. He'd been through this before.

• • •

"General quarters! General quarters!" announced Sinclair's voice over the PA. No one could ignore him, or the honking alarm, or the flashing lights. "This is not a drill! All hands to general quarters!"

Everyone in the galley rose from their seats. Some pulled their helmets off their shoulder slings; others grabbed them from under their seats. Tanner snatched the MA's beret off of his head before shoving his own helmet into place. "Where are you guys headed?" he asked Sullivan and the others at the table.

"DC Team Nine," answered one of the other engineers. "Lower midship."

Sullivan and his friends said no more than that. Tanner saw them take off toward the far exit in the galley. He stepped up onto the table and looked out across the dining hall for any trouble spots. Unlike most ratings, many of *Beowulf's* MAs didn't have a specific place to be during general quarters. Their first job was to make sure everyone else got where they were going.

Training held. None of the exits looked choked. Nobody tripped or fell. Tanner saw no signs of panic. He hit a button on his holocom to join his department's communication network while he walked toward the nearest exit.

"—still waiting," came Jacobson's voice over the receiver in Tanner's helmet. "All I know is we've got a friendly ship under attack and we're going in hot to provide help. Lewis, Cruz, you're closest to the armory, so head straight there. Brig watch, we've got nobody in custody. Seal it up and reinforce the guard by the bridge."

Tanner took one look back at the dining hall as he got to the exit. He saw the galley crew closing the other exits behind them, including those leading to the chowlines and the heads. He lingered at the hatch as the last few non-rates on mess duty ducked through the other exits. Tanner waved to the last storekeeper to leave through the opposite end of the galley before stepping out and sealing the hatch. Dishes, cups, silverware, and food sat abandoned at almost every table. Tanner didn't envy whoever got to clean up the place after a battle sent everything flying.

"Malone," Jacobson said over the net, "I've got you in the galley?"

"Portside exits, sir," replied Tanner. "Galley secure."

"Right. Upper port decks, then. Standard sweep."

"Aye, aye, sir."

As an MA under arms, his role included keeping order and providing security. Down in the armory, Lewis, Cruz, and other MAs would issue small arms to designated officers and enlisted personnel. The marines would do the same from their own stores.

At the outset of this war, Archangel scored a major coup in pulling off two successful combat boardings. The navy had no intention of allowing that tactic to be used against them. That much Tanner agreed with wholeheartedly.

The MAs also had the task of dealing with those in the crew who froze or dropped out of their posts from panic or disobedience. He found that part of the job far less appealing.

• • •

Argent's circling maneuvers bought her thirty seconds. Her sudden speed won her almost another full minute on top of that by the time the NorthStar vessels spread out and reoriented their lines of fire. Life depended on avoiding the enemy's cannons.

Secondary armaments, like the turrets and laser batteries that lined the hulls of any warship, dished out plenty of punishment. Clipped and tagged again and again, with the electrostatic reinforcement of her hull shrugging off many lesser blows, *Argent* finally suffered a serious explosion. Everyone on the bridge felt an upward lurch before the ship's artificial gravity systems could compensate.

"What the hell was that?" Casey asked. He saw power output, acceleration and weapons conditions on his screens. Nothing had fallen there.

Santos had a better view of damage control from his station. "Something pierced the hull under the shuttle bay," he explained in a loud but controlled voice. "Think it took out fuel storage or the oxygen tanks. DC team is en route now."

"That's great," Casey muttered, then raised his voice again. "Helm, come about a full 180 and charge in through the middle. Guns, focus on that fucker to high starboard. Every gun that can get a bead should turn on him. Lay off on the drag drones for a second. We need to hit 'em back a bit."

"We giving up on running, captain?" asked Santos.

Part of Casey wanted to slap down the question, but he realized the whole bridge crew could stand to hear the captain's thinking. If nothing else, it would show that neither he nor the ship was flailing around in a panic. "They haven't fired any missiles at us because they don't want those drag drones caught in the blast. If that happens, we have a chance to go FTL. If we can evade their main guns and keep 'em from lobbing missiles, we'll stay alive."

The ship dove into a half-circle cutting under her previous trajectory, trailing smoke and burning gases from her shuttle bay and several smaller wounds. The drag drones matched her speed and course tightly while she spun and reoriented. *Argent* spat out fire in four different directions as she moved into the diamond-shaped formation of vessels now trying to turn inward to catch her.

As usual, each ship was too distant from the others to see with the naked eye. Computer models offered up images that seemed dramatically closer to those on the bridge, but trained eyes understood the illusion. No one held out any hope of one enemy ship striking another by accident, no matter how close it all seemed on the screens.

Holding to Casey's instructions, the bulk of *Argent's* fire went toward a single ship as she came through the center of their loose formation. All four ships turned inward to catch *Argent* with their main guns—a much easier task at this distance—but Casey's vessel held the edge in speed. Moreover, his plan had a secondary tactical purpose.

"Missiles by the ripple on that bastard, now!" he demanded on the bridge. *Argent* let six missiles fly in rapid sequence. Their range made it too easy for the enemy's computers to plot intercepts with chaff missiles and defense guns, but Casey counted on exactly that. The cloud of chaff missiles made *Argent* almost impossible to target for those few vital seconds.

By the time the enemy ship cleared the mess, *Argent* had pulled the same tactic on the next vessel in succession. *Argent* spat out more missiles in her wake which detonated not far behind her to spread more sensor-scrambling chaff. Some of those missiles exploded so close that *Argent* herself felt the blast against the hull, but it was a calculated risk—and one that failed. The drag drones held on in their chase. *Argent* poured on the speed, soon taking her to long range from two of her attackers. The pace, distance, and evasive maneuvers proved too much for the computers and the gunners on those vessels.

The cruiser's powerful engines closed that distance faster. Her crews were better trained and more experienced than their comrades.

Casey had bought all of three minutes and fifteen seconds before the cruiser's main cannon landed a hit that ran thirty meters along *Argent's* starboard side. It was more than the ES systems and the hull's natural resilience could handle. Magazines feeding defense turrets exploded. One of *Argent's* missiles burst in its launch tube, not yet armed but still yielding enough force to rip a large hole in the ship's side and kill dozens of crewmen.

Argent reeled from the blow, turning and twisting in space. The cruiser's main guns weren't ready to fire again before *Argent* corrected, but her lighter turrets still worked. With the ES system buckling, *Argent* suffered another tag from a red beam that cut into her hull at her fore, drawing out another series of small explosions. This time the damage reached her bridge.

On reflex alone, the captain ducked and covered his head as the world seemed to roar around him. The sound vanished as quickly as it emerged. When Casey looked up a second later, he realized that all the air had left the compartment.

Santos lay on his back, charred and bloody, still strapped to a chair that fell three meters away from his station. Artificial gravity held on. A hole that had been burned through three bulkheads and the hull offered a view of the void outside.

The captain's eyes darted over to the tactical display. Raphael lay seven point one light minutes out. *Argent* had been fighting for three and a half. This whole show would be over by the time Raphael saw it start. The enemy would be long gone with *Argent* reduced to a cloud of debris not worth searching.

That gave him an idea. "Play dead!" blurted the captain. He buckled himself back into his chair. Schlensker turned his head in confusion. He wasn't the only one.

"Next time they hit us, don't try to correct our course. Let the ship drift like nobody's at the helm, got it? Guns!" said Casey, shifting his attention, "drop off fire one or two turrets at a time. Nobody's alive on the bridge to coordinate, okay? And everybody start shutting down displays! Anything that gives off light in here. If you don't absolutely need it, turn it off! Renaldo, cut off any distress calls."

He was barely done with his instructions before another vicious blast struck *Argent* above her aft quarter. The cruiser's main guns strained the ES systems to the breaking point once again. Though the powerful lasers offered no kinetic force, the resultant overloads and explosions caused plenty of problems for a helmsman—if he were trying to maintain control. Instead, Schlensker shut down automated compensation systems. *Argent's* speed dropped as she fell off course.

Everyone on the bridge held their breath. The storm of light laser fire continued from all four pursuing ships. More of it missed than connected, but no further cannon shots followed. Soon, the enemy's turrets and batteries fell silent. All four ships closed in.

"Cannon One, Cannon Two," Casey said, switching over to a direct channel override, "evacuate your compartments. I say again, evacuate. Get out of there." He heard the crew chiefs acknowledge his order and comply, but he already had his attention back on the tactical screens. "If they fall for this, they'll take out the main cannons before risking a closer approach," he said, explaining his thinking to no one in particular. "No sense losing the crews with 'em."

The incoming fire continued to diminish, along with the ranges between *Argent* and her pursuers. The die was cast; all Casey could do now was brace his ship for the consequences. "Guns, make sure we don't have any missiles armed. In fact, if you've got any in the launchers, pull 'em back. They'll probably target those, too. Let's not make this easier for 'em."

"Captain, Okeke in engineering," spoke up another voice on the command channel. "I have crews in Thruster One trying to get it online."

"Right. Get 'em out," said Casey. Okeke's concerns were plain: the exterior thrusters were also a likely target if the enemy wanted *Argent* completely disabled. Casey hadn't realized anyone was in there until Okeke spoke up. Santos had been the one coordinating damage control.

"I assume we will not go so far as to kill the ES system?" asked Okeke. The chief engineer's question was largely rhetorical. Okeke signed on with *Argent* after the Union fleet had pushed him toward retirement, making him the most experienced person in the crew. Casey often wondered how much Okeke knew about Casey's origins. He doubted the old man would approve, but at least the chief engineer trusted Casey's ability.

"Yeah, that's a bigger gamble than we need. Besides, there's no reason that would shut down even if the bridge crew was dead." Casey's eyes remained on the tactical screens. The enemy slowed to match *Argent's* drifting speed rather than closing in.

"Okay, they're gonna need another minute to investigate and think this over," Casey said to a darkened bridge. He looked over at the hole in the bulkhead. Beyond that hole lay another one in the corridor outside, and an even larger tear in the hull past that. "One ship or another will swing around here and take a good scan, probably let the captains see the hole there and identify the bridge. That'll buy us at least another two minutes. Maybe two more while they chew on whatever they see. Sit back and stay still, people. You're all strapped into your chairs. Let 'em think you died there."

"You think they'll see right into the bridge, sir?" asked Renaldo.

"With a hole that big in our side?" grunted Casey. "Might take 'em a minute or two to line up a good angle, but their optics are as good as ours. Hang in there, guys. They aren't done shooting us up yet."

Chatter over the bridge comms channels fell off. Casey heard the main cannon crews report evacuation. He listened in on other chatter from DC crews now coordinated by Renaldo instead of his dead XO. Beyond that, he could only play dead in his chair and wait.

Casey frowned at Santos's corpse. He'd been less uptight than his predecessor. Santos kept Casey locked up on the ship, to be sure, and provided an obvious block to any real fun Casey might have, but at least he didn't freak out about every little thing or constantly remind *Argent's* lone prisoner of his authority. Under Santos, Casey could get a good drunk on now and again. It was better than nothing.

Now Santos was dead. God only knew who Kiribati would replace him with, assuming *Argent* got out of this current mess.

Even at long range, nobody could see a laser flash before it hit the target. The red beam cut into the center of Cannon One on *Argent's* bow. With the crew evacuated, the resultant damage brought fewer screams and alarms that one might expect, but the cannon was down for good.

On one dim viewscreen, Casey saw the brief rush of atmosphere and debris through the breach. He scowled deeply, hating this but seeing no alternative. He sucked up his frustration as Cannon Two suffered a hit that left the anterior weapon inoperable.

On the aft end of the ship, a single missile flew close and detonated a few hundred meters out from the thrusters. Though the missile blast didn't cause much serious material damage, Casey understood its purpose, confirmed by status readings on his displays. Engine systems went into emergency shutdowns and reboots. *Argent* slowed dramatically.

"Okeke," Casey spoke up, "do what you can to fix that shit, but don't try to build up any steam. We need to look like that hurt us worse than it did."

"Understood. Did that blast catch the drag drones?"

Again, Casey scowled. "No. Doesn't matter anyway. We'd never accelerate fast enough to slip out of this spot now. They'd shoot us to pieces."

Though Casey heard continued background chatter from DC parties over his comms net, a sense of pensive silence washed through the ship. No more enemy fire struck the hull. Renaldo went quiet, having no transmissions to report.

Casey left one holo screen up where he could see it. Any starship could see fine details many thousands of kilometers out, but people died with their holo screens on all the time. All the other vessel needed was a solid line of sight…which, as he saw on his screen, one enemy liner maneuvered into now.

"Bridge crew, hold still," he reminded calmly. "Don't turn anything on. Don't move."

The liner settled into place. Casey watched on his tactical screen. Though his enemy lurked much too far away to see with the naked eye, Casey knew full well he was looking down the barrel of a gun.

"Talk it over, captains," Casey murmured. "Take your time. We'll wait."

Seconds ticked by all too slowly until Casey's display showed the critical mark: eight minutes since the battle began. By now, his back-up had to have seen the opening salvos of the fight. If they were ready as planned, they'd appear any second now.

Only seven and a half light minutes away, he thought. *Fuckers should already have been at GQ from the start. It wouldn't take even a piece of shit civilian freighter more than the blink of an eye to cover seven and a half light minutes in an FTL jump.*

The enemy liner held her position. The other two took up flanking spots, well clear of one another, as did the cruiser. Nobody came in closer to attach grapples or launch shuttles.

They weren't taking the bait.

"Guns," Casey spoke up. "Defensive fire and chaff missiles on my mark. Helm, get ready to burn." He held his gaze on the tactical screen, giving orders and making plans while knowing he didn't have any real hope of fighting his way free. Not now. He'd go down shooting, but either the cavalry arrived or *Argent* was dead. No other way out of it.

Everything happened at once: two new contacts appeared, well out of weapons range from *Argent* and most of her enemies. Bridge officers called out warnings. Casey shouted over them all. "Fire!" he roared. "Full speed! Go! Go!"

The last order was almost overwhelmed by the rumble of multiple hits along *Argent*'s hull. With no air on the bridge, the strikes made no sounds, but the vibrations were terrifying as the ES systems strained and meter-thick hull plating bent and peeled away. *Argent* spat defensive fire and chaff missiles in almost every direction, working to throw off enemy targeting computers as she fled the kill zone.

One enemy liner turned to face the pair of destroyers that had just appeared on the screens. *Belfast* and *Madrid* would keep that one ship busy, but the other three—including the cruiser—were clearly of a mind to finish *Argent* off. Casey spat in frustration.

Then *Beowulf* appeared on screen in the middle of the pack. The captain gasped, knowing all too well that the battleship's location was nothing but blind luck, but he'd never complain. *Beowulf* opened up. The enemy scattered.

Argent had a chance.

. . .

"Helm, get on that cruiser!" ordered Admiral Branch. "Stay on 'im! Run his ass down!"

"Ma'am?"

"I'm—what?" Perez blinked and looked down toward Sinclair.

Sinclair was glad for the faceplate that hid his grin. Perez had her eyes on the admiral and the bigger tactical screens since a few seconds before the jump. He understood. He'd had the same problem in his first real shipboard engagement. "Damage Control board is up and ready," he repeated helpfully.

"C'mon, missiles," Branch called out. "One, two, one, two, like you're throwin' punches! Keep 'em wasting their chaff!"

"You'll learn to tune him out when you need to, ma'am," Sinclair said when Perez looked back at the CO again. "It's the asteroid accent. Comes out when he's excited. Helps you focus on your own job."

The ensign shook herself out of it. "Thank you, Sinclair," she mumbled before *Beowulf* endured a small shudder from its first hit. Compartments outlined on the DC board offered color-coded condition readings. Though none showed serious damage, the hit reminded everyone that worse would come. *Beowulf* held the edge in power and armor, but she wouldn't come away unscathed.

Sinclair watched Perez as she took in the info and tried to focus on the task at hand. The continued excitement behind her made that difficult. It showed in her body language.

"Ma'am?" he asked, and then called up the same tactical screen she'd asked him to close down moments before—providing them with a view of the action without needing to turn around.

Perez gave a brief, somewhat apologetic nod of approval this time.

Sinclair grinned. Neither of them had anything to do with maneuvering or firing, but it was natural to want to keep track of the battle as it unfolded.

If anything, Sinclair felt bad for the thousands of other poor sods on the ship who had no idea what was going on.

"Comms—Perez!" Branch called out. "Tell Wingless or Broken Wingtip or whatever the hell that ship's name is to throw some chaff missiles our way! The bad guys are worried about us now, not them! See if they can take some heat off of us."

• • •

"Hell with that," grunted Casey. He'd gotten exactly the same read on the situation as *Beowulf's* CO. In seconds, the enemy cruiser had gone from the pursuer to the pursued. Two of the smaller enemy vessels joined the chase, trailing behind *Beowulf* with guns blazing to take some of the heat off of their leader.

None of them were out of firing range from *Argent* yet, but they no longer considered her a threat. Casey agreed with their assessment. Still, *Argent* had chaff missiles to offer up for *Beowulf's* protection and several of her light laser turrets still worked. She could follow behind the chase while lending what support she could at a distance. Or she could look after herself. *Argent* sure as hell didn't need any more attention.

Besides, Casey knew all too well who served on that ship.

"Renaldo, tell 'em we got nothing to spare. Too much damage as it is. Helm! Maintain course."

• • •

"Critical in Battery Six! Battery Six!" Sinclair's voice announced through the DC channels. "We've lost contact and atmosphere is venting."

Beowulf shook from another hit, but nothing burst or collapsed in front of Tanner. He picked himself up off the deck and looked at the hatch down the corridor from his position. The flashing red sign on the door panel indicated a lethal loss of air pressure on the other side.

"DC Central, DC Team Two," came another voice on the net. "We're still tied up with this fire. I can't spare any of my guys."

"DC Central, Malone," Tanner spoke up. "I'm right near there. I'll take a look."

"Acknowledged," said Sinclair. "Be careful."

Tanner lost the other replies in the rumble of another impact on *Beowulf's* hull. He hustled over to the door panel and checked the readings. Power and gravity both remained online on the other side of the door, but he read no air pressure at all. Tanner keyed in an override code. "DC Central, Malone. I'm emptying Passageway One-Six to access Battery Six."

"Confirmed," acknowledged someone else on the line. "I read One-Six as clear. Go ahead." Not wanting to put too much faith in the remaining life support functions nearby, Tanner grabbed a couple of spare air cartridges for his helmet from a nearby emergency panel. He then double-checked the magnetic grip relays in his vac suit while the air rushed out of his compartment. With venting complete, Tanner hit the last command on the door panel.

Flickering lights and bent metal offered an eerie, unsettling welcome. He still felt vibrations through the deck and heard chatter over the comms net, but without any air, his surroundings fell silent.

Though the magnetic relays slowed his stride, Tanner made his way through the wreckage toward the blasted-open hatch leading into Battery Six. Orange light pushed back the shadows for a brief second as something exploded outside the ship. Thankfully, the light didn't carry anything lethal with it. Tanner anchored himself with one magnetized glove against the bulkhead as he came around the corner.

Battery Six contained a pair of quad-laser turrets pointing out of *Beowulf*'s port side. The compartment reached from Deck One to Deck Two, with much of the turret situated on the upper deck. The power supply, controls and other necessary machinery and maintenance space sat on Deck Two. The set-up allowed the turrets to swing up over the top corner of the hull, offering a broad field of fire. In the scope of *Beowulf*'s size and power, Battery Six was a mid-tier gun emplacement.

Tanner found destruction and debris inside. The battleship's hull was a meter and a half thick in most spots, yet Tanner saw a gaping hole out into space on the other side of the dark compartment, with the hull around the breach burned down to jagged metal shards like monstrous teeth. Deck plating was gone. Ladders were cut. Sparks flew from the primary control panel. The guns up above looked intact, but inoperative. No one remained of the gunnery crew.

No one except the body impaled on one long sliver of the shattered hull. The warped shard of metal ran straight through the crewman's torso, leaving the body dangling two or three meters up from what remained of the deck plating below.

Beowulf shook again. The crewman's limbs flailed lifelessly along with the motion. Tanner knew the crewman was already dead. Even if the metal hadn't gone through a vital organ—which seemed unlikely—the tear in the vac suit and the resultant exposure to space would have been fatal by now.

He activated the flashlight on his holocom to survey the remains of the compartment. Down and to the left of the jagged shards of the hull where the body hung, Tanner saw the curve of a helmet but couldn't make out the rest amid all the shadows and wreckage. Continuing his sweep, he realized that underneath more overturned metal, the ready lights of the turrets' power supply units still glowed. He swept his light left and right. While the covered power leads running on one side of the compartment had lost almost a full meter of their length, the other side looked to have survived the explosion intact. He saw banged-up shielding panels, but no obvious cuts.

A strong hand clamped down on Tanner's shoulder from behind, causing him to yelp. He turned and found a pair of faceplated helmets and blue Archangel marine vac suits, one of them distinctly taller than the other. "Tanner, it's us," said Ravenell. Physical contact created a person-to-person channel over their helmet comms, which the other marine joined by briefly grabbing Tanner's arm.

"Thought you might need some extra hands," said Alicia Wong. "Shouldn't try to do damage control alone, right?"

"I didn't even realize anyone else was nearby," Tanner admitted.

"We spoke up, but I think the ship took a hit while we were talking," explained Ravenell. He nodded toward the compartment. "Looks like everyone's gone. Anything we can do in there?"

"Yes!" Tanner guided them around the blasted-open hatch and pointed at the lower level. "I think the power supply is still running. That lead on the opposite side looks like it's intact. If you can get down there, I'll double-check the cables. We might get the gun operating again."

"Sounds like a plan," said Alicia. She and Ravenell took to climbing down the wrecked steps down to Deck Two while Tanner headed to the other side of the compartment. Like Tanner, the marines kept the magnetic relays on their vac suits active in case of gravity loss, making for somewhat slower but safer going.

"I thought you two were on the boarding team roster?" Tanner asked as they made their way to their separate destinations.

"That's Third Platoon," corrected Ravenell. "Changed out last week. They've got us on ship's security for now."

Once again, *Beowulf* shook from an impact. Alicia reached down to Ravenell as they climbed, more out of protective reflex than need. Predictably, he had his hand on her calf, too. Magnets, artificial gravity, and handholds aside, neither wanted to see the other flung out into space. "When did you get back?" Alicia asked when she caught her breath.

"Right after breakfast." Tanner crawled across the deck to the power leads and started popping open the dented panels to check inside.

"Nice welcome home, huh?" muttered Ravenell. He jumped the last open meter to the deck and pushed aside some of the debris from the control panel. "Hey, half of this is fried, but I think we can get the rest working. How are the power leads?"

"They're good," Tanner declared, then shut the panel again. He turned back to the exterior bulkhead and the dangling body. Another jarring impact against *Beowulf's* hull left everyone fighting to keep their balance. Tanner gave up on the fight and knelt down to the deck, perfectly happy to have his hands and knees keeping him connected along with his feet. Outside, the stars spun and orange light flashed as missiles burst.

He looked back to the body and noticed it had slipped part of the way back off the shard of the hull. It left a trail of blood that immediately froze on the metal. He could also make out a little more of the body's shape this time, but he couldn't read her nametag.

"You okay up there?" called Alicia.

Tanner glanced over the edge of the deck to see her working with Ravenell to clear up the control panel. "I'm good," he replied. "Just checking something out."

Stars continued to fly past outside. *Beowulf* was spinning. Tanner saw the woman's limbs sway. Part of his mind wondered if that could really be happening. Like Tanner, the body was much more under the influence of the ship's artificial gravity than its momentum. Still, she'd already slipped part way off the shard.

She was dead, but for now, she was still inside the ship. Barely.

Tanner swallowed hard and pushed himself upright, moving step by step toward the bent and jagged shards of *Beowulf's* armor. He moved over to the remnants of lockers and machinery along the remaining hull, and there he found the helmet that he'd seen before, looking back at him.

The helmet was still attached to a body, which sat huddled in the dark corner before him.

Tanner reached out to touch the body and felt the crewman jerk in reaction. His helmet beeped as their comms system established a person-to-person connection. "Hey, are you alright?"

The crewman's faceplate turned away. His arms, already wrapped around his knees, seemed to only tighten his body into something of a ball.

"Are you hurt?" Tanner asked.

The crewman seemed to hesitate, but shook his head.

"What's your name?"

Again, the helmeted head shook.

Though Tanner couldn't see the guy's nametag with him curled up like this, the markings on his vac suit offered some information. He bore a third class gunner's mate insignia on his arms. Bloodstripes on his leg denoted combat experience. Together, that meant he might be new guard or he might not, but this wasn't his first engagement. He appeared to be the only gunner left alive.

"I've got a survivor up here," Tanner reported.

"Oh shit, is he okay?" Ravenell asked.

"Think so. How's it going down there?"

"We've got a solid connection!" declared Alicia. "The gun's running a diagnostic. I think we can get it going."

"Are you checked out on this thing, Tanner?" Ravenell asked. "Can you operate this?"

"No way," Tanner answered, his eyes still on the huddled gunner.

"We'll see if we can route fire control to another battery crew, then," suggested Alicia. "Maybe they can run it on one of their back-up terminals or something."

Tanner hardly listened. He looked back to the impaled body, still hanging precariously over the edge of *Beowulf*'s hull and the void outside, and then scanned his surroundings for options. Plenty of now useless cables lay nearby. He started pulling. Within only a couple of seconds, he had enough to work with. Tanner cut the cable free with his knife and then turned to the huddled gunner.

"Hey, I need your help with this," Tanner said, gripping the gunner's shoulder again. That got a silent response, at least: the gunner's wide eyes stared up at Tanner through the lenses of his faceplate with obvious fright. Again, the gunner shook his head.

"What's up?" Alicia's voice broke in.

Tanner blinked. He forgot his helmet defaulted to putting him on all personal channels at once. "Talkin' to the survivor. I think he'll be okay. Keep working on the gun. I've got this."

He saw Alicia nod and wave in agreement before she turned back to her task. Only then did it occur to him that while Alicia equaled him in rank, he held seniority. It meant little to him. He couldn't imagine himself actually giving orders to either Alicia or Ravenell.

"Listen," he said to the gunner, "we've gotta get her down."

The gunner's eyes followed Tanner's pointing finger, then shut tight as he shook his head once more in refusal. "She's dead," he argued, his voice shaking. "They're all dead!"

His eyes, his voice, and his body language all testified to his fear, and his shame. Tanner knew the feeling. He wanted to explain that he'd been there, but doubted any of that would matter. Still, he knew from experience that fear was always worse when he thought about himself. The best way to break out of the spiral was to focus on someone else.

"She's still one of ours," Tanner tried. He held the bitter end of the cable out to the gunner. "You're never gonna forgive yourself if you leave her. She needs us right now."

The gunner looked back at the body hanging lifelessly not ten meters away. Tanner put the cable in his hands. "Wrap this around your waist and stay put," said Tanner. "If you've got another mag relay to turn on, hit it and stay stuck to the deck. You don't have to move. You're my anchor. Okay?"

He saw a nod. He didn't wait for anything more. After wrapping the other end of the cable through his belt a couple of times and tying it off, Tanner put one magnetized palm on the inside of the hull and started walking.

Brilliant flashes of red light almost gave him a heart attack. So did a triumphant cry over the comm. "We're online!" shouted Alicia as the battery turrets above Tanner fired again. "We did it! Battery Four has fire control!"

Tanner swallowed hard. He saw the lasers flash out into the void. All that meant to him was that *Beowulf's* port side now faced something worth shooting at, which would probably shoot back. As soon as he made that realization, he saw more laser fire flash through the darkness and felt *Beowulf* shudder.

He edged out toward the breach in the hull, his hands on the shard that held the body and his feet barely touching the twisted skeletal remnant of the deck below. *Beowulf* would keep turning during the fight. Her port side wouldn't be exposed to fire for more than a few breaths at most. His heart pounded in his chest as he shuffled along toward the body and the gap out into space.

Soon enough, he didn't even have much to stand on. Tanner hung onto the shard and kept moving. The magnets in his gloves kept him securely attached to the metal. The last few inches left him wiping away frozen blood as his hand slid within reach of the body.

"Hey, Tanner," Ravenell spoke up, "you there? Tan—Tanner, what the *fuck* are you doing?"

His hand gripped the dead woman's belt. He gave her the gentlest push, but found that her blood had frozen around the shard through her chest.

"Aw, Jesus, hang on! We're coming!" called Alicia.

Tanner heard the huff in her breath as she started her way up the broken ladder. He didn't risk a look back. He let go of the dead woman, shifted his grip on the shard to get a bit closer, and then reached for her again.

Gonna have to shove hard to break the ice, Tanner considered, but that would only make her harder to control once she came free. He didn't know if she'd fall inside *Beowulf* or tumble outside. If she went the wrong way, the ship's artificial gravity wouldn't necessarily pull her back in. Certainly not if the ship took a hit or a sharp turn in that moment. Artificial gravity wasn't perfect in combat conditions. If she fell out in Tanner's grasp, she could well take him with her. He had the cable, but…

Orange bursts of light along *Beowulf's* hull decided the issue for him. He shouted out a curse as the explosions hit and the vessel shook. One hand gripped the hull shard while the other hand held her belt. He shoved firmly.

Beowulf lurched. The body fell, taking Tanner with him as he lost his grip. It all happened too fast for Tanner to track. He felt the pull of the cable on his belt, but he also felt a strong pair of hands on his left ankle. "I've got you! I've got you!" cried out an unfamiliar voice.

Tanner tried to look back. He saw only *Beowulf's* thick but broken hull and his own legs. He felt one of those hands shift from his ankle to his leg to pull him back inside. He realized that his rescuer had to be lying on his belly to reach all the way through the hull and still keep hold of him. With another tug, Tanner felt himself pulled further back inside.

"You stupid asshole!" Alicia shouted at him once both his legs and his hips were back over the edge and more than one set of hands had a good hold on him. Alicia, Ravenell and the gunner's mate pulled Tanner back inside, dragging him and the dead gunner around the breach to safety before the whole pile of them collapsed on the deck. "You could've said something!"

"I did," Tanner gasped, his heart still racing. "I had...I had help. This guy," he babbled, waving his hand at the gunner's mate. "Whatshisname."

Alicia stared at Tanner while she caught her breath. "DC Central, this is Sergeant Wong," she reported. "Battery Six operational, fire control routed through Battery Four. One survivor and one body recovered. The hull's open to space in here. We're pulling out."

"Wong, DC Central, confirmed. Get out of there."

Tanner sat up. He found the gunner's mate on his hands and knees, staring at his comrade's body lying on the deck. "Thanks for that," Tanner said.

"I would've left her there," confessed the other man. He sounded every bit as young and bewildered as Tanner felt. "I was gonna leave her."

"Yeah, but you didn't." Tanner patted the gunner on the back. "You didn't. That's all that counts. C'mon, let's get out of here."

The gunner's faceplate made his expression impossible to read, but his tone spoke volumes. "I couldn't move," he said. "I didn't want to move."

"Neither do I, most days."

• • •

"—still says she's too damaged to lend any aid," relayed Perez on *Beowulf*'s bridge. "They're giving me the laundry list now."

"Aw, bullshit," grumbled Admiral Branch. "They aren't too damaged. They're too chicken."

Sinclair shared the skipper's frustration. Given the task of coordinating damage control on *Beowulf*'s top decks, he saw the impact *Beowulf*'s chasers had on the battleship. While *Beowulf* continued to run down the cruiser, the other two vessels shadowed along, hanging just far back enough that they could bring their main weapons on the battleship while evading the heaviest return fire.

The converted liners had little chance of bringing *Beowulf* down, but they made the battleship and her crew bleed regardless. "Alicia, you guys out of there?" Sinclair asked over the DC channel.

"Almost," she responded.

"Hey, that chaser on our port side is backing off a little more now that you've got that gun up," Sinclair told her. "Good work in there."

"Thanks! Just climbing out and—woah!" his friend blurted.

Beowulf shook. Sinclair's eyes darted from the DC board to the tactical display and back again. The ship's systems registered a nearby missile detonation. "Alicia, you okay?"

"Yeah. Okay, we're out," she huffed in time with a flashing indicator on his viewscreen. "Hatch sealed."

"Understood. Hold tight. I might need you somewhere else in a sec." He looked over the DC status boards once more. Plenty of other problems awaited. While he wouldn't have called the partial recovery of Battery Six a critical matter, his friends had probably saved *Beowulf* some further grief.

The skipper hardly noticed. He had larger concerns than a single gun. "Okay, I've had enough of this," he grumbled. "Lieutenant Blair, put every missile launcher we've got on that bastard in a single salvo and spread 'em out all around. Just blast the hell out of 'em."

Sinclair looked back over his shoulder at the larger tactical screens as the missiles flew. He heard no rebuke from Perez, since she couldn't help but look up, too.

The cruiser had no trouble intercepting the first few missiles. She couldn't shoot down all eight. Battered and blasted at several sides, her acceleration faltered, as did her defensive fire. Only two seconds later, *Beowulf*'s main guns scored a hit, and then another.

Cheers rang out across the bridge as the cruiser exploded. Immediately thereafter, both of the other two ships peeled off and ran in opposite directions. The skipper ordered the helm to give chase, but everyone knew it was over. Not far away by the standards of space combat, *Belfast* and *Madrid* finished off their opponent. A moment later, the remaining enemy vessels disappeared into FTL speed.

Sinclair's DC board looked under control. Lives had been lost, but at least *Beowulf* came out of this with a victory to show for it. He smiled and let out a deep breath, accepted a pat on his shoulder from his new boss—now a combat veteran—and glanced at the boards run by the signalman to his left.

His smile vanished.

• • •

Tanner practically dragged himself back to his quarters from the MA office.

Beowulf remained at general quarters long after the fight. Search and recovery operations for lost personnel proved fruitless as usual, though that was never something anyone took for granted. Even with that completed, *Beowulf* had wounded allies to escort back to safer space. The skipper opted not to risk an FTL jump given the damage on each ship. That meant a long run home with the chance of another encounter.

By the time the skipper could release his crew from their stations and put the ship back to some semblance of regular operation, Tanner's watch with the MA department was long over. Even then, he still had to report back for an after-action check with his shipmates. Once he was free, he staggered off to the lifts and headed for his berthing area.

He'd gotten lucky in the last personnel shuffle. No longer the least-senior second class on the crew, he finally merited a spot in one of the four-person berths rather than the larger bays shared by mobs of non-rates and third-class enlisteds. Then Sinclair, still a third class himself, landed the same exact room through some arcane bit of wheeling and dealing. It reminded Tanner how important his second class standing wasn't.

Tanner found his friend sitting on the deck against the bulkhead outside their berth. His pace slowed in anticipation of bad news. "Avery?" he asked.

Sinclair glanced over at him and shrugged. "Hey."

The hatch leading into their berth stood closed. Tanner knew the schedules of the other two guys they shared the space with. Both would be on watch right now. Yet Sinclair sat outside.

"You okay?"

The signalman nodded. Tanner waited. Finally, Sinclair said, "Laser poked through the hull on Deck Nine. Set off an oxygen line. Pedro didn't make it." He gestured with his thumb over his shoulder. "Couple yeomen are in there collecting his stuff."

Tanner's eyes shut tight. He took a deep breath, let it go, then put his back against the bulkhead and slid down to sit on the deck beside Sinclair.

He wanted to find tears, and couldn't, and that scared him more than anything. "God, I thought we got off so lucky."

"Did a good job in Battery Six," offered Sinclair.

"Thanks."

"Thought we'd lost everybody. Maybe we would've, if you guys hadn't gone in so fast. Saw you got one of the bodies, too."

"I'm always so scared of leaving nothing behind when I go," Tanner mused, staring at the overhead. "Stupid, really. Not like I'm gonna be there for my funeral. Not like I'll know the difference. But I just…the idea of floating around out there forever…"

"Yeah," Sinclair said.

"The hell happened today, anyway?"

"Somebody went fishing again. Caught a bite this time. Not really sure who. Definitely wasn't a navy ship. Maybe Ministry, maybe something else. We weren't supposed to be the cavalry, but the skipper saw they'd bitten off more than they could chew, so…" He held up his hands, then let them drop. "We took out a cruiser this time, so there's that. One of their destroyer-liners, too."

"How many did we lose?"

"Including Pedro and most of Battery Six? Twenty-nine so far. Dunno if that's gone up yet. Docs still have a few in surgery."

"Shitty trade."

"Yeah."

They sat together in silence until the hatch to their berth opened. Two enlisted men carried out a couple of bags and some boxes. "You can go back in now," said one. "Sorry about your roommate."

Neither young man moved. Sinclair offered a bit of a wave in acknowledgement. Tanner just blinked harder, grateful that he'd managed at least a tear and a lump in his throat. They sat until the footsteps faded. With the yeomen gone, Sinclair produced a small bottle of whiskey from behind his back. "I got to Pedro's stuff first," he explained. He opened the bottle, gulped down a mouthful and then offered it to his roommate. "He wouldn't want it to go to waste."

Tanner accepted it without comment. They all knew about Pedro's stash behind the little shrine he'd built in his locker. Possession of alcohol would get a person on report, but as long as no one got stupid, Tanner and his fellow MAs didn't much care. It hardly seemed any worse of a sin than date night in the engineering spaces. He took only a quick pull, more out of memory for his friend and contempt for their shared lifestyle than any desire for a drink.

He thought about writing a letter to Pedro's family. He thought idly about his own mail, and from there he remembered Vanessa's teasing.

The lump in his throat faded.

"You get a good look at what went on out there?" Tanner asked.

"Yeah. Had a tactical screen going again, like usual. Thought Perez was gonna tell me to shut it down, but once the fight was going, she understood."

"…you think you could put the video from that screen on a data file for me?"

CHAPTER FOUR

There but for the Grace of God

Dear Captain Kelly,
Short engagement tonight. BM3 Bhatia and I are fine. I'll explain when I can, but it might be a couple more days. We took some hits on this one.
Sincerely,
MA2 Tanner Malone
ANS Beowulf

--Personal Letter, April, 2279

"Jesus said to her, "I am the resurrection and the life; he who believes in me, even if he die, shall live; and whoever lives and believes in me shall never die. Dost thou believe this?" She said to him, "Yes Lord, I believe that Thou art the Christ, the Son of God, who hast come in the world."

The chaplain's voice resonated across the audience of officers, marines and crew standing in formation in the hangar bay without need for artificial amplification. Built much like any of the marines and sharing all the same vitality and energy, Chaplain Corleissen had a strong, solemn voice. Everything in the hangar bay that hummed or blew or tapped was turned off. The deck department had these ceremonies down to a well-rehearsed process.

One might have reasonably expected a misstep or an awkward beat. No one would have held it against the presiding officer. Still, he pronounced every name with familiarity, knew whose eyes to meet when he spoke of each individual in the thirty-one flag-draped caskets, and clearly didn't need the small, leather-bound book in his hands. Corleissen wasn't just confident in his knowledge; he was personally invested.

It was only Corleissen's third day on *Beowulf*. His predecessor lay in one of the caskets before him.

Standing in the middle of the two lines of caskets, Tanner watched and listened for the familiar steps of the ceremony. No one here would be buried or cremated today. Rather than a full funeral, the navy called this a "ramp ceremony," a term borrowed from pre-Expansion Era military customs. The ramp ceremony offered the crew a final chance to say goodbye.

Of the thirty-one men and women in the caskets, most would go home to Gabriel, Uriel, or Raphael for their final rest. Those from Michael would be interred at Veteran's Memorial Cemetery on Raphael. One came from an asteroid mining colony not far from Ophanim. She, too, was bound for Raphael. NorthStar had ensured she had no such home anymore, nor anyone to receive her.

The passage from the Gospel of John cued the final pieces of the ceremony. Corleissen had mentioned something short but memorable and significant about each of the lost, from the widely beloved Chaplain Ochoa to Crewman Apprentice Daniels. He quoted the Gospels and the Hebrew Bible as appropriate out of respect for each individual. The final passage from John brought the ceremony to this traditional ending point.

"Let us pray," intoned Corleissen.

Tanner bowed his head per the requirements of military drill, waiting in silence as the Chaplain led the assembled in the Lord's

Prayer. The war had done more than a little damage to his sense of faith. He'd never been all that solid of a Catholic before joining up, yet he was never ready to call himself an atheist, either. The trials of the last few years had pushed and pulled his sense of spirituality all over the place. Some days he believed. Other days he didn't.

Today, standing with Sinclair over a flag-draped box containing their roommate of fourteen months, Tanner was in no mood to talk to God.

Chaplain Ochoa's casket went first. Her pallbearers included *Beowulf*'s captain, who led the procession. Admiral Branch turned his head over his shoulder and called out, "Bearers, atten*tion*! Ready, *take*!" The detail came to attention, turned to face their caskets, and knelt to lift them. "Ready, *lift*!"

In sequence with the bearers of the other caskets, Tanner and the men and women around him took up their burden. The move was less crisp than other close-order drill motions. Few people received formal training in this task. Yet with proper solemnity and precision, the line of caskets started on its way up the cargo ramps of the two shuttles. Each casket was turned to carry the dead feet first, excepting Chaplain Ochoa's. Custom and her duty held that chaplains should face their flock even in death, and thus hers was reversed as it led the way.

Inside the shuttle, Tanner's group found their designated slot. They set the casket down, leaving the shuttle's loadmaster and crew to secure it to the deck. The pallbearers had one small privilege for their work: they could break from the stiff formality of drill for little more than a breath to say farewell. Tanner put his hand on the casket, like so many others did, and said, "Bye, Pedro." Along with others, he took the few extra steps to touch another casket. "Goodbye, ma'am," he said to Chaplain Ochoa's casket. As he moved back to rejoin his formation, he paused to touch one last casket. He'd never met the gunner's mate inside until her death, but he touched the flag and said, "Goodbye, Holly."

The ceremony wrapped up quickly and proficiently. Apart from the newest transfers, everyone on *Beowulf* had enough practice with it. Most of the crew had transferred over from *Los Angeles*, where all had returned, just once, for a similar ceremony honoring shipmates who'd perished in her first fight.

Tanner remembered the sight of it all too well. There hadn't been enough flags to go around.

• • •

"They really ought to let us drink for these things," complained Ravenell. He sat in the couch with a glass in his hands. In accordance with navy regulations, his glass—like every other glass in the junior enlisted lounge—contained not a drop of alcohol.

Tanner sat in the couch opposite Ravenell's with a small table between them. Unlike the others in the lounge, he wore his beret and a sidearm. Per Commander Jacobson's policy, an MA was on duty as long as he was awake. Even if, as Tanner asked Ravenell, "We're at a thing?"

"Well, yeah." Ravenell gestured to the other men and women in lounge. Apart from regular watch sections, most of the ship's crew knocked off from their regular work shifts after the ceremony. The group only snagged couches by virtue of Ravenell and Alicia heading straight there after being dismissed. "Isn't this basically a wake?"

"Nah, wakes are an old Irish thing. Pedro was Colombian. I think. Maybe Venezuelan. We talked about it once, but I forget. Anyway, his family's all from someplace in South Am—"

"So he can't have a wake?" asked Alicia, seated beside Tanner.

"I'm not saying he can't have a wake. Just sayin' it's an Irish thing."

"What, you need to defend your heritage, Mr. *Malone?*" joked Ravenell.

Tanner made a face. "I'm Mexican-Irish by way of America," he said. "My grandparents came out here from San Diego and Tijuana. I'm not even sure how long their families had been there. That's about how connected to Ireland I am."

"I'm drawing a blank on those names," said Alicia.

"Coastal cities, really close together," Tanner explained. "They all grew up something like twenty miles apart on Earth. Never heard of each other. Then they came all three-hundred some-odd light years out here and their kids got together."

"Who the hell uses 'miles' anymore?" asked Sanjay as he joined the group.

"My grandparents did. It's how they always said it in their old holo-recordings, anyway. You guys all know Sanjay?" Tanner asked the others as he and Alicia shifted to make room.

"You're one of the shuttle drivers, right?" Sinclair reached out to shake hands. "I'm Avery."

"That's one of my jobs. Good to meet you. Think I've met everyone else once or twice."

"Y'know, I'm not actually sure how far twenty miles is." Tanner noted. He opened up his holocom's interface screen.

"Okay, schoolboy," Ravenell droned teasingly, "we'll take your word for it. You don't have to look anything up to make your story stick. Nobody's checking you for proper citation."

"I'm not—whatever." Tanner grabbed some peanuts off the table to toss at Ravenell. Then he sank back into the couch and got back to the interface. "I've got a message to put out, that's all." It required only eight words: "Starboard lounge with Rav and Alicia. He's here." Then he closed up the screen.

"Where's your family from, anyway?" Sinclair asked Ravenell.

The tall marine shrugged. "Gabriel. Grandparents were from Gabriel. And my great-grandparents, too. I tried to go further back than that for a school project once and found out some of my family came from Atlanta or Georgia or some—okay, don't correct my Earth geography, wise-ass," he said when he caught Tanner's grin. He threw back some of the peanuts.

"That why your family name pops up so much on news out of Gabriel?" Sinclair wondered. "Isn't there a senator or something?"

"One senator, one mayor, and a former governor from before I was born, yeah," Ravenell confirmed with open pride. "Family's been on the planet long enough to be part of the history. Barlow River was named after one of my great-grandmothers before she got married. One of the other early surveyors had a crush on her or something."

"No shit? Hey, if your family's so connected, how'd you wind up a marine grunt?"

"Because believe it or not, *honest* politicians don't usually get rich. Not the kind of rich that buys all the kids out of educational debt, anyway. I had a couple of small scholarships to run on, but I wanted to pay my own way." Feigning embarrassment, Ravenell looked down at his bottle and muttered, "Plus there might have been patriotism or something silly like that."

"Ha ha, sucker!" teased Alicia. She, too, threw some peanuts at Ravenell.

"Anyway, what were we talking about?" Ravenell asked. "Oh yeah, Irish stuff."

"How'd we get on that?" Sanjay asked with a quizzical frown.

"Ravenell wants a wake for Pedro," said Tanner. "Only a wake is where you get drunk and tell stories about whoever died. We don't have anything to drink, and we're talking about ourselves. We suck at waking."

"So someone tell a story about Pedro, then," suggested Sanjay.

Alicia shook her head. "We barely knew him," she replied, gesturing to include Ravenell. "Seemed like a good guy and all, but we only knew him as Tanner and Avery's roommate."

"He was actually kinda quiet," said Sinclair. "Religious sort. He prayed and went to every mass and had a little shrine in his locker." He glanced at Tanner, who knew that Sinclair was deliberately leaving out the part about the whiskey hidden behind that shrine. "But he didn't push it on anybody."

"Last Christmas," Tanner went on for Sinclair, "he won the holiday leave lottery. When he found out a couple other guys who'd won were gonna give up their passes 'cause they were from Michael, he brought them home with him. Didn't even know either of 'em before he offered. He was like that."

"Got a bronze for the moon raid, too," Sinclair added. "Dislocated his shoulder brawling with some NorthStar jackass and still wound up carrying a wounded crewman out on his back."

Tanner found himself staring at the table. He'd lived with Pedro for over a year and now found it hard to talk about him. He felt like he should have more to say, but the stories didn't come. As much as he generally avoided drinking, he wondered if maybe the Irish were onto something by making that part of a wake.

He didn't notice the silence at the table until Sanjay asked, "How much did he owe?"

It wasn't the sort of thing people talked about a few years earlier. Everyone had debt. One could just assume it. Yet unless obligated or put under duress, people rarely spoke of it freely.

The war changed all of that.

"One hundred, forty-eight thousand," answered Tanner. He glanced up at Sanjay's whistle of surprise. "Early longevity treatments. This wasn't his first job, but he kept sliding further in debt. He enlisted 'cause he couldn't keep up."

"What do they want from you, Alicia?"

"Thirty-eight."

"Forty-three thousand, one hundred twenty-two," offered Ravenell. "Sinclair's got it worst. Three years of college on top of the rest? Where's that put you again?"

"One hundred, seventy-two," answered Sinclair.

Eyes turned first to Tanner. "Fifty-three thousand, nine hundred seventy-four," he said. "And that's after giving them sixteen and a half thousand credits."

Alicia grinned. "It's like they were out to get you right from the start. I mean you really got screwed." She glanced over to Sanjay. "What about you?"

"Fifty-one thousand, nine hundred seventeen," he said. "Only I didn't pay like Tanner did."

"How much are you gonna give 'em?"

"Not a God damn thing," declared Sanjay.

"Not a God damn thing," Ravenell agreed solemnly.

The others said it, too, completing the ritual: "Not a God damn thing."

They fell silent until Alicia asked, "How much does a cruiser cost?"

Tanner frowned. "Not nearly as much as we paid to take it down."

"Think it'll make any difference?" Ravenell wondered aloud.

"Ah, I dunno," said Sinclair. "I mean at some point, this whole mess can't be cost-effective for those assholes. Even so, they've got more shipyards and more resources and more systems by the balls, so maybe they can keep crankin' out ships and troops. The rest of the Union is pissed at 'em, but everyone keeps buying their products and contracting their services. We're the only ones doing anything about them."

"Hey, 'licia. Guys," greeted Baldwin as she arrived. Tanner's semi-regular partner had bonded with Alicia after the Battle of Raphael, largely over similar experiences growing up on Raphael and any number of interests that had nothing at all to do with the military. Soon, she was a solid part of Alicia's social circle, along with Tanner's…although there was one person in particular she wanted to be better friends with. "Hi, Sanjay," she all but sang out as she sidled up beside him.

"Oh hey, uh, Jesse," Sanjay replied. "How's it going?"

Tanner suppressed his grin at the awkward, almost embarrassed tone in Sanjay's voice. He'd been on liberty at shore stations with Sanjay and seen people fall all over him. Baldwin seemed to be the only person who could put the good-looking bo'sun at a loss for words. So far, Tanner couldn't figure out why, but he found the mystery hilarious.

"Just getting off duty. I didn't know any of the outgoing today, so I volunteered to take watch in the brig." She kept her eyes on Sanjay. "Got kinda lonely. Thought I'd come see who was up here."

"Wow, I thought everybody on the ship knew Chaplain Ochoa," said Alicia.

"I'd met her," said Baldwin, "but we never actually talked or anything." She looked at Sanjay with her big, blue eyes. "Did you know any of them?" she asked with a flawlessly soft, empathetic tone. She placed one hand on his.

It was all Tanner could do not to laugh out loud. He put his glass on the table and stood. "I'm out, guys. Things to do."

"What?" Sanjay asked. "Really? You aren't even done with your drink."

"Yeah, but I've got letters to write and stuff. You guys have fun." Amusing as it was to watch Sanjay pretend not to notice Baldwin coming on to him, Tanner wasn't sure he was up for a one-sided romantic comedy. He slipped away from the couches and his friends, maneuvering through numerous marines and navy ratings until he escaped out into the passageway.

His berth was the last place he wanted to be. Tanner had the lower rack under Sinclair's. That meant that he could see the bare mattress on the top rack across the room where Pedro used to sleep. With others in the berth or when Tanner felt tired enough to go straight to sleep, it wasn't so bad, but the last thing he wanted now was to sit in silence with his roommate's ghost. Tanner went right past his berth and kept going.

The lounges would be full. The galley wouldn't provide the solace he'd want for writing. He had no idea what to say to Pedro's mother, but it seemed decent to send her something. Even if all he could do was to put down one word after another until he could at least say that her son was well-liked and already missed, it seemed like the right thing to do.

Maybe I shouldn't start with that one, thought Tanner. *Get rolling with something easier first.*

He found all too many people in the enlisted gymnasium. The chapel, he figured, would be quiet but far from empty. Tanner wandered through passageways, keeping his eyes open for a corner he could claim as his own for a bit. Warships made use of all available spaces. No one placed random benches or picnic tables anywhere. Every compartment was either secured for the day by its department, busy with people on duty or on watch, or just full of people coming together after the ramp ceremony. Before long he began to seriously consider holing up in one of the empty cells in the brig.

By the time he found an open space he could use, he was practically in marine territory. Officially, no one would tell him he couldn't be in that end of the ship. Unofficially, he needed an escort or an invitation, or at least to be on patrol as an excuse.

Navytopia and marinopolis, Tanner grumbled inwardly. *This job is ridiculous.*

Just shy of the imaginary border, Tanner found a briefing room with its hatch open. Nothing marked it for current use, nor was it any department's specific territory. Tanner poked his head in, found only a couple of people in the audience chairs minding their own business, and realized they likely came here with needs similar to his.

Tanner sank into a corner seat near the entrance. He flicked on his holocom and nearly started with his mail, but paused and opened up the ship's file interface. He doubted he would find anything new, but sooner or later, there had to be *some* opportunity for a few days on Uriel to follow his leads.

The temporary duty rosters showed little change from the previous day. *Belfast* needed people for a three-week personnel rotation gap. Apostle's Station likewise had a few holes to fill. The usual suspects all turned up. Few of them would bring him to Uriel, and none asked for anyone in Tanner's rating, anyway.

Course listings showed little promise as well. Polar survival course? As much as Tanner liked the outdoors, he wasn't a masochist. The Naval Justice School was on Uriel, but all of its offerings were for officers and chiefs. Everything else seemed to be about engineering, or flight, or other things that he'd never get his bosses to sign off on. He closed up the file directory and moved over to his personal mail to open up a new message...and stared at the blank screen.

The letter he dreaded but felt obligated to write wasn't ready to come out yet.

The letter he wanted to write, to the person he wanted to talk to, also needed to wait. She'd understand.

Dear Dad, Dear Sharon,

Thank you for writing so often. It feels like I don't say that enough. Sorry I haven't written for a few weeks. I'll explain someday. I got all of the letters you sent, though. They mean a lot.

We had a fight here a few nights ago. They put a hold on outgoing communications long enough to notify the families of anyone we lost first. I could've written after that, but we took some ugly hits in this last one. I guess I needed some time to get my head together before writing.

My roommate, Pedro didn't make it. We sent him off today with the other people we lost. He was a good guy. I wasn't nearby when he died, though. I was in another…

Tanner's fingers stopped moving over the holographic keyboard. In a previous letter, long ago, his step-mother told him to say whatever he wanted and not try to sanitize or sugarcoat anything for them. No worries about language or too much detail or keeping anyone's spirits up. Sharon wanted to provide a safe place to vent, she said, and he believed her—or at least, he believed that she believed that.

He didn't believe she wanted to hear about the dead woman he'd pulled off of a shard of the hull, or how he and Sinclair drank their roommate's secret stash of whiskey before his body was cold. She knew about the blood on his hands. Dueling propaganda narratives in the first year of the war made sure of that. If it wasn't NorthStar putting him up as an example of Archangel's thirst for blood, it was "friendly" media in need of a "hero." Either way, anyone who cared knew how many people he'd killed.

His parents didn't need to hear how good it felt to come through fight after fight alive, or how bad he felt for that when others lay dead. They didn't need to hear how sometimes he was damn proud of the things he'd done. *Yes, I killed all those fuckers. You know who's still alive because I did that? Besides me?*

Tanner stared at the blank screen. Before his enlistment, before pirates and Scheherazade and the war, Sharon would have been the first to point out that most of "those fuckers" felt like they were doing the right thing, too. She didn't say things like that anymore, and why? Because her stepson's feelings were more important than their right to live?

A silent buzz on his holocom and a brief flashing indicator on his screen interrupted those thoughts. The regular personal mail drop came through, delivering two messages. He opened the first without a second glance at the next.

Dear MA2 Malone,

Haven't heard from you since your last. Message traffic on my end makes your ship look pretty good in this one, but that's nothing new. Ordoñez is complaining that we missed it.

My sympathies about the hits. Drop a line when you can, details or no. I know it can take time. I remember how I felt about Joan's losses when I was in the infirmary on your ship after Raphael.

I also remember who came by to see me every day, whether I talked about it or not.

Sometimes it's good just to say hi and put off the rest.
Sincerely,
Lt. Kelly
Captain, ANS Joan of Arc

Tanner didn't have to hide his smile here. Their letters never crossed the line into outright flirtation. They never got dry or impersonal, either, and they only stopped or slowed when one sender or the other had good reason. *What's that, sir?* thought Tanner. *Fraternization, you say? How can that be? We're not even on a first-name basis, sir!*

The dodge wasn't entirely facetious. He took nothing for granted. Kelly had gone out on dates and such. Officers were almost expected to maintain a certain level of social engagement. Kelly wasn't living with her life on hold.

But she kept writing.

Tanner closed up the message, planning to fire off a reply soon—even if, as she suggested, all he could manage was something short. He looked to the second message, expecting something from his parents or perhaps one of his friends from school. What he found was closer to the latter, and yet entirely different:

> *Dear Master at Arms Tanner Malone,*
> *At the behest of Midshipman Nathan Spencer, the Superintendent and the Class of 2279 of the Archangel Naval Academy requests the honor of your presence at the graduation and commissioning ceremony of May 20th, 2279.*

Tanner sat back in his chair and stared at the invitation. The attachments doubtlessly included stuff about hotels and schedules and how he was absolutely required to wear his full dress uniform and every single medal.

Midshipmen got a limited number of invitations to give out. Originally, second-year transfers like Nathan expected to get half the usual allotment. The Academy only accepted such transfers at all as an emergency measure after the Battle of Raphael and the obvious need for an expanded officer corps. Naturally, those midshipmen who attended all four years took some precedence in ceremonial matters. Tanner had written off any hope of being there.

The last time they were together, Tanner was covered in blood, wearing a jacket from someone he'd beaten to death and kneeling over another man he'd just stabbed. Nathan wore only swimming trunks, sandals, a towel, and a horrified expression. They didn't see each other after that—not with Tanner needing medical attention. Nathan got herded into a transport bound for Augustine with all the other civilians. Now Tanner's childhood friend was about to become Ensign Nathan Spencer.

He wondered how much influence his own example had over Nathan's decision to transfer into the Academy. He'd wondered that ever since Nathan first told him in a letter after Raphael. That was unfair, though, and Tanner knew it. Their home planet was under occupation. Unlike Tanner, Nathan still had family trapped there. Had Nathan been at one of Michael's universities instead of enrolling at a university on Gabriel, he'd have been trapped there, too.

Nathan had other relatives outside of Michael. "Clan Spencer," as Nathan's mother always called it, was both wealthy and large. Plenty of names to put on an invitation list. Yet Tanner's invitation glowed at him in blue holographic light.

He wanted to see his friend. Much as it pained him to see Nathan get roped into the military, Tanner knew this had to be a proud moment for Nathan and his family. If being there meant that he had to put on his dress greys and endure ceremony and pageantry, it was a small price to pay.

The invitation also gave a path to Uriel. Short of legitimate operational needs, his bosses would never turn down a request to attend the academy graduation.

Wasting no time, Tanner opened up a leave request template screen. He'd have it logged in the system in minutes—or he would have, but for the sudden, loud squelch and vibration from his holocom.

Even the other two guys in the briefing room looked up from their own matters at the noise. Everyone's holocom was attached to the ship's internal comms net to allow for certain remote functions in case of an emergency. The system helped ensure everyone in the crew would always hear the call to battle stations, or abandon ship, or in Tanner's case, an emergency call from his department.

"Malone, dispatch," said the familiar voice of MA3 Farina. "Locker Room Charlie, deck seven. It's forward and starboard from your position. Go. Go *now*."

Tanner took off running. Whatever was going on couldn't be a shipwide emergency or he'd hear alarms, but it was clearly serious. "Gangway!" he shouted to clear people out of his path. Bodies moved aside. No one questioned him or his flight. The beret on his head answered anything that might have been asked. "Dispatch, Malone," he said to the holocom on his wrist. "I'm on my way. What's going on?"

"One suspect, armed and threatening," answered Farina. "Nobody hurt yet. Back-up is coming but you're closest and they asked for you."

The wheels turned in his head as Farina spoke. Aside from a few specific areas, deck seven was marine territory. He couldn't imagine them calling for help if one of their own did something crazy. More likely, they'd call it in after it was handled. Still, there was no mistaking the urgency in Farina's voice. "Did they say why they wanted me?"

"No, they didn't," Farina replied. "I figured they just knew you were close by. We're getting back-up on the way, but it might be a few."

He fairly jumped down the ladder leading to deck seven and kept going. Up ahead, he saw marines standing around pensively in the passageway. "Gangway!" he demanded again. "MA coming through!" Heads looked up as men and women in blue vac suits stepped aside. The loose crowd near his destination made room to let him through.

A marine corporal stood outside the hatch with her hands out to shoo away a couple of other marines. She looked up at his arrival and said, "Glad to see you. Might wanna hold up a sec." He wasn't used to marines keeping their voices down like this.

"What's going on?" he asked.

"Got a guy sitting with an armed grenade in there," explained the marine—Padilla, according to her nametag. "Says he doesn't want to hurt anybody, but he's not letting go. Sergeant Collins is in there with him. Made us all clear out and wait for you."

Tanner blinked. Brent Collins knew Tanner personally, so that explained why he'd been called by name. Still, he felt surprised that nobody higher in rank was on hand. On paper, at least, he and Collins stood at the same level. The marines tended to invest more responsibility and higher expectations at each rank step than the rest of the navy, but even so, this seemed a bit much to put on someone at the same level as Tanner…who, despite his trepidation, stepped up to the problem.

"Okay, you all need to move back," he said to the other marines. "Clear out both of these passageways for responders. Go."

Thankfully, the marines obeyed. Tanner wasn't sure they would. He was used to getting more grief and resistance than this, but as they moved, he understood they only wanted some way to help. Tanner turned to the woman at the hatch and asked, "Who is this guy? Do you know what's going on with him?"

She shook her head. Her eyes told Tanner she wasn't comfortable with her lack of answers. "I didn't see a nametag and I don't think Sergeant Collins knows him. He's not one of ours. Either he just came on board or he's in one of the other companies. Pretty sure we startled the guy by coming into the room in the first place."

"How long has this been going on?"

"A few minutes. Called right away. Dunno how long the private's been there."

"Okay, thanks." Tanner's mind raced. MA school had a few hours' worth of classes for such incidents as this, but it wasn't a major focus. He forced himself to take a breath and run through a list of basic steps in his mind, wishing he had something better to go on than vague memories of a written exam. He supplemented it with a little common sense. "Listen, you're gonna have to move back, too. At least to the corner bulkhead. We don't want people out here if he throws that grenade."

"You got it. Good luck." The lance corporal moved without another word.

"Dispatch, Malone," Tanner said with one finger on his holocom. "I'm on scene. I think we've got a suicide threat. Suspect is armed with a grenade. Sergeant Collins from Bravo Company is in there alone with him right now and needs support."

"Understood. Back-up is on the move, but Chief Lockwood was in the infirmary for something and…shit, it's gonna be a few minutes before anyone ranking gets there." It was a reminder that *Beowulf* was a big, busy place. Gaps and delays happened. Getting from one end of the ship to another didn't happen in an instant.

"Okay. I don't think we can leave Collins on his own. I'm moving in. *Do not* send me any more screamer calls. Don't want to startle anyone. Including me," he added. His fingers hit some other holographic buttons on the interface screen before he killed the projection. "I'm recording and transmitting for you."

"Copy that. I've got your signal. Be careful."

He glanced around one last time to make sure the passageways were clear. He also checked—or perhaps hoped—for someone higher-ranking to take this off his hands. No one appeared. He couldn't leave Collins in there alone. Tanner cautiously moved in.

Locker Room Charlie felt much more like a storage space than anything attached to a gym. It offered benches, but no showers or the like, and the lockers were wider and thicker than the usual athletic storage types. Marines used the space to keep equipment sorted for planetside expeditions or extended deployments. The lockers contained weapons, ammunition, backpacks, field rations, and other infantry supplies.

As Tanner moved through the rows of lockers and benches, he could hear Collins speak. "…always got other options, buddy." His voice carried all the stress one might expect, but the sergeant kept his cool.

"I just wanna go home," pleaded another voice—a deep voice, with too much bass for anyone to ever call it whining.

Stopping at the corner before the last row of lockers, Tanner caught sight of Collins standing nearby with his hands open and outstretched. "Hey, I'm here," Tanner announced in the same low, calm tone that he heard Collins use. The last thing he wanted to do was surprise anyone in this situation.

"Aw man," the voice around the corner groaned.

"No, it's okay," said Collins. "Nobody's here to rush you. It's only one person. C'mon out, Tanner." The young sergeant beckoned with one hand. Tanner followed. "He's from Michael, too."

The comment offered another explanation as to why Tanner had been called. The man on the bench at the end of the aisle was not small. He was young, with brown hair shaved down almost to stubble and the same tan that so many people from Michael bore all their lives. He looked stronger and fitter than Tanner had ever been. Bloodstripes ran down the legs of the guy's vac suit, but other than that and his rank, Tanner could read nothing from his clothes. His posture covered up the nametag. He sat hunched over roughly ten meters away.

One of his thumbs partially covered up the glowing indicator of the grenade's arming key. The red color indicated that it was live. Tanner didn't know how much of the five second timer might have already elapsed. With both hands covering the orb, Tanner couldn't be sure of the grenade's type, but it was surely the lethal sort.

"Hi," Tanner began hesitantly. The look of despair on the man's face seemed to increase as he made the predictable inferences from Tanner's beret and sidearm. "I'm not here to bust you," Tanner said quickly. "You're not in any trouble."

"That's bullshit," the guy muttered.

"What's your name?"

The marine shook his head. Tanner glanced to Collins, who did the same. "Think you've heard pretty much everything he's said to me," Collins noted quietly. "He said before that he wanted to go home, so I thought maybe he should talk to someone in the same boat. Only other thing he's said is, 'Get out.'"

"I'm Gavin, okay?" said the marine. "I'm just…Gavin. You'd figure it out anyway."

"Gotcha," Tanner replied. He needed to know other things, like what unit Gavin belonged to. Still, if he was in here and this wasn't his locker room, and neither Padilla nor Collins knew him… "You came here hoping to be alone?"

"I didn't want to hurt anyone," mumbled Gavin.

"Where on Michael are you from?"

Gavin took a quick, sharp breath. He stared at his hands. "Saguaro."

Tanner winced. Saguaro was one of the larger cities on the planet. It had taken a beating during the initial bombardment. "I've been there. A few times. I'm from Geronimo."

Gavin nodded, but didn't respond.

"Are you new on the ship?"

"Eight months."

The surprised look Tanner saw from Collins confirmed that Gavin had to be from one of the other companies. "You were on the moon raid, then, huh?" Tanner asked.

Gavin shrugged. "Closest to home I've gotten since I joined."

"Yeah. Yeah, me, too."

"I just wanna go home. But I can't, can I?"

"Hey, we're all workin' on that, right?" Collins asked gently.

Gavin shook his head. "I can't do this anymore. I don't belong here. I never did." He took another shuddering breath. "Please get out. Leave me alone. I don't want to hurt anyone."

"You don't have to hurt anyone," said Tanner. "Nobody's gonna touch you. We can just talk, okay? All the time in the world. Is there anyone you'd be willing to talk to?"

Gavin shook his head. "I don't want to talk to anyone. Not my unit."

"Then we'll keep them out." He glanced to Brent. "Maybe you ought to make sure of that?" The sergeant frowned, which Tanner fully expected. Collins had seniority, and whether or not Gavin was part of his company, he would still consider any marine to be one of his people. He also wasn't the sort to leave someone to face danger all alone. "We don't want anyone out there to do something jumpy," Tanner added. "And they'll listen to you before me."

Though still reluctant, Collins couldn't disagree with that. "Yeah, I'll be outside, Gavin," he said before slipping out.

"You should go, too," the private tried again.

"I kinda can't do that, Gavin," said Tanner. "Whatever's going on, it's my job to help, y'know?"

"It's your job to bust me."

"I'm not gonna do that, and I'm not gonna let that happen." In truth, Tanner knew that a lot of other people, even MAs, would see it differently. Gavin could easily hurt more people than himself with that grenade. By the strictest reading of rules and procedure, it would be perfectly legitimate to simply shoot Gavin and then flee before the grenade went off. Training even specified that this was—sometimes—the right thing to do, but the trainers conceded that every situation was different. Tanner considered it unacceptable. He didn't want anyone else to step in and take that option, either.

"Yeah, but I'm fucked anyway, though, right?" asked Gavin. "Sitting here with a live grenade. It's not like I can go back to work and everything will be fine."

"It kinda sounds like everything isn't fine there to begin with, though, right?"

Gavin shook his head. He didn't speak right away. "I'm a shitty marine. Ask anyone."

"You made it through basic and weapons. You got assigned here. And you made it through combat. I know what all that takes. You were on the moon raid, and you're still alive. That says a lot to me."

"We lost that fight."

"Yeah, we did. We lost that fight before it started, and we lost it together." He paused, wondering if this was remotely a good path to take. "Anyone can make mistakes. And you can do everything right and still lose sometimes. Losing that fight doesn't make you a shitty marine. Surviving it means you aren't bad at all."

The marine didn't respond. Each second stretched out into eternity. Tanner felt like he'd been with Gavin for an hour already, even if it had only been a minute. "Have you thought about doing this before?" he asked. Gavin nodded. "Told anyone about it?" The marine shook his head. "You don't feel like you've got anyone to talk to, huh?"

"Who am I gonna—?" Gavin snapped, finally looking up in response. Tanner saw tears. "My whole unit barely talks to me at all! The only guys I could talk to died on the moon, or went home on medical! Everyone else wishes they had left me behind on Port Astonaco, too!"

"Did something happen? Some big accident? Or an argument? Or was it always like this?"

"I *don't know!*" the marine all but pleaded. "I showed up and they all gave me the cold shoulder, no matter what I did. Anything goes wrong, or turns up missing or doesn't get done, it's always on me. They say it's always on the new guy. But I'm not even the new guy anymore, and…"

Tanner's jaw clenched up. One of his hands balled into a fist. "And sometimes you believe it really is your fault, right?"

"Maybe it is."

"You get made fun of a lot? Catch all the shit jobs?"

Gavin looked away. "It's just words. Chores that somebody's gotta do. Nothin' to cry over." He took in another shaking breath. "Couple of pranks. Same stuff everybody goes through, like they said. Just gotta suck it up."

"That's what people tell you when they don't want to get nailed for shit they know they shouldn't do. It's so you don't say anything. So you don't stick up for yourself."

"I *did* stick up for myself! You know what it got me? I was on track to make lance corporal before I got here. I pushed back and told those assholes to quit messing with me. Next thing I know, I've got a 'bad attitude' and I 'don't show military bearing,' and…" his voice cracked. He struggled to find words. "I came in from a shore station, sure. I did my job there. I do it here, too. But the platoon sergeant and the lieutenant took my stripe and said I had to 'earn it for real.' They say I'm not up to snuff. And now…Look at me." Gavin sniffled. "God, look at me. Some warrior."

"You shouldn't have to handle this alone. Nobody should."

"That's what I'm saying, man. There *isn't* anyone else. I started going to Mass so I could talk to Chaplain Ochoa, but there were always thirty fucking people standing around after she was done. I finally put in a request for an appointment, and then my platoon sergeant told everyone that I'm excused from PT so I can go talk to her about my *hurt feelings*.

"I sucked that up, and all the shit everyone else gave me for it, and I started talking to her," he said through quivering lips. "She was listening. I didn't tell her everything yet, but the more I talked, the more I thought maybe… And now she's dead."

"Hey, listen. I'm sorry she's gone, Gavin. I'm so sorry. I didn't know her well. I'm not the church-going sort, y'know? I know she was great, and everybody loved her. But listen, if you could talk to her, you could talk to Corleissen. He's good. I knew him on my first station. He helped me out a lot, too."

"With what?"

"Oh man. Everything you've said…Gavin, my first ship was fucking awful, almost exactly like you're saying. They didn't beat me up and I didn't lose any friends, but I didn't *have* any friends there. Just a big pack of assholes making me miserable. I know how that hap—"

"Aw, bullshit!" Gavin snapped. "You think I don't know who you are? I saw all the stuff they put out about you and *St. Jude*! That crew was top-notch! All the stuff on the news said so. Now you're trying to tell me that they were like my platoon? Why, so you can show some made-up sympathy?"

The response stole Tanner's breath and everything else he tried to say along with it.

"That's what I thought," fumed the marine.

"Gavin," he tried again, "look, the point is there are people you can talk to, and you don't have to go back to—"

"*Obviously* I'm not going back! Not after this! They're not gonna put me in a combat unit now!" He held out the grenade, his thumb still on the activator. "The best I can hope for is a medical discharge. And then what? How do I get a job unless it's someone pitying the fuck-up? I can't even go home! Shit, I don't *have* a home to go back to anymore!"

"You don't know that," Tanner argued, almost pleading with him. "Gavin, listen, I believe you, okay? It's gonna be—"

"Get out," Gavin demanded. "Stop lying to me and get out of here."

"Listen, Gavin, we can fix this. We can fix so much of this."

"I don't want it fixed! I want *out*! Get out of here!"

Tanner opened his mouth to plead with Gavin to slow down, but the marine pulled his thumb off of the grenade's activator and screamed, one last time, "*Get out!*"

Tanner dove out of the aisle of lockers. He saw others in the locker room in the one heartbeat that he had. Brent had found the chaplain and Chief Lockwood, but it was all too late. "Down!" he yelled, still rushing to gain any distance he could.

The explosion shook the entire room. Even with two or three rows of thick lockers between himself and the detonation, Tanner felt the heat. Something hit his legs as he fell to the deck with his ears ringing. The world went dark with smoke.

Hands snatched Tanner's wrists and dragged him away. Almost as suddenly as the explosion, Tanner felt freezing wet foam all over him as the fire suppression system came on. He looked back toward the corner where Gavin had been and saw one man rush past, fighting through both the smoke and the spray to look around the fallen lockers. The air beyond that still gave off smoke and intense heat.

Collins turned back from the destruction, picked up Tanner's ankles and helped haul him the rest of the way out. Seconds later, Tanner was on the deck outside the locker room with people standing or kneeling all around him. "You okay, Malone?" asked one voice, while another one asked, "Are you hurt?" and a third urged him to speak up. The ringing in his ears diminished.

"Something hit my legs," said Tanner, but as he spoke, he bent them at the knees to pull them close. They seemed to work correctly.

"Probably debris. You're not cut. Can you sit up?" Chaplain Corleissen's voice came through the din. He looked like he'd been in the room when the blast went off, too. Tanner realized he must have been the one to drag him out. "We should make sure nothing hit you in the back."

Someone heaved Tanner up by the shoulders before he could move. "Think he's good, sir," the marine at his back reported.

"I can stand," said Tanner. He looked around again. For a hallway right outside an explosion, the place felt pretty crowded. Lockwood stood beside him, calling in the situation on his holocom. Aside from him and the chaplain, Tanner saw most of the same lower-ranking marines as before, likely Collins's squad, but he saw more stripes in the mix, too. It hadn't taken long for people to come down. They must have been getting organized when Gavin…

Tanner looked back toward the open hatch. Smoke drifted out at the top and foam spilled into the passageway. Collins stood near the hatch, sadly looking inside. "I'm sorry," Tanner said to him.

Collins shook his head. "Wasn't your fault. You did your best. It's not about you."

A damage control team in full protective gear pushed through the passageway and plunged into the locker room. Lieutenant Commander Jacobson arrived and took charge, sorting people out while Chief Lockwood shooed away unnecessary bystanders. The corpsman assigned to Collins's platoon arrived to look him and Tanner over.

All along, Tanner's eyes drifted back to the hatch. He knew, intellectually at least, that Collins was right. None of this was about him, no matter how familiar it felt. No matter how close Gavin's story was to his own. That didn't make him feel any better about it, though. Nor did it mitigate the one small part of it all that really did feel personal.

• • •

"You had absolutely no way of talkin' Private Foster down off that ledge, Malone," declared Admiral Branch. "You didn't, Sergeant Collins didn't, and I don't think anyone else would've, either."

Personal visits from a ship's captain weren't common for someone at Tanner's rank, but Branch wanted it clear that he saw this as no ordinary matter. The admiral sat across from Tanner in the master-at-arms ready room with Jacobson, Lockwood, and Farina.

The younger man's vac suit and scalp still bore the marks and scrapes of the incident. He sat somewhat hunched over, a little too weary at this point for proper posture. Neither the admiral nor anyone else seemed bothered by it.

"I've listened to the recording from your holocom four times," Branch went on. "We'll have a full investigation an' all that, but nothing from the moment Sergeant Collins found that poor guy until his death is all that complicated. Collins did what he was supposed to, and so did you. Any missteps were made in good faith. It's not like we practice for this all that often.

"Nobody else got hurt. You both contained the damage, you both made sure Foster wasn't left alone and you held on as long as you could. I came down here to tell you that, and I'm gonna go see Sergeant Collins and Corporal Padilla and tell 'em the same thing."

"Yes, sir," Tanner managed. His throat felt dry. "Thank you, sir."

"I'm sure everyone's gonna get some refresher training in suicide prevention. You might see something you could've done differently. I don't want you or anyone to use that to second-guess yourselves over this incident. You gave it your best. Nobody can ask more than that."

Tanner nodded and quietly said, "Understood, sir."

"I have been in uniform a long time," Branch said, showing a little weariness himself. "This is not the first suicide to occur under my command. It's never been anyone under my direct supervision, and it has not happened often, but that doesn't make me less responsible. The one thing that I can tell you from all the investigations and all the studies is that you cannot take any one case as an example of how they all play out. They're all different. This happens to new people and old and men and women and combat troops and non-combatants. The truth is that every one of us big bad military sorts is just as vulnerable as anyone else, only when you're in a culture that pressures people out of admitting that and asking for help…well, this is what we get.

"I also heard what you said about having common experiences with Private Foster. Him going down a different path than you doesn't mean he was weak. It also doesn't mean what he dealt with was worse. Shit's all more complicated than that."

"Begging your pardon, sir," Tanner replied, looking up soberly, "it sounds like what Foster dealt with *was* worse than my problems."

The admiral frowned. "Well, we're gonna look into that, too. I am not happy with what I heard. Rest assured, there will be an investigation into Private Foster's claims, and we will have a full court martial if necessary." Again, Branch cast a meaningful glance toward Jacobson. "That whole platoon is coming off the line until I am satisfied with its leadership regardless. But that's someone else's job, not yours. This needs to be done right or it won't get done at all, so you stay clear of it. Understood, Malone?"

"Yes, sir."

"I'll coordinate with the marine company CO, sir," said Jacobson.

"I guarantee you she's ready to crack skulls, too." Branch stood, and naturally so did everyone else. He paused to give Tanner a thoughtful look. "Like I said, I listened to the whole conversation several times. It would be cold and cynical for someone to suggest that the stories around the loss of *St. Jude* were good for recruitment. Maybe even politically exploitative. But we're in a cynical business, aren't we, Malone?"

"Yes, sir. We are."

"I imagine there was a lot of pressure on you not to correct the things you saw and heard about your shipmates. Lotta guilt, too. Grievin' families and all that."

Tanner looked the admiral in the eye, but said nothing.

Branch nodded. "Private Foster's last moments are confidential per regulations. If you ever feel the need to set the record straight on your own experiences...well, nobody on this ship will tell you to keep quiet."

"Understood, sir," Tanner acknowledged.

With that, the admiral said his farewells. Chief Lockwood turned to department business. Jacobson moved closer. "You've written down enough to serve as a report. Go clean up and get some rest. It's been a hell of a day."

"Aye aye, sir," Tanner replied. He looked over as Jacobson turned away. "Sir? Have you…this wasn't the first suicide you've seen either, is it, sir?"

"No. It happens in civilian life, too."

"Does it happen as often?"

"I haven't looked at any studies lately, but…I don't think so, no. My guess? The war is what killed Foster. Or maybe the navy. I know a lot of people are going to want to blame him, and it's natural to be angry. Deaths like this are hard on everyone. But it might be past time we gave Private Foster a break."

• • •

"Bearers, atten*tion*!"

The pallbearers, almost all of them marines, turned to face the casket. Major Crenshaw took the lead. As with the captain's service as a pallbearer for Chaplain Ochoa, the major's participation was unusual, but so were the circumstances. Crenshaw plainly wanted to impress the significance of this particular loss on her marines.

Sergeant Collins stood opposite the major. He volunteered, as had Corporal Padilla. A great number of *Beowulf*'s marines had also volunteered. Some came from the deceased's company. None came from his squad, nor his platoon.

The investigation was three days old. Major Crenshaw needed only the evidence gathered on the first day to declare that no one from the platoon would speak at the ramp ceremony, nor would they touch that casket, but they would damn sure stand front and center.

"Ready, *take!*"

With the other pallbearers, Tanner bent at the knees and took hold of the casket.

"Ready, *lift!*"

The casket rose. Holding to a precise step, the pallbearers carried it past Admiral Branch and Chaplain Corleissen into the waiting shuttle. Inside the shuttle's cargo bay, they settled the casket into a space marked out for its dimensions.

Tanner put his hand on the casket. "Goodbye, Gavin." He swallowed hard, unsure if he should add that he was sorry. Someone put a hand on his shoulder. He didn't see whom. He stood, joined the pallbearers in formation, and marched off the shuttle.

"Detail," called out *Beowulf*'s captain, "dismissed."

Officers, ratings, crewmen, and marines fell out of formation. Tanner watched the platoon that stood closest to the shuttle. Some of them looked remorseful. The rest looked tense, even defensive—particularly the platoon sergeant and their lieutenant.

"You can't fight every battle for everyone, Tanner," said someone behind him. Tanner expected Chaplain Corleissen would be busy with others, and indeed, it looked as if a number of other officers had gathered to speak with him. Instead, Corleissen left them waiting.

"Yeah," Tanner replied.

"I don't believe there was anything you could have done."

Tanner glanced once again at the platoon as they shuffled out. "First thing Chief Everett told us when we started with first aid training in basic: 'You can't save everyone.'"

"No, you can't," Corleissen agreed.

"I'm glad you're here, sir. The ship could use you. I'm sorry about the raid on Augustine Harbor, though. Should've written or something once I heard that you made it out okay."

The chaplain shrugged. "The war had just started. Although I can tell you one bit of good news from the whole thing: that painting of Christ in my office that you hated so much was among the casualties."

The news drew a small, brief smile. "Better that painting than you, sir. Sorry I haven't had a chance to come say hello."

"You've been busy. I'll admit, as welcoming as the crew is, this has been a rough first week. I imagine it's been rougher on you, though." He paused, looking at Tanner carefully. "I heard the recording from the incident. Are you alright?"

Tanner looked around the hangar bay. This wasn't *St. Jude*. He knew he would never be that same lost and overwhelmed crewman again…and yet he had to remind himself of it all the time. Years and medals and battles won didn't set to right the problems he'd had since he first put on the uniform.

He looked back into the shuttle's open cargo bay.

"I want to go home, too, sir."

CHAPTER FIVE

Reunions

"Continued peace along Union borders cannot be taken for granted. Protracted warfare and destabilization within the Union will inevitably attract alien interest. Further losses of ships and military strength may encourage aggression. Command encourages any and all reasonable indirect action to reduce tensions. All available paths of influence should be pursued."

--UNION FLEET INTELLIGENCE MEMORANDUM (CLASSIFIED), MAY, 2279

"Repairs to thruster one and two are complete. I still feel that many of the new components are not ready for heavy combat," warned Okeke, though with less of the urgency than in earlier meetings. At this point, he merely needed to state the problem as a matter of due diligence. Shipyard repairs and refits were a done deal.

His captain agreed entirely. "I hear you, Okeke," grumbled Casey at the head of the conference table. "Still no explanations from on high, though. Non-answers and static, every time."

"It is worse in other areas of the ship," Okeke pointed out. "We've found many second-hand parts. My electronics techs found nothing installed to military specifications. Power, internal sensors, comms—all of it decent and working, but not ready to take the pounding of a serious fight. If we leave the shipyard on schedule, we'll spend weeks tearing everything out and re-installing it on our own while underway."

"Hopefully we *have* weeks," Casey fumed. "Then again, maybe there's a reason they're being cheap and sloppy with us. You think maybe they plan on putting us in non-combat roles? At first I figured they wanted to get us out of here as soon as possible, but now…"

"It seems unlikely," said Okeke. "We were not so beaten up after our last fight that full repairs were impractical or too expensive. Archangel has barely produced enough frigates and destroyers to keep up with losses. Expansion has been impossible. If we are to retake Michael, the navy can't afford to waste any available warships."

"Well, we don't exactly work for the navy."

"We're close enough." Okeke gave a shrug. "From what I've gathered here in the shipyards, it is not like the navy is trying to cut costs or short-cut ship repairs. Much the opposite, in fact. No one in this business is short of money."

"You'd know more about what's going on outside this boat than I do," Casey replied. He hadn't been off the ship since he first came aboard. Okeke surely knew that by now. "Okay. We can sit here and speculate all day, but it doesn't get us anywhere. I'll report in that we're ready to go and we'll see what happens."

Knowing that the captain was not one for explicit dismissals or other formalities, Okeke murmured farewell and disappeared through the conference room. That left Casey to review the rest of the reports.

The task took little time, since Casey cared only about the ship's stats and supply readiness. He had complete faith in Okeke's evaluations. The chief engineer was as diligent an officer as he'd ever met.

Few of the other reports mattered to the captain. He didn't give a damn about anyone's performance evaluations. That was an XO's job, and he didn't have one of those. Was he short on crew in any department? Yes? No? Fine. Details like departmental budgets and who got mouthy with whom were someone else's lookout.

For all that the ship beat being in a real prison, he was still a prisoner. Casey had a vested interest in keeping his own prison running well, but he'd be damned if he was going to pick up the slack when it came to anything outside of combat and general safety.

The door chime rang. Casey decided he didn't give a damn if any of his own crew found him in an improper posture. "Come on in," he said.

He didn't pull his feet off the desk, but his eyebrows rose as David Kiribati stepped in, along with a large, muscular man with dark hair and facial stubble. "Wondered when I'd hear from you again," said Casey. "Didn't expect you'd drop by in person."

"A visit seemed appropriate." Kiribati offered a smug grin as he took a seat. His companion remained standing as the door closed. "I take it no one told you I was here? You must be disappointed that you haven't won greater personal loyalty from your crew."

"*Your* crew," Casey countered, though he felt less annoyed by Kiribati's needling than he let on. He knew he'd never be able to trust the ship's security personnel. The rest of the crew was an open question. "That doesn't bother me nearly as much as all the cheap repair parts and half-assed work your guys here in the shipyards have put in."

"Is it not up to your standards?"

"It's not up to military standards, no."

"Funny that you should use those words. It took us a few weeks, but we figured out why NorthStar reacted so forcefully to your last fishing expedition."

"Was it 'cause they knew we were trouble?" Casey replied with a dry tone.

Kiribati pointed to Casey like a proud teacher hearing the correct answer in a classroom. "They did indeed. That much is obvious. The question, then, was *how* did they know you were trouble? It turns out they ran a spectrographic analysis of the emissions coming off your thrusters and realized you were running military-grade power and fuel. That's not something they normally look at. I mean, who cares what a ship's emissions look like? That is, until someone starts running frequent covert ship operations." Kiribati held his hands out innocently. "Who knew they would catch on so quickly?"

"It's been two and a half years," noted Casey with narrowed eyes.

"Yes. Pretty good run, I have to say. Anyway, you got out alive and with your ship intact, the navy bagged a cruiser and a destroyer, and here we are. Overall, I'd say we came out ahead this time. But it left us with the question of what to do with this ship going forward, since they seem to have it in for you. It occurred to me that maybe they knew exactly what sort of readings to look for because they knew what sort of work gets done here on Uriel. Maybe they have sources inside our supply chain. Maybe they got to someone inside the yards. We haven't found anything yet, but it's a concern.

"So that's why we're patching you up the way we are—decent, serviceable work, but not the whole nine yards of military-grade refits—and sending you on a long trip. I need this ship off the grid for a while, Casey. Far outside of Archangel, and long enough for people to forget about her.

"You're headed for friendly territory. It turns out a lot of other states in the Union are happy to see us fight it out with NorthStar, and they're willing to help as long as nobody knows about it. You're going to Quilombo for a full refit using some of their tech and their engines. That'll take some doing, obviously. Think of it as a vacation. By the time I call for you again, you'll have a new power plant, new thrusters, and a significantly different profile for the hull. New paint, too," Kiribati added playfully.

Despite the fact that this was all relatively good news, Casey scowled. "And here I thought you had turned into a cheapskate on me."

"Archangel is a modern, developed star system. Plenty of industry, with motivated citizens eager to chip in for the fight. This is a fully-mobilized wartime economy. I've almost got more money than I can spend. Almost. But have no fear, I can always find a way."

"How great for you."

"Isn't it?"

"I take it this also means you and the navy don't plan to be ready to take back Michael in the next couple of months?" Casey asked.

"Correct. Don't worry, I won't let you miss any big parties. Not the ones we plan ourselves, anyway. Can't speak to what NorthStar plans, but I doubt you'll miss out on much. I could tell from the play-by-play of your last engagement just how eager you are to fight," Kiribati said, his tone finally growing more serious and even irritable.

Casey remained unbothered. "You've got a problem with how I handled the ship?"

"You and I both know you could have stayed in that fight to give *Beowulf* some extra cover. Even at long range, you could have made a difference while keeping yourself out of the line of fire."

"That's some tough talk for a desk jockey," replied Casey. "Did you take a good look at our condition readings from the fight before you decided to come bitch about it with your bodyguard to protect you? Did you see what we had left in our magazines and our power output? See our casualties? NorthStar came at us like mad dogs. We were on our last legs. It was better to get out while we could."

Kiribati smiled again, this time without the feigned warmth he'd shown so far. "Yes, I have, in fact, looked over those stats. I looked over everything. *Beowulf* took damage and casualties, too. She might have taken less of both if you'd stuck it out."

Casey shrugged. "I'd play you a sad song, but I never learned the violin."

"A skill you might have learned in prison." Kiribati dropped his insincere smile. "You owe a great debt to society, *Captain*. We wouldn't be in this situation if you and yours hadn't run clear off the reservation with the hit on *Polaris*. The body count and the complications you racked up for us with that stunt more than justified a fatal 'accident,' but I took into account all the good work you'd done up until that moment, so here you are. Don't make me regret it."

The pirate's glare held, but he said nothing in response.

Kiribati regained his pleasant demeanor. "I think partly you were prone to make such a decision because you no longer had an executive officer to advise you and keep the team spirit strong. Funny how that's not the first XO you've lost."

"People die on warships in battle, *Dave*. It happens. Come out and see for yourself some time."

"Oh, I've got too many other things to manage. However, I don't want to leave you without an XO. Since it's such a dangerous job, I thought I'd assign someone with good survival instincts. Casey, meet Ezekiel. He's been running covert operations for some time now, and he has plenty of shipboard experience. More than Hawkins had, in fact. I thought he'd make a fine addition to your crew as your new jailor—sorry," Kiribati corrected without a shred of contrition. "I mean as your new XO."

Only then did Casey bother to look the other man in the eye. "Welcome aboard," Casey said without warmth or an outstretched hand.

• • •

For all that the PR people billed the event as an "open house," Tanner knew it was more like an open foyer, or maybe only an open front lawn. Showing off the military-industrial might of Uriel Shipyards to the general populace was good for morale and public support, but there was simply no way any tour group full of starship enthusiasts and wide-eyed school kids would ever get in to see the good stuff.

Standing in the wide entrance hall full of holograms, physical models, and artifacts showing the history of spaceflight, Tanner felt surprised these tours happened at all. Still, he saw plenty to justify the endeavor in the form of young boys and girls who might get inspired to sign onto a life in the stars, not to mention adults who might become vocal supporters or even investors. The whole business of war needed money and it needed recruits. Events like this one helped draw in both.

He'd already been sucked into the machine as a recruit. They wouldn't get his money, though. *Joke's on you guys,* he thought sarcastically. *Military passcard gets me in for free. Suckers.*

Tanner didn't wear his uniform for the tour. He jumped at any chance to wear civilian clothes like a normal person. Active duty or no, he was on leave. Given his itinerary, he couldn't get really crazy and go to a salon to have his hair grown out past his shoulders like it was before he enlisted, but he took what opportunities he could.

"Please have your holocom or other personal electronics out for deposit," explained a uniformed guard as the crowd shuffled through the entrance queues. "Each bin will be coded to your holo-com. No recordings of any kind are permitted."

Though he expected as much, the rule put a frown on Tanner's face. Security on such a big facility couldn't be airtight, but any decent scanning tech would certainly catch his regular old holo-com. Life as a junior master-at-arms was often more about security duties than police work. His training had focused on that from the beginning. Any security system could be circumvented—it was an unending arms race, after all—but Tanner didn't have any of those ways available to him, nor did he want to take any big risks.

In truth, he came only to get a sense of the location…and, if he got very lucky, to locate one particular ship.

"Holocom and other electronics in the bin, please," said a uniformed guard as Tanner came through the queue. Tanner pulled his holocom off his wrist—he still couldn't afford any of the swanky, miniaturized jewelry-mounted models—and deposited it in the bin provided. He heard a beep as the bin's ID reader added his info to the screen at the guard's side. The young guard was pale-skinned, fit, and to Tanner's eyes somewhat innocent. He blinked and did a double-take at the screen.

"Hey," spoke up the guard curiously, "you're Tanner Malone?"

Tanner didn't expect recognition. He'd gotten no special attention after leaving *Beowulf*. Even the hotel staff treated him like any other random guest when he checked in. His fame had limits—but, as Captain Madinah had pointed out, some people still remembered him.

"Hey, there are eleven billion people in this system," he said. "There's gotta be more than one Tanner Malone out there, right?"

The guard grinned back. "Head on through." Tanner didn't stop to chat any further or hold up the line. Following the crowd as instructed, he casually glanced back over his shoulder and caught the guard leaning over to say something to one of his co-workers, eyes following Tanner through the crowd.

"Welcome to Uriel Shipyards, the largest joint civilian and military ship facility in the Archangel System," began a feminine voice over the hall's PA speakers. Tanner cringed: she sounded exactly like the insufferable computer voice from the Test before graduation years ago. "At Uriel Shipyards, we construct and deliver the military technology that protects Archangel and the civilian solutions that keep us connected in a challenging galaxy. The business of Uriel Shipyards is the business of Archangel."

Tanner immediately reconsidered his stance on giving up his money. He decided he'd gladly pay a fee to shut that voice down. Still, he paid attention and stayed with his tour group. They gathered around the big model of the colony ship *Agnus Dei*, which brought the first colonists to Archangel a century and a half ago. He listened to the opening bit about the shipyards' ninety year history, the parent corporations making up the facility's management, and how wonderful the whole cooperative venture was.

Uriel Shipyards sprawled for several kilometers in a full arc outside the yard's entrance hall. Tanner and the other tourists saw numerous office buildings and large enclosed hangars that filled the landscape, along with the open-bay facilities that housed shuttles, freighters, and even a couple of navy corvettes. The frigate *Virtuous* and some civilian freighter sat in the monstrous "cradles" able to keep a ship as large as a destroyer suspended in an anti-gravity field around the clock for any number of vital tests and repairs. The cradles appeared to be the facility's pride and joy.

The group stopped at a broad balcony for a moment of recent history. Holographic display generators in the safety railing superimposed images in the crowd's field of vision to recreate the sight of *Los Angeles*, savagely battered after the Battle of Raphael, as she slowly descended to earth along the shipyards' broad central flight line. She'd been too big to fit within the space, explained the tour guide, leading the shipyard to hurriedly empty and demolish a couple of buildings to make room for her.

Tanner paid little attention. He had a personal interest, of course; *Los Angeles* had been his ship. Yet he didn't know when he would get here again. The shipyards represented one of the few leads he could find.

Looking out over the facility, Tanner saw color-coded lines along the pathways and roads that guided people to various locations. Even in the age of personal holocoms, Uriel Shipyards was the kind of place where a visitor or even a regular worker could easily get lost. Sometimes a low-tech solution like paint on a sidewalk or avenue offered greater security and surety than anything else.

"The weirdest thing about working there is the blue zones," Rob Sullivan had told him weeks ago in *Beowulf*'s junior enlisted lounge. It was their third game of pool. Sullivan still felt the need to impress. Tanner let him. "That's where they keep the hush-hush projects. So, one day I'm walking along outside a blue zone. Everyone is acting ordinary, no big deal. It's just some blue paint on the deck, right? Only I dropped a couple tools—simple hand tools—and they fell onto the blue paint. I bent over to pick 'em up and suddenly I had a gun in my face. I mean, that's where they do all the secret stuff, right? So secret they don't even want to take a chance that a guy reaching for a wrench might have some sort of recording device."

Tanner considered it with a frown. "Seems like a terrible way to keep a secret. Wouldn't you want to make it look completely normal? Security like that *draws* attention, y'know?"

"Well, sure, when your secret's small enough to put someplace out of the way. But when it's the size of a frigate, and you need a box big enough to house it? Can't really dress that up as something that it isn't, can you?"

Tanner couldn't ask the obvious follow-up questions. He couldn't ask what Sullivan thought might be in those blue zones, or if he'd ever gotten in to take a look. Not without looking too nosey. He had to let the electrician's mate offer all that up himself. Remembering his training from MA school, Tanner took a shot in the dark: he kept watching Sullivan as if waiting for him to say more.

"I mean, you can't move whole *ships* without people seeing," Sullivan continued after the unspoken prompting. "Plus things get moved around while they're there."

"What, they just jump from one parking spot to another?"

"Kind of like that, yeah. Different facilities do different work. There's also the need to shift priorities if there's an emergency—like after the Easter Blitz last year, when we had to take in all those damaged ships and get 'em turned right back around and running again? Even the spooks will move their shit out and let someone else have the parking spot in a real crisis."

"Doesn't everyone see what was going on in the secret box if that happens?"

"Well, again, it's a shipyard," Sullivan answered with a shrug. "Anyone a few kilometers away with a halfway decent set of optics is gonna get a good look at everything going in or out. They've gotta *know* they're being watched, right? So it's a matter of doing what you can. No reason to make it easy for the bad guys. But knowing a ship is in a building for a week or whatever doesn't tell you what's going on *inside*."

Walking away from that conversation, and again in reflecting on it as the tour group moved on, Tanner felt a little silly for not having come to that conclusion on his own. MA school offered more than a little training in investigations, though it was geared toward comparatively small crimes. A few class sessions glossed over counter-espionage principles. Information security was more often about curtailing sloppy behavior than catching spies. Undercover work and serious investigations—and the training to go with it—were at least one enlistment term away if not more.

Tanner paid close attention to the painted lines on the streets and walkways and took note of the buildings with their grounds outlined in blue. He noted the hangars with open bay doors, and those with their doors closed. Even if he couldn't see through walls, he could at least consider size and shape.

It had been over a month since the engagement in the space between Michael and Raphael, which was more than enough time to repair the damage done at the pace offered by Uriel Shipyards. *Even if it is here, I'll never find it,* Tanner concluded. *I'd get caught trying. I don't have the skills for this kind of thing. I don't have the tools.*

The tour group continued on, allowing Tanner and his thoughts to remain alone in the crowd.

• • •

Garrett Masters started his morning with the usual routine. He silenced the alarm, stretched, and checked messages on his holo-com while still in bed. The screens provided the only light in his comfortable bedroom. The first holo screen showed messages from his superiors marked "high priority," but not, he dutifully noted, "urgent." He therefore ignored them in favor of the daily message from home.

The second holo screen showed his wife still in bed with their baby crawling toward the camera. "Morning, Garrett," said Robin. She laughed as little Timothy practically reached through the screen with a happy baby smile on his happy baby face. Garrett knew

Timothy was only reacting to a holographic trick projected in the bedroom, but he smiled uncontrollably just the same. "Timothy says good morning, too," Robin added.

His wife wore no cosmetics. Her hair was unkempt. She wore one of his old shirts and the blankets. They couldn't wake up together, but they could still share the first few minutes of the morning—even if those minutes were, in fact, weeks apart.

"He's threatening to take his first steps any day now," Robin said. "Might happen by the time you get this." A yawn overtook her, and then she reached forward to gather Timothy into her arms. "We're planning to go to the park this morning. I stayed in yesterday to finish up some analysis stuff. Honestly, as much as I want to see you again, I'll be happy when you're back home so I can have a whole day at the office or maybe even a little field work…"

When Robin's message finished, Garrett opened up his own. He faced the recorder with a broad smile. "Hey, Robin. Hi, Timothy. So I had my own day in the park yesterday, working with that volunteer group from the church I told you about. We had a lot of kids there for the carnival, and I won the award for Best Adult Costume." He held up the cheap, gaudy ribbon bestowed upon him by the cheers of a couple hundred pre-teens. "I'm up a little late today, so I don't have much time to chat. Gotta get to the office. Love you both! Bye!"

He routed the message onto the next available packet relay drone before turning back to business traffic. Decryption of the message contents required multi-layered passkeys, including retinal scan and a voice stress test.

"Given recent developments within your region, management authorizes a change in posture," began the message. "Accordingly, your recommendations within report #25256. A are hereby adopted, specifically regarding acquisition of high-value personnel.

You may exercise command judgment following the guidelines listed below…"

Garrett cheered in triumph. Even for a natural morning person, he felt greater energy than usual as he leapt out of bed.

He jogged to the office as part of his weekday routine. Today's run felt lighter and shorter. Plans and possibilities crowded his mind. Ideas kept coming as he enjoyed the morning light and the fresh scent in the air. Only when he cut through the park did he think more about his faraway family. He'd do them proud here, he thought. Robin was proud of him for getting this assignment in the first place, but this was the sort of opportunity he'd reached for ever since arriving on Uriel.

The working-class neighborhood stirred with its workday morning grind. Garrett took every grumpy face and bleary look in stride. He jogged with a new spring in his step. He made a pit stop on the way to the office, thinking this would be a good day to show a little extra appreciation for his co-workers and their efforts. Twenty years of working in human resources before this new phase in his career provided Garrett with a lot of great experience in managing people. A little bit of effort and a dash of personal touch improved the work environment for everybody.

His "office" looked to ordinary people like a regular, modern, two-story home. He arrived as the younger kids of the neighborhood headed off to school. He waved to a couple of little girls from the door with a flat cardboard box balanced in one hand.

They waved back with their little faces full of smiles and sunshine. "Thanks for buying cookies for the fundraiser!" they called back.

"Aw, you bet, Julieta! I love 'em! Have a good day!"

His holocom and his vitals checked out on the home's security systems, all of them more advanced than anything available on the civilian market. He moved straight through the living room to the stairs, passing another virtually instant, high-quality security check on the way to the extended basement.

The usual media channels played on holo screens against one wall. Jim and Lori sat at their desks, working on reports or maybe goofing off before the morning meeting. Garrett couldn't tell from here. He set the box down on the table.

"Hey, guys!" Garrett greeted them brightly. The other two faces turned toward his, looking neither happy nor sad, but he knew he would turn that around. "Listen," he said with obvious energy, "we're gonna have to call everyone in. I'm gonna grab a quick shower upstairs, and then we'll get right down to business. Oh, and pull up the local talent files, would you please? The deniable asset stuff?"

"Sure," Jim yawned.

"Everybody?" asked Lori. "Is something happening?"

"Big things, yeah!" Garrett assured them. "I got the authorization. We've still got two passes for the academy graduation tomorrow, right? Great! That'll be Lori and I. Jim, I need you to put together some local resources for a personnel acquisition right away."

Lori blinked. "You mean we're kidnapping somebody?"

Garrett made a playful face. "Well, we don't call it that in this business, do we? Anyway, like I said, call everyone in." He pointed to the box on the table. "I brought donuts!"

Jim and Lori stared at him until he bounded back up the stairs. "I swear to God," Jim murmured, "I really think he's a double agent for Archangel and he's just fucking with us until we all get arrested."

• • •

Civilians in the audience outnumbered those from the military. Most wore formal clothes. The military guests—overwhelmingly officers—turned out in full dress uniforms. Not all of the uniforms were native to Archangel, either; Tanner saw guests from New Canaan, Quilombo, and others, along with a small contingent from the Union fleet. For many, this was one of life's big milestones. For Tanner, it was something to sit through until he could meet his friend, though he had the fortune of being seated with Nathan's attending relatives.

"We're still not sure where Nathan will be assigned," said Anthony Spencer in the break of applause between speakers. The greying *paterfamilias* of the Spencer clan was accustomed enough to power and influence that he seemed perfectly at ease here. He didn't even care about the stature of the keynote speaker. To Anthony, the only important person here was his great-grandson.

Tanner could sympathize. Besides, he'd seen the president speak in person plenty of times. Aguirre took the podium and accepted the usual cheers and applause. Tanner clapped as a matter of rote behavior. "Wait, you don't already know?"

"Oh, he put in a wish list," explained Anthony. "They don't get told their assignments until they get the diploma and the commission here at the ceremony. With the third-year transfer status and all the politics there, who knows how it'll shake out?"

He smiled as he spoke, like a parent teasing at a good birthday gift. Tanner had only met Anthony a few times as a child: a commencement ceremony here, a basketball championship there. Nathan's parents usually invited Tanner's family to their extravagant Christmas party, where they spent more money on catering than Tanner's parents earned in a month. The old man always attended, relishing the role of the generous elder.

Many of Anthony's children and grandchildren were trapped on Michael. His wealth and influence couldn't get them out. It left him fewer descendants to dote upon. He sat holding his wife's hand as Aguirre opened his speech with the usual thanks and platitudes. The opportunity for quiet chatter had passed; anything more now would be impolite.

Tanner opened a holo screen, mindful to keep the size and brightness turned down lest other guests notice him sending out a message while President Aguirre held forth on the honor and tradition of the Archangel Naval Academy. He missed Aguirre's first jokes while he keyed up the presets for personal messages.

The current adjusted time for Fort Stalwart on Raphael popped up as he routed a note to Lieutenant Lynette Kelly. "What's the best first assignment to get coming out of the Academy?" he wrote, then quickly sent it off and closed the program. The holograms vanished.

As soon as he looked up, he noted a couple of disapproving glares from people around him. Some of those people wore officers' insignia. Tanner dutifully if grudgingly turned his attention to the President's speech.

"Many of you here have already seen combat and earned your bloodstripes," noted Aguirre. "This class has known combat and sacrifice. Sixteen of your classmates gave their lives during their summer service cruises in defense of this system. Their war is over. For the rest, even those who have seen combat before today, this is only the beginning. You're doubtlessly wondering when it might end. I don't know the answer to that. I can only promise you that we will prevail. Today, I want to talk about what happens next.

"We must look not only to our final victory in this conflict, but *past* this war and into the Union and the greater galaxy beyond it. We must consider how to defeat NorthStar and Lai Wa, and also how to protect ourselves when they are no longer a threat. We are still a part of the Union. We may make stronger alliances with our neighbors. In the end, though, we must rely upon ourselves.

"Before this war, NorthStar, Lai Wa, and CDC provided an illusion of security. They sent occasional patrols, backed up with a great deal of hype and rhetoric. We saw how hollow that protection was not only through our own experience, but through events like the vicious pirate raid against Qal'at Khalil. That illusion is gone now, replaced by a genuine threat from our alleged protectors. But the price we paid for that illusion is gone, too. We now carry the burden of our own protection, and indeed, we have become stronger for it.

"That is why I am calling upon the Senate to make our current force metrics permanent. We must keep the Archangel Navy and the Civil Defense Force strong. The numbers of men and women in uniform and the warships in service must be our new standard. When this war is over, parties outside Archangel and perhaps even beyond the Union will believe we are weakened and vulnerable. We cannot afford to let that perception attract new threats.

"We will have peace. We will have security. This war will end. We will move on to a brighter tomorrow. *This*," Aguirre emphasized, gesturing to the assembled graduating midshipmen in their expanded numbers, "this is part of that tomorrow."

Cheers and applause built, but Tanner felt a growing pit in his stomach. The reaction of the audience didn't surprise him. This was a navy establishment in a shipbuilding city. All of these families, by virtue of these graduating midshipmen, were now navy families. A great many of them had probably been navy families already.

Lost in his thoughts, Tanner paid little attention to the rest of Aguirre's speech. He'd done his policy bit, anyway; from there, Aguirre returned to congratulating the students, encouraging them for the days and years to come. He stayed with his audience.

Tanner's concerns took him well beyond the academy. For all its faults and shortcomings, the one true accomplishment of the Union—apart from creating a unified front *vis-à-vis* the known alien states—was that it prevented a serious arms race after the Expansion Wars. Treaties limited the size of militia fleets of individual Union states. Despite the drastic losses of ships in the Battle of Raphael and the months that followed, those treaties flatly prohibited a system like Archangel from fielding a battleship, let alone the pair that she now held. Archangel's state of war qualified as an extraordinary circumstance. Even the Big Three corporations couldn't muster enough support to make the Union Assembly declare otherwise. But what would happen to those ships after the war was still in question.

The Union's treaties on arms limits were designed in part with a reliance on corporate security fleets. While other corporations wielded military might, the Big Three easily held the largest forces outside of the Union Fleet itself. If the last few years had proven anything, though, it was that the Big Three—now the Big Two—could not be trusted.

The status quo lay in ruins. No one knew what would rise up in its place. The vast distances between Union systems meant that chaos spread quickly, while order only grew over time. Aguirre wasn't wrong, at least assuming Archangel did somehow win the war. Even after the war was over, the Union would probably be a rough place for years to come.

Tanner didn't know how he felt. He wanted his home system to be strong. He understood the notion of deterrence through strength. Yet he couldn't shake the feeling that something about this was all wrong.

Applause shook him from his thoughts. Aguirre remained at the podium, now joined by the academy commandant. Anthony smiled proudly. "All graduation ceremonies are the same," he said. "You wait through a lot of speeches for this one part."

"Midshipman Ricardo Gonzales," read the commandant. A young man in dress greys marched from the graduate formation to the smiling president and commandant. "Midshipman Gonzales," continued the aide, "you are hereby commissioned Ensign Gonzales and assigned to the operations department on *ANS Roland*. Midshipman Jennifer Adams…"

It was impossible to make out Nathan's face from Tanner's seat. At first, the names seemed to have been randomized. Decorations on the uniforms offered some hints as to who had completed a full four years and who had transferred in after the war started. From that, Tanner figured out the order of precedence. Despite his solid performance, Nathan would likely be among the last called.

As the wait dragged on, Tanner felt the buzz of his holocom on his wrist. He glanced around to see that his would not be the only open message screen in the crowd. As he hoped, he found a reply from Lt. Kelly.

Looking at the timestamp, he noted a two-minute turnaround from when she'd received his last message—and she was in the middle of the work day. He reminded himself twice not to read too much into that.

"Depends on your career goals, of course," her note read, *"but the fastest advancement happens on destroyers and cruisers. You get more chances to check off all your qualifications. Groundside posts and support ships slow you down because you don't get the right experience. It's also a matter of shining in front of the right people. Operations and Weapons are good, Supply not so much. That sort of thing. I'm guessing the battleships are great if they give you a lot of chances to look good in front of senior officers. Our promotions are usually more political than they are for you enlisted guys, too.*

"I'll assume you're asking about your friend. *If you're actually considering a shot at the academy, I won't know what to believe in anymore. The shock might kill me.*"

Grinning, Tanner looked back to the stage. As if on cue, he heard, "Midshipman Nathan Spencer." He saw Nathan step out, looking as sharp as the rest in his clean-cut uniform. "Midshipman Spencer, you are hereby commissioned Ensign Spencer and assigned to the Operations Department on *ANS Beowulf*."

Tanner's eyes widened. Operations would put Nathan into rotation on the command bridge. The department handled all kinds of matters throughout the ship, too, but at the moment Tanner saw everything through the lens of Kelly's message.

He felt a pat on his back. The influential patron of the Spencer clan favored him with a grin. "I'm glad you'll be on the same ship," Anthony said a little too proudly.

The ceremony concluded before Tanner overcame his reaction, which varied between sympathy for Nathan—whose family had always pushed him a little too hard—and the resentment of wealth and privilege. Nathan would already get the opportunities and advantages reserved for officers. Was that not enough? Didn't some midshipman who'd spent all of their college years in the regimented academy environment do more to earn that billet than Nathan had as a third-year transfer?

The ceremony ended with loud cheers, hugs, and smiles. Stiff decorum crumbled as graduates and their families rushed to reunite. Tanner pushed his irritation aside. His friend may have had little or no say in the matter, and in the end Nathan would still be put in harm's way like anyone else in a combat billet. He bid Anthony a momentary goodbye and started working his way through the crowd. Many of the new officers headed straight into the audience. One human wave met another in a mess of hugs, bumps and apologies.

Tanner managed to track Nathan as he left the stage. He gently shouldered past a graduate kissing her civilian boyfriend, dodged a crying mother, and then found himself stuck behind a wall of lieutenants and lieutenant commanders who likely wouldn't grant any pardon to an enlisted man who pushed through them regardless of his impressive medals. As he turned back to find a way around, Tanner bumped into a lovely blonde who grabbed onto his shoulders to keep from falling.

"Oh, I'm so sorry about that," he said, gently holding her arms until she was back on sure footing.

"No, it's my fault," she laughed, "I was following too close. You blaze a good trail." She patted his collar smooth and then shrugged. "This is a mess. Maybe I'll wait out the crowd."

With an understanding smile, Tanner plunged back into the mob. Soon enough, he broke through the worst of it and weaved his way up near the stage.

"Tanner!" someone shouted. Nathan's embrace nearly threw him off balance. "Aw, man, I'm so glad you made it."

"I am, too," Tanner said, clapping Nathan on the back before letting go. "Congratulations. It's really good to see you."

"You, too."

"I was sitting up there with your great-grandparents," explained Tanner, gesturing with one thumb over his shoulder. "I don't think they wanted to try to get through that crowd."

The comment seemed to reduce Nathan's excitement. While he didn't quite lose his smile, the hesitation in his nod and his simple, "Yeah," spoke volumes.

Tanner let it drop. Family influence or no, the academy was no cakewalk. "You did good. I'm proud of you. *Sir*," he teased.

"Oh, god, I don't know how I'm gonna get used to that," Nathan groaned. He then regained the bit of excitement he'd lost with the mention of his relatives. "Hey, guess who else is here?" Nathan led Tanner's gaze to one side.

She stood apart to allow the two their brief moment, grinning with a mixture of amusement and pride. Her blue Union fleet marine dress uniform stood out among the greys of the Archangel Navy. Unlike the graduates, she'd been wearing her second lieutenant's bars for over a year now.

Tanner rushed forward to throw his arms around her. Music blared over the PA and people shouted all around them, but Tanner heard only Madelyn Carter's happy laugh.

• • •

Lori didn't conceal her irritation as she walked off the academy grounds among a throng of other attendees. To be sure, most people looked happy and excited for the new graduates in their family or friend circle, but hers wasn't the only annoyed face in the crowd.

Someone was grouchy about putting up with extended family. Someone else loudly complained about the president's politicization of the event. And *someone* had been pushed by her boss into getting up close to a known mass murderer. She wasn't terribly thrilled by it. Unfortunately, her boss was over the moon.

"You did a great job in there," he gushed. Garrett was careful not to say anything incriminating or attention-grabbing while walking through the security gates and out onto the street that made up the academy's north border. "This is exactly the sort of chance we were hoping for!"

Lori grimaced in disbelief. The team's instructions offered considerable leeway in terms of choosing a target that was both high-profile and vulnerable. This wasn't what she'd expected at all. The chances of grabbing one admiral or another had been slim to begin with, and they'd already known Admiral Yeoh and her chief deputies wouldn't be in attendance. Going after the president was never in the cards. But *this*?

"There had to be a dozen senators and five CEOs in there," she pointed out, "not to mention all the senior officers. Any one of them would be less trouble than what you're planning."

"Nah, it'll be fine! We can do this. Look, we know the hype machine exaggerates the stuff he's done for the sake of propaganda. That's the whole point, though. Think of what a PR coup this could be! And think of how good we'll look for pulling it off!"

She bit back her immediate responses. There was no dissuading him when he got like this. On the contrary, she'd only earn herself another "honest, one-on-one conversation" about her attitude and her semi-annual review. "So what's the plan now?"

"I've got to go meet with our outsource assets," he said. "You stay on our target. You might want to put on a coat or something. Change your hair a little, maybe, so you don't look quite the same."

Lori's pace slowed considerably as he relayed kindergarten-level shadowing techniques to the most experienced agent on his team. "I'll go get right on that, Garrett," she said subtly enough for him to miss her sarcasm.

"Great!" he waved, trotting off to the event parking area down the street. "Reach out on your holocom when you have news!"

• • •

"You're kind of a big deal at the academy, Tanner," said Nathan. He pulled the cloth napkin from his lap and put it beside his plate. The waiters wouldn't be long in sweeping up the remains. Service at this restaurant, as with everything else, was impeccable. "I had whole class sessions about you three times this year. Crisis management, leadership…did you know your jump from *St. Jude* is a physics lesson?"

Tanner couldn't help but glance at Madelyn across the table, who seemed to enjoy seeing him blush and wince at the same time. "Yeah, I got a letter from Mr. Chao before the invasion saying he was using that as a physics lesson back in school," Tanner admitted. "He asked if I could send him the actual numbers from my helmet. What sort of 'leadership' lessons did they use me for, though? I can't even manage a cleaning detail."

"It was an ethics discussion. Not much of a debate, since everyone took your side of things."

Madelyn gave a snort. "That must have been nice."

"They talk about that at Annapolis, too?" Nathan asked her.

"Are you kidding? They talk about all of this non-stop. Archangel tops the interstellar news almost every other day. People feel like this is the focal point of all the Union's problems. Even more than Hashem. They might be bigger, but that's still seen as an internal fight. We're the ones messing with the whole economy," she added with clear sarcasm.

"Yeah, but they talk about Tanner?"

"Sure. He's a part of this. Honestly, Tanner, the day after you finish your enlistment here, you could walk right into the next class at Annapolis. You'd have to set the record straight with some people, but they'd be happy to have you."

"What would he have to set straight?" Nathan asked, skipping right past Tanner's surprise.

"Oh, two years ago someone started up an ethics debate about *Polaris* and *Vengeance* and whether Tanner took things too far. I didn't get to see much of it. The instructor asked me to step out after I said I'd actually been there. He didn't want to 'taint' the debate, he said. I saw the blood and I pulled the trigger myself, so obviously I'm biased."

"Well," spoke up Nathan's great-grandmother, "it's getting rather late, wouldn't you say? For us, at least, Anthony?"

"I suppose you're right, Sophia," Anthony agreed.

Tanner noticed the subtle tightening of Madelyn's mouth. He'd seen this before. Medals and memorials and ceremonies were all fine. Most civilians seemed eager to show appreciation as long as they didn't have to actually listen to veterans speak about combat. *We're so grateful for everything you've done. Please don't talk about any of the uncomfortable parts, you monster.*

Whatever her reactions, Madelyn kept up a polite and gracious face. "Thank you very much for having me along for dinner, Mr. and Mrs. Spencer," she said, standing along with everyone else.

"Oh, of course," replied Anthony. "We're glad to know Nathan has good friends like you. It makes all the difference in the world when you know the right people."

"I hate to say it, but I need to go, too," Nathan confessed. "There's too much to get done before checking out."

"That blows my mind," said Madelyn. "They at least gave us the night after our graduation to go out and see family or get stupid with friends."

Nathan gave a shrug. "Your class wasn't already at war."

"Fair enough," she said, and then gave him a tight hug.

Tanner held off on the goodbyes until Anthony and Sophia had shuffled off to retrieve their coats. "I don't get up to the bridge much at all, but I'm sure I'll see you on board sooner or later. Don't be surprised if it takes a while. *Beowulf's* a big ship."

"Yeah." Once again Tanner saw that drop in his mood. Madelyn seemed to notice it, too. Nathan admitted, "Listen, I wanted

Beowulf, but I knew I shouldn't actually get it. It's the old man. He never leaves well enough alone. I never should've said anything to him about it."

Madelyn understood. She shook her head. "This is nothing new. You've got to expect some degree of politics when you're an officer. It happens."

"Yeah, but how many other third-year transfers got their first choice?"

"Did you meet all the academy's requirements?" Tanner asked. "Did you bust your ass and earn that diploma and that commission? Was *Beowulf* on your wish list?" His questions, of course, were all rhetorical. No one skated through the academy, no matter how connected. "Then don't worry about it. Your assignment was out of your hands either way."

He glanced over Nathan's shoulder at Anthony and Sophia, who graciously waited a little further off to let childhood friends say their farewells. "Listen, whatever you do, always play it straight with Admiral Branch. Officer life may be all politics and bullshit like they say, but that guy means what he says. Don't try to impress him. That'll just piss him off. Do your job and don't worry about the rest, okay?"

Their handshake quickly became another hug. "Gonna be weird calling you 'Malone,'" said Nathan.

"Gonna be even weirder calling you 'sir,'" Tanner countered.

"Nah, it won't be that weird," Nathan teased. With that, he gave Madelyn one last hug and left.

"He'll be alright," said Madelyn. "You won't have to look after him. Not on the bridge."

Tanner shrugged. "He wanted this. Lots of people wanted this after Michael. Some of our class from Geronimo dropped out of college to enlist."

"Are you proud of that? Or sad?"

"Little of both. More sad, I guess, but once you face up to what's happening, what else is there? I'm not talking about you," he added quickly. "I mean, you're—"

"I made my commitment," Madelyn cut him off. "Made my peace with it, too. It's okay. If I'd known this was coming, I would have done everything differently, but I'm doing what I can where I landed. When this is all over, I'll probably do more good in the Union fleet, anyway. It's a matter of how large of a lens you want to look through, y'know?"

"Fair enough. Pretty good surprise seeing you here, though. I knew you were friends with Nathan, but I didn't think you were that close."

"We're not," Madelyn answered. "I came to see you."

• • •

The restaurant's bar gave Lori a good view of the exit. Music and conversations covered her holocom calls. The presence of so many uniforms kept her on her toes, but everyone was busy drinking and socializing.

She sat up in her seat to look over the bar patrons and other minor obstructions as if waiting for company. "Looks like the grad and his family are done for the night. He's still with that fleet girl. They're moving out, too. Seem to be sticking together."

"Can you get a read on them?" asked Garrett over the holocom. "Are they friendly?"

"I'm getting a puppy love vibe from him, at least. They both have that Michael tan, too. They're friendly. Don't know how friendly."

"Shit. I hope they're not too friendly. We can't move on him if it means getting some fleet officer tangled up in it."

"They're leaving together. No holo screens open, so I don't think they're calling a cab. Starting to rain, too," she warned. "Forecast said it could get heavy before long."

"Yeah, I saw that. It could work in our favor. Okay, keep following. There are a lot of hotels in this area. He might be staying nearby."

"I'm on it." Lori left her drink behind, throwing on her coat as she walked. Her civilian holocom, mounted on a stylish bracelet, paid the bill on her way out. The other holocom, mounted in her brooch, provided the signal security and other less ordinary options required in her line of work. She gave the glittering jewelry a slight squeeze once she was out on the street. Following behind her targets at a safe distance, Lori quietly said, "Audio relay. Dual human targets twenty to twenty-five meters ahead. Filter ambient noise."

The computer did the rest. Within seconds, she had a clear read of the officer's voice, along with the young man beside her. "…wasn't even sure if I would make it here," he said.

"I figured it was worth the gamble to see you," she replied.

"Isolate and track," murmured Lori. "Relay to group channel B and record."

Her target turned his head curiously. "Hell of a gamble to come all this way from Zheng He to see me. That's nine days from here. Lot of leave time to burn."

Lori's eyebrow rose. Already she knew where the lieutenant was stationed. Located on the *de facto* border of Krokinthian space, Zheng He held a major Union fleet base. That didn't mean much, though. A base that large had thousands of low-ranking officers.

"Well, it's not *just* to see you," said the lieutenant. "Uriel might not be *home*, but it's closer than I've been in a couple years, and it's still Archangel." Her head casually turned as they walked. She kept track of her surroundings, which made Lori a bit wary. So did Malone, for that matter. Yet they didn't seem worried about anything.

The lieutenant brought her hands behind her back. The fingers of her right hand slipped up under the cuff of her left sleeve, and then Lori's signal dropped out as her holocom ceased tracking. "Oh, shit," she grunted, tapping her earring to check its systems, but she already knew what happened. "Hey, it's me," she said, turning back to her comm channel with Garrett. "That officer turned on a white noise field. I can't hear a damn thing now."

• • •

"My bosses took a good look at my personnel files when I got to Zheng He," Madelyn explained, walking somewhat slower. "They read my report on the *Polaris* incident and asked me about it while I got settled. '*Hey, how well do you know Tanner Malone?*' Harmless, except…well, I'm not naïve enough to think anything is harmless when you work in intelligence. But I had nothing to hide. I told them you're my friend. Told them we stay in touch."

"This was a year ago?" asked Tanner.

"Yeah, thereabouts. They didn't ask again, which seemed normal. You aren't exactly a mover and shaker, right? Just an enlisted guy. NorthStar likes to use you as a punching bag for their propaganda, but my department knows that for what it is. Sometimes they tease me about being friends with you when the PR gets really shrill. Everyone busts your chops in the military, right?"

Tanner listened and watched her carefully as they walked to the hotel. A few raindrops fell between them. Madelyn didn't pick up her stride. Neither did Tanner.

"They're watching Archangel as closely as you might imagine. I know it seems like the fleet's staying out of it and they can't publicly take a side, but they want Archangel to win this thing. Nobody in the fleet felt good about sharing so much of the defense structure and strategy with the Big Three. The civilian leadership decided all that. Nobody in the fleet really trusts them.

"On the other hand, this whole thing has everyone worried, Tanner. Yeoh scared the living hell out of a lot of professional naval masterminds with what she did at Raphael. The whole establishment was focused on figuring out how to prevent another Qal'at Khalil from ever happening again. That was scary enough. Then this war breaks out and Yeoh *wrecks* a whole century of tactical thinking in a single battle, along with one of the main arms of the Union's defenses." She shook her head. "They're watching like hawks. It's not just here and Hashem. Lots of other places are getting worrisome."

"I've heard," said Tanner. "We're not entirely in the dark out here. We still get news."

"Sure. Anyway. They watch things here. They watch Hashem." She paused to glance around again, entirely subtle except for Tanner's interest. She was good. "They don't spend much effort watching you, but it's not like they haven't noticed."

"Noticed what?"

"You're a player in all this, Tanner," Madelyn told him. "It might not seem like it, but you are. You've been close to the top. You're one of Yeoh's favorites. You're always *there*, Tanner," she pressed when he made a face at the idea of Yeoh singling him out. Her voice stayed low and her demeanor remained perfectly calm. "Shit hits the fan and everything's going to hell and oh, look, there's Tanner Malone in the middle of it. *Again.*" She fell silent long enough to take his arm and lead him over to an awning that offered cover from the rain.

"So a couple of months ago, after everyone hears Prince Khalil is dead, this idle research station out in the ass end of Hashem gets hit. Murtada's guys try to keep the whole thing quiet: the base, the fact that it got hit, what they were doing out there. Only my bosses caught it. They called me in from my normal job, which doesn't have anything to do with this. They asked if I'd gotten any letters from you in about that time period—and I hadn't—and then they asked if I figured you'd know anything."

Tanner's face darkened. The rain fell a little harder. "You aren't on leave at all, are you?" he asked. "They sent you out here to pump me for intel?"

"Hey, Tanner, listen," she tried, pointedly keeping her voice down. "You're not letting me finish—"

"Finish what? Making your pitch? Why the hell would you think you could turn me into a source?"

"Because you're one of the smartest guys I've ever met," Madelyn hissed, finally mirroring some of his stress. "Because I know you can see a bigger picture here than just Archangel versus NorthStar and Lai Wa over debt payments." She took a breath, trying to dial back the tension. "I'm not asking you to betray anyone. I'm asking you to think of—"

"That's exactly what you're asking, and you damn well know it!" snapped Tanner. Unlike Madelyn, he didn't try to hide his anger, or his hurt. "You really came out here for this?"

Her face turned apologetic. "They asked me if they should try it. I told them if they were going to do it, they'd better send me instead of someone else, because—"

"Why, because you're such a good friend?" Tanner jerked his arm out of her hand and strode away into the rain.

"Yes, because I'm your friend," she protested, following closely. "Because I wanted to play this straight! Tanner!" He kept moving, saying not another word to her as he blew through the hotel lobby, came to the elevator, and hit the call button. "Tanner, please."

He said nothing. He looked at her only after the elevator doors opened, giving her a glare that made his unwelcoming mood plain before he stepped inside alone and closed the doors.

Madelyn's eyes shut tightly. She slammed her fist against the elevator. "Dammit!" No one bothered her. A breath or two later, no longer hiding her distress, she walked out into the rain.

• • •

"He's in Room 2172. He's the only registered occupant and he's got no reason to expect trouble. We have our people working things out with the concierge and hotel security now."

Isaac's dour face stared back at Garrett with a skepticism built up from eighty years on the wrong side of the law. He didn't need to glance back at his compatriot in the passenger seat of the hovercar, or the three others in the backseat. They knew to back him up. If they had objections, he'd hear them once their employer of the moment was out of earshot. Still, he had plenty of concerns of his own. "By 'working things out,' you mean money, right?"

Garrett flashed his charming smile. It didn't work on Isaac. He was well past the days where charm worked on him. "Money and computer code, yeah," Garrett replied. "We're sliding a bug into their system. Their cameras won't see what goes in and out of the hotel for a while. They won't pick up any alarms when you kill the lock on his door with that bumper unit, either. Should be at least an hour before the security systems spot and kill the bug."

"Yeah? And what happens after that?"

"After that it won't matter. If you do your part right, no one will know the guy is gone until sometime tomorrow morning. Then they won't find any faces or voiceprints. The concierge won't know who you are. He'll only know he wasn't supposed to send anyone up or down the freight elevator for a little while. This sort of thing happens in hotels, you know? People need to hide their naughty affairs somehow."

"This seems a little low-tech for you guys, apart from taking care of the security systems," noted Isaac. "I like low-tech. That's fine by me. I'm not so sure I like you guys acting out of the ordinary."

"Hey, if we had more time to plan this, we'd do it ourselves," said Garrett. "That's why we came to professionals like you, and that's why you get paid the big bucks."

"Don't patronize me, kid. You need a cut-out in case things go wrong. Let's not pretend it's anything that it isn't. Who's taking the hand-off?"

"Me. I'll be in that garage tower with the airvan. You call and I'll meet you on the rooftop. I wouldn't ask anyone to take risks that I won't share."

Isaac nodded. Bullshit about sharing risks aside, he figured Garrett wanted to take charge once their target was in hand. Most likely, Garrett would skip right off of Uriel with his target and hopefully be long gone from the system long before morning. "Okay, then. Jimmy," Isaac said to one of the men in the back seat, "you go with him in the airvan."

Garrett's smile vanished. "Now, waitaminute—"

"You want the job done? Then I want one of my guys with you in case it goes wrong."

"Well, sure, but…" Garrett reached for a counter-argument. "We told you this guy's military, right? You don't want every one of your guys there?"

"Listen, pal, military don't mean shit when it's four to one. Especially when you don't see it coming. This guy up there, he doesn't have any reason to see this coming, right?" He paused long enough to read the answer on Garrett's face. "Joey and I are ex-military, too, and I actually fought in a war. A real war, with the fucking aliens. We know how it is. Soldier boys train for unarmed maybe two, three hours a week. He's got nothin' that's gonna surprise us. Neil and Clayton here? They've been bouncing at bars since they were eighteen. Bars that military guys liked, too. Soldier boys train and they play war, sure, but these two have *actually fought* almost every damn day. Besides, nobody gets up after a shot from a stunner. You just be there when it's time."

"Okay," said Garrett, holding up his hands. "Only trying to be helpful."

"You be helpful by doing your part. We'll do ours."

CHAPTER SIX

No Time for Hurt Feelings

"Often, you will hear experienced investigators refer to a pivotal moment in a case as a 'lucky break.' To be sure, luck plays its role. However, a critical eye will show that luck is rarely the deciding factor in most investigations. Remember that a 'hunch' or a 'gut instinct' is usually a connection that our mind has made but cannot yet articulate. Likewise, most 'lucky breaks' only happen because the investigator actively searches every possible avenue.

"Whether you uncover clues through your own actions or you receive information through seemingly random circumstance, you must recognize opportunities when they appear. Ultimately, you must make your own luck."

--MASTER-AT-ARMS RATING SCHOOL MANUAL IV:
INVESTIGATIONS

Tanner held onto his rage long enough to shut the fancy sliding door behind him before he started shouting. "Fuck!" he roared, looking for something in the small, sound-dampening hotel room to throw or kick or smash. He found nothing—or at least nothing that he wanted to pay back the hotel for, anyway. Just a comfortable bed set too close to the entrance, minimal furniture, his bags, and the floor-to-ceiling plasti-glass door to the balcony outside.

He saw his stupid reflection in that balcony door, wearing his stupid uniform with his stupid fucking medals that marked him as being so very important. The Archangel Star was the biggest. It was almost as big as his fist, hanging closely around his neck rather than on his chest like all the others to make sure everyone would see how very *special* it was.

Every now and again he almost felt proud of it.

Tanner tore the Archangel Star from his neck, snapping off a button and ripping some small bit of the seams along the way. He threw the medal across the room at his reflection.

Wait. No. The tumblers on the nightstand were made of actual glass. He could afford to pay for those. He threw one against the balcony door hard enough that it shattered against Tanner's reflection. The other glass, in his hand a second later, soon fell onto the bed. Tanner stared down at it, and then looked back at himself on the balcony door.

"Well, *this* is stupid," he fumed. *Good job, Malone. Feel better?*

He didn't sit on the bed, instead slumping down onto the floor with his back against the mattress and frame, staring back at the door out to the hallway.

They'd hardly talked about anything. Not family, not their worries about home. Not even her boyfriend. For a second there, when she said she came out to see Tanner, he thought—ever so briefly—that it might be about that. He'd actually felt awkward about it, too.

He was over her. Over his crush, anyway. He sure as hell wasn't over their friendship…which at this point might well *be* over.

Nothing about last few years felt worse than the sense of loneliness. The violence and fear couldn't compare. He'd had friends all his life. Good friends. Even in basic training, he'd made friends. And then came *St. Jude*, where the best that he could hope for was to be alone, right up until its destruction. Before the navy, the only funeral he'd been to was his mother's. He'd lost count of all the funerals in the last two years. Many of those buried were friends right to the end.

He'd never walked away from a friendship before.

Tanner touched the holocom on his wrist, opening up his message file. Nothing new turned up. Nothing from the ship. Nothing from any of his friends. Nothing from Kelly, nor anything from Madelyn, who used to be the first name he hoped to see.

And then her name appeared as he stared at the screen. He hesitated, but brought his finger to the highlighted line in the air.

"Tanner," read the message, "I'm so sorry. I didn't mean what you thought I did. There's so much more I wanted to talk about that has nothing to do with my job. This was hanging over my head and I wanted to tackle it head-on. I'm sitting in the hotel bar and I feel like I'm about to fall apart. You don't know what you mean to me. I won't bring it up again. Please talk to me."

The lump in his throat grew as he read the message. He was still mad. He had every right to be angry at her for taking on a job like this. Her plea made him reconsider the words she'd said in the street outside. Maybe he had misinterpreted? Jumped to conclusions?

He hadn't denied anything or feigned ignorance like he should have. Had anyone else in the galaxy asked him the same question, he'd have thought to play dumb. That only proved she was the right person for this job, though…which made him angry at her again, and angry at the people who'd picked her out for it.

"…I feel like I'm about to fall apart," read the message. "You don't know what you mean to me."

Tanner fumed rather than exhaled, but as he focused on his breath, the swelling sensation in his throat diminished. *Maybe we can both learn to shut up about some things,* he thought. *God knows I keep my mouth shut about enough stuff already. What's one more stupid secret between friends?*

The anguish faded, but the anger didn't. It held as he stood and surged again when he glanced in the mirror next to the bed and saw the tear in his collar. The war and the military might still cost him one of his dearest friendships because of what they couldn't talk about. But he had to try.

Opening up his door, Tanner found four rough-looking men right in front of him. One held a stunner pistol. Another busily keyed up a small bumper unit. The men blinked in surprise. Tanner didn't.

He had considerably more training for this sort of trouble than for post-adolescent drama. He was also already pissed off.

Tanner launched his fist at the older man holding the bumper without a second thought, crushing the man's nose. The bumper unit fell to the floor as its owner stumbled backward into his friends' arms. Tanner grabbed the one holding the stunner by the wrist and pulled, keeping one foot planted firmly where it would trip his victim.

"Neil!" blurted out one of the bigger men. Neil tumbled over Tanner's outstretched leg into the hotel room, flopping awkwardly onto the bed. His stunner fell to the floor. Tanner slapped his hand over the door controls to shut the portal behind him, leaving the other three men out in the hallway.

Aw shit, he realized. *Why didn't I grab the guy with the bumper instead of the guy with the gun? They can't shoot through the door with a stunner!*

Rising to take his first swing, Neil accidentally kicked the weapon under the bed before Tanner could grab it. Tanner ducked the blow and forcefully planted his fist straight into the bigger man's crotch. Following up with moves drilled into him since basic, Tanner went for Neil's jaw with his left hand, catching the bigger man with the heel of his palm in an open-hand uppercut. He closed his fist and brought it back down in a hammer blow against the collarbone. Neil's right arm went limp as he let out a grunt of pain. Tanner promptly seized the limb, twisting it painfully and punching Neil's neck and side with his other hand. In another well-practiced move, Tanner twisted the arm and held it against his hip, pushing Neil's face down on the floor.

He forced himself to think: fight, flee, or talk? Fleeing seemed impossible. The bathroom door wouldn't hold any better than the hallway door, his chances of slipping past all three guys outside and then outrunning them down the hallway looked slim, and the balcony offered only a lethal fall. Fighting looked just about as bleak. It seemed too late to talk, but he didn't even know what this might be about.

"Who are you guys?" Tanner demanded. An alarming thought occurred to him—one without much to back it up, but the consequences made it an urgent concern: "Are you police?" He didn't know what the police could want him for, anyway, but police could make mistakes. Tanner sure made plenty.

The door behind him beeped. He slapped the control panel to reset the lock. Neil stirred. "Ugh, fuck police," the big man groaned. "Fucking kill you, man." Though his right arm was both useless and restrained, Neil reached for something in his pocket with his left hand. The door beeped again, and this time it didn't respond to the reset button.

Can't flee. Can't talk. Out of time. Damn.

As the door opened, Tanner pulled on Neil's right arm and kicked hard at the base of his skull. Neil went limp.

"You motherfucker!" someone shouted.

Tanner dove to his right to evade the stunner blasts he knew would come. He only thought to get around the foot of the bed, but he swept up the second drinking glass that lay on the blankets as he moved. At such close range, his speed did less to save him than the shooter's broken nose. Tanner threw the drinking glass. Though he missed by a mile, the effort still made his enemy flinch, ruining the second stunner shot.

No third shot followed. One of the other, bigger attackers charged in. Tanner's right foot came up to meet the incoming threat with a side kick intended to drive the attacker back, but it wasn't fast enough. Broad shoulders and strong arms lifted him up off his feet and then brought him down hard past the foot of the bed. The back of Tanner's head slammed into floor, which for all its lush carpeting still hurt like hell.

Tanner didn't even think about wrapping his legs around his attacker's waist, preventing the other man from getting too much leverage or control. Janeka's regular training sessions turned such moves into rote behavior.

"Clayton," yelled the older man, "check on Neil!" Tanner caught a glance of the others behind his attacker. One of them, bigger and younger than the rest, turned to check on their fallen friend. The older man came up behind Tanner's attacker. Blood flowed from his nose and his eyes were still blurry with tears. He held his stunner ready for a clear shot. "Hold 'im down, Joey!"

A grapple was both good and bad: a hit from a stunner would knock out Joey, too, but wrestling with one enemy made Tanner an easier target for a beating by the others. Joey was bad enough alone. He caught Tanner across the cheek with his elbow. Tanner got his left arm in the way to block a second blow, then clawed viciously at Joey's face. He didn't get a good grip, nor did he catch his foe's eyes, but Joey brought both hands up to pull the grasping attack away—which left him open for a nasty right hook to the temple, and then a second similar blow.

"Oh shit, Isaac," came another voice—presumably Clayton's—from the back near the door. "I think Neil's dead! I can't get a pulse!"

"What?" the older one asked in disbelief.

Shaken by the blows to his head, Joey put one hand down on the floor to steady himself. Tanner grabbed Joey's wrist, then wrapped his other arm over and around Joey's shoulder, locking in a hold that gave him control of Joey's arm. Tanner followed through with the same viciousness the gunny instilled in all her students, twisting Joey's arm around his back while rolling sideways into a dominant position. In training, the "Kimura roll" usually ended with the opponent tapping out unless they managed a clever escape. Tanner couldn't allow either outcome. Now adding leverage to his lock, Tanner twisted and strained hard. He felt and heard Joey's arm snap.

Both that noise and the resultant cry of pain brought Isaac's attention around again. Tanner lunged for him, sloppily crossing the minimal distance and the corner of the bed. He caught the barrel of the weapon and turned it aside. The electric crackle and white flash of the stunner inflicted a small scorch-mark on the nearby wall.

The stunner offered the best hope of ending the fight. Tanner held to keep it turned away from himself, but he couldn't wrench it free. Rather than waste time on the struggle, Tanner brought his other fist down in the same sort of hammer blow that he'd first used on Neil. As the weapon fell onto the bed, Tanner yanked and twisted Isaac around, sending him stumbling face first into the glass-framed picture hanging beside the bathroom entrance.

That was when his momentum ran out. A heavy, brutal fist collided with his cheek, then right under his ribs. Another blow knocked the stunner from his hand. He heard someone shout at him—"sick" and "fucker" were definitely among the words coming from the fourth and biggest of his opponents—while he suffered a few more blows that he couldn't block. Things got even scarier as Tanner felt himself yanked up off his feet. He regained his sense of direction right before he was thrown straight into the transparent balcony door.

He struck against it with a loud crash. The door buckled under the impact but thankfully didn't shatter. Pieces of the door's frame fell around Tanner as he lay half on the hard balcony deck and half on the carpeted hotel floor. This side of the hotel room offered little in the way of weapons. He saw only shards of glass too small to be of use, broken debris from the door frame, and his stupid star-shaped medal sitting in the center of the stupid black ribbon meant to hold the gold-plated steel in place around his neck.

Tanner rolled over and grabbed for the medal.

"Dammit, my arm!" screamed Joey from one corner of the room.

"Isaac, are you okay?" asked Tanner's last attacker.

"Clayton," gasped the leader as he picked himself up off the floor, clutching at his bloody face, "don't worry about me! Fuckin' finish him!"

Rising to his feet just as Clayton arrived, Tanner blocked the first punch with his left arm, then came back with his right fist. The star-shaped medal now covering Tanner's knuckles landed a stunning blow on Clayton's jaw. Tanner hit his opponent again and again, first across his temple and then over his eye. The arms of the star bent as he struck. Clayton seemed to shrink in height with every blow as the repeated punches left him staggered and disoriented. Tanner soon found himself punching downward, pounding Clayton to his knees until he could push his enemy's head back and deliver a crushing blow to Clayton's throat.

The big man fell backward without another sound. That allowed Tanner to see Isaac bracing himself against the bathroom doorway, blood streaming down his face from a dozen cuts in addition to his nose. His right arm hung limply at his side, but Isaac had his left arm twisted to reach for something in a shoulder holster under his jacket. Tanner's eyes went wide as he identified the small, sleek laser pistol. He rushed forward to turn the weapon before Isaac could point it at him.

He'd seen such a struggle play out in a dozen films and thought it silly and unrealistic every time. Two opponents struggled over a weapon until it went off, usually with both combatants making strained faces at one another to increase the suspense over which got shot. The reality of it played out a little clearer as a blast of red light cut into the wall behind Isaac—on its way out of the older man. He stared at Tanner in shock as he slumped to the floor, smoke floating up from his side where the blast had burned through his chest.

Everything went quiet. Wearily, Tanner picked up the laser pistol from Isaac's corpse and the stunner that lay inside the bathroom. Then he turned to Joey, who huddled in the corner clutching at the shoulder of his broken arm. The big man watched Tanner, saying nothing and making no threatening moves.

"Are we done?" Tanner huffed.

Joey didn't quite whimper, but his emphatic nod wasn't exactly silent, either.

Tanner rolled his neck and his shoulders. His side hurt like hell. His head hurt, too. He took a long, deep breath and let it out, four times as he'd been taught. He raised the holocom on his wrist to call for help…and then stopped.

What do I say? I was attacked in my room by whom? Four guys. Hitmen? They had nonlethal weapons. Spies? The last seemed unlikely.

Tanner knew a spy. Direct action like this wasn't part of her usual method—or at least not direct action all alone. One of these guys might be a spy, but something about it all made that seem unlikely. "Stay," he warned Joey.

He made the necessary rounds, both for the sake of procedure and a bare minimum of ethics, and found he'd have considerable explaining to do after this. Neil turned out to be as dead as his friends feared. Clayton offered no pulse, having asphyxiated from the final blow to his Adam's apple. Blood flowed freely from Clayton's mouth with Tanner's first efforts at resuscitation. Medics wouldn't arrive in time to revive him. With a frown, Tanner closed Clayton's lifeless eyes.

Joey watched in obvious concern. "Holy shit, are they all dead?"

"Looks like," Tanner admitted with a weary sigh. He went through a second round of checks, this time patting the men down for anything valuable or suspicious. Each had a civilian holocom. They all carried knives, but hadn't used them. Isaac had a pair of handcuffs. Only the older man packed a lethal firearm.

He had to call in local police. He and his surviving opponent needed medical attention, too.

But the moment he called for help, this would be taken out of his hands.

"So, hi there," Tanner huffed, crouching down in front of his prisoner. He neither smiled nor snarled. Though Tanner had never conducted a real interrogation, he'd gone through the training in MA school. He knew better than to commit to one approach or another right out of the gate. Tanner needed some interaction with the suspect—other than the punching and kicking—to know where to go.

"You're Joey, huh? Or at least that's what we're calling you?" He watched Joey's eyes. The wounded man could clearly see all three of his friends where they lay dead. "It's fine. I'll call you Joey. You obviously know who I am."

Joey made a face. "What? No, I don't."

The quick reply made Tanner blink. It sounded honest. "You sure? Take a good, long look. It might be the blood throwing you off. No? Huh," he grunted when no recognition dawned in his prisoner's eyes. Tanner didn't expect that wrinkle. Then he remembered how his trainers admonished their students never to show surprise. He'd already dropped that ball. Now he had to roll with it. "I'm Tanner Malone."

Joey didn't seem to recognize the name right away, either, but soon his disdainful expression turned grave. Tanner fished the battered Archangel Star out of his coat pocket and held it up for Joey to see. "Aw shit," the wounded man grumbled.

"There you go. So, you're Joey, and from your accent and your clothes, I'm guessing you're local. And you didn't know who you were coming after? That's interesting."

"I haven't got anything to say to you. I need a doctor."

He knows the arrest routine, Tanner thought. *That's something.* "That'll happen real soon. I'm a cop. Well, I'm a military cop—yeah, didn't know that either, did you?" Tanner put the medal back in his pocket and then called up the ID screen on his holocom to offer some proof. "The procedure's all the same. Well, mostly," Tanner corrected. "You've got all the same rights and such, but…" He shrugged. "You attacked a military cop, so this is going to be a bit more complicated."

He watched Joey's reactions carefully. The look on his face suggested Joey didn't know such details. "So which one of you is in charge?" Tanner asked. "Was it the old guy?"

Joey didn't flinch until Tanner's suggestion led his gaze. "Right," said Tanner. "Did *he* know who was in this room? Did he talk to you about it, at least? Or are you only muscle?"

The prisoner's scowl darkened. "Listen," Tanner pressed calmly, "all I care about is whether you're all spies or if he's the spy and you're just hired muscle. We can wait for you to talk to an attorney, but it's the difference between treason or simple felonies."

"Treason?"

"Well, *yeah*." Tanner feigned surprise that Joey didn't already know. "You see the uniform," he said, gesturing to the tattered remains of his dress coat. "It didn't occur to you that you're attacking a serviceman in a time of war? Unless you've got a hell of a story or something to offer, you're looking at a treason charge. They don't give parole for that. You just go away forever."

"What the fuck are you talking about? I know my rights!"

"You know your rights for civil courts and ordinary crimes," Tanner corrected. "Treason's a different animal, Joey. Besides, I told you who I am. That's a whole aggravating factor on top of all this. We can wait and you can ask your lawyer if you want, but by then everyone's going to be wondering why you didn't speak up as soon as you could."

Joey glanced at his fallen comrades. "Aw Christ, man, all I knew was that Isaac got hired to grab somebody out of this room!"

"Isaac's the old guy?" Tanner asked. "You work for him? Who does Isaac work for? Who hired him?"

"Some guys," Joey protested lamely. "For all I knew this was some gambling debt that didn't get paid, y'know?"

"Right, so you've decided not to cooperate. I'm sure nobody will be annoyed that the real bad guys got away while you stalled."

"No! Isaac said it was best if he didn't tell us too much. I saw the guy who hired him. Short red hair, decent shape. Looked like he was about thirty, but how can you tell age for sure, right? Isaac has worked for the guy before. Said his name's Garrett. He planned everything."

"What was the plan, Joey?" Tanner watched him sweat. "Joey, this is the difference between spending your life in a military holding cell or going to a civilian rehabilitation center and maybe parole. You understand what I'm saying? I'd guess that *maybe* you didn't know what you were getting into here, but unless you back that up with something concrete in the next few seconds—"

"Isaac didn't know everything either, okay?" interrupted Joey. "None of us did! This was just a job, y'know? We were supposed to grab whoever was in the room and take 'em to an airvan outside!"

"Where outside?"

"Upstairs," Joey admitted, losing more of his bluster now that he'd gotten talking. "Up to the roof in the freight elevator. That smiley motherfucker who hired us is in the van waiting on a signal. I don't know him, but he's with one of ours—Jimmy—and Jimmy doesn't know any better than we did," he added, realizing his mouth was now outrunning his brain.

"What's the signal?"

"I don't know, a wave, maybe? Isaac was gonna call Jimmy on his holocom."

Tanner tore Joey's holocom off his wrist. "It won't be weird if he gets the call from you instead of Isaac, right? What's your access code?"

"Hey, you can't do that! Jimmy will think I flipped on him!"

"Well, Joey, you kinda did. So either you tell me your access code to your holocom, or I can tell the judge that you decided not to help me at the last second and that's why the actual spies got away. I bet that will help your case a whole bunch."

Joey winced. "Fuck, it's my fingerprints on the reader. Pinkie and ring finger. Here." He squirmed painfully to offer his right hand. "You're not gonna kill Jimmy, too, are you?"

"It won't be my first choice." Tanner looked at the holo screen projected by Joey's reader and set it to unlock.

Then he heard the door chime. Joey seemed just as surprised as Tanner. Turning back to the door, Tanner activated the hallway viewer to find a lone woman in a dress Union fleet marine uniform on the other side of the doorway.

He considered the possibilities of a con or a trap, turned and shot Joey with the stunner, then turned back again. Joey slumped over on his side unconscious as Tanner opened up.

"Tanner, I'm so—holy shit!" blurted Madelyn.

"Apology accepted. I gotta go deal with the rest of these assholes. Right now."

Madelyn glanced briefly at the smashed room and the bloody bodies. Then she shrugged. "Let's go."

• • •

Lori expected to take the front passenger seat when she got to the airvan in the high-rise parking structure. The unfamiliar man in the chair gave her pause, but Garrett looked up from the pilot's seat and waved cheerfully.

His goddamn cheerfulness irritated her even more during an op than in the office.

The wind maintained a steady whistle high up here in the air-vehicle terrace. Fortunately, the rain eased over the last few minutes. Garrett's parking space offered a great view of the city, which Lori would have appreciated but for her concerns about the passenger. She made a show of keeping her coat closed against the wind to cover up the grip of her fingers around the gun in her pocket.

The airvan's side door rose up under the thruster pods that spread out from the top of the vehicle like short, stubby wings. "Come on in!" Garrett called.

"Who's this guy?" Lori asked.

"Oh, this is Jimmy. He's one of our contractors. They wanted a liaison."

Jimmy looked at Lori with cold eyes. He didn't look like a liaison. He looked like a hitman. Lori slid inside and took up one of the back bench seats.

"Great view up here, huh?"

"Garrett," said Lori, "shouldn't we talk in private before this gets rolling?"

"Not time. Isaac should call in any minute now. We'll drop Jimmy and the other contractors off as soon as we do this pick-up."

"Great." She considered her options, but decided she'd have to risk saying more than she wanted to in front of the hired help. Garrett would be headed off-planet with Malone in less than an hour. "So that fleet marine friend of his? She's stationed in Zheng He. That's all I caught before they had an argument and split up." Lori called up the audio file on a holo screen and routed it to Garrett's holocom. "Definitely some personal connection. I couldn't make out more than that."

"Hey, that's good to know. We may be able to use that later when we start the 'interview' process. Every little bit helps." Garrett leaned over to look down through his side window. "Man, this is a great view, isn't it?" he asked again.

Lori heard a beep from the front of the van. Garrett looked over at Jimmy, who now had a holo screen opened up in front of him. "They're ready," said Jimmy.

• • •

The hotel's rooftop didn't offer much in the way of scenery. It wasn't intended for guests. Lights and painted lines marked out parking spots for air vehicles. The only standing structures on the rooftop were the freight elevator terminus, a couple of bulky ventilation intake units directly opposite the elevator, and two-meter perimeter walls to serve as windbreaks.

Tanner and Madelyn crouched between the ventilation units, grateful for the shadows and the clear line of sight to the parking spots. "Still don't know whether it's better to stick together or split up and hit from two sides," said Tanner.

"Well, too late now," Madelyn replied. "We made the call. Don't want to get spotted moving around when they come in. At least here we back each other up." They had both left their uniform dress coats in Tanner's room, reducing them to dark, long-sleeved undershirts. "This better not get to be a pattern with you," she said, giving his shirt a small tug.

"What? My shirt?"

"Every other time I see you anymore, you're covered in blood and surrounded by dead people. Next time we meet should be fine, but after that, I'm gonna have to remember to pack bandages."

Tanner grimaced. "I'd be perfectly happy to break the violent part of the habit."

"Hey, again, for the record: I was way out of line before. Honestly, I didn't mean to actually ask anything, but even bringing it up...I'm sorry."

"We're good. I should have hashed it out instead of walking away," He gave a small shrug. "We both signed up for jobs that ask us to do shitty things all the time. I shouldn't take it personally."

"Right. Anyway, like I was saying, about seeing you when you're all beat up and stuff…" Madelyn took in a deep breath. Tanner glanced at her curiously. She seemed even more nervous now than when she'd brought up the intelligence-gathering questions. "Rick and I are getting married. And I want you to be in my half of the wedding party."

Tanner choked. "*Now?*"

"No, dummy, not now. My family's trapped on Michael. I can't get married with all this going on."

"No, I mean you want to talk about this now?"

"One of us might get shot here. I didn't want to do this without at least asking first. Things tragically left unsaid and all that bullshit, y'know?"

"You're not even twenty-three yet and you're already deciding to get married?"

"Hey, I don't need to wait until I'm going on my second longevity treatment to know he's the one."

Though his mouth hung halfway open, Tanner found himself surprisingly undisturbed by this news. His affection for Madelyn didn't include romantic angst anymore. "You want me to be your maid of honor?"

"No." Madelyn rolled her eyes. "That has to be Becky, my roommate from the academy. She and I have been through a lot together. You'd be there between her and…" Madelyn shook her head. "Look, Tanner, I've seen the things NorthStar says about you in the media. I've heard people make psycho jokes and I've heard all the talk about war crimes. We grew up in the same city, on the same planet, and you're my friend. I want everyone to see you there with me at my wedding so they'll never doubt where I stand. In your uniform, even, if you're willing."

He let out a long breath. "Honestly? I hate wearing uniforms."

"No pressure, then. Tuxedos are fine."

"...is Space Marine Becky single?"

Madelyn snorted, then laughed, and cut herself short when Tanner put his hand on her arm. Lights floated straight over the rooftop, swung around and turned back, this time accompanied by the sounds of an airvan's antigrav systems and maneuvering thrusters. "Shit," Tanner hissed as he guessed the airvan's flight path. "This is inconvenient."

• • •

Garrett loved piloting air vehicles. Sixty years ago, coming out of school on Fairhaven, he'd worked as an air courier. Atmospheric flight offered far greater joy than traveling through space, which was so big and empty that it rarely felt like one was going anywhere. Even a simple airvan like this, so similar to the one he piloted in his first job all those years ago, gave the right sense of freedom and power.

On most worlds, the special license and personal insurance required for air vehicles went above and beyond those for ordinary ground transports. Garrett gladly paid for the classes and permits and all the other details. His first license set him back quite a bit on top of his educational debt, but it was a good job for a kid just starting out. Cruising in over the hotel rooftop, with his mind mostly on the task at hand, Garrett idly imagined himself someday teaching his son to fly.

Until yesterday, Garrett figured it would be a long time before he got to hold his boy or his wife again. He hadn't considered this caper as his ticket home until he had to work out transportation. Even when he and Lori first spotted Malone, he thought only about what a coup his capture would be. It wouldn't turn the war around or anything. Malone was all about propaganda and hype. But because of all that hype, the PR value of his capture would be huge. NorthStar understood PR.

For something like this, Garrett had to conduct and supervise transportation to Fairhaven personally. Heck, he would probably get the stink-eye from his bosses if he *didn't*. He might only be home for a few days, or he might be there for weeks. Either way, he'd see his family again soon.

That was all in the back of his mind, though. Garrett did his job well. He considered his best path to the spaceport, the timing of his chartered flight out, and the necessary risks for evading interception by naval patrols. He brought the airvan over the parking spots once, doing a quick sweep of the area. He didn't see Isaac or his guys, but figured they could be waiting in the elevator rather than standing out in the open. Despite his good cheer and friendly demeanor, he never let his guard down, especially with a hired gun like Jimmy seated next to him.

He smoothly brought the airvan down in the parking spot, situated in a wide open space between some boxy air intake units on the east side of the rooftop and the freight elevator on the west. Garrett parked with the airvan turned south to bring the driver's side cargo door to face the elevator. He backed off on the power and set the thrusters to idle, hoping to see his four other hired guns and a bound—probably unconscious—prisoner appear once the elevator doors opened.

Instead, he saw movement out of the corner of his eye. Garrett turned his gaze to the front of his airvan, where a deeply tanned and somewhat bloodied young man came to the end of a headlong sprint. The agent immediately hit the power to go airborne again, but the kid in the windshield already had his holdout laser pistol up and firing. "No no *no!*" Garrett shouted.

Malone blasted away at the airvan's right thruster pod. Sparks flew and metal screeched as the vital component burst. Suddenly, Garrett believed the hype.

• • •

He considered grounding the airvan his first priority until it lurched up at him from its parking space. That turned his biggest priority into not getting hit.

Tanner didn't know whether to blame his inaccuracy on his holdout pistol or his own aim, but either way, it took him three blasts to hit the thruster pod. He turned the weapon on the other pod as the vehicle revved up and rose. Once again, he needed more than one shot. By the time he struck the pod, he was firing at a moving target. Tanner threw himself out of the airvan's way as it dropped back down onto the concrete and skidded toward him.

The vehicle came to a halt just before it hit the windbreak wall. Tanner scrambled back to his feet and advanced on the open side door, but the smoke and sparks of the thruster pod obscured his view within. He moved quickly, hoping to end this while anyone inside might still be off-balance.

Madelyn saw everything from her vantage point at the air intake units until the airvan flew shakily forward and obscured her view of Tanner. She started moving as soon as she lost sight of him. Even after the airvan stopped, she still couldn't see him, but other matters demanded her attention. The front passenger door flew open, allowing a man in a dark coat to tumble out with a gun in one hand and a frantic look in his eyes.

The stunner limited her to a range of only a few meters. She'd have been more comfortable with Tanner's crappy holdout pistol. Still, her involvement here was questionable enough—to put it lightly—without using lethal weapons. Madelyn closed the distance as her target caught sight of her. An electric crackle and flash of white light burst from her weapon, striking her target in the chest. He jerked, spun, and flopped ingloriously onto the deck.

The airvan's rear hatch opened up as she fired. A blonde woman leaped out, barely keeping her balance as her feet hit the deck. She, too, held a weapon in her hand. The blonde spared only a moment to fire off few rounds at Madelyn without serious aim. She only wanted to keep Madelyn down. The young lieutenant understood that as soon as the blonde fled toward the elevator.

Madelyn rushed after her, but the blonde was already halfway to her escape. The stunner couldn't shoot that far. Luckily, Madelyn had two such weapons, along with a stellar record on the pitching mound. She drew back with her right arm and hurled her stunner.

With over a kilogram of solid metal hitting her on the back of the head, the blonde fell to her knees, but forced herself back up despite disorientation and pain. She made it to the elevator controls before turning to squeeze off one last burst of suppressing fire.

As she turned, Madelyn shot her with the spare stunner at point-blank range. The blonde slumped to the deck as the elevator doors slid open.

The sparks and smoke from the overhead thruster pod prevented Tanner from seeing the blonde escaping out the back. Movement in the front of the vehicle caught his attention as the man in the driver's seat tried to climb out through the passenger's side. Tanner dove in after him. He managed to grab the driver by the collar with his open left hand, bringing his gun down hard on the man's head. The seats between them made it difficult to do much else. Tanner pistol-whipped his target again. He remembered Joey's description of Garrett's red hair before the driver managed to slip free from his jacket.

Neither combatant moved with grace or elegance. Garrett escaped from Tanner's grasp and the vehicle only to step on an unconscious Jimmy. He flopped to the ground while Tanner fumbled his way over the airvan's front seats. Before Garrett could get to his feet again, Tanner came flying out of the vehicle to tackle him. The agent's face hit the concrete deck, leaving cuts on his forehead and cheek.

It wasn't the worst of the punishment he suffered. Tanner slammed his gun hand into the side of Garrett's head. He heard the loud bang of gunfire on the other side of the airvan, but couldn't afford to split his attention from the fight at hand. The agent managed to turn over and throw another punch. It didn't do him much good. Tanner absorbed the blow and drove one knee into Garrett's gut, then struck his head once more, this time hard enough to knock Garrett onto his back.

The gunfire had Tanner worried. He stomped on Garrett's right hand to keep it pinned to the ground while he looked up and around the airvan. The thruster pod overhead stopped sputtering, allowing Tanner to see Madelyn swing around the back of the vehicle with an automatic pistol in her hands rather than her stunner. "Jesus, you play rough," she observed as Garrett curled over his crushed fingers.

Tanner didn't respond. Her posture told him she was fine and that there were no more hostiles to worry about. He released Garrett's hand and quickly stuffed the holdout pistol into his belt at his back.

"You're under arrest—" Tanner began.

Garrett surged up, simultaneously grabbing at Tanner's throat with his wounded hand while reaching around his back for the weapon. Tanner drove another uppercut into Garrett's jaw, knocking his opponent back onto the deck. With no further trouble from the agent, Tanner set to patting the unconscious man down.

"There's one more by the elevator doors," said Madelyn. "I hit her with the stunner."

Glancing over at the man laying by the passenger door, Tanner mumbled, "Think that's Jimmy. This one has to be Garrett." He took the pistol from Garrett's concealed holster under his arm, thankful that the agent never had a chance to draw it, and handed it to Madelyn. He didn't find much else other than the sturdy, high-quality holocom mounted on his wrist.

Several things came back to Tanner then: Scheherazade, his fight inside a tank, conversations with Vanessa Rios, and his own frustrating lack of knowledge and skill with the cloak and dagger aspects of war. He tore the holocom off Garrett's wrist and stared at it silently. More things fell into place. None of them made him feel any better.

"Tanner?" asked Madelyn.

"These guys are Risk Management," he said.

"How can you be sure? I mean, it makes sense, but—"

"This is exactly the sort of piece Risk Management guys like to use." He turned the holocom in his hand. "Sturdy, high-capacity, specifically not a NorthStar brand. I've seen it before. And espionage is all about deniability, right? Those assholes downstairs were hired muscle. This is the guy who hired 'em. So unless there's another cut-out along the way, he's the ringleader. I can't believe I'm valuable enough for something like this, but I guess that's up to the police or naval intelligence or whoever to sort out. Still, it's the only thing that makes sense."

Madelyn nodded. "They wouldn't have handed you off to some other hired goons to bring you in, though. They'd have taken over from here. And whoever brought you in probably would've brought a data-dump of whatever other ops they've got going on. Probably a lot of info on that thing." She winked as he looked back at her. "I know a little about how these things work."

"Yeah. A lot more than I do." He looked back at the holocom. He'd never be able to crack it on his own, and nobody who could—not the police, not the Ministry or naval intelligence—would share its contents with him. "How much trouble are you gonna be in for all this?"

As the words left his mouth, the two heard the soft ping of the elevator doors open on the other side of the roof. "Holy shit!" someone blurted.

Tanner looked up through the airvan's windows to see a couple of men in hotel staff suits. "It's all over!" he shouted. "Navy incident here! Call the police!"

The two men withdrew into the elevator, letting the door close behind them. Local authorities would soon be on their way if they weren't en route already.

"Doesn't look like I'll be able to slip away now," Madelyn grumbled. "So yeah, jumping into someone else's war? Putting my personal relationships before my duty? This mess?" she added, gesturing to the airvan. "Lots of trouble. Probably a whole lot. I knew that going in."

"Probably less if you don't come back empty-handed." Tanner took hold of her wrist and pushed back her sleeve to attach the holocom.

"Tanner, what—" she began.

"You're a fleet officer. Local police need permission from the fleet reps to give you more than a pat-down for weapons. There's no way the fleet okays a search through an intelligence officer's belongings. You can tell your bosses you did all this to cultivate an intelligence source. They'll understand that."

"Why are you giving this to me? You don't want to turn it in?"

"They'll get all the same info out of interrogating Garrett, anyway," Tanner explained. "By the time he admits he doesn't know where his holocom went, you'll be long gone."

"Okay." His plan didn't allay her concerns. "That doesn't explain why."

"What do you know about the *Argent*? From the Battle of Raphael?"

"Same things as everyone else," she answered with a shrug. "Covert Intelligence Ministry ship, fired the first shots. Kept the invasion occupied until the fleet moved in. Her captain died during the battle. She was so beat up they scrapped her afterwards, didn't they?"

Tanner shook his head. "I don't think so. And there's no way Aaron Hawkins was her captain." He glanced at the elevator, knowing he had little time for this. "That ship was on Scheherazade. Nobody I know ever saw her captain. Even Admiral Yeoh didn't know who was in charge of her. *Argent* took a shot that nearly killed me and the rest of *Joan of Arc*'s shore party during the evac. I didn't freak out about it at the time, but looking back I don't think it was an accident.

"I watched the media stories and replays of *Argent*'s performance at Raphael over and over again. At first I couldn't put my finger on it, but I knew I'd seen those moves somewhere. It was weeks before I figured it out. I should've known all along, because I haven't ever studied all that many space battles. *Argent* used some of the same maneuvers that Casey pulled as the captain of *Vengeance* during the raid on Qal'at Khalil."

Madelyn's brow darkened. "Tanner, Casey's dead. He died in the invasion when NorthStar hit Fort Bradley on Michael."

"Yeah. Fort Bradley. Where they held Lauren Williams and some of the other pirates. When it comes to groups like that, the Prison Authority keeps the leaders separated. Casey was held on Raphael until all of a sudden he was blown up on Michael with the others. They'd never have put them all in the same prison together. I've looked it up. And moving Casey would've been a media story. I had alerts set up on all my media subscriptions for him and the others. *Someone* would've reported it, only nobody did, and then the war hit and no one cared about old news like pirates anymore. Except me.

"Madelyn, I've been trying to run down anything I could on this since Raphael. I hardly get off my ship. I can't exactly ask around. People keep track of me. I've had a Ministry agent tell me that somebody reads my mail, and that might've been a joke but it might not. It's taken me two years to figure out even this much."

"Oh man." She nodded despite her discomfort. "What do you want me to do with this?"

"The covert ops ships get repairs and refits done at Uriel Shipyards. NorthStar's gotta be watching that place. I need whatever's on this holocom about the shipyards, especially anything about liners coming in with battle damage over the last few months. I don't think *Argent* got scrapped at all. I think she's still operating with a new skin and the same captain."

"Okay," said Madelyn, trying to catch up with his thoughts. "You figure the Ministry cut Casey some sort of amnesty deal if he worked for them?"

"No. I think he's been working for them since before I ever ran into him."

She stared at Tanner, blinking in disbelief. "Holy shit."

"I can't ask anyone in the navy for help. Not short of Admiral Yeoh herself, and it's not like I can knock on her door. It's one thing for her to talk to whoever she wants, but it doesn't work in the other direction. Anyone else would get into nine kinds of trouble for getting involved, but you're not part of all that. And it's like you said: the fleet has to think about more than just us against NorthStar."

Madelyn frowned. "I meant what I said before, Tanner. I didn't mean to actually ask, let alone… Are you sure you want to do this? I mean, they could call this treason."

"Nobody told me *not* to look into this. Far as I'm concerned, I'm investigating a war crime."

CHAPTER SEVEN

Misdirection

"She's Union fleet, guys. I don't like it either, but those are the rules. Turn her loose and let her own people deal with her. Same with that Malone kid. At least we should get some follow-up on him, right?"

--Inspector Courtney DeLandro,
Uriel Investigative Service, May 2279

"It's a 'special session' of the Union Assembly, but hardly any rules or protocols change. Delegates have standard rights and responsibilities. We've been assured by the Assembly president that we have the top item on the agenda. It doesn't mean we run the show. Border worlds still have priority privileges. Proposals go through ordinary channels. Assurances are not guarantees."

The nineteen junior staffers and honor guard troops in the conference room gave Theresa Cotton their full attention. Usually Andrea or one of her deputies handled this sort of thing. Everyone present was a solid, reliable professional, right down to the lowest-ranked uniform and the staffer with the most menial job. Still, Andrea wanted to ensure nobody got complacent. Having the foreign minister herself conduct the briefing seemed a good way to drive home the seriousness of it all.

That didn't mean they couldn't allow for a little levity. "Think of it like a traditional Catholic church wedding," Andrea chimed in with a smirk. "Standard Mass, but with added matrimony."

Theresa smiled. "Actually, it's rather the opposite. The last five special sessions have had an average of 2.2 divorces among combined delegation staff. Someone did a study," she added once she saw surprised looks from her small audience. "That brings us to one of our serious hurdles: many people in attendance *won't* take this seriously. The sidelines are one great big distraction here, people. Everyone who is anyone or *thinks* they're anyone will try to get a piece of this.

"You may receive invitations to glamorous private parties. Turn them down. You might get notes from admirers wanting to meet with you when your shift is over. Show them to your supervisor and do not respond. There will be glitzy social functions. There will be receptions. I swear to God, someone threw a masquerade ball during the last 'special session.' *Don't go*. Don't even say you'll consider going. It's a trap. Politely turn it down and walk away."

"This is dangerous territory, people," Andrea agreed. "No one from the president on down goes to any parties. We're at war and traveling almost two weeks from home to make this mission happen. The after-hours social stuff is usually a big benefit of the job. But there's PR value in catching even a junior baggage man from our delegation in an embarrassing situation. We're all business on this one. No distractions. No cheap stunts. Clear?"

"Yes, ma'am," responded the audience. Andrea and Theresa saw all the seriousness they needed. With that, the briefing broke up. Men and women, most of them young, left the conference room to pack for a month-long trip that only a couple of them knew was coming before this morning.

"Honestly," said Andrea, "I would feel better if we had a few cheap stunts up our sleeves."

"We'll have our hands full reacting to whatever gets thrown at us," countered Theresa. She sank into a chair and let some of her weariness show now that she was with a trusted peer and not in front of subordinates. "Besides, you said yourself that you didn't want the president caught at some glitzy party while people on Michael are living under NorthStar's guns. The truth is, we could get a lot done at those social functions. Diplomacy happens at receptions and stupid masquerade balls. You think the Congress of Vienna worked any differently?"

Andrea quirked one eyebrow. "The Congress of Vienna?"

Theresa sighed. "Earth, 1815. After Napoleon was defeated, the big powers of Europe met to draw up a new map and prevent another huge war. Most history books only talk about the outcome, but if you actually study it? Every power player and petty noble who could be there was. They all wanted in on the action, so they threw big, gaudy social functions. There was intrigue, scandals… the whole thing was a circus. Just like this will be," she grumbled. "We can't get sucked into the stupid stuff."

"We need to assign someone to keep you from getting sucked into pre-spaceflight trivia."

"You laugh. I'm a diplomat. We study things like this. You study media stunts."

"Yeah, and I'm telling you, we could use some media stunts."

"Ah. Back to this again."

"Theresa, everyone's eyes will be on us. We've got to time everything just right and keep the attention off our real plan until it's ready to go. Wouldn't some misdirection help?"

"Our plan goes into action as soon as the Assembly convenes. We'll know in the first ten minutes if it will work or not. At that point the only thing that'll stop it is if the building catches fire. Or are you proposing arson?" Theresa teased. "If our plan doesn't work, I suppose that might distract from our colossal failure."

"I'm not talking about a safety net. We need something that will grab attention as soon as we step off the shuttles. Something to keep the other side a little distracted. You know, let 'em think they see a knife sticking out of our pocket so they don't bother looking for the gun?"

"We've got less than twenty-four hours. You think you can come up with something?"

Andrea fell silent. Her eyes drifted to the conference room table as her expression changed to a frown.

A knock on the door interrupted her thoughts. The door opened only a second later to reveal one of Andrea's chief assistants. "Sorry for interrupting," said Ellen.

"What's going on?" asked Andrea. Her people held to clear rules for both privacy and urgency. Ellen would have stayed outside if this could wait. Her assistant's expression seemed more awkward than urgent, though, so it couldn't be a disaster. Scandals fell into the press secretary's lap almost weekly, and sometimes more often than that. It was her job.

"Just got word from Uriel. Apparently Tanner Malone was at the academy graduation for a friend. Some NorthStar agents tried to kidnap him in his hotel room after the ceremony."

"Is he okay?" Andrea asked with wide eyes.

"He's fine. The guys who tried to grab him, though…" Ellen winced. "It got messy. He killed three of them. Local police only released him a little while ago. He's probably back on his ship already. They're holding details out of the media right now at the

Intelligence Ministry's request, but it won't stay quiet long. The Ministry warned us as a courtesy."

Andrea's thoughtful frown returned. This was a news story, certainly, but she would normally direct questions to the military or Uriel's police. Ellen plainly brought it straight to Andrea because of the press secretary's past relationship with Tanner. He had a famous name, to be sure, but he was old news to everyone except NorthStar's propaganda machine.

Her thoughts ground to a halt. She turned to Theresa. "Okay. One stunt." Then she looked to Ellen. "Ask the Ministry to leak as much as they're willing. No, wait—I'll talk to them. Tell the honor guard CO I need to talk to him right away. We're adding someone to the guard detail."

Then it was Theresa's turn to frown. "I thought we'd ruled out arson?"

• • •

"I'm surprised you didn't burn the fucking building down."

"Gosh, there just wasn't time," Tanner grumbled through a swollen lip, then looked up at Lieutenant Commander Jacobson's scowl. "I'm sorry, sir. What would you prefer I do in this sort of situation in the future?"

Jacobson released a slow, rumbling breath. Tanner's departmental CO sat behind his desk with a spread of holo screens floating before him. Each screen held a different complaint or damning detail about Tanner's night and the endless hours of civil and military police investigation that followed. Tanner stood in front of Jacobson's desk in the tattered remains of his dress uniform, mostly because MA1 Lewis had said he'd better put it on even if it looked like hell. Tanner still looked like hell, too. For all the wonders of modern medicine, cuts, scrapes, and bruises didn't vanish instantly. Nor could anything replace a night's lost sleep.

"I'm not second-guessing you for using lethal force, Malone," said Jacobson. "That's still the biggest issue. But you were outnumbered and unarmed and had no idea what was going on. You saw no other way to control the situation, and neither do I, so I'll back you on it. Command will back you."

The officer waved a hand through one of the holo screens, killing it as if checking off a bullet point on a list. "Leaving a suspect unattended with broken bones and other serious trauma is a problem, as is interrogating him before medical treatment," Jacobson noted with a frown. "However, you did not use medical attention as leverage. You didn't threaten him with violence. You promised he would receive treatment, and you had *arguable* cause for delay. I've also gotta say that lying your ass off about treason charges was creative. Not the cleanest interrogation, but it isn't exactly a war crime, either. You might receive a formal reprimand. Probably nothing worse."

Tanner couldn't object to that. Everyone felt strongly about such things, from command to the MA department on down to Tanner himself. He'd half-expected to face a captain's mast over it.

Jacobson killed that holo screen. Another one blinked into existence as he opened his mouth for his next point. Tanner felt his holocom buzz on his wrist, indicating that he'd received the same message. He didn't dare open it while talking to his boss. Jacobson glanced at the new screen and then ignored it. Tanner saw the weariness in his superior's eyes. Long nights and unexpected wake-up calls were all part of the job, and Jacobson handled them well, but that didn't make them pleasant for anyone. "You should have called for help. I get what you were trying to—sorry, what you *did* accomplish," Jacobson corrected. "It's hard to argue with the results. But you took huge risks, Malone. If you'd died on that rooftop, or if the bad guys came out on top and took you away like they'd originally planned, we still wouldn't know what happened to you.

"I want to make one other thing absolutely clear above all else, Malone." Jacobson paused for a breath to make sure he didn't shout. "You're a *second class* master-at-arms. You didn't even have anywhere near enough time in grade as a third class to move up to second, either. You're an officer of the law by virtue of the responsibilities of your rating, but you are not a *commissioned* officer and you are not a civil police officer. You do *not* have the authority to fucking deputize *anyone*, under *any* circumstances, especially not an officer in a foreign military. Is that understood?"

"Yes, sir."

"I can't even imagine the shit your friend will get from her command, but that's her problem. I'm glad she stepped up to help. It's complicated and it makes for a longer report and I'm fine with that because you both got out of it alive. But don't try to bullshit civilian authorities with something like that, okay? She helped you out based on friendship. The rest is for her and the Union fleet to work out. Don't try to cover for her."

"Aye, aye, sir."

"I honestly don't know whether you're going to get a pat on the back for this or a foot up your ass. It might wind up being both. In the meantime, I'll tell the chief to take you off of the watch rotation today. Hell, it's almost time for chow. If you go throw on a vac suit right now, you might make it for breakfast. Then go get some sleep. I want a full report from you in department format before 1900 hours, understood? Dismissed."

Surprised at Jacobson's magnanimity, Tanner said, "Thank you, sir," and headed out as his boss turned his attention to the new message. "It's nice to get back to the ship in time for a meal for once," Tanner added as he walked away.

"Belay that," Jacobson spoke up. Tanner stopped in his tracks, wondering why the hell he had to jinx himself. He turned see Jacobson staring at his holo screen. "You've got orders. Temporary Duty, Ascension Hall Honor Guard, diplomatic detail underway. Estimated five weeks." His eyes rose. "Full ceremonial dress uniform required. Your shuttle is in two hours."

Tanner looked down at his tattered, blood-stained clothes. Even his shoes had nasty tears in them. A decidedly unheroic noise escaped his throat. "Seriously?"

"Don't worry about the rest of this." Jacobson clearly appreciated the challenge laid before his subordinate. "Get moving. You don't have much time."

Tanner ran. *Beowulf*'s MA offices lay halfway across the ship from the storekeepers' supply holds, three decks down and far from any shortcuts. Signs of ongoing repair work turned up as he closed on his destination. He saw work benches and heavy tool sets, replacement parts neatly stacked against the sides of the passageways, and bulkheads still discolored by welding torches. This side of the ship had taken a hit during the last skirmish. *Beowulf* got back into top fighting shape within a day, but low-priority repairs still crawled along. He took it all as a bad omen.

Coming around the last corner, Tanner saw the door latched open at his destination. His hopes rose. Even now, with the mid-watch about to expire and the majority of the ship still not yet out of bed, someone was on duty here. The ships' stores were open for business.

He loved the supply guys. He loved them so much.

Tanner found a bored man in a vac suit sitting behind a counter reading a holo screen. Beyond him, Tanner saw racks holding boxes and barrels—and other racks that sat empty.

The Storekeeper Third Class looked up and blinked. "What the hell happened to you?"

"I need a full dress uniform," Tanner gasped. He could easily run a lap of the ship on an ordinary day. The morning after a sleepless night and two desperate fights made it a little harder than normal.

"Yeah, you do. You can put in an order through the ship's—"

"Sorry," he interrupted, shaking his head. "I need it in time for a shuttle in less than two hours."

The SK3's pained, sympathetic expression said it all, but he explained anyway. "Oh man, all of our service and dress stuff went up in smoke in the last engagement. And the original supplier was based on Michael. The navy's still got a backlog of replacement orders. We're on a waiting list."

"They make these stupid suits on *Michael*?"

"I know, right? Wool coats from a planet that's half desert. You think they shear those sheep every other day to keep 'em from dying of heat stroke?" A moment of realization crossed his face. "Hey, are you from Michael? You've got the look."

His shoulders sank. His level of stress didn't. "Yes. Yes, I'm from Michael."

"Wow. I guess you can't catch a break, huh?"

Tanner's jaw set. He hated the supply guys. He hated them so much.

The storekeeper winced. "Guess you'd better start begging and borrowing."

With nothing more to be gained, Tanner bolted out of the compartment. He almost made it to the nearest lift before he heard the storekeeper call out, "Hey, wait! I've got shoes! Does that help?" It brought Tanner to a halt. He turned and ran back, stopping in the open doorway. The storekeeper's face offered up a hopeful expression. "What's your size?"

"Eleven," said Tanner. "I need an eleven."

Once again, the storekeeper winced. "Oh. I've got everything but elevens."

"*Fuck!*" Tanner took off running once more.

The early hour gave him one small advantage: Tanner encountered sparse traffic, and virtually none of it wore officers' insignia. He didn't have to ask for permission to pass anyone by. Tanner vaulted up the steps of each "ladder," still resenting how the navy refused to call them "stairs," and swiftly traversed the passageways leading to his berth.

By the time he arrived, he'd forgotten to enter with any consideration for his sleeping roommates. The soft red lighting required by regulations as a safety measure should have reminded him. Instead, he went straight for the standing lockers near his bunk and threw open the door bearing his name.

"The hell time is it?" mumbled a voice from one bunk. Sinclair already had his wrist up as he asked, answering his own question with his holocom.

"Sorry, personal crisis," explained Tanner. "Reveille's in fifteen minutes or so." He devoted most of his attention to his frantic search. Regulations demanded he keep his gear neatly sorted and organized. As much as he hated the micro-management of his personal property, he had to admit it made for easy packing. Those same regs allowed for a small section of personal gear, however, and the manner of storage there was not so regimented. That small bit of personal storage would either save or wring Tanner's neck. "Wait. No," he grunted to himself. "Pack what you can first, then freak out." He yanked the navy-issue travel bag down from the overhead compartment.

"What's going on?"

"I got back an hour ago and now I've got orders for temporary duty with the honor guard. They want me on a shuttle in less than two hours and I need my dress uniform."

"So?" Sinclair reached for the light switch near his bunk. The room went from red to normal. "Shit, man, what the hell happened to you?"

"I got jumped by some assholes on Uriel," Tanner explained as he stuffed two vac suits into the travel bag. "Ought'a be on the news later. I spent five hours answering the same questions with 'I don't know' before I came back up here. And now I've got this temp duty and it says five weeks with vac suits and ceremonial, which has to mean a presidential trip, which I've never been on, and it's gotta be the Assembly negotiations and I don't know why the fuck they'd want *me* along, but here I go."

"You know the ship's stores are still out of uniform pieces, right?" Sinclair propped himself up on both elbows, his face still somewhat twisted into a squint as his eyes adjusted.

"Yup! That's why I'm so screwed," Tanner answered with grim energy. "I might have an extra pair of trousers and a shirt in here from when I was in the honor guard, but I'm not—yes!" he hissed, tugging a white shirt out from under his paltry collection of civilian clothes. "One part down. Still, it's not like I have an extra coat. Things are expensive."

"I'm sure someone has a coat that fits."

"Even if I find one that fits, it won't be *fitted*. This is honor guard stuff. Every button has to be shined 'til it glows. Things have to fit right down to the millimeter."

"I thought you hated all the parade standards and uniform bullshit."

"I do."

"Then why'd you go for the honor…?" Sinclair's question fell off. He knew the answer to that one. "Oh. Right. Is she gonna be on the trip?"

That made Tanner stop and take a breath. "I dunno. Probably. I can't think about that right now. I need shoes and a coat and all the stupid little pins and accessories." He popped the last surviving button and shed his ruined coat. "A vac suit's fine for the shuttle, but it's not like I can stop at a uniform store on the way to wherever we're going. It's 2279, and we're still wearing wool coats, for Christ's sake." Tanner flung the tattered rags to the deck, but stopped cold when he heard the resulting soft metallic thump.

Sinclair watched Tanner reach down and pull the misshapen and blood-stained medal from his coat pocket. "Oh wow. Is that your Archangel Star?"

"It's a fucking albatross is what it is," Tanner growled. He flung the medal into his locker. His hands came up to rub his temples. "I gotta get on a holocom message and start asking people for help. Maybe I can get Baldwin's patches. They're the same as mine, at least. Have to sew 'em on later. That means I need a sewing kit, too. And pants. Damn it." Tanner pulled the medal from his locker and looked it over again. "Not like I can borrow one of these from anyone. Maybe I can bend it back into shape."

"Put out the message," said Sinclair. He rolled out of his bunk and sealed up his vac suit, scooping his helmet up off of its mount nearby. The young signalman opened up his locker with a touch of his hand. "My pants might work if you hem 'em. Take whatever works. We've got most of the same medals and badges, at least. I'll be back."

Tanner already had his eyes inside Sinclair's locker. "Hey, thanks," he said, but his roommate was already gone.

• • •

"All hands, morning meal will secure in ten minutes."

"Shit."

"Shuttle Bay Two, prepare for arrival."

"*Shit.*"

"It's gonna be fine," Baldwin assured him. She sat on Tanner's bunk with her dress uniform coat on her lap, now devoid of patches on the sleeves and several pins from its collar. She mounted the last qualification badge on Tanner's magnetic "rack," with most of the other badges taken from Sinclair's collection before help arrived. "You've got pretty much everything here, right?"

Collins had dropped off a pair of dress shoes. The coat came from one of the non-rates currently assigned to the MA department, whom Tanner now considered the biggest hero on the ship. Between Baldwin, Collins, and Sinclair, he had most of his lesser medals and decorations replaced. The patches from Baldwin's coat now sat in the borrowed one's pockets. He would need to put some care into the shirt and pants stuffed into his bags. Presumably he would find the right tools among the presidential entourage if he approached a fellow menial servant nicely enough.

He had the belt. He didn't have the gloves, but the guard detail always carried spares. He had as much of the uniform as he could scrounge. The outlook for the final piece remained grim.

Tanner sat on the bunk opposite Baldwin in a standard vac suit. He held his gaudy, bent and bloody medal in one hand and a pair of pliers in the other. His initial attempts at repairing the bent arms didn't look too good. "I'm so grateful that you came down to help me with this," he said. "It means a lot."

"Don't sweat it. Happy to help. Think I'm done here, though. How's that coming?"

He sighed, put down the pliers, and held up his medal.

"Maybe you just need to own it," Baldwin suggested. "Put it on the way it is. If anyone asks what happened to it, tell 'em."

"Nobody's going to ask," replied Tanner, "and I won't be free to answer even if they do. I'm going with the honor guard. I'm supposed to stand there and look pretty."

Baldwin made a face. "They hired you for that? Listen, you're good looking, but I like my men pretty, and you're not exactly… y'know?" She held off her grin until Tanner threw a pillow at her. "At least you're spunky, though. I'll give you that."

"Okay, I gotta go face the music, I guess. You've got the morning briefing, too."

"Right." Baldwin stood, flinging her jacket over her shoulder. "Take care of yourself out there. Try not to get jumped again. Or try running if you do."

"Pretty much my plan. Thanks, Jesse."

"Anytime." She lingered long enough to give him a hug before she left.

Tanner dropped his medal into a side pocket of one of his bags for the sake of visual proof. He shouldered one bag, hooked a hand through the straps of the other, and picked up his helmet. He'd hoped Sinclair would come by again before he left, if only to say thanks for the loaners, but he was out of time. Tanner moved out into the passageway.

He heard her voice before he'd made it ten steps: "Malone."

Tanner stopped and turned around. Almost five years on, he still couldn't say he was comfortable in any encounter with Janeka. It didn't matter how much he respected her. The gunny remained an enigma. "Morning gunny," he said, and then took a risk in the interests of time. "I hope this isn't rude, but I've got a shuttle waiting for me."

"I know. It isn't rude," she said in her usual flat, serious tone. She came to a halt within arm's reach. "Sinclair came to find me. And I saw the news. You okay?"

He gave a slow nod. "Yes, gunny. I think I am."

"You don't have much experience in covert ops and espionage bullshit. I do. When you're back, we should talk."

"I...thank you, gunny," he said. Her thoughtfulness still surprised him. Then her previous statement clicked in his head. "Sinclair came to find you?"

"He said you might need this." She held out her hand. Resting in her palm was her Archangel Star.

Tanner's heart virtually stopped. "I can't..."

"You can. Technically, you're the only other person on this ship who can." She waited until his gaze met hers again. "This ship should be filled with these things. You should be able to borrow one from Wong, or Ravenell, or Lieutenant Thompson, or a dozen others. Hell, maybe you should have a spare. But somebody decided to limit how many of these they handed out after Raphael to make sure they stayed special. So there's only yours and mine."

"Yeah," said Tanner. "Yeah, you're right about that."

"You also know that yours isn't just about you. Mine isn't just about me, either. Take it. Bring it back to me when you're home."

Tanner's load of bags and his helmet left him with one hand free. He accepted the medal and put it in one pocket. "Thank you, gunny."

She paused. "Show me the other one," said Janeka.

Suddenly embarrassed by it, Tanner pulled his own medal out and held it up by its neck ribbon. The star turned freely, showing off the bent arms and blood stains on both sides.

"Four men, huh?"

"I didn't have to take them all on at once. I managed to split them up, but even so…The things you taught me saved my life. Again."

"I would imagine. You have a shuttle. I have a meeting. Bring my medal back, Malone."

"Aye, aye, gunny."

• • •

The summons led her to believe that she would be one of many in the CO's office. She found no one waiting in the passageway outside, but that didn't seem odd. Perhaps they were still on their way. This meeting came on short notice with no indication as to its purpose.

Janeka gave herself a good up-and-down glance to make sure her vac suit was in order. Younger personnel sometimes thought there was some trick to keeping oneself spotless, but in truth it was simply a matter of habitual vigilance. Janeka got her hands dirty all the time. She wouldn't have it any other way.

She pressed the door controls. "Gunnery Sergeant Janeka, reporting as ordered," she announced when prompted. The door slid open. Inside, Janeka saw Admiral Branch at his desk along with a single visitor sitting in one of the two seats opposite the CO's.

That explained everything.

"C'mon inside, Gunny," said Branch. "At ease. This isn't exactly formal."

She entered as requested, and did not stand at attention, but Janeka did not go so far as to adopt the CO's carefree manner. The phrase "at ease" did not mean the same thing in all situations.

"Did I take you away from anything important?" asked the admiral.

"No, sir. The company will do fine without me. Anything that falls through the cracks while I'm away will become a learning opportunity, sir."

Branch couldn't help but smile. His other visitor's smile was somewhat muted, but Janeka noted it. "That's what I like to hear," he said as he stood. "I've probably been tucked away in here for a little too long myself, so I'll let you two talk. I believe you've met. Ma'am. Gunny," he said to each in turn. He closed the door as he left his two visitors behind.

Admiral Yeoh nodded to the other chair in front of the admiral's desk. "Have a seat, gunny," she said calmly. "It's good to see you."

"Likewise, ma'am," said Janeka as she sat down facing the other woman.

"I'm not here to promote you," Yeoh assured her.

"Thank you."

The slight twitch at the corners of Yeoh's mouth and in one eyebrow spoke volumes if one knew her well enough to read her properly. "Heaven knows you aren't ready for that level of responsibility," the admiral said with a masterfully straight face. "Not nearly enough professional knowledge. And you're so detached from your job and your subordinates."

"Yes, ma'am. I would embarrass the navy, ma'am."

Yeoh's eyebrows rose. "Threats, Michelle? How long have we been friends?"

"You brought up promotions, ma'am," Janeka deadpanned.

"I suppose I did," Yeoh relented, and then released a wistful sigh. "Some dreams die hard, you know. The thought of you standing at the sort of rank you deserve…"

"Yes, ma'am, because you have *so much* respect for military etiquette and the chain of command," Janeka replied with the sort of undisguised smirk that few others in uniform ever saw from her.

Yeoh's eyes widened. "I beg your pardon," she shot back with equal sarcasm. "I went through your CO to see you. You saw him yourself."

"You threw the man out of his own office."

"Politely." Yeoh shrugged in the face of Janeka's friendly frown. "It's my navy. I can slip on board unannounced just to say hello if I want. Oh fine," she said as that frown grew ever more skeptical. "I'm here on business."

"What can I do for you, ma'am?" asked the gunnery sergeant.

"I need you in a field op," Yeoh explained, her tone growing more serious. "I may also move onto the flag bridge again soon. Seemed like good reasons to visit."

"We're ready to move?"

"Depending on the Assembly negotiations, yes. Ultimately, we have three possible outcomes. One is a negotiated peace, which seems unlikely but let's not give up hope. Another is an ongoing status quo, which seems to me the most likely. The third outcome will give us an opportunity to move if we're lucky. We must get ready for that now.

"That possible opportunity puts a critical and potentially ugly job on the agenda. It will fall to either us or the Ministry of Intelligence, or most likely another joint operation." She noted Janeka's now genuine scowl. "I know how you feel, and I agree. We'll need some Ministry support regardless, but the more of this we can take on ourselves, the less ugly it will turn out. I hope."

"Understood," said Janeka. "What do you need from me?"

"I need you to put together a ground team for an operation in advance of a fleet action. Yours won't be the only one, but the risks are high enough that you need to be ready to handle this on your own. And again, it could get ugly. I want you to mitigate that as much as possible.

"Unfortunately, none of the specifics that I have to offer are entirely reliable. Locations, targets, and timelines may change. The opposition is difficult to accurately estimate. You will also need to have at least one officer along," she warned, again with a hint of good humor, "but I will make sure they know who to listen to. Beyond that, I do not care about rank or assignment. Tell me who you need. I don't care if you choose them for their specialties or for their experience or just because you consider them lucky charms. I'll make sure you have them. I have a couple of suggestions, but I trust your judgment."

Janeka's eyebrow rose. "What am I looking for?"

"Independent thinking. Talent for improvisation. And above all, trigger discipline."

• • •

"NorthStar has never made *demands*. We have *requirements*, but we have always been open to any chance for negotiations. We have made ceaseless overtures." Anton Brekhov leaned back in his chair with his hands out in a practiced gesture of openness. In the window behind him, Saturn's rings swept upward to offer a visual effect that relied heavily on computer enhancement. The spectacular gas giant did indeed loom outside that window, but not far enough away to offer the image provided.

Seated in the chair across from NorthStar's CEO, Charlotte Robinson tilted her head to acknowledge his point. "I'd like to go over your requirements for our viewers, if I could," she said. "In straightforward language, and without legalistic fine points."

Brekhov flashed a tight, good-humored smile at the journalist. "Legalistic fine points are at the heart of this dispute," he observed, "but please, go on."

"I should note for viewers that you support these same demands from Lai Wa and some of CDC's creditors. You've made joint statements regarding a collective grievance. Feel free to correct me if you feel any of this misrepresents your position.

"You have called for an end to hostilities and the return of NorthStar property, staring specifically with all captured warships. You require the release of all prisoners held by Archangel, and the arrest of a list of people you consider war criminals."

"Yes."

"You have sixteen names on that list, ranging from government ministers and high-ranking military officers to enlisted personnel."

"Being at the top does not make one's hands any less bloody. Being at the bottom does not make an individual less responsible for his or her actions."

"Agreed. And as a related issue, you have demanded—sorry, you require—compensation for the deaths of your personnel in the line of duty, both for their families and for NorthStar. But you haven't put a monetary figure on that."

"We understand that this will require negotiation," Brekhov conceded. "We should never truly be comfortable or casual with the idea of putting a monetary value on human life."

"Don't all NorthStar security employees acquire life insurance policies as a standard benefit?"

"They do, but the nature of this conflict makes those policies problematic. These lives were not sacrificed defending the Union from aliens or criminals. Archangel is liable."

Again, Robinson gave a slight nod. "Finally, you require that Archangel accept its original primary debt obligations. You've also stated that you want an agreement to re-negotiate terms of educational debt. How far are you willing to give on that?"

"Unfortunately, that's the sort of legalistic fine point that I think would bore your viewers," Brekhov answered. "We don't require an immediate monetary agreement. We instead expect Archangel to agree to come to the table and to accept that they must, in fact, pay their debts. We are willing to compromise. At no point has NorthStar broken any laws, nor have we acted in bad faith, but we recognize that the dispute over our educational policies is a key issue. In the interests of peace, we are open to renegotiation of terms, including individual debts.

"However, primary debt—the debts owed by the state of Archangel for its initial terraforming and settlement—is simply not in dispute. Archangel decided to abandon those obligations without cause. And as you stated, NorthStar and Lai Wa are united on this issue."

"Final thoughts, then: how high are your hopes for this special session of the Assembly?"

Brekhov sighed as if to remind viewers that he carried the Union on his back, but he smiled despite the burden. "You know, my hopes are always high, Charlotte. I don't know if we'll find a path to peace and prosperity here, but I know that we can. These last two years have been terrible for the whole Union. It's time to get back on the right track. I hope that President Aguirre will feel the same way."

She smiled back at him. "Thank you for your time, Mr. Brekhov."

"Thank you, Charlotte."

Lights rose throughout the plush hotel suite. Charlotte rose and turned to face the half-dozen men and women observing outside of the camera shots. "And thank you, everyone. I thought that was great. Emily, any concerns?"

Charlotte's technician shook her head. "Everything is good. Hardly needs to be edited."

"Then I think we've taken up enough of your time, Mr. Brekhov." She accepted the older gentleman's handshake.

"I wish I could invite you to stay," he replied, "but I could see my staff over your shoulder during the interview. They have plenty to talk about with me already. It is always a privilege, Charlotte."

The journalist turned for one last handshake and warm farewell with Christina Walters before she and her technician left. Brekhov's eyes never left the two until they were out the door. He then turned his gaze to a man among his waiting staffers. Like every other man in the suite, Jeff O'Neal was well-groomed and dressed in a sharp, expensive suit, but his broad shoulders and tight haircut left him easy to identify as a personal security consultant. O'Neal checked a reading on his holocom and then nodded, confirming that his team could detect no listening devices or other toys left behind by their guests. "We're clear," he said.

Walters gave a teasing frown as she walked over to her boss. "Somehow I don't think the most recognized journalist in the Solar System wants to be tied to an eavesdropping scandal."

"Neither do I," he replied, "but after the last few years, I think we have reason to be careful. We will have fewer lapses if our security is disciplined." Brekhov put one gentle hand on Walters's arm as he walked her back over to their other associates congregating at the hotel suite's tasteful bar. As usual, he saw several active holo screens before them. "So what's so important that you were all making faces while I spoke with a reporter?"

"Aguirre's ships arrived," explained Maria Pedroso, longtime head of Risk Management. "You have good timing. They're exiting now." She broadened one screen with a wave of her finger across its intangible control board, but kept the sound off. Several camera angles provided full coverage of a trio of shuttles, all with their ramps down. A group of people in civilian clothes and a few in uniform emerged from one of the shuttles.

"They're not slacking on security, either," Pedroso commented. "Multiple ships, multiple shuttles, all the usual scouting and arrangements."

Terry Donaldson let out a snort. "You'd think someone would have reason to kill him off," said the company's chief financial officer. "He only started a war and tanked the Union's economy."

"This is live?" asked Brekhov.

"Sure is," Walters confirmed. Her eyes narrowed as she saw the usual entourage of security and assistants that accompanied a head of state file out of the shuttles. "Curious to see who they brought. There's Theresa Cotton, Andrea Bennett—"

"Bitch," grumbled Jon Weir.

Walters threw a teasing look toward the company's chief administrative officer. "Don't worry, Jon, I won't let the bad lady embarrass you again." Her attention returned to the screen before Weir could retaliate. "If they brought both of them, they'll probably have left Victor Hickman at home to mind the store. Hrm. There's Kiribati. I didn't think he'd…wait…"

She reached for one of the other screens and expanded it. They all saw President Aguirre come out of the shuttle to accept the welcoming handshake of the Assembly's vice-chairman. Walters ignored that in favor of an angle showing the uniformed troops lined up beside the entry ramp. "Freeze frame," she ordered. "Huh. Speaking of war criminals."

Pedroso looked over. Her face darkened. "Why would they bring *him*?"

"That's a deliberate provocation," murmured Walters. "Why would they do that?"

"They don't have him out front, though," Weir observed.

"No, they don't," Walters concurred, "but they know we'll see him. And they know every media outlet will catch on sooner or later. This is on all four local news channels. It seems passive-aggressive to stick him with the other uniforms, but they know we'll see him…"

"This is their answer to our complaint about war crimes," said Brekhov. "They knew they could bring Kiribati without much of a fuss because he is a senior official. No one realistically expects Archangel to hand him over. Not even us. They brought a second criminal to drive the point home.

"Pay it no mind, Christina," he continued. "Either they came to deal or they didn't. If they came to deal but refuse the war crimes requirements, then they will have to give on something else. That works in our favor. We added that to our list as something to be bargained away, anyway. Aguirre is the real concern. Aguirre, Cotton, and their spymaster."

"I don't think so," Walters murmured thoughtfully, then blinked and shook her head to bring herself back into the conversation. "You're right about Aguirre, of course, but I think this might be more of a hint to their strategy. They're waving the bloody shirt. *Look what happens to little boys and girls who blow the Test.* To Archangel, he's an example of how the Test was so unfair."

"They turn into uniformed psychos?" Donaldson asked with a frown.

"It's a little more woe-is-me than that, but yes. That's how they'll play this back home. And they have to play for the audience back home, whatever their strategy is here."

"Little psycho is right," said Pedroso. "You saw that story on the last media drone out of Archangel, didn't you, Christina? We can deny it for now, but that will be an embarrassment for us before long."

The PR chief shrugged. "We can change the subject easily enough."

"How? We'll deny that those were our agents, obviously, but what then?"

"He killed three people. Anyone capable of murdering three men with his bare hands is capable of *not* murdering them. It's as simple as that."

"Still, this...The whole entourage is Bennett's show. I don't think she brought the mad dog along for nothing. She's got a plan for him. I just don't know what."

• • •

"Walk beside us and look pretty, Tanner," she joked. "That's all you need to do."

All the windows and balconies of the station's promenade probably gave the president's bodyguards quiet fits, though none of them complained. The honor guard acted only as a back-up to the regular security detail, having less specific training for situations like this. The party moved in something less orderly than a march yet more organized than a stroll among friends. Tanner walked on the group's outer perimeter. He was surprised that Andrea stuck close to him, but he didn't mind.

Visibility was apparently a virtue here. Rather than taking unmarked vehicles to their destination, President Aguirre and his entourage walked openly through the street-like passages of Assembly station. The Assembly's vice chairman and Archangel's delegate walked at Aguirre's side.

The "boulevard" provided opposing lanes for limited vehicle traffic along with simple sidewalks. Currently, the way lay clear of trams and cargo haulers. Signs advertised limited hours for vehicles to keep the streets pedestrian-friendly.

Assembly Station did not disappoint. The facility was immense and varied, having grown in size and complexity right along with the Union. Unfortunately, Tanner was too preoccupied with security concerns to appreciate the tourist spectacle. A great many people watched from those windows and balconies. Any number of weapons could easily handle the range between the "street" and the shadows of the domed ceiling far overhead.

"I'm pretty sure I should be doing more than looking pretty," Tanner grumbled.

"Maybe later," said Theresa Cotton, who seemed more inclined to walk with Andrea than to stick close to the president. Andrea's presence and casual manner was enough of a distraction. Now he also had a cabinet minister talking to him like they were pals. "For now you really are part of the spectacle," advised Theresa. "I know you should be on your toes, but protection isn't all on your shoulders. That's up to the Assembly staff. They haven't had an assassination here in a hundred years, and they won't let one happen now."

Tanner risked a questioning look. The foreign minister smiled. "I won't to tell you to relax, Master-at-Arms, but I've been a diplomat long enough to recognize that look on your face. It really is out of your hands right now. Let it go."

"I'll try, ma'am."

"You're here to be seen, Tanner," Andrea explained. She kept her voice low enough not to carry. Subsonic white noise generators scattered among the security detail diminished the threat from surveillance devices. "That's why you're on the outside, and it's why we're walking close to you. They're not going to shoot at us. This is how diplomacy works."

"Diplomacy works by putting the wanted criminal where everyone can see him?"

"Sometimes."

"Great. Because I love being a public figure." He knew despite Andrea's practiced poise that he'd cut her without meaning it. "Sorry."

"Trust me on this, okay? Besides, you always wanted to travel. This is only your second trip outside of the system, and here you are at the Assembly, right? They're looking at us. It's only fair if you look back at them."

His gaze swept their surroundings again, taking in towers with glittering lights and the décor and architecture of a dozen cultures. "Been a long time since my social studies classes," said Tanner. "Almost feels like I don't even know what I'm looking at."

"I find that hard to believe, schoolboy," Andrea quipped.

"We're coming into Embassy Row," explained Theresa. She slipped around Andrea to come between her and Tanner. "One hundred twenty-five member states have a presence on this station, but obviously they can't all be on this one level. And let's face it, a lot of those member states are still small colonies. You're seeing the oldest of the established embassies here, and some of the strongest.

"The layout of embassies generally follows the flow of human expansion. Those three tall towers in the distance are the embassies for Earth, Luna, and Mars. They're all in such a lock-step alliance that they should hardly count as independent worlds," Theresa added with a frown. "But there they are. Three separate embassies, three separate delegations."

"My social studies teachers always said Earth made that move to grab some extra voting power for itself at the founding of the Union. Is that a fair read of it?"

"Absolutely. Independent in name only." Theresa gestured to the right and left of the towers. "Immediately around the Solar System worlds, you've got the first nine states established in other star systems, all of them settled either by old Earth nation-states or multinational corporations."

"Where's Quilombo?" asked Tanner.

Theresa grinned. "They're on the other side of the Solar embassies. Everyone asks about that. First colony to revolt and declare independence. You know why they changed the name from New Brasilia to Quilombo?"

"Yeah, it was a shot at how badly the Brandao-Alegre Company treated the colonists," said Tanner. "A *quilombo* was a settlement built by escaped slaves in old Brazil. Should've been an omen for what would happen later with the other big corporations."

"Who says it wasn't? By then, everyone felt like humanity needed the corporate powers to keep us expanding into space. Nation-states couldn't afford it, but multinationals could."

Andrea laughed. "I knew you two nerds would get on like a house on fire."

"Quilombo puts on the best embassy parties," noted Theresa. "Not that we'll be going to any on this trip. Anyway, we have that ring of first colonies, and then it spreads out from there. Real estate deals on a space station get complicated, but the embassy placements mostly reflect the timeline. The next ring of embassies represents all the settlements that grew up after we made our first alien contacts and the Expansion Era began."

"What, they set everything up to mirror a panicked land-grab?" Tanner asked.

"Again, it's complicated," Theresa said. "That's why Archangel is so close to the inner ring without actually being inside of it with the 'First Worlds'—seeing as it wasn't exactly founded until the

Krokinthians started trying to stem the tide and the Expansion Wars began. The second 'ring' of embassies is all the colonies that started up during the Expansion War, and then the ring outside of it is all the ones established after the Krokinthians stopped shooting at us…more or less."

By then, Tanner couldn't help but ask. "Are there Krokinthians on the station? Nyuyinaro? Others?"

"There are usually a couple of aliens here, yes," answered Theresa. "Don't get your hopes up about meeting them, though. It's not like they get social. They're here mostly as observers."

Tanner saw more than embassies as they walked through the street. No embassies stood side by side. Interspersed among the impressive structures, Tanner found restaurants, hotels, retail stores, corporate offices, and even a nightclub or two, along with every sort of station facility he would expect. None of it looked inexpensive. It reminded him of life in Salvation as a member of the honor guard—and of being a low-ranking enlisted man at many high-powered functions. "How can anyone afford to be poor here?" he wondered aloud.

"What do you mean?" asked Andrea.

"Office-workers and waiters don't get paid like executives or ambassadors," Tanner explained. "Somebody cleans the floors and takes care of the office equipment at Noble-Dawn Holdings over there, whoever they are. Am I missing something?"

"Well, you're in the Embassy Core here," said Theresa. "The other habitats aren't this glitzy. Still, many people would jump at the chance to live and work on this station, even for only a couple of years."

"Seems like a great way to slide into debt," Tanner replied. "*Another* great way."

"With any luck, what we're doing will change some of that."

Tanner fell silent. Despite his concerns about the cost of living here, the station's glamour was undeniable. He wished he could wander through the stores and visit the restaurants. Many of the embassies stole his breath away.

New Canaan's embassy rose like a temple behind formidable walls. Its ancient, almost religious shape was tempered by modern sensibilities and open, welcoming gates. The embassy of Shanfang looked like some palace from a history book, except for its façade built from blue-tinted metals rather than masonry. The embassy of Anambra, built to mimic the ancient ruins of a pre-industrial civilization that died out before humanity settled on the planet, shone like a jewel in the station's lights. Tanner's heart skipped a beat when he saw Arcadia's embassy, with its terraces and greenery reminding him of all the holo-vids sent to him by his parents now living in one of the Union's most popular vacation hubs.

He saw beautiful people and fine clothes, and figured that anyone living at the center of the Union probably thought it worth the extra money to always look their best. Cosmetic physicians and image consultants here probably raked in a fortune.

"There's Hashem, obviously," the foreign minister added with a nod to Tanner's left. "Not the only minarets you'll see here, but theirs are the prettiest. Ugh. Murtada came up with such an ugly flag, too."

Tanner glanced up to the Hashemite embassy. He couldn't make out the faces of the people looking looked down from the windows. Rumor had it that Murtada's takeover of the embassy had been bloody. Since the embassy was considered Hashemite territory, nobody could enter to investigate. Nor could the station's authorities hold the Hashemites accountable for anything that happened inside.

The party slowed as they turned in toward Archangel's embassy, which faced Hashem's in one more perpetual reminder of how intertwined the two states had become. Hashem was a "founder," while Archangel was the first among the second wave of extra-solar colonies. While the building's exterior bore clear similarities to a cathedral, Tanner found no gaudy crosses or other Catholic iconography. No bell tower rose above the edifice. The glass in the windows was tinted for privacy rather than stained for artistry. *Thank God.*

Though he heard no beep of approval as he passed through the entrance, Tanner knew he must have been scanned by a security system. The embassy would have at least the same state-of-the-art protections as Ascension Hall. The foyer provided plenty of space. Its décor, like the exterior, leaned away from religious influences. Social conservatives pressed for that sort of thing back home. Out here facing the rest of the Union, Archangel preferred to dial back the displays of piety.

Everyone seemed to know where to go as the group entered. Tanner felt a soft touch on his arm as Andrea said, "See you later." Farther away, he caught a beckoning gesture from one of the other honor guardsmen. Tanner glanced back to Andrea to see her and Theresa join Aguirre and Kiribati. Casual conversation and slumming it with the help had to end sooner or later. The foreign minister and the press secretary had jobs to do.

• • •

"Mr. President, I should take my leave," said Terrance Jackson. The Assembly's Vice-Chairman warmly shook hands with Aguirre. "I truly hope this is a productive visit. We all hope so."

"Indeed we do, Mr. Vice-Chair." Aguirre mirrored his smile. "Always good to see you."

"Take care. Minister Kiribati, Ambassador Rojas," Jackson added, nodding his farewells to the Intelligence Minister and Archangel's resident delegate. He turned to leave, only to find himself facing Andrea and Theresa as they came over. "Ah. Minister Cotton. Secretary Bennett. I'm sorry we don't have more time to talk."

"Likewise," said Theresa.

Andrea's smile relayed a bit more mirth. "We'll get together and 'tear down the fabric of the Union' again another time, Mr. Vice-Chair."

Jackson winced—barely, but Andrea noticed. Jackson's historic meeting with these women two years ago clearly burned in his memory. "That quote didn't come from anyone in my office," he grumbled quietly. "We were trying to prevent all this."

"I know," Andrea assured him. "I'm sorry. Gallows humor. Sometimes I can't help myself."

"Does that explain your choice of escorts?" Jackson asked with a raised eyebrow. "The earbud from my holocom might not be easy to see, but it nearly rattled itself right out of my head once the media got a nice close-up of your honor guard detail."

"Mr. Vice-Chair, I can assure you that every member of our delegation was hand-picked with deliberate care," said Andrea. "I'm sure you'll find your callers all have the same friends in common."

Jackson let out a mild sigh rather than debate it further. "I'll let you get back to your work, ladies. Good evening."

As he passed, Andrea saw her boss's professionally pleasant expression fade as a more honest mood took its place. She and Theresa joined Kiribati and Ambassador Rojas for a huddle with Aguirre. "Bad news, Mr. President?"

"Yeah. We've got a big problem. Murtada's here."

Theresa almost spat in frustration. "When did he show up?"

"Yesterday," said Ambassador Rojas. She had served as Archangel's delegate to the Assembly since before Aguirre took office, giving her experience and knowledge that few in the administration could match. "He went straight into his embassy and hasn't come out or met with anyone as far as our people know. Technically, any head of state can assume their delegate's seat at will, just like President Aguirre will be doing tomorrow. Per Hashem's charter of membership, the head of state is the ruling member of the royal family. Murtada has the capital, so his claim is solid."

"And they know we have Khalil?" Andrea wondered.

"They've known it was us all along," Kiribati grumbled irritably. "The rescue was botched from the start because of—" He stopped himself. "Anyway, here are the consequences."

"There was always a risk that Murtada would come to this regardless," Theresa noted. "Plenty of other heads of state have shown up."

"Did any of those other heads of state walk away from a civil war to be here?" Kiribati countered. "This is a calculated move. He knows his seat is at risk. The only question is whether he told his NorthStar buddies or not. We have to assume that he has."

"He might not have," Theresa considered. She held up a hand at Kiribati's scowl. "No, you're right, we should *assume* he has, but… he's kept it a secret this long. It's a gamble. He knew Khalil was in bad shape. If he hasn't said anything yet, he's probably hoping to ride this out. He might even be waiting for a ransom demand from us. Even so, he won't spoil his advantages. Not preemptively. As Ambassador Rojas said, he has a perfectly solid claim to the seat here regardless. He needs to be here so no one else can pull rank on his delegate."

"Then we need to come up with a way to pry him out of that seat before we get started tomorrow," Aguirre broke in. "You're all smart people. Think of something. In the meantime, Ambassador Rojas tells me the ambassador from Quilombo is here," he said meaningfully.

"And the Pope," Rojas reminded.

Aguirre rolled his eyes. "Like anyone listens to the Pope anymore. We see the ambassador from Quilombo first. Are we all ready for this?"

"I should hang back with my staff and see how our arrival is playing with the locals," said Andrea. "I'll be right outside within a few minutes."

"Suit yourself," replied Aguirre. "Let's go."

• • •

They found the ambassador in one of the embassy's comfortable living rooms. He sat at a window overlooking the embassy's inner atrium, along with another man whose chair was turned slightly away from the entrance. "Cristiano," said President Aguirre, offering a warm handshake as the ambassador stood to greet him.

"Mr. President," said Ambassador Goncalves, "it is always good to see you."

"I can't tell you how grateful we are for your role in arranging all of this."

Goncalves shook his head. "We are happy to help. To do anything less would fly in the face of Quilombo's history and our heritage. However, I believe we can all agree that your situation and our past are…not entirely the same," he added gently, glancing over his shoulder.

"No argument here," said the president.

"With that in mind," Goncalves continued, "I believe I should attend to my own matters. I'll be nearby when it's time to go." He exchanged the briefest of greetings with Aguirre's advisers as he left. The door closed behind him.

The advisers hung back while Aguirre stepped around to the empty chair. The other man did not rise. No one called out the obvious snub. A cold shoulder was more than expected.

"Mr. Lung-Wei?" asked Aguirre. He gestured to the chair.

Lai Wa's chief operating officer nodded his head slightly. "President Aguirre."

"It's good of you to meet with me." The president sat in the empty chair facing Lung-Wei's. "I also appreciate your willingness to keep this meeting so discreet."

"I came disguised as one of Ambassador Goncalves's aides. I did this understanding that diplomacy is built upon discretion. Lai Wa wishes to see Archangel return to diplomacy and civility."

"It may be some time before we can establish more than that," noted Aguirre.

"More than that is not obligatory," said Lung-Wei. "You and your administration have said from the outset of this conflict that no state and no individual should be forced to engage in business with any corporation or entity against its will. You object to the use of force to compel business arrangements. In this, Lai Wa finds no fault."

Aguirre didn't try to hold back his cynical smile. "The presence of Lai Wa's warships in Archangel space may have contributed to some misunderstanding on that point."

Lung-Wei's eyes finally turned from the view of the atrium. "We joined with our peers to object to the seizure of our property. When an individual's property is unjustly taken, that individual has every right to retrieve it, or to demand recompense. If you had been willing to negotiate, we would not have resorted to such measures."

"I seem to recall you brought three assault carriers filled with troops. Were they all coming to make nice as a show of solidarity?"

"It was not Lai Wa's personnel that fired the first shots or took the first lives. That blood is on your hands, President Aguirre. Further, we have not returned since our withdrawal. It was not Lai Wa who assaulted your worlds and still occupies Michael."

"No, it's not Lai Wa," Aguirre conceded. "Although your fleet picked up a lot of the slack so that your allies in NorthStar could manage all of that. Yours and CDC's."

"CDC has paid for its mistakes. NorthStar continues its aggression, while Lai Wa does not. Any and all hostile actions taken between Archangel and Lai Wa since the Battle of Raphael have arisen as a result of your initiative, not ours."

"We'll have to agree to disagree, Mr. Lung-Wei. I concede there is room for debate."

"Will an apology be forthcoming?"

"That depends on what you would consider an apology," replied Aguirre. "You may not hear that word, but I believe you will be satisfied with what we have to say."

"You have no evidence that Lai Wa ever cheated any students on their final examinations. You made accusations based upon the wrongdoing of one of our peers and questionable statistical studies made in haste rather than a full investigation. Is this what you have to say?"

Aguirre slowly nodded. "We did not have direct evidence to implicate Lai Wa. Correct."

"Your government unilaterally broke contracts with Lai Wa, deliberately harmed our stock on the open market, and seized our property? You will admit this?"

"We did, and we will."

"Your ships fired the first shots? Ships that were, in fact, disguised as civilian vessels?"

"That is a matter of public record, yes. We feel justified. We will own our actions. Let the rest of the Union and history judge us however they will."

"You will end your accusations in the media?"

"Archangel defends the right to free speech," said Aguirre. "I can't promise anything about what my fellow citizens will say. I can tell you that my administration and my colleagues in the Senate would be glad to put this behind us. This administration will not accuse Lai Wa of crimes for which it has no solid evidence."

"And the indemnity?"

"We will agree to sixty percent of what you ask for."

Lung-Wei's eyes flared. "This is already a fraction of the actual value!"

"And the Union's economy is in chaos. Archangel has obviously suffered great hardship as a result of this conflict. So let's skip the bartering where you demand more and I try to slip away with less and agree to sixty-five percent, shall we?"

"I find no humor in this."

"You don't see me laughing, Mr. Lung-Wei. But I do see you and your company making an incredible profit if our agreement works out. I also believe you will save face through this arrangement. More than you would by pursuing our current conflict. Our action will not affect Lai Wa. We've been careful to ensure that."

"If your ploy targets Lai Wa, it will go nowhere," said Lung-Wei. "I do not see that as a concession."

"Not a concession. Merely an assurance."

Lung-Wei watched the president carefully. "It falls to you to create the opportunity you have promised. Lai Wa and its allies will not engineer it for you. The rules of the Assembly are also clear. Tomorrow's agenda is already written."

"Let us worry about that, Mr. Lung-Wei. If and when the opportunity arises, do we have a deal?" The president stood and offered his hand.

Lung-Wei rose and took it. "We have a deal."

"Good. You'll know your moment when it happens. I won't take up any more of your time, Mr. Lung-Wei. I'm sure Ambassador Goncalves is just as eager as you are to make a discreet exit. Thank you for your courtesy."

"Thank you for yours, Mr. President."

Aguirre waited until Lung-Wei left the room before he addressed his aides. "That brings us back to the other thing. Any thoughts on dealing with Murtada? David?"

Kiribati shook his head. "No, sir. I'd need my best people and a month for recon and intel before I could work out an op on that embassy. Staging anything between here and the Assembly hall is… it's not possible, Mr. President."

Aguirre snorted with grim amusement. "Sorry, Ambassador," he said to Rojas. "David doesn't usually come right out and say these things."

"Don't apologize on my account, sir," she replied. "You think nobody's tried any shenanigans in the embassies before? Sometimes people even get away with it. But Minister Kiribati's right. It's not something you try on the spur of the moment. Station security is top notch. Hashem's embassy has to be at least as tight as ours. I wouldn't recommend it."

"I haven't come up with anything less shady yet either, Mr. President," Theresa admitted. "Not short of delaying until Murtada has to go back home, but that hurts us, too."

"Yeah," Aguirre agreed wearily. "Well, I had hoped we could all get some sleep tonight, but it looks like we've got about eleven hours to come up with something, so let's start talking about it."

A knock on the door interrupted further conversation. Kiribati turned to open it, allowing Andrea in along with the holo screens floating beside her. Each of them carried a muted video still in motion. "Come on in," said Aguirre. "We're getting nice and gloomy."

"Did your meeting with Lung-Wei go poorly, sir?"

"He says he'll deliver if we do," Aguirre answered. "We still need to come up with some sort of plan for our new little wrinkle, though. How do things look on your end?"

Andrea's smile reflected satisfaction rather than happiness. "All seven media outlets on the station seem to agree that your arrival is concerning. You look too relaxed, you look like you might not take this seriously, and so on. Apparently everyone expected you to arrive with your hat in your hand."

"Is that what we did wrong? Why didn't someone bring me a hat?"

"We're also seeing a growing narrative that says your arrival implies defiance. You brought the intelligence minister, whom NorthStar and Lai Wa both consider a war criminal. You walked to the embassy in the open rather than arriving quietly. They also saw Malone in the honor guard. NorthStar's outlets are making exactly the mountain out of that molehill I expected. They're replaying news about his incidents and doubling down on the war crimes talk. It's only color commentary, but it's sexy since it involves violence. They're already playing clips of the news from the Uriel incident that went out before we left Raphael."

Aguirre's eyes narrowed. "So you don't think they picked up on the other thing?"

"No, sir, it doesn't look like it," said Andrea. "They spotted one blemish and they seized on it without looking for another one. It's possible that they'll still catch the other thing, but I think we slipped that in without tripping any alarms. The distraction seems to have worked. Sir," she added, "I've been chewing on our conversation downstairs. I have a suggestion."

CHAPTER EIGHT

Say it to my Face

"No, that video from Uriel doesn't surprise me. Not at all. Look at Malone's public record. In all the PR spin from Archangel about the Pride of Polaris incident, people missed an important point: Malone never gave the suspects a chance to surrender. Not once. The moment he had control of their ship, he vented the entire thing. Rather than negotiate for a peaceful release of hostages, he murdered hundreds of people. And during the seizure of NSS Hercules, Malone used captured guns to target not one of the vessels directly engaged in combat, but instead the largest ship carrying the greatest number of personnel. He didn't want to affect the battle; he wanted to kill. Just like he did in that hotel video you showed earlier.

"Archangel trained thousands of Tanner Malones. This is what we're up against."

--CHRISTINA WALTERS, ASSEMBLY NIGHTLY ROUNDUP, JUNE 2279

"Ruiz. McCrea. You're the designated escorts. Walk with the president and the ambassador to their desk and then return here. You probably won't be at the desk for even thirty seconds. Understood?"

"Yes, ma'am," replied the two men in flawless dress uniforms.

Marine Captain Katrina Brown gave a curt nod. Her dark eyes looked over the small huddle of her honor guard detail. "We'll be up here with the rest of the delegation. If something happens, deal with it under the usual protocols. We follow the protection detail's lead. Past that, we have to let the Assembly staff take the lead on security. Remember, we're here as a visual reminder that Archangel is at war. If we become functional rather than ornamental, something has gone wrong."

The collection of marines and navy ratings could see the Assembly floor through the window behind her. Desks representing every sovereign state of the Union spread out in an arc before a raised dais with podiums. A tall screen behind those podiums currently showed the Union's ornate seal. The far wall towered over the Assembly floor like a single sheet of obsidian, but in truth it was all tinted glass covering several stories of observation lounges much like this one. Each of those rooms held more delegations, along with some that hosted groups of observers from major corporations and, of course, the media.

Almost everyone on the floor dressed in civilian clothes. Tanner saw suits, a few unique fashions that looked like modern robes, and in one case even a pair of delegates in shimmering silk togas. He saw only a few military uniforms, all from worlds with dictatorships or oppressive regimes like Izumoto's Star. The delegation from Hashem had arrived, too: Murtada, one of his generals, and two bodyguards, all of them in uniforms. In all, being in uniform at the Assembly didn't put the honor guard in good company.

"Okay," said Brown, "the president's ready to go. Head out." Ruiz and McCrea stiffened to attention, "getting into character" as the honor guard often termed the demeanor they took on while in the public eye, and moved off.

Their departure left Brown with only three other guardsmen. They would all stand quietly while the civilian staffers observed the proceedings. Tanner watched Ruiz and McCrea move out with Aguirre and Rojas, wondering why the rest stuck around. They provided an escort for the walk over from the embassy, sure, but they could have returned and waited there until the delegation was ready to come back. The protection detail provided all the actual security. The honor guard wasn't even armed. As Brown said, they were window-dressing.

Not for the first time, Tanner wondered why he was here.

"Captain Brown?" asked Minister Cotton. The captain walked over to her and Andrea, leaving her remaining detail waiting and watching through the windows. As with so many large and formalized events, arrivals held to an established protocol. Delegations generally took their seats in something of a reverse chronological order, with the youngest member states arriving first. A few founding member states, such as those of the Solar System, had the privilege of arriving more or less when they wanted. Murtada, for instance, showed up earlier than needed. The arrangement meant that Aguirre and Rojas would take their seats with almost all of the other delegates watching.

Chairman Dhawan would give some predictable opening speech calling for an end to the fighting and a return to peaceful stability. That seemed impossible. Many other conflicts and crises had erupted in the last two years. The third largest corporation in the Union lay in ruins, and the interstellar economy still hadn't recovered from the shock. Even if Archangel, NorthStar, and Lai Wa all agreed to put down their guns, that wouldn't make everyone forget the malfeasance and dirty tricks the Big Three had pulled on the entire Union that kept so many in debt.

Unless, Tanner considered, people genuinely wanted to forget. Perpetual debt had been a way of life for a clear majority of people across most of the Union. They were used to it. They were also used to having jobs and a relatively predictable economy. How many people preferred stability—even unfair stability—over the turmoil of honesty?

"Master-at-Arms Malone," said Captain Brown. Tanner got into character and walked over to the captain and Andrea. "You've got a job. Escort Secretary Bennett downstairs. She'll explain the rest."

"Aye, aye, ma'am," he replied. Brown's orders couldn't have made her happy. Her job was to lead the honor guard detail, not farm them out to Ascension Hall staffers. Everyone would jump at the president's every word, of course, but his advisers generally weren't entitled to anything more than the honor guard's exceptional courtesy.

He knew better than to ask any questions here. Tanner looked to Andrea, gave her a curt, military nod. "By your leave, ma'am."

"Let's go." Andrea waited for him to open the door for her with the touch of a button. The tall, wide halls curved around the observation lounges. No one else accompanied them as they walked. "So we've had a slight change of plans," Andrea told him quietly enough that her voice wouldn't carry.

"Won't throw me off," said Tanner. "I've been in the dark for this whole trip, anyway."

"Yeah, sorry about that. I didn't want to telegraph anything."

He kept to a stiff and formal posture, but his eyes continually searched the halls as they walked. "How have you been?"

Andrea blinked. "I'm sorry?"

"I didn't want to ask in front of others. Brown already said I was too familiar with 'the president's advisers' as if she could mean anyone else in the group. No, don't worry about it," he said, knowing an objection would leap out of her mouth if he didn't stop it. "Don't get involved. You didn't do anything wrong. It's her job to say things like that. It feels a little weird calling you 'ma'am,' but a lot of things feel weird, I guess. Anyway, how have you been?"

"I'm…fine," she answered. They came to the end of the circular hallway and descended a long, curved staircase toward another similar passage. "Things are the same as they've been, except for how the war takes away most of the fun parts of my job and replaces them with ugly parts. Obviously I've still got it better than a lot of other people, but there it is."

"You look like you're holding up okay. You still plan to run to get your senate seat back again when this term is over, right?"

"I'm not sure we should make small talk at a time like this, Tanner."

A faint smile broke through his honor guard demeanor. "I said sort of the same thing to Admiral Yeoh once. She told me there wasn't really a 'time like this.' There's just now. 'Crises come and go. Life moves on. Move with it.'"

Andrea's frown remained. "Is that how you look at things now?"

"I'm trying. I'm not very good at it."

He wanted to say more. He was over Madelyn. He wasn't over Andrea.

She didn't break her stride, but she asked, "How are you?"

"Getting by. I didn't want to come all the way out here with you and hardly talk."

"Yeah. I'm sorry. Look, I pulled you away to do something for us. You might not like it, but I need you to trust me."

"What's the job?" he asked as they came to the bottom of the last staircase. The grand entrance of the Assembly Hall spread out before them. Dozens of people milled about.

"Escort duty, like Captain Brown said. We need you to walk someone to their seat."

"Okay," Tanner said, trying not to frown. He was out in public. He was supposed to be in character: firm military bearing, but otherwise emotionless. "Who am I escorting?"

"Andrea Bennett?" called out a cheerful woman's voice from across the entryway. Andrea stopped in her tracks. The crowd parted as if everyone rehearsed it. The presence of that crowd made some sense once Tanner saw the tall, grey-haired man at the center of it, but it wasn't Anton Brekhov or any of the journalists, aides, or bodyguards who now strode toward Andrea with gleaming eyes and a broad smile.

"Christina Walters," said Andrea in a guarded tone.

"I'm so excited to finally meet you!" Walters declared. A couple of aides followed her, but nothing like the entourage that she'd left behind. Tanner thought he saw Brekhov glance their way. He didn't focus much on that in light of the newcomer. Walters beamed with a smile that seemed utterly genuine. She stuck out her hand. "I've followed your career for a long time. Especially the last couple of years, as you might imagine."

Andrea shook her hand. "Likewise."

Tanner stood more or less at attention, looking out at the crowd watchfully as he'd been trained to do. This wasn't about him.

"This is such an amazing place, isn't it?" Walters asked wistfully. "Here we are, two people on opposite sides of an unfortunate conflict, but we get to put down the swords and talk. I have to say, I admire what you've accomplished since things turned sour. Not the easiest hand to play, yet you've played it well."

"Thank you."

Walters paused for only a beat before she could tell that Andrea wouldn't say more. "Listen, you should know I don't take any of this conflict personally," Walters continued. "We're both professionals. Someday when this is all settled, I hope we can get together and talk about things. I'm sure we have a lot in common."

Andrea didn't exactly smile. "It's a thought."

"And this must be Tanner Malone! I couldn't believe it when I heard you were part of the delegation. You've made quite the impression over the last few years."

"Ma'am," he grunted without looking at her. Rules of etiquette obligated him to a minimal response when directly addressed. His job was to stand guard, not socialize.

"Tell me," Walters asked the unmoving young man in front of her, "how are your parents? They're on Arcadia, right? A program designer and an art teacher?"

People were watching. He was probably being recorded. This was the most important diplomatic setting in the Union. He was a member of the honor guard.

He suddenly couldn't give a damn about any of it.

His eyes turned down to meet her radiant smile with a cold, murderous glare. "I've heard the things you say about me," Tanner replied in a quiet rage. "You couldn't come up with bullshit like that unless you knew the truth about who I am and the things I've done. You also couldn't have your job unless you were a smart person, so I don't see how you could ask me such a *stupid fucking question.*"

She didn't flinch. She didn't seem to move at all. But something changed behind her eyes.

"I don't *have* parents," said Tanner. He didn't move, either, though he felt like he might at any second. "My parents don't exist. *Do you understand?*"

To her credit, Walters remained in place. Her smile widened and brightened just a little bit more. She replied cheerfully, "My mistake!"

"We should go," said Andrea. She took the risk of touching his arm. "Tanner?"

None of them said goodbye. Walters remained almost frozen in place as Andrea led Tanner away.

"That couldn't have gone better if we'd rehearsed it," Andrea quietly declared.

"You know why she asked that," Tanner seethed. He looked back over his shoulder, but he saw only random faces in the crowd. His eyes remained wide and his breath tense. "She threatened my parents."

"Yeah, she did, and she sure as hell won't ever do that again," assured his companion. She did a double-take as soon as she looked away from the crowd back to him. "Oh my God, that wasn't an act at all, was it?"

Tanner's angry expression barely twitched with confusion. "What do you mean?"

Amazed, Andrea shook her head. "Wow. I couldn't have *scripted* that better."

"Andrea, if she's—"

"She's not going to do anything, Tanner. Not to your parents. Hell, I'd bet the only thing she's considering right now is a resignation letter. Tanner, look at me. Focus. I need you here with me. You've got a job to do, okay?" She paused. "Might want to let the anger hang around for a minute or two, though."

"What do you need me to do?"

Andrea looked past him to one of the side entrances. "Escort duty."

Tanner followed her gaze to the side entrance. A tall, thin woman with short black hair stepped through, dressed in a conservative but feminine suit. The man who followed her in was all too memorable.

"Secretary Bennett," said Prince Khalil, greeting her with a nod. "Master-at-Arms Malone, allow me to introduce Ambassador Halima Al Farran. She was my father's official delegate here before the war."

"And grateful to be here again," she added.

"I believe you were right about the timing of my arrival, Secretary Bennett," Khalil went on. "We seem to have drawn considerably less attention than I expected."

"The reporters around here have had a lot to occupy them, and they're waiting on the main event," agreed Andrea. "Still, plenty of others can see us. Facial recognition programs will have kicked out alerts by now. Word will spread quickly. This ball is rolling, Your Highness."

"Then let us waste no time."

"You have the files? You're all set to go?"

"Everything is in order," said Halima. "It will be as we rehearsed last night."

"Thank you again for that," added Khalil. "Your aid in our preparation was most helpful. We need only claim our seats." His eyes turned to Tanner. "Are we ready?"

Tanner's head turned halfway toward Andrea, but his gaze stuck with Khalil. "Isn't your government in exile, sir? Do they have a section for that?"

"Ah, we didn't exactly have time to talk this over, Your Highness," explained Andrea. "But I've found that Master-at-Arms Malone here is excellent with improvisation."

"I understand," said Khalil. He regarded Tanner with a tight smile. "Our seats are occupied by some unexpected guests. We go now to resolve this, and we would greatly appreciate your company. As you may remember from our last meeting, I am somewhat short on escorts from my own domain. Would you be so kind?"

He blinked, looking to Andrea. "I think you're in exactly the right mood to do this," she told him. "I've got to head back to our observation room. Your Highness, ambassador: good luck." With that, she turned and walked away.

Exactly the right mood? Tanner thought. *Like the mood to strangle someone?* "Is there a plan, Your Highness?" he asked.

"Yes. We walk in, I tell Murtada to step aside, and we take it from there."

"That doesn't sound like much of a plan."

Khalil flashed him a quick smile. "It is the best we could do. Shall we?"

"By your leave, sir."

They walked. As Andrea said, most of the media and other delegations had already found their seats or settled into observation spaces. Overhead screens along the walls showed Chairman Dhawan take the podium.

A small trickle of journalists began to gather before they made it halfway across the floor. Tanner noticed the subtle rise in the intensity of light around himself and his charges created by the miniature video relays hidden in the jewelry and buttons worn by the reporters. No one used handheld microphones anymore, but he had no doubt that everyone there was now recording.

"Prince Khalil! Can you tell us where you've been since your reported death?"

"Did you fake your death to escape capture?"

"Ambassador, is it true you've hidden in New Canaan since the outbreak of the war?"

"Are you here to petition for Assembly support against your brothers?"

"Your Highness, is it true that you've begun surrender negotiations?"

"No questions," Halima quietly prompted Tanner.

"Ladies and gentlemen," Tanner bellowed, stepping in front of the prince and Halima, "please move aside! We are not taking questions!" The honor guard occasionally trained for such moments in role-play exercises, but they never actually happened. The protection detail took care of this sort of stuff. Furthermore, it wasn't as if Tanner was a big guy. Standing only slightly above average height and tending toward a slim figure rather than bulk, he wasn't built for plowing through a crowd. Yet while the reporters continued shouting questions, they obediently moved aside.

The security guards at the main hall's closed doors weren't so quick to move away. Tanner had no idea how to handle them. If someone wanted him to do the talking, Tanner figured, they should've given him a script.

"Gentlemen," Halima spoke up. "I present Prince Khalil of the Kingdom of Hashem. We are here to represent the Kingdom in the Assembly per our charter of membership. Please allow us to pass."

"Your Highness, Ambassador," said one of the guards, "Prince Murtada has already claimed Hashem's seat for this session by that same authority."

"That is a matter for he and I to discuss," said Khalil. "I somehow doubt he will come out here for that conversation. As the ambassador states, my rights per the charter are clear."

The guard hesitated as he listened to instructions over an earpiece. His posture shifted. "Of course, Your Highness. Do you or your aides require a translation unit?"

"Yes, please," Tanner answered with his hand out. He didn't bother to wait for Khalil or Halima. The guard gave him a small black earbud. Tanner inserted it and felt it swell inside his ear to secure itself. A soft beep assured him that it was on. He tapped the earpiece twice to select English per its instructions, then moved forward with the prince and Halima as the doors opened.

Dhawan's speech continued. From Tanner's viewpoint, he guessed that every seat on the floor was filled. Here and there a couple of pages in suits moved up and down the aisles. Aside from them, everyone's attention was focused on the chairman.

That changed as Khalil and Halima strode down the aisle leaving turned heads and murmurs in their wake. They didn't look back. Neither did Tanner.

"We must recognize the nearly unprecedented nature of this conflict," Chairman Dhawan carried on from the podium. "Many have observed similarities between the current crisis and the revolution of Quilombo over a century ago, but those similarities are only superficial…"

Tanner didn't get to listen much. He had to watch Khalil and the audience. He felt more and more eyes upon them as they closed on their destination. Hashem held a seat near the front of the hall, off to one side of the arc formed by the delegation desks. Off to the other side, behind Tanner, sat Archangel's desk. Its president and its ambassador surely watched this now rather than the chairman.

More and more delegates made the same choice. Eventually, a halting note of concern crept into Dhawan's speech about peace or human suffering or some such. Tanner didn't know. He was more concerned with the two uniformed men standing to either side of Prince Murtada at his desk. The prince rose as Khalil approached through the row of other delegations with Tanner beside him.

He'd seen Murtada in holo-videos. The man made the news often enough. Yet despite all the exposure Tanner had with mass media in the last few years—seeing himself in the news, serving in Ascension Hall, briefly dating a media expert—Tanner could still be surprised by how differently famous people could look in person. Murtada had that same hard expression on his face. He wasn't as tall as Tanner expected, though. His curly black hair wasn't exactly cut to suit his military uniform. Tanner couldn't help but think that Murtada probably didn't earn the medals on his chest the old-fashioned way.

The other two uniformed men with Murtada, however, gave exactly the opposite impression. He didn't like the look of them at all. *I have no idea what the fuck I'm supposed to do here*, thought Tanner.

Dhawan's speech faltered, then ended. No one seemed to be listening, anyway.

"Brother," Khalil said in Arabic. Tanner's earpiece helpfully translated. He knew that word, but his understanding of the language was still choppy.

"Khalil," replied the other prince with a sneer. "I'd heard you died with Father. Have you been hiding in Archangel all this time?" he asked, gesturing to Tanner. "Hoping to find some friends to rescue you from your incompetence?"

Khalil shook his head. "That's my chair, Murtada. Step aside."

"I am the rightful King of Hashem," shouted Murtada. "The Assembly recognizes me!"

"Look around. You're a monster. Everyone here knows it. They don't want you in this seat. No one wants you watching the borders. No one trusts you. Your armies may be propped up by NorthStar and whatever other companies will take your money, but no one here respects you. No one is coming to help you." He paused to let it sink in. "Step aside, Murtada. Go home."

"And how do you plan to make me?"

"Christ," Tanner muttered without even realizing it. "That's how we're playing this?"

Murtada glanced at him in surprise when he spoke, but the prince quickly turned his attention back to Khalil. Tanner's mind raced through plans and outcomes. *These two bodyguards look like the real deal*, he thought. *No way can I protect Khalil and Halima from both of them.* His heart beat heavily as he considered the space between himself and his likely opponents, the distance and obstacles that the Assembly security guards would have to cross to get to them, and how he could possibly keep his charges alive and in one piece.

Stress and danger made for rapid thinking. To Tanner, time seemed to slow down into an agonizing and suspenseful pace.

No. I can't take the bodyguards out. I'm not even sure I can take one of them. His eyes and his attention focused on Murtada, who wore no body armor, who stood with his weight unevenly distributed, and whose hair looked like a great hand-hold.

Murtada's bodyguards watched closely. Tanner kept track of them, making sure they hadn't moved yet, but he fixed his attention on their boss as his hands clenched and unclenched. His breath steadied with his strengthening resolve.

The only way to protect Khalil and Halima is to go straight for Murtada, decided Tanner. *They're here to protect him. They'll have to focus completely on me as long as I'm a threat to their boss...*

"You play at being a soldier, Murtada, but we both know better," said Khalil. "You don't fight. You send others to do that for you. Unfortunately, I've had a very different experience. Step aside."

Tanner caught the note of finality in Khalil's voice. He took a deep breath, shifting slightly on his feet into a ready stance instead of the ridiculous position of attention expected of the honor guard.

The bodyguards reacted as if they'd read Tanner's mind. One stepped in front of Murtada while the other pulled the prince back, much to his surprise. "What are you—?"

"This is not safe, Your Highness," declared the bodyguard tugging him away. The other, backing up along with them, kept his eyes on Tanner as if to warn him not to try anything. They almost bowled over Murtada's adviser, who stumbled out of their way and then did his best to keep up with them.

The sudden change didn't catch up with Tanner until he'd taken a couple of steps forward. Then he blinked in surprise. Murtada's party backed up beyond the last desk in the row and its shocked delegates. They kept moving into the aisle.

Tanner felt a gentle tug on his sleeve. He glanced back to see Halima gently shake her head. "Well done, my friend," she murmured.

Murtada pushed once against his bodyguards, who dutifully held him back. Tanner thought the prince and his men looked like a drunkard being pulled away from a stupid bar fight by wiser friends. Murtada pointed over one bodyguard's shoulder and shouted something. Chatter from audience drowned it out.

Assembly security guards appeared. They calmly ushered the prince and his bodyguards toward the exit, resulting in an even more animated discussion—one that moved farther and farther away.

Tanner watched in shock. Khalil and Halima took their seats. Reaching forward to press the small amplifier button on the desk, Halima said, "Mr. Chairman, ladies and gentlemen, please accept our sincerest apologies for the disruption."

Turning around to look at his companions, Tanner asked, "Holy shit, did that just happen?"

Halima removed her hand in time to avoid projecting Tanner's question across the hall. "Yes, I believe it did, Master-at-Arms Malone," she said with a slightly bemused smile.

Tanner shook his head and realized the whole Assembly was watching. He stepped behind his charges and tried to assume a dignified, watchful posture. It wasn't easy. "Did you plan that?" he hissed.

"No," Khalil chuckled, clearly worked up with a bit of adrenaline himself. "No, I did not."

Halima leaned over. "You might consider that the local media spent all night warning everyone of your past exploits," she suggested. "I understand you recently put down six assassins with your bare hands?"

"Wha—no, I didn't! It wasn't six! Nobody could do that!"

"I suggest you hold off on correcting the record," said Khalil. "Embellishments like that seem to be working in our favor."

"Ambassador," boomed Chairman Dhawan's voice across the hall, "is the Kingdom of Hashem ready to continue with the Assembly's business?"

Halima looked to Khalil, pointedly deferring to the prince. "We are, Mr. Chairman," Khalil responded with a graceful, apologetic bow.

"Thank you, Your Highness," Dhawan replied. He opened his mouth again as if to continue on with his speech.

"On that note, Mr. Chairman," Khalil interrupted, "and with further apologies, the Kingdom of Hashem must invoke its border state priority to bring business to the floor."

Murmurs swept through the crowd of delegates, mostly with frustrated tones. Journalists and others on the floor shifted their attention. "Your Highness," said Dhawan, "I am sure you are aware of the focus of this special session. While it is your right to exercise your priority privileges, I must implore you to allow the current agenda to continue."

"Mr. Chairman, I believe once I have made my proposals, all will understand why I feel this timing is appropriate."

Dhawan bowed his head and made a gesture of concession toward Khalil's desk across the floor. "You are within your rights. Please proceed."

Khalil faced the majority of the gathered delegates. "I shall not attempt to replace the chairman's fine oratory. We are all aware of why we are here. NorthStar, Lai Wa, and the now defunct CDC have made war upon Archangel, as they have made war within my own kingdom.

"To some extent, this is nothing new. All three corporations have hired out their forces to individual states and organizations many times. Other corporations of lesser size and stature also provide military services.

"Yet almost all examples of corporate military action have had one critical common aspect: such force has been exercised at the behest of a sovereign state or the Union as a whole. Even in Hashem, Lai Wa and NorthStar serve claimants to the throne who have at least arguable legitimacy. Corporate forces fight piracy under state and Union contracts, but under specific limits and with government oversight.

"In Archangel, we saw something quite different. These three corporations acted on their own. They attacked a sovereign state, knowingly claiming false authority, for their own reasons. No state requested this. No government established their rules of engagement or any other limits. Lai Wa quickly saw the error of its ways and broke off. CDC collapsed as a result of this and other rash decisions. NorthStar, however, continues.

"These are not the acts of a corporation. These are the acts of bandits, or of pirates, or terrorists—yet no one sees NorthStar as any such thing. Alternately, these are the acts of a sovereign state." Khalil looked around the hall. "Few would claim that a corporation and a state are the same thing. In this case, I disagree. That is exactly what NorthStar has become."

Khalil paused again, giving his audience and the translations a chance to catch up. "NorthStar would claim that it is simply a company organized to turn a profit like any other, but they are unlike the rest. They influence every facet of our interstellar economy. They negotiate and enact treaties with other states—except they call them contracts. NorthStar holds territory on 'unsettled' worlds as if their colonies don't count as settlements, where they lay down their own rules and regulations…which we here would otherwise call laws.

"Diplomacy. Trade. Laws. Territorial expansion. These are the powers and defining traits of states.

"NorthStar even wields the power to explore and terraform new worlds. To this day, the world of Fairhaven is largely owned and run by NorthStar. Fairhaven's independence is a polite fiction. Only a fortunate few states can manage such a feat without corporate help. Indeed, in the early days of interstellar exploration, no Earth government wanted to take on the full burden of risk and expense to develop terraforming technology. That is why these great corporations were allowed to grow so freely and so large. It is why we let them arm themselves as a state would arm itself.

"Yet now, unlike any other corporation, NorthStar has taken on that most fundamental and most dire power of a sovereign state: it wages war."

Again, Khalil paused for the translators. "A great many of you here today are heads of state. You know the challenges of leading a government. You know how hard it is to provide for your people, to meet unlimited desires with limited resources. You know the nightmare of raising taxes. NorthStar avoids all of that by clinging to its labels. They make laws and treaties and war, and they dodge the burdens of nation-states by claiming to be a mere 'corporation.'

"I submit to you a proposal," Khalil said, nodding slightly to his side. Halima keyed several quick instructions into her holocom, sending a file out to every delegation, every media service present, and each observation lounge. "It is time that the leaders of NorthStar took on these burdens. It is time to see NorthStar for what it is: a sovereign power equal to any state in the Union. It is time that NorthStar's personnel recognize their employer as the state that holds their allegiance—or deny it and hold to the states of their birth, and limit their services and obligations appropriately."

Murmurs swept the hall, some shocked, others mocking. He continued on undaunted. "Let us grant NorthStar a seat in the Assembly. Let us hold them to the responsibilities of any other state—and the same restrictions. The arms limits that bind us all must bind them as well. Should any state of the Union choose to host NorthStar's operations, it must do so with the full knowledge that it is hosting a foreign power. Let them re-negotiate appropriately."

Khalil fell silent. He watched the delegates all around him study their holo screens. Some scowled in disbelief. Others laughed. A few argued among themselves. The prince turned to face the dais. "Mr. Chairman, I hereby move that we adopt this measure for consideration and for a vote at the earliest possible time before this special session continues."

Chairman Dhawan stepped up to the podium to answer, but hesitated as a new wave of activity passed through the audience. Some opened up holo screens and read. Others seemed distracted by audio calls. Several turned to speak with pages. To be sure, not every delegation showed such activity, but from Dhawan's viewpoint perhaps a third or even half of the Assembly was distracted… while Khalil patiently watched.

Automated lights illuminated another delegation's desk as its speaker—another head of state—claimed the floor. "Mr. Chairman," said Prime Minister Corina Gosnell in a hesitant tone, almost as if she could not believe she would say the words, "the sovereign system of New Corsica supports this measure."

Lights shined down on other delegations. Further support rang out, soon tallied on the screen behind the dais. Within moments, the motion carried enough support to push it through to debate on the floor—and after that, a full vote.

The chairman hardly spoke. Other delegations, clearly blindsided, signaled their outrage with shouts and waving arms. Khalil took his seat and then glanced back to a visibly stunned young man standing behind him. He gestured to the walls and ceiling around them. "It is larger than it looks in the news videos, isn't it?"

• • •

Most of the light in the room came from the view into the Assembly hall on the other side of the glass. Numerous holo screens provided a little more illumination. Some were lined up along the top of the window. Others floated around with the room's occupants.

Seated in a plush black leather chair, Lung-Wei kept an open holo screen at each side. The woman seated beside him had none. A quirk of her last longevity treatment left her sensitive to bright lights. That her treatment had involved any "quirks" at all presented a grave problem for her doctors, but she graciously assured them they would not be punished. She understood that even her vast resources could not cheat time forever.

"Please inform Chancellor Dupont that his support for this measure will aid his campaign for reelection next year," Lung-Wei said to the face on one of his screens. "Remind him, as well, that the textiles his system produces would sell poorly on the open market without efficient shipping." He waited for an acknowledgement before dismissing the holo screen with a wave of his hand. "This will cost us more than we expected," he warned soberly.

"Our opponents are vulnerable," observed the woman beside him. "They have committed too much to their current endeavors and cannot respond to a strike. If we must reach farther to accomplish our goal, we can and we will. No one is in a position to take advantage of us. We will be stronger for the gamble."

"If it succeeds," noted Lung-Wei. "I am still unconvinced."

Ji Xue smiled. "You said this was impossible."

"I did."

"Do you still?"

"My opinion is no longer the one that matters." Lung-Wei gestured toward the window and the muted debates raging on the line of holo screens above it. "The sky doesn't change colors simply because we agree it should, no matter how many incentives we might offer."

"No, it does not," conceded Lai Wa's oldest and most influential director, "but the sky is a physical thing. It has always existed. Corporations and nations have not. These are constructs of the mind. They exist only because we agree they exist. They may therefore be changed however we agree to change them." She, too, gestured toward the window, but spread both of her arms wide in a grander move than Lung-Wei's. "This is the greatest legislative body in human civilization. If they say a company has become a state, then it is a state. The change is not impossible. It is simply *unprecedented*."

Lung-Wei's eyes shifted to his remaining holo screen. "Brekhov has stopped calling."

"Of course. Anton is an intelligent man. He understands math."

• • •

"The measure will pass."

Brekhov stood close to the window of the observation lounge, watching the Assembly floor while delegates argued and colluded. No one in the lounge seemed to hear his words or see him as he loosened his collar and rolled his left shoulder to relieve the tension in his chest. They, too, were engulfed in discussion and debate, along with the task of absorbing the text and meaning of Khalil's measure.

"This is ridiculous," scoffed Weir. He read aloud from a holo screen. "They even included requirements for who has to be offered citizenship. Listen to this: 'Citizenship is to be offered by said corporation to—'"

"Wait. 'Said corporation?'" asked one of Weir's assistants.

"Well, yeah. They can't pass a law for one entity or individual. This is a law designed for any corporation that fulfills its criteria. That criteria just happens to exactly fit us."

"How can anybody *force* state sovereignty on…on anyone?"

"Plenty of nations were created out of whole cloth by treaty conventions in pre-spaceflight days," Weir said. "Some countries were born or erased without ever having a seat at the table. And it's not like non-state entities haven't been given recognition before."

"I never figured you'd be the one offering up historical context, Jon," said Donaldson.

"He worked in politics before he went into business." Pedroso's lips curved into a smirk. "Nobody gets into a C-level position through connections alone."

"Your backhanded compliments never get old, Maria," Weir fired back with similarly false warmth. "By the way, great job on confirming Khalil's death. I could swear I read a memo from your department saying we'd never see him again."

"We'll have a discussion with Murtada about that," Pedroso answered without humor. "It might come as a shock that Murtada has his own secrets. Maybe this will discourage him from keeping so many from us in the future."

Weir waved off that concern. "Look, ludicrous or not, Khalil is saying this with a straight face. He obviously has backing. We need to take this seriously, but we also need Christina to get out there and make everyone else think it isn't serious." He glanced toward their PR expert. "I think we need to fight this as… Christina?"

Walters sat nearby, hunched over a holo screen while she typed. She sat upright at the sound of her name and promptly closed her request for a personal security upgrade. "I'm sorry?" she spoke up, blinking and looking from one fellow exec to another. "I was…I agree with Jon. I think we need to take all of this seriously."

"Christina, are you alright?" asked Pedroso.

"I'm fine. Sorry. It's a lot to catch up on. This diplomatic stuff isn't my field."

"It's not our shareholders' field, either," grumbled Donaldson. "Communication delays from here to Earth are a little over an hour right now, but with regular drone updates, we could see our stock prices take a hit sooner than that. People are going to get jittery if they see this thing has legs. It could be as bad as Aguirre's opening salvo over the Test."

"It could be worse than that if some of our bigger shareholders actually fancy the idea of buying into a new state," Weir pointed out. "Don't forget how many colonies get funding from the first colonists. *'Hey, I have a half-percent stake in the company,'*" he said, affecting a new voice. "*'Doesn't that entitle me to at least a barony in NorthStar Land?'*"

Donaldson scowled. "This won't get that far. It's no different than the vote for punitive sanctions that Archangel whipped up last year. We're the biggest corporation in the Union, they can't just—"

"The measure will pass," Brekhov repeated, this time loudly enough to be heard. Discussion stopped. "Pay attention to who speaks in support. This is not Archangel's doing. Not alone. This is Ji Xue.

"Jon, you have the text. Do the details fit Lai Wa as well as us?" He didn't bother to look to Weir. The question was purely rhetorical. "I suspect not. Our 'allies' in this struggle have made a separate peace.

"The earlier punitive sanctions did not pass because Lai Wa and a hundred other major corporations stood against it. None of them wanted the Assembly to set a precedent that could one day affect them. This…as Jon says, this targets us specifically, no matter what the legal language says. This measure draws a line which only we have crossed. Every other power in the Union will know how to play around this new line, but that still leaves us on the other side of it.

"Everyone who stood with us to protect their own interests now sees us set apart. The sharks smell blood in the water. Lai Wa backs this measure. Their investment in swaying votes will cost them in the short run, but they see the long term benefit. Others will fall in line. They know this will impact our stock value. We will have to work hard and fast to retain shareholder support.

"And when this is done, our fleet will fall under the same limits as the rest of the Union's systems," Brekhov added quietly. "That is what Archangel stands to gain. Even holding our stolen ships, they can't overcome us, and they know it. But as one state against another, even a more powerful state as we would doubtlessly become…that brings us down to their level. That makes us an enemy they can fight on their terms."

Silence followed until Donaldson spoke up. "Not if we walk away from the fight," he pointed out. "If we pull out of Archangel now—"

"We will not have terms dictated to us," Brekhov cut him off. He looked from Donaldson to Weir. "Let's not wait on the votes and the formalities. Call a shareholder meeting right away. Get me a meeting with Governor Heath before we leave, too. We need to discuss the status of Fairhaven in light of these new developments. NorthStar *built* that world out of rock and dry ice. I'll not have our 'capitol' be placed in some asteroid mining colony.

"And send word to our people in Hashem. Have them pull out immediately. Murtada can deal with his brothers on his own."

• • •

"You might be surprised how many parliaments and other such bodies have seen brawls, even in recent years," said Halima. "Usually it's only pushing and shoving. But it happens. It has even happened here. It is always an embarrassment."

Tanner appreciated the conversation from Halima and the prince in the frequent lulls in activity on the Assembly floor over the course of the morning. Much of their time and attention was devoted to small discussions with others who came directly to their desk. In their spare moments, however, they were mindful of their uniformed companion.

"If it's always an embarrassment," Tanner asked, his voice low while he stood tall and vigilant, "why did you risk it?"

Prince Khalil let out a snort of grim amusement. "Because the only thing worse than having such a brawl is *losing* such a brawl. To be honest, I did not expect a fight. I expected the dispute would go to a floor vote. Given Murtada's reputation, I believed that would turn out in my favor, but it would take time. You have saved us hours, and perhaps protected our element of surprise. This is all unfolding much faster than I had hoped."

The prince's words ran counter to Tanner's mood. Though he was engaged and interested in the situation, time didn't exactly fly. He'd stayed in place without a break since they arrived. Absurd as it seemed, Tanner presented a deterrent to another confrontation, which meant that he couldn't step away until they knew Murtada and his people had left the building. His feet ached, his back grew stiff, and he needed to find a bathroom.

As the morning wore on, Tanner began to believe the proposal would go all the way to a full vote. The outcome was always in doubt. He knew enough about the Assembly's rules and politics from his days in school to keep his hopes in check. Still, Khalil and Halima seemed pleased.

"Delegates," came a voice over the PA and the individual translator, "we will recess for ninety minutes."

Khalil and Halima stood. Tanner's hopes of relief rose. "We don't have to stand guard over the desk?" he asked.

Halima smiled back at him. "No. Our proposal has passed the first phases of debate. The process would continue even if Prince Murtada somehow reclaimed the seat. The call for recess was the first finish line of this race."

"I do not expect my brother to return during this session, regardless," said Khalil. "He knows he has lost the day. He will not waste effort on this now."

"So we can leave?"

"I think it's about time we did," said Khalil.

A breath of relief escaped Tanner's lungs. His shoulders dropped. "Oh thank God. I'm dying to find a restroom. Sir," he added.

Khalil chuckled. "Halima, you are the only one who knows this place. Show us the way?"

"Of course," Halima replied with a smile.

Naturally, Khalil was delayed by other delegates who wanted to speak with him on his way out. He kept moving, bringing the interested men and women along with him, while Halima played the part of guide and Tanner did his best to keep a watchful eye. Assembly Hall's own security personnel stayed close, and none of the delegates looked physically dangerous. Their political muscle might be another matter, but that went far above Tanner's rank.

"Sycophants," said Tanner's translator after they left the last such group behind. "Small fish who think of themselves as sharks," Khalil grumbled further.

Tanner responded with a nod. "I'll take your word for it, Your Highness."

"You need not be so polite and formal with me, Tanner," Khalil told him as they moved through the halls. "If I may call you Tanner?"

"Whichever you prefer, your high—" Tanner began, but he stopped himself. "Sorry. It's part of the job. Sir," he added, though he grinned a bit. "What you call me is up to you. To be honest, I prefer my first name. 'Master-at-arms Malone' is a bit much."

"I had the same thought."

"It's appreciated, sir. I made a personal connection or two while serving in Ascension Hall, but usually guys like me…" Tanner shrugged. "I was a special case because people sometimes wanted my picture, but usually the honor guard's job is to stand around like furniture. It's amazing how many people play right along with that. You and Ambassador Al Farran have been very different. Thank you."

Khalil's smile turned a bit sad. "You have been a special case for us as well. Regardless, I learned early that those who guard are no less important than anyone else. One of my closest friendships came from my bodyguards."

"It sounds like you miss him."

"I do. His name was Samir. He died in defense of Qal'at Khalil when the pirates attacked. In defense of my family and I. By the grace of God, his wife still tutors my children." He paused, and then said, "He had two adult children. His son died in the war. I do not know where his daughter is now."

The younger man didn't know what to say. "I'm so sorry."

"You have done more for his family and his memory than anyone else I could name, Tanner. My people have all suffered in this war. For Samir, at least, there was some measure of justice." He let out a deep sigh. "You know, since coming to Archangel and seeing your struggles, I cannot help but think sometimes that your war began at my doorstep."

Looking out ahead as they walked, neither the prince nor Halima saw the way Tanner's eyes widened. He said nothing, merely walking along and listening. Suspicions that had plagued him for months twisted around in his gut like a snake threatening to bite.

Khalil didn't seem to have such suspicions, given his thoughtful but casual tone. "The pirate attack exposed our vulnerabilities," he continued. "It showed how corporate navies left us unprotected. It forced other systems to tighten security on their own, especially yours. The military build-ups, the political friction, the suspicion and espionage. All of that began with the attack on my little world."

Halima touched Tanner's shoulder and gestured toward one doorway. "I believe we have found the restrooms…and the media," she said with a sigh. A dozen men and women hurriedly approached with shouted questions on their lips.

"We'll be fine out here," Khalil said as he stepped past.

Though professional training and a sense of obligation made him hesitate, Tanner allowed Khalil and Halima to move on without him. Hall security was near, and Tanner's personal needs wouldn't take care of themselves. He gave the crowd of reporters one more appraising look before slipping through the door. If anything happened to the prince at that point... *Well*, he decided, *I'll feel awful about the timing, but how many people would really blame me?*

Not my fault nobody assigned him more than one bodyguard.

The thought brought him right back to what Khalil had told him. Samir, was that it? Not for the first time, Tanner noticed the way he'd so quickly shifted mental gears away from talk of death and loss. He didn't always do that. He didn't want to be able to do that. So many of his friends and comrades could, though. Shipmates died, sometimes right in front of them, and the only measure of the depth of their friendship was the number of minutes that would pass before the banter started back up again. Even that measure wasn't all that reliable. Some people could joke right on through it all. Some people needed to do that.

Everybody had their defenses. Some people used humor. Others relied on faith.

By the grace of God, Khalil had said, Samir's wife was still around. Yet didn't God have anything to do with Samir's death, too? Or his son's? Or this whole mess? Bad as things were for Archangel, Khalil's people had it worse. He'd seen that war up close, too.

Staring at himself in the mirror as he washed his hands, Tanner heard Khalil's words echo in his mind: *I cannot help but think sometimes that your war began at my doorstep.*

Heading out of the bathroom again, he found more reporters, all obviously recording every word from the prince. Tanner knew how to stay out of a camera shot during a moment like this. It was something else he'd learned in Ascension Hall, both from the honor guard and Andrea's casual commentary. He simply shifted out of the way.

The reporters shifted, too. Each of them subtly turned, still listening to Khalil speak about the war in Hashem and the suffering of his people at the hands of his brothers and their corporate allies… and never let Tanner out of their sight.

No journalist would break away from a prince of Hashem, but Tanner understood what he saw. He'd become part of this story.

Whatever Khalil's opening statement was to the media, Tanner had missed it while in the bathroom. He stood by as Khalil fielded the sort of questions that one would expect: Where have you been since your brother announced your death? Are you in alliance now with Archangel? What are your plans for this? For that? For the other thing?

Halima leaned over to Tanner amid the din and said, "We are safe here. Assembly security is present. They have offered escorts. Would you be willing to let your delegation know we will be delayed? This was expected."

Tanner couldn't turn down such a request. "Yes, ma'am."

No one followed as he slipped away. He caught plenty of wary looks from security officers, both uniformed and those in suits, along with several interested glances from the reporters. Again, Khalil was plainly the bigger draw.

As he left the crowd and the voices behind, Tanner felt only a little bit of relief. The implications of Khalil's words haunted him up the stairs and through the quieter hallways.

He found no reporters outside Archangel's observation suite. Two members of President Aguirre's personal protection detail guarded the door. The man and woman, both wearing suits, gave Tanner a slight nod as he walked up. One reached for the controls.

Laughter and lively conversation spilled out through the open door. Tanner found more people here than when he had left. He recognized a few of the faces as semi-regular visitors to Ascension Hall. Some people consulted with faces or text on holo screens. Others held drinks in their hands. Aside from the honor guards and protective service people sticking close to the walls, it felt like an impromptu office party.

Tanner scanned the room. He saw Aguirre and Kiribati toward the center, talking and even laughing with others. Andrea stood nearby, obviously part of the conversation but also monitoring local media as usual. He didn't see either Captain Brown or the protection detail lead, leaving him wondering who should get his report.

"Secretary Cotton?" he asked, finding her free of high-level discussions—if Tanner could call it that. "Ma'am, Prince Khalil and Ambassador Al Farran are with some media downstairs. They wanted me to relay that they'd follow soon. Assembly security is taking care of them."

"Thank you," Theresa acknowledged with a nod. "I'll—"

"Hah! There he is!" interrupted the president's voice. Tanner and Theresa both turned as Aguirre and his immediate circle came over to greet him. "Hell of a job you did out there, Tanner!"

"Sir?" Tanner asked. "I just stayed with my charges, sir."

"Oh, come on, you did a little more than that," Aguirre chuckled. Tanner had seen Aguirre many times while serving on the honor guard, but the president never spoke to Tanner again after the ceremony for his Archangel Star. Suddenly Aguirre grinned at him like Tanner was an old buddy. "I wasn't sure that whole stunt was a good idea until I saw it play out," said the president, "but you did a great job of scaring off the bad guys."

Tanner glanced around awkwardly, realizing now that he—by virtue of talking with Aguirre, anyway—was at the center of attention. Andrea looked like she was trying to slip through the crowd to come to Tanner's rescue. He tried to stall. "Sir, that's not what I was there to do."

"Well," spoke up Kiribati, "it was and it wasn't. Andrea suggested we send you in, actually. She saw the media spin on your presence in the delegation party and realized we could make some use of it, and you *were* there in a protective role."

"Yes, sir," Tanner replied, waiting for him to say more.

Andrea slipped into the conversational circle. "We knew things could get a little heated," explained the one person present whom Tanner could call a friend. She didn't seem quite as high-spirited as the rest. "We thought, knowing what we know of Murtada, that having you there could prevent that."

"And as it turns out," Aguirre continued, "Murtada's bodyguards are professionals. They know what it looks like when someone is right in front of them doing—what did you call it, David? 'Murder math?' Yeah, doing murder math in your head."

The polite deference in Tanner's expression wavered. "The whole Union saw that, Mr. President."

"Well, yes." Aguirre laughed. "Lots of cameras on you. I thought you handled that well."

"Mr. President, I'm sorry, but I don't see how this is funny," said Tanner. "I know what the media does with my name and video like that. Andrea can try to spin me as a good guy in Archangel, but the rest of the Union sees me as some monster."

A hush came over the room, and with it, a chill. Even Tanner felt it. Angry as he was, his awareness of his surroundings remained sharp. He'd relied on such senses too heavily as a matter of survival to lose track of them now.

President Aguirre's cheer disappeared. "You make a good point, son," he said all too tactfully. "It's easy to lose sight of such things in times like these. We're all fighting to end this war as soon as possible. We all make sacrifices."

"What sacrifices have *you* made, Mr. President?"

The question came out of Tanner's mouth before he could stop it, and then he couldn't take it back. In truth, he didn't want to—and that made the rest impossible to hold back, either.

"I can't count how many friends I've lost since all this started. I've been shot and hunted and bombed. I've been in and out of therapy for *years*. My face is plastered all over the media as a mass-murderer and a lunatic. There isn't enough soap in the galaxy to wash all the blood off my hands. And I'm one of the *lucky ones*. I can't count the funerals anymore, sir. Too many of them have happened in group ceremonies."

He watched Aguirre's eyes grow colder and firmer, as if the president were silently ordering him to stop any time now. Tanner felt a hand on his arm. Andrea suggested, "Maybe we should step—"

"Malone," interrupted Captain Brown's voice. "Outside."

"Aye aye, ma'am." He turned and walked out. The president caught the captain's eye, but Tanner didn't linger; Brown had given him an order.

A single glance from the protection detail sentries told Tanner all he needed to know as he came through the door. Their earpieces were good. He couldn't even see them. Tanner kept walking to give them some distance. The door opened again a few seconds later as Andrea emerged with a concerned look.

"Tanner," she asked, keeping her voice low, "what's going on with you?"

"I'm not sure how to answer that, Secretary Bennett."

"Don't do that," Andrea shot back. "Don't talk to me like we don't know each other."

"Then why do you even need to ask?" he hissed. "What do you think is going on with me? You think I didn't mean what I said?"

"No, but we thought you did good out there! Everyone's proud of you! Why are you mad?"

"I thought I made that pretty clear. If you want the whole list, you might need to clear a couple days off your schedule." He didn't know why he was trying to match Andrea's volume. It wasn't as if the protection detail wouldn't hear him. Or any listening devices in the halls, if that was the sort of thing the Assembly used.

Andrea shook her head. "I'm sorry. This wasn't the president's idea. I'm the reason you're out here. And it's like Kiribati said. Once I saw how all the station media sources played up your reputation, I thought—"

"Yeah, thanks for that," he fumed.

"—I thought you'd want to help!" she shot back. "You always wanted to help!"

"I wanted to help *you*."

"And you did. You helped all of us. Don't you understand? Walking right in and claiming Hashem's seat like that—Tanner, if that had gone to a floor vote, we'd have lost the whole day. NorthStar would have had that much more time to shore up support and develop a new game plan."

His scowl deepened. "It's not what you had me do," he explained, and then pointed at the door. "It's coming back here and seeing that fucker *laugh* about it."

"What are you talking about?"

"Nothing I can talk about here."

"What—Tanner, I thought we were still at least friends."

"Then stop *using* me, Andrea."

She winced. The door opened just then to reveal Captain Brown with two other members of the honor guard detail. "I'm sorry. It's not about you," Tanner muttered. "Your boss is not a good man."

The comment left Andrea all the more shocked and bewildered.

"Secretary Bennett," Brown spoke up, "I apologize, but I have to interrupt, please."

Andrea blinked. "I've got to get back inside," she said to no one in particular. She glanced at Tanner. "We'll talk later?"

"That may not be up to me," Tanner answered.

"Ma'am," said Brown.

Frowning uncomfortably, Andrea walked away. Brown waited until she was through the door before she turned her attention to Tanner.

"You're done, Malone. I won't waste time tearing you the new asshole you deserve. My first priority is to get you the hell away from any opportunity to further embarrass yourself or the honor guard. Gutierrez and O'Neal here will take you to the shuttle bay. You're going straight onto the escort frigate to stand mess cook duty in the galley or clean toilets or whatever the hell they decide to do with you until we get back to Archangel. And you will under no circumstances repeat to anyone what you said in there until and unless ordered by an officer who outranks me. Do you understand?"

"Yes, ma'am."

Brown reached up and yanked a small pair of emblems off the upper shoulders of his dress uniform. "You are out of the honor guard, Malone. Don't even think of trying to come back."

Tanner nodded once. "Aye aye, ma'am."

CHAPTER NINE

Invitations

Dear Shareholder,

Please read this communication thoroughly, as it directly impacts the status of the NorthStar Corporation and your investments.

As of this writing, the Union Assembly has passed an unprecedented measure that effectively forces NorthStar to adopt sovereign statehood. Despite widespread opposition, the measure is now Union law and NorthStar must move forward.

NorthStar is not going out of business. All of our operations and policies remain in effect. Your investment is safe with us. NorthStar is still the top manufacturer of industrial and consumer goods, the largest provider of educational, military/security, and financial services, and a leader in scientific and technological development. However, this development will obviously bring great changes and create new responsibilities.

Our fiduciary duty to our shareholders remains our greatest concern. Your presence is requested at an emergency shareholder meeting at NorthStar's headquarters on Fairhaven to address these developments...

--LETTER TO SHAREHOLDERS, JULY 2279

For once, Tanner arrived on *Beowulf* an hour before the galley would open again.

He came aboard *Beowulf* via a straight-level airlock vestibule link-up with the escort frigate. The two ships came close enough together that Tanner hardly even felt the lurch of passing between two artificial gravity fields. He walked through the vestibule in a regulation vac suit, helmet slung in place over one shoulder and bags in hand as he came back to the closest thing he had to a home in the last two years.

That particular thought had him torn between resentment and relief. He decided, quite deliberately, to focus on the latter. For all the drawbacks of life in the military, let alone being at war, *Beowulf* held a few people who meant the world to him. The last few years had taught him the importance of being in good company when stuck with a bad job.

The first face he saw brought that consideration home. Nathan—Ensign Spencer now—stood with a bo'sun and a crewman at *Beowulf*'s end of the vestibule. The crewman ran a sniffer unit as part of the ship's routine security checks for arriving personnel and passengers. The bo'sun was there to assist Nathan in his duties as deck officer—on paper, at least. In reality, Tanner knew the bo'sun was there as the trainer. This would be one of only a couple dozen crummy new-guy chores an ensign could expect.

On the bright side, it beat scrubbing toilets. Presumably officers did plenty of that in the academy, far from the eyes of the enlisted rabble who couldn't be shown evidence that any officer was once as lowly as the people they commanded. That wouldn't do at all.

"Request permission to come aboard, sir," Tanner said at the end of the vestibule.

"Permission granted," replied Spencer with a professional but sincere smile. "Welcome home, Malone. Good job out there."

Tanner didn't mind the use of his last name. Presumably, Nathan was better off not making their connection obvious to everyone. The comment, on the other hand, made him wince. "Thank you, sir. I take it I made the news broadcasts?"

"Yeah, you did," chuckled the bo'sun.

Nathan plainly read the concern on Tanner's face. Given their letters back and forth over the years, he knew Tanner's feelings didn't match the spin that the media and the PR machine put on his moments in the public eye. They couldn't talk here, though—not as officer and enlisted man. *Malone* and *Sir,* standing right in front of one another all too far from home.

"Everyone here is behind you," offered Nathan. "Probably won't be too long before the rest of the world forgets about it all, anyway. Crewman, are we clear?"

"Yes, sir," replied the young woman with the sniffer.

"Thanks. Malone one quick note: *Beowulf* has gone quiet. Receive-only, nothing going out."

"Understood, sir. Thanks." He continued on, but looked over his shoulder as soon as he was past. Nathan didn't look back. He had two subordinates to "manage" and duties to perform.

Coming into the passageway, Tanner noted a number of men and women from the frigate standing off to one side as if waiting for someone. They carried bags, too. He'd wondered why they went to the trouble of establishing a nice, stable link-up rather than opting for a shuttle transfer. Seeing others come over, Tanner understood that this was a bigger deal.

He heard the ship's bell and glanced over his shoulder as the PA announced, "Now, *Virtuous*, arriving." Tanner popped to attention along with everyone else as the captain of the frigate and his ops boss passed by with the bo'sun from Nathan's gangway detail acting as a guide.

Tanner's eyes narrowed. He didn't know where exactly *Beowulf* was. Life on a ship often meant not knowing such simple details. He didn't even know for sure if *Virtuous* had escorted the president's ship all the way back to Raphael or if they'd broken off before then, but that now seemed likely. *Virtuous* was transferring people off to *Beowulf*, its captain and third-ranking officer were on board presumably to meet with *Beowulf*'s CO, and the battleship was in "quiet" status yet again. Something was up.

Though his curiosity rose, his first priority was to get back to his berth and drop off all of his gear before anything silly happened to him or the ship. His holocom would already be synching up with the battleship's internal comms systems and loading over a month's worth of internal traffic, subscription media, and personal mail.

He made it to the nearest lift before his holocom buzzed with a live call. Tanner reached out to hit the call button for the lift, then tapped the device on his wrist to answer. A screen opened up to reveal Baldwin's cheerful face. The smudges on her forehead and cheek suggested she was doing the sort of work that masters-at-arms generally didn't get stuck with. "Hey, are you back?" she asked.

"Nope. Sorry. You're still asleep. This is a dream. A dream about me, no less. So we should ask what this tells us about Jesse Baldwin. Her hopes, her desires, her secret—"

Rolling her eyes, Baldwin grumbled, "It's a rhetorical question, ass. What I mean is, are you back on board for real, or are you popping in and out again for something else?"

"I'm back. Soon as I drop stuff off at my berth, I'll—"

"Cool. Meet you there." Baldwin cut off the line.

Meet me at my berth? Tanner wondered. *Why not meet me at the MA office when I check in? Is she not on watch or something? She looked like she's working.* He stepped into the lift and hit the button for his deck. No one else on the lift had much to say. The quiet atmosphere held as he walked off the lift.

A light outside the hatch into Tanner's berth indicated someone was sleeping inside. He took care to keep the wheel on the hatch quiet as he opened it and stepped through. Someone new lay in Pedro's former rack over Sinclair's, opposite Tanner's side of the berth. The other racks were empty. Only Tanner's was made up to pass inspection—as it had been when he left for Nathan's graduation ceremony. He hadn't slept in it since.

Unpacking could wait until the new roommate was up again. Tanner found Baldwin outside as he left, wearing her beret and sidearm as *Beowulf*'s MAs almost always did. "Get the medal," she whispered to him, patting at a spot below her neck.

Tanner blinked, but turned back to the duffel bag on his rack and did as she asked. Maybe she'd heard something from Janeka. Tanner pulled the borrowed Archangel Star from the bag, slipping it into one of the side pockets at his thigh as he came out again.

"What's going on?" Tanner asked.

"I didn't want you to forget it."

"How did you even know I had—?"

"C'mon, this is me here. I'm in everyone's business," Baldwin reminded him shamelessly.

"Why are you dirty?" he asked, gesturing to her still smudged-up face.

"Because I've been playing engineer, sort of. Come with me, I'll show you."

"What, are we re-modeling the brig or something?"

"Nope. Extra-curricular stuff."

Tanner threw her a wary glance as they walked together. "Extra-curricular" was Baldwin's term for things that took her outside the usual shipboard MA duties—usually combat missions like the moon raid and the boarding during the Battle of Raphael. He was almost always stuck right there with her. "So I'm not imagining things? There's a big operation coming up?"

"You could say that," Baldwin answered.

"Then I'll probably wind up involved anyway. I ought to go check in with the MA office first. I've gotta talk to Commander Jacobson."

"Oh, he's where we're going," said Baldwin. "The MA office knows you're with me. I called it in already."

His suspicion grew. "What's going on?"

"You'll see. All your favorite people are there." She guided him around a passageway corner and then down the steps to a lower deck. "So how'd the trip go? I mean other than the bit they showed on the news with you on the Assembly floor? That had to be amazing."

"A bit, yeah," Tanner admitted. Baldwin gave him a nudge. He winced, knowing exactly the reaction she would have. Nothing entertained her more than a scandal as long as it didn't involve her. "I'm under strict orders not to talk about it."

"Wow, seriously?" asked Baldwin. "Is it classified?"

Tanner sighed. "No."

Baldwin chewed on that. "So that means it's...*embarrassing*?" Her eyes lit up when she saw Tanner wince again. "Oh, now I really want to hear it!"

"You didn't want to hear it before?"

"No, before it was a rhetorical question like 'how are you?' It's the sort of thing you ask for the sake of asking and showing you care, y'know?"

"Ah. How silly of me."

"Besides, I'm obviously making small talk to avoid questions about where I'm taking you. Can't talk about it in the open. I figured you'd catch on to that by now. But if you can't talk about what happened…" Her voice drifted off thoughtfully as they descended through more decks. "Did you sleep with someone you shouldn't have?" Baldwin ventured.

"What?"

"Nah, couldn't be that. I've seen you try to pick up."

"You have not!"

"I have, too. We've hung out on plenty of liberty calls together. Hell, I even went out with you once myself. I've seen how you operate."

"Bullshit. I took you to the Annual Address, and *you said* it wasn't a date."

"Woah, way to announce it to the whole ship, loudmouth," she teased. "Seriously, just because you came with someone doesn't mean you couldn't have tried picking up while we were there."

"I'm not gonna 'pick up' at a political function," Tanner protested.

"That's kinda what I mean, though, so obviously you didn't sleep with anyone. Oh, did you get drunk at an embassy thing, maybe?"

Tanner almost objected to that absurdity, too, and then caught on to what she was really doing. The dark cloud hanging over his head for the last couple weeks already felt lighter. "I missed you, Jesse," he said. "Wish you'd been there."

"I know, right?" she agreed. "Missed you, too."

"Anything happen while I was gone?"

"Well, yeah," said Baldwin. "Nothing really good, but there's gossip you haven't heard, sure. Oh, you mean like battles and stuff? Couple minor engagements. Have to tell you about it later, though. We're here."

They came to a halt before a hatch along a wide passageway. Nearby stood large sliding doors opening into the same compartment. "Cargo loading six?" Tanner asked. "What are we doing here?"

Baldwin answered by tugging off her glove and placing her palm up against the security scanner by the wheel for the hatch—a scanner that wasn't there a month ago. She waited while it verified her DNA and beeped a welcome. Then she threw open the hatch.

A yacht took up almost half of the available space within the cargo bay. Her disassembled thrusters lay in two orderly lines spilling out from under the ship's aft section. Almost every access panel was open. Her starboard laser turret stood exposed from its recessed home within the yacht's "wing," with one barrel removed and the other looking like it wasn't a factory original.

All around the cargo bay, Tanner saw familiar faces. On top of the ship's bridge, Sinclair and Ravenell worked on installing a new comms module. Sanjay stood on the yacht's lowered cargo ramp doing calculations with his holocom. Chief Everett talked with some engineers amid the pieces of the yacht's thrusters. Tanner was fairly sure that was Mohamed and Baljashanpreet from Oscar Company there with him. On the other side of the cargo bay, past the bow of the yacht, Alicia packed several boxes of personal gear along with DC3 Fuller, a young woman from Oscar Company whom Tanner hadn't seen since the Battle of Raphael.

Baldwin hadn't exaggerated. He didn't know everyone in the cargo bay, but he almost never saw so many friendly faces all in one place. His brow furrowed as questions came to mind. The answers arrived before he spoke.

"Malone," said another familiar voice. "Glad you're back." Lieutenant Commander Jacobson looked like he'd been doing physical labor, too. Several dark smudges marred his normally pristine vac suit. He'd even loosened his collar.

"Thank you, sir," replied Tanner. "What's going on?"

"Covert operation, first off," the officer explained amiably. "You are to tell no one about what's going on here and you do not talk about it anywhere outside this cargo bay unless specifically authorized. Understood?"

"Yes, sir." Tanner made a bit of a smirk. "Kinda took the covert bit for granted."

"Yeah, it does have the look, doesn't it?" Jacobson nodded. "The second thing I need to tell you is that this is strictly voluntary. We'll give you the summary and you're either in or you're out. It's your call. Everybody was hand-picked, but no one is pressed into this one."

That made Tanner blink. In five years of service, nothing had ever been strictly voluntary. He'd never had reason to doubt Jacobson's word, yet he still had to look to Baldwin for confirmation. "Everyone here is already in?"

"Correct."

"Are you in charge, sir?"

The good-natured grin that crept across Jacobson's face spoke to his humility. "Technically."

"Malone," said someone behind him.

Should've guessed she'd be here, Tanner thought as he turned around. "Gunny Janeka."

"Commander, am I interrupting?" she asked Jacobson.

The officer shook his head. "Not at all. I was about to give Malone the general summary. If you're interested, I should probably leave it to you."

"Yes, sir," she replied. With that, Jacobson stepped away. Her gaze slid toward Baldwin, who departed without *quite* making a grumbly face about it. "He already told you this is covert, classified, and voluntary?" Janeka asked Tanner.

"He did."

"This mission is exceptionally high-risk. It is also ethically questionable, or will be to some. But it may be the best way to end the war."

Tanner's eyebrows rose. He didn't hear "ethically questionable" very often. "I don't suppose we're prepping to re-take Michael?"

"No," Janeka answered evenly, "we are not."

"What's the mission?"

"The Archangel Navy is going to invade and take NorthStar's headquarters on Fairhaven. By the time we get there, the whole planet may be under the corporate flag," she continued, not stopping for his shocked expression. "Obviously, this is one of the most fortified targets in the Union. Admiral Yeoh believes the navy can pull this off, but it will be an ugly fight. Our mission will be to cut that fight as short as possible.

"NorthStar has scheduled an emergency shareholder meeting on Fairhaven. Sovereignty or no, they do not want to give up on the corporate game. They need to keep their financial backers happy. Senior leadership will have to attend. This must be done in person, so Fairhaven is about to see a good deal of civilian traffic from liners and private spacecraft like this yacht.

"We will slip onto Fairhaven among that traffic in advance of the navy's attack. When the invasion gets underway, we will seize control of that meeting and capture as many senior corporate leaders and major shareholders as we can."

Tanner was stunned. He couldn't even figure out where to begin. A dozen questions tried to escape his mouth all at once, but they could only get out in single file. "We're going in with whoever we can cram into that?" he asked, pointing to the yacht. "There's gotta be hundreds of security people at an event like that, plus all the random bodyguards and local police and who knows what else, and however many thousands of non-combatants!"

"We won't be the only team," Janeka answered, unsurprised by his skepticism, "but we'll need to be ready to take this on ourselves if something goes wrong with the others, yes. Ideally, this will be timed with the navy's attack. Their civil defense and security people will have an awful lot on their hands when it happens."

"Okay, but…" Tanner ran his hands over the short black stubble on his scalp. He looked at the ship again and at the collection of friends and people he genuinely admired. Several of them seemed to be split between their work and not-so-subtly watching his conversation with Janeka from afar.

Practical questions and objections flashed through his mind. Some of them he answered on his own as quickly as they popped. Like Janeka said, the mission was high risk, yet planning and preparation were already underway. The calculations had been made. He wondered when that happened. Passage of the measure in the Assembly had been a shocker. Clearly someone had planned several steps beyond it. "How long have you all been working on this?"

"Admiral Yeoh approached me right after the president's delegation left for the Assembly," said Janeka. "If the measure failed, the mission would have been scrapped. We were instructed to be prepared in case things fell into place, and so far they have."

"This is Admiral Yeoh's idea?"

"Yes." She watched him carefully. As usual, she betrayed no particular emotion. "What do you want to ask me, Malone?"

He paused, looking her in the eye and hoping once, just once for the love of God, that he could read something from her calm expression. "We're going to attack a civilian target?"

She nodded—not in confirmation, he realized, but approval. She knew this would be on his mind. "This is the ultimate command and control of our enemy. NorthStar's executive leadership ordered the invasion of Archangel. Their shareholders have repeatedly voted their approval. They represent a massive portion of the enemy's backing and its will to fight. They are a legitimate target."

"They're a bunch of suits," Tanner countered. "You're talking about rich businesspeople and lawyers and third-generation high society. They don't know they're military targets, and they're not going to see us as a military team, either. They'll think we're a bunch of thugs with guns. I've *been* to that party, gunny. That's the kind of party we're supposed to prevent."

"We are not criminals," Janeka said with surprising patience. "We are not pirates or terrorists or a death squad. Killing is not our goal. We will secure the site and we will sue for peace. As soon as they order their forces to stand down and the occupation of Michael ends, we go home. Our rules of engagement are clear. We will not harm anyone who doesn't present a violent threat. We will not abuse captives."

"You honestly think it'll play out like that?" Tanner asked. "Bring a bunch of people with guns and grudges like ours into that city and you think nobody will do anything bad in the heat of the moment?"

"That's why Lieutenant Commander Jacobson is in command. That's why Baldwin is here. Everyone here has an individual role and contribution, but across the board, these are all people that I trust to do this right."

"You picked the team?"

"I did. The only person on this team I did not know personally was Bo'sun Bhatia. Admiral Yeoh recommended him based on his experience on Scheherazade. After reviewing his record, I agreed. I believe you know his value."

Again, Tanner glanced around the cargo bay. His friends—so many of these people really were friends—made almost no effort at all now to hide their interest. "If Jacobson and Baldwin are here to keep everyone honest, why am I here?"

"The same reason they are."

"That's my job, then?" he asked. "I'm there as an MA?"

"That, too." Janeka held out her hand. "You borrowed a medal from me. Do you have it?"

Tanner blinked. He reached into his pocket and pulled out the Archangel Star, holding it out for her. She placed her hand over his and held it there before taking it.

"Something will go wrong on this mission. Something always does. On a mission like this, it will likely be something bad. *That's* why I picked you, Malone."

He felt a lump in his throat. It seemed to appear out of nowhere as she spoke. Clearly, it was the result of another of Janeka's endless supply of dirty tricks. How could she keep doing stuff like this to him? At some point, shouldn't he learn to counter, or dodge, or something?

"Okay. I'm in."

"Malone!" shouted Jacobson suddenly. He stormed across the bay, followed by a floating screen of text from his holocom. "What *exactly* did you say to the president?"

• • •

"I told him to get off his high horse and quit pretending he's something special. People like that can't stand being told they aren't the most important person in the room." She took another sip of her drink, then shook her head at the way the subject of her disapproval harangued the attendant at the far end of the exclusive spaceport lounge. "Half a million shares. Should that impress anyone?"

Her companion—of the moment, at least—managed not to visibly choke. "It's more than anyone I know. Individually, at least." He looked young and fit, with his blond hair cut close and his tailored suit advertising a trim figure. "I'll confess, I'm attending as a representative rather than a shareholder myself. I have shares of my own, sure, but not in those kinds of numbers."

"Oh, that's nothing to confess." The glamorous, golden-skinned woman seated beside him waved off his humility. If anything, her smile seemed only to brighten. "You work for a living. It should be a point of pride. Especially in here. So are you an attorney, or a broker, or…?"

"Both, actually. At my level, you can't get by on only one and not the other." He flashed a practiced smile. "I'm sorry, was that a brag?"

"It's adorable, whatever it is."

"Excuse me, Ms. Cortez?" They both looked up to the sight of another woman in the same black business casual wear as the other lounge attendants. "I'm sorry to interrupt, but if you have a moment, could we take care of your boarding check-in?"

"Of course. Would you excuse us?" she asked her companion.

"Sure. I'll…talk to you later," he mumbled uncertainly as he walked away.

She turned back to the attendant with a sly grin. "He needed time to recover his nerve, anyway. What can I do for you?"

"We know this meeting comes on short notice and that it's an inconvenience for many," said the attendant. "The crew of the *Bird of Paradise* wants to make sure the trip is as pleasant as possible. Shall we begin?"

"Please."

"My information says you're a Platinum-Series shareholder, correct?"

"That's correct."

"Excellent. That entitles you to a number of special benefits on the liner and at Fairhaven. I've been informed that you'll get priority entrance to shareholder events, too."

"That was the whole point of it," smiled the woman calling herself Ms. Cortez.

"And according to my screen here, you're traveling to Fairhaven alone. Is that correct?"

"For now, yes." She winked at the attendant's quizzical expression. "Give me a chance to evaluate my fellow passengers."

"Yes, ma'am," the attendant chuckled. "What I mean is, do you have any personal staff that you'd like to have quartered near your suite?"

"Is that something you're arranging for everyone?"

"Gold Series and up, ma'am."

"Ah. Well, again, I'm on my own for now, but we'll see who I can poach along the way."

This time, the attendant couldn't hold back a full laugh. "I'm glad you're in such good spirits, ma'am. Not everyone is today."

"I've noticed. People are stressed, I take it?"

"You could say that, but I probably shouldn't talk too much about it."

"I'm more than happy to listen. Maybe once we're on our way."

"That's so kind of you, Ms. Cortez. Maybe later? We're on a tight schedule."

"Of course," Vanessa agreed. "I wouldn't want to be late for this party."

• • •

"Four weeks doing refit in drydock, a cargo run to Edison, a cargo run to Anambra, and here we are picking up yet another cargo load for God knows where. This is becoming a normal job."

Lounging in the captain's chair with his feet up on the console, Casey glanced over his spread of holo screens at the duty helmsman. "Not enough action for you, Schlensker?"

"I didn't leave the Union fleet voluntarily," the younger man replied with a shrug. "It doesn't have to be life and death all the time, but about the most dangerous job on this ship right now is running all those crates and shit up the loading ramps. Somebody might trip and the safeties on the anti-grav dollies might not kick in before someone gets bumped a little."

"He's speaking for himself, cap'n," said Renaldo at the comms station. She seemed about as relaxed as Casey, short of having her feet up on her console. "That last fight was as close to getting blown up as I ever need to be again."

"Okay, I'm not saying things need to get *that* exciting," Schlensker clarified. "But when they hired me for a covert ship, I figured we'd be, I don't know, raiding commerce outside Archangel and stuff."

Casey wondered if Schlensker meant that as a hint. The captain no longer wore his hair long and his face bore no stubble, but it wasn't as if he'd undergone serious cosmetic surgery. He could still be recognized by anyone who'd seen the media coverage that followed his capture.

Three years was a long time to keep one's guard up in such a close environment, and all the more so in the face of a leader who'd carried everyone through danger time and again. Casey saw that opportunity all the way back on Scheherazade, and here sat the results. Schlensker, Renaldo, and others had to know who Casey was by now. He was on their side. He looked out for them. He treated them with respect.

They had to know the truth, but with time and shared dangers, they no longer cared.

"Well, we lost a couple of our guns in the refit, but they were harder to hide or disguise than the rest," said Casey. "We've still got our full missile payload, just hidden away better now. Our armor only got stronger and the ES generator is better than what we had before. That wasn't done to take us out of action for long. In the meantime, running contraband is still a way to be a part of things. Ask yourself how bad it would be if we got caught by some boarding team. Maybe that'll help your sense of excitement."

"Are we taking on anything illegal?" Renaldo wondered.

Casey's eyes turned back to his holo screens. Two of them showed surveillance feeds from the cargo bay ramps. Another showed a scrolling manifest that updated as each new piece of cargo came on. "Five pallets of cots, five others with matching blankets and pillows. Prefab shelters, a couple hundred portable generators, fuel cells, a whole lot of first aid kids, and tons of pre-packaged food…still gonna be plenty of room left in our holds when it's all loaded up. Not so much with the contraband, no. Sorry."

"What, are we doing an emergency aid run?" asked Schlensker.

"We're not exactly in a rush about it," Renaldo noted.

"No, we're not," Casey agreed.

"And yet we're not running any liberty rotations, either," said the helmsman. "Everyone's still on board or right outside. Anambra's a first-tier world. Plenty to see and do here, but we're all cooped up."

"Yeah, I hear you." Ordinarily, a captain was every bit as obligated to back up his superiors as any member of the crew. Casey, however, felt no such obligations to those who gave the orders. "Doesn't do *me* any good to keep you all restricted to the ship. Busywork doesn't help anyone. Hopefully we'll get some sense of where all this is leading soon."

As he spoke, his eyes drifted back to the screens showing the cargo bay. A woman in a long, dark coat walked confidently up to the security troopers at the top of the loading ramp. Casey couldn't make out much of her face, but everything about her suggested she wasn't one of the port workers. She and the troopers exchanged a few words. He watched her step aside with one of the men where they could speak out of the way of anyone else going in or out of the ship. She flashed him some holographic identification, and then the trooper spoke into the holocom at his wrist.

Casey glanced over to Renaldo's station. She didn't appear to receive any new signals. As far as he could tell, she was playing some game to pass the time. On his screen, the newcomer strode across the cargo bay with that security trooper acting as her escort.

As the captain's eyes drifted over to the command status board, one of the hatches at the aft end of the bridge opened up. Casey waited as the sounds of footsteps came to his chair. "Captain," said Ezekiel, "could I speak with you in the wardroom?"

Casey killed his holo screens, pulled his feet up off the console, and stood. "Renaldo, Schlensker, try to keep the party up here from getting out of hand."

"Talk to you later, skipper," replied the comms officer. Schlensker merely waved.

"Let's go," Casey told his XO.

The pair exited together, with Ezekiel closing the hatch behind them.

"So where are we invading?" asked Casey.

Ezekiel glanced around the adjoining passageways as they came to the first intersection outside the bridge. "Who said anything about an invasion?"

"A cargo like ours is all stuff you want available as soon as possible after you've invaded somewhere and smashed up the place." He glanced back at the agent, who said nothing in response. "Up to you whether to talk or not."

They walked in silence only long enough to cross the next intersection, where no one else was in earshot. "You'll find out where we're going and what we're doing when we get our orders," said Ezekiel. "Until then, as I've told you before: I don't want you idly hanging around with the crew. You need to *act* like a captain, and that means you need to act professional. This isn't a pirate ship."

"I'm not unprofessional, I'm informal. And it's *my* ship." Casey's casual stride never wavered, nor did he look back. He refused to be upset or intimidated. "You don't like it, go cry to your fuckin' boss. Good luck finding someone better than me to take the reins here."

Ezekiel grabbed Casey by the wrist, turning it painfully and yanking him around to throw him against the bulkhead, but Casey got one leg in between the XO's to disrupt the move. The two wound up on the deck in a tangle. Though the larger man lost his grip on Casey's arm, he still managed to claim the superior position. Keeping Casey pinned to the deck, he drove one elbow down hard on Casey's jaw. His follow-up was blocked.

That was when he noticed the sharp bit of metal against his throat. Ezekiel grabbed for it with his punching hand, but Casey tangled that arm with his own while holding the blade firm against Ezekiel's neck. The XO realized he wouldn't get it away cleanly.

They stopped struggling and instead glared at one another.

"It's *my ship*," Casey seethed. "Keep pushing and you'll see how I deal with mutiny."

The glare held. Casey waited. Ezekiel released him and stood. Casey got to his feet.

"You'd never make it off the ship," said Ezekiel. "Even if you did, you'd never get away. We don't go anyplace where you could disappear."

"Are you trying to convince me, or yourself?"

Ezekiel held out his hand for the shiv. The pirate defiantly tucked it back into his sleeve.

"I'm a prisoner, not a victim." Casey's gaze never wavered. "Neither of your predecessors was dumb enough to make that mistake. Do your math before you come at me again."

They stood for another long moment, simply breathing and watching one another warily. Casey waited as Ezekiel considered his responses and his options. Ezekiel seemed to understand now that he would have to think more than one step ahead. "You said something about business in the wardroom," Casey prompted.

Ezekiel grunted. He touched the side of his neck, scowling when his fingers came away with blood. His clothes were as disheveled as Casey's. "We have a contact in with intel and orders. Soon as we—"

"Then let's go." Casey continued on his way without a second thought to the tear in his shirt, the reddening spot on his face from where he'd been punched or the rest of it.

Ezekiel cursed under his breath as he followed, pressing his fingers to the cut on his neck again. The bleeding wasn't dangerous, but he would need clotting gel or a bandage to stop it. Bloodstains marred his shirt. He didn't open his mouth fast enough to stop the captain. Casey threw the wheel on the hatch and stepped inside. Ezekiel had no other option but to go in after him.

The brunette from the cargo bay now sat at the wardroom conference table. Her breathing filter lay on the table. Casey didn't recognize her. He gave no reaction as she did a double-take at the sight of the two men, merely taking his seat at the head of the table beside her. "My XO tells me you have intel?" he said without introduction.

"I—yes," she replied, her eyes on Ezekiel as the bigger man settled into his chair.

"And instructions?"

"Yes," she answered, and then opened her mouth to speak again.

"What do I call you?"

"Nicole."

"Where's the invasion?"

That stopped her cold. "I'm sorry?"

"He's making a wild guess," said Ezekiel. "What are our orders?"

"Planetary invasion," she conceded, then paused for Casey's derisive chuckle. "Action in the Union Assembly has opened up our options. I'm sure you'll see it the next media drop. I have a legitimate special cargo order from a friendly source at your destination. It's on the way over now. You will to deliver it to Fairhaven and remain there in advance of an invasion by the navy."

"Fairhaven," Casey repeated.

She confirmed it with a cool nod. "We don't have a firm date and hour for the arrival of the invasion, but there's a solid timeframe. I have the relevant passwords and protocols, including contingency plans in case the invasion is canceled."

"They're gonna invade Fairhaven," Casey muttered. "And they want to slip us in past all the security NorthStar has in that system? Right at their home base?"

Nicole shrugged. "It's no more of a risk than you've taken in flying this ship through boarding parties in other systems. NorthStar's security forces are vigilant around Fairhaven, but short of actually tearing into this ship's bulkheads or taking systems apart, they won't find anything worrisome. Your obvious weapons appear to be well within legal limits, the hidden systems are well-concealed, your records are all in order, and you don't carry anything to make them suspicious, correct?"

"I dunno," Casey said, his eyes narrowing. "What's this other cargo you have on the way?"

"Livestock. Crustaceans out of Fremantle, all in compartmentalized tanks. It fits our needs. Livestock arriving on Fairhaven has to undergo a ten-day 'health and safety' quarantine before offloading, along with a stiff tariff. That gives you reason to park on the surface and wait through the invasion window without raising suspicion."

"If we're on the ground ahead of the invasion, what are our objectives?" asked Ezekiel. "We must be there for more than an advance landing of supplies."

"You will set down near the primary spaceport. Once the invasion arrives, you're to prevent any other vessels from launching. Aerial vehicles, too, if you can manage it. Ideally, you will take control of whatever spaceport you occupy."

"Makes sense," said Ezekiel.

"Sure." Casey sat back in his chair, folding his arms across his chest. "So. Lobsters and crabs and shit, huh? Fremantle's critters are good for snobby restaurants, I'll give you that. Now what else is in those tanks with the livestock?"

Nicole smirked back at him. She no longer showed any surprise at his pointed questions. It almost seemed to amuse her. "Chaff missiles modified for surface action and small arms for advance landing parties," she said.

"Surface action?" Casey slid a dry glance toward Ezekiel. "I guess I'll get to see how you handle a real fight after all."

• • •

"I got sixteen different ass-chewings from people outside my department, but everyone who gets an actual say in this says no harm, no foul. I'm officially Not In Trouble. Hopefully you can say the same on your end by the time you get this."

"Cleared for launch," announced Mohamed's voice over the PA. Tanner glanced up from his holo screen as *Mansa Musa* lifted off from *Beowulf*'s hangar. He hadn't been in on the practice flights, but now he understood what Mohamed and Sanjay meant about how the yacht handled. Were it not for the announcement or a look out the portholes, Tanner and his teammates in the ship's comfortable lounge might not even have noticed their departure.

No one had much to say. Plans were set. Watch stations were filled. Every bit of gear was stowed. Like Tanner, his teammates generally had their eyes on the last batch of personal mail to arrive before they got underway—which they'd all have to purge from their holocoms before they made it to the Endeavor system.

For most, it was good to hear from friends and family one last time on their way out for the mission. With the fleet in quiet status, though, they wouldn't be able to respond. Tanner wound up with mixed feelings as he read Madelyn's letter.

"As usual, I still can't talk much about actual work stuff. Still get to be just as vague as I was on Uriel. I can tell you I've done a lot of follow-up research to help investigations that aren't mine. The bosses say, 'Hey, we've analyzed what you've told us and holy crap it all lines up, you really are onto something but we still need more.' I get told to

keep at it, that I'm doing big favors, and people will pay me back…and then it's out of my hands again. The big thing I do, apparently, is that I prove other people aren't crazy with their work. I guess that makes me a corroboration specialist?"

Tanner understood her perfectly. Madelyn knew his mail might be read. If that NorthStar agent's holocom had anything truly useful on it, she wouldn't be able to send it to him, anyway. He had realized that almost as soon as it was too late to change his mind.

Yet Madelyn's letter provided vindication. Her bosses analyzed what he'd told her and their research backed him up. He wasn't crazy. Her superiors took this seriously—and he'd gotten her out of any trouble for helping him. Given the way his perspective on events kept changing, he considered that a solid success regardless of his sins.

His holocom buzzed with a call from *Mansa Musa*'s bridge. Tanner answered it with the touch of a finger. "Hey."

"Take a look out to starboard," Sanjay told him. "Timing, huh?"

Tanner followed the tip. Not far away, he saw a familiar corvette pass by on its way into *Beowulf*'s hangar bay. His shoulders slumped. "Yeah," he grumbled, glancing from the ship to the holographic letter and then back again. "Timing."

• • •

"You could get lost on that ship," said Lt. Kelly. "I thought *Los Angeles* was big, but yikes."

"Haven't you been on board *Beowulf* before, ma'am?" asked the woman standing at *Joan of Arc*'s helm. Ops Specialist Third Class Renata Montes seemed perfectly comfortable balancing conversation with manual control. It spoke well of her. The question, however, illustrated how new she was to *Joan*'s crew.

"I was a little worse for wear the one time I was here." Kelly's eyes drifted involuntarily to a spot on the deck behind Montes. She blinked, told herself for the millionth time to stop doing that, and looked away. The captain caught the gaze of her XO from his seat on the other side of the corvette's small bridge and understood his unspoken message. He'd tell Montes the story later, in private.

"We all were," Lt. Booker said to ward off the uncomfortable silence. "Pretty sure all I saw was the passageway to the infirmary and back and the two wrong turns that poor marine took us through. The only one of us who saw more than that was Ordoñez. Speaking of her, captain, she asked if she can jump ship long enough to say hi to some friends here."

"At least one of us should get the time for that," mused Kelly. "Might as well be her."

Joan flew gracefully into *Beowulf*'s cavernous landing bay. All of the battleship's shuttles were cleared out to make room for visitors. The space usually occupied by Beowulf's companion corvette, *St. Catherine*, was occupied—but not by its usual resident. "Is that *St. George*?" asked Booker.

"Sure is," Kelly confirmed. "Guess their patrol got cut short."

"And *St. Nicholas* is coming in behind us," noted Montes. She brought *Joan* in for a smooth landing, hardly needing to look at the computer screens on the helm. "Docking complete. Clamps secured. Powering down."

Kelly appreciated the other woman's natural aptitude. Her last junior ops specialist had trouble taking his eyes off the numbers during fine maneuvers like this. That worked fine while flying in open space, but it didn't bode well for tighter work. Montes seemed born to the helm. "That was the last thing to check off on your qualification list, right?" Kelly asked.

"Yes, ma'am."

She opened up a new holo screen, quickly navigating through the menu to *Joan*'s personnel files. "At the first chance we get, we'll run your board exam and write you in as a full-duty helmsman. I'd have the XO do it right now, but he's in this meeting with me." Both officers stood from their seats. "Montes, you have the in-port watch."

"Aye aye, ma'am. I have the watch."

"You need to grab anything before we go?" Kelly asked in the short passageway outside the bridge. Each officer had a cabin close by.

"No, I'm good to go," said Booker. "You?"

"Yeah, I'll be ready in just a second," she said. Booker gave her a simple wave and continued on to the lower deck. Inside her cabin, Kelly stopped for a quick look in the mirror to ensure she was presentable and then flicked on her holocom for one last message check. With so much activity and so many ships in close proximity, she fully expected changes of plans, cancelations, redirections, and all the other "hurry up and wait" of the navy.

Joan of Arc went quiet as of yesterday. *Beowulf* was in quiet status, too, and had been for some time. Even with *Joan* on board, personal traffic from anyone on the battleship wasn't likely to show up in her messages.

She looked anyway, of course. It only took the touch of a button.

Less than a minute later, Kelly found the XO waiting for her at the bottom of *Joan*'s cargo ramp, chatting with one of *Joan*'s bo'suns. Docking chores already looked complete. The pair got on their way, only to come to an almost immediate stop in front of a frowning gunner's mate.

"Something wrong, Ordoñez?" asked Kelly.

"Sanjay's not here," she replied. "They've got him listed on temporary duty. Tanner, too."

"Huh. That's too bad," said the captain. "I'd like to see them."

"Yeah. Wonder where they're off to with all this going on?"

Kelly shrugged. "We'll let you know if we hear anything."

"Captain Kelly?" asked a voice to her side. A yeoman walked up to her with a deferential nod. "I've been sent to direct you to your briefing, ma'am."

"Thank you," she replied with a smile. "It's appreciated. I wondered how we'd find it. Please, lead the way."

The walk across the docking bay gave a better view of all the activity. Load-lifters shifted stacks of fuel and ammunition. A crew seemed to be rearranging the shuttle landing markers. To Kelly's surprise, she saw a platoon of marines in full combat gear formed up on one end of the bay, though she couldn't hear a word from the NCO speaking to them.

"Is it always this busy?" Booker asked their guide.

"Yes and no, sir. It's always a busy ship, but this is a bit much. We've been laying in supplies and new units all week."

"Units? You mean tech?"

"No, sir. Personnel. Mostly marines and civil defense grunts. If this isn't something big, it sure is serious practice for the real thing."

Kelly and Booker shared a pensive look. As they walked, Kelly's curiosity grew. Their journey took them into areas typically reserved for *Beowulf*'s marines. She kept expecting the yeoman to lead them back out toward navy territory, but eventually they came to "Briefing Room Charlie," according to the placard on the hatch leading inside. The yeoman wordlessly opened up the hatch and stood out of the way.

They found a couple of marine officers waiting, along with a handful of sergeants—and Admiral Yeoh. "Ah. Captain Kelly,

Lieutenant Booker," she said, looking up from the holographic star system projected over a center table. "It's good to see you both."

"Ma'am," Kelly replied as they walked in. This wasn't her first meeting with the admiral, but every other encounter involved a much more populated room than this, and usually someone higher in rank did the talking for her.

"How are your ship and your crew?" Yeoh asked pleasantly.

"Fine, ma'am. Ready for duty."

"That's what the files say," agreed Yeoh. "You have a full crew. Maintenance is up to date. But we all know not all matters fit into the paperwork. I ask because I'm about to present a vital and dangerous mission. Effectiveness is far more important for me than resolve or a can-do spirit. If you tell me anything is wrong, I will value your honesty and think no more of it."

Kelly shook her head. "Ma'am, we're in the best shape we've been in since the start of the war. If there's a party in the works, we wouldn't miss it. Where are we headed?"

Yeoh greeted Kelly's answer with a crisp smile. "Fairhaven." Her smile grew a touch wider as she saw Kelly blink. "Captain, Lieutenant, I want you to meet Lieutenants Thompson and Craig, and Sergeants McAllister, Rodriguez, and Collins. They're most of the leadership of Bravo Company's Third Platoon from the ship's marine regiment. The rest of their platoon is in the docking bay now. You may have passed them on your way here. *Joan of Arc* is needed in the vital role of troop transport.

"If our experiences on the Astonaco raid are any sign of what's to come, you can expect to take heavy fire on your way in. But I imagine it will be an easier maneuver than dropping off troops on a moving battleship." She paused. "Slightly, anyway."

• • •

"That expeditionary load-up exercise is still running. Raphael, Uriel, and Gabriel sources all report movement and our ships in orbit see it as well. Navy, Civil Defense, Independent Shipping Guild. The whole nine yards, just like the one we saw last month."

"Uh-huh."

"The anti-occupation rally in Crystal Falls occurred overnight as planned. Nineteen arrests, couple of damaged vehicles, no serious injuries on either side. Risk Management says their undercover agents can probably use this to co-opt the protest leadership."

General Carruthers didn't look up. He kept typing. "Hrm."

"Ranger Team Delta is prepping for a fugitive pick-up in the northern hemisphere. It's the getaway drivers from the detention center hit last month. They should have a pre-strike estimate for us in the next hour."

"That's fine," the general muttered. In the windows behind him, savannahs stretched out toward distant red and brown mountains under a beautiful morning sky. Birds flew. Tall, golden grass rippled in the breeze.

Neither the general nor his nervous aides would get to enjoy the view. "Also, we had another strike at the spaceport outside Geronimo. Three smaller—"

"Oh, God damn it!" Carruthers burst. He slammed his hands down on the table. His glass of water bounced and rolled through the holo screen that had kept his attention until now, causing it to blink out of existence. Under the angry flare of his nostrils, the general's bushy blond mustache seemed to mimic the flow of the grass outside. No one laughed, of course. The general's sense of humor didn't allow for laughs at his own expense, particularly not at a time like this. "How many ships did we lose this time?"

"Three smaller craft and two shuttles, sir. Two of our corvettes were also hit badly enough that they'll be grounded for a while."

"Corvettes? What the hell weapons did they use?"

"Infantry-portable missiles, sir. They were powered down for routine maintenance. It's not like they kept the ES systems running."

"Where in the hell did they—oh, nevermind where they got missiles." Carruthers sat back in his chair, rubbing his bald head in aggravation. "How many dead?"

"Only thirteen, sir, with about twice as many injured."

"*Only* thirteen! These people are incorrigible!" He glanced from one aide to the next. "That's not the worst, is it, Trent?" he asked of his senior deputy.

"No sir. The, ah, main power grid for the spaceport was sabotaged as well. We think there's a layered problem, both hardware and software. The combination makes it tough to run it all down. Critical systems for running the port can go on back-ups or portables as needed."

"But? I hear a 'but' in there, Trent."

"Major Greenly at the spaceport warns us that the problem is widespread. Both anti-orbital plasma cannons near the port are offline. The power problems might, um…cause an explosion."

"And you people didn't wake me up? You didn't even have someone call me as soon as I was up and moving this morning? You know my schedule!"

"Sir, the damage assessments are still coming in and the sun isn't up over Geronimo yet. Also, you said not to wake you unless we were under attack from the navy—"

"Don't tell me what I said! And what the hell is with those people there, anyway? They know these attacks don't make any real difference. We're only occupying the vital spots. Hell, we don't even have a whole regiment in Geronimo."

"Sir, Risk Management has a report on Geronimo's—"

"Screw Risk Management! We're god damned NorthStar Security, we should have our own intelligence and our own reports." Fuming, Carruthers looked out his window. Everyone knew his patterns. He fumed, and then he seethed. Once he fell to seething, he was less likely to fire anyone or give them a shitty assignment.

"We've got three other working spaceports on the planet, sir," Trent reminded him. "They can pick up the slack."

"The other spaceports have all been hit in the last few months, too. The one in the capitol is still under a workforce walkout. The only people there are our own guys. But that's not the point to attacking at Geronimo, Trent. Have you looked at a map or a globe lately?"

"Sir?"

Carruthers sighed. "It's the only one in the southwest quadrant. This puts a hole in our defense screen."

"The fleet can move other ships over there to cover it."

"You mean they haven't already? This is why you've always been a staff officer and never gotten your own command, Trent. Get Captain Sokolov on the line. Tell him we need coverage over that spaceport. Then get your ass out there and start relaying reports to Martha," he added, gesturing to another aide. "Every half hour. Go."

"Yes, sir," Trent mumbled. Carruthers didn't quite hear him add, "Chickenshit," as he left.

"Me, sir?" Martha asked.

"I don't want him calling *me* every half hour." Carruthers let out another sigh. "That was unprofessional of me," he said as he opened up his holo screen again. "I shouldn't reprimand an officer in front of others. I apologize."

Martha glanced at the other remaining aide. Neither of them pointed out that it was Trent who deserved the apology, but… "He really was waiting for complete information before notifying you, sir," Martha ventured.

"He's a kiss-ass," grumbled the general. "Never should've gone beyond Lieutenant. He's only here because of politics." His fingers paused over the holographic keypad laid out on the table. "A lot of staffing here happens because of politics."

He didn't see Martha swallow her response. "Yes, sir."

"Put in that call to Sokolov. I've got a letter to write."

Martha and the other one staffer left with politely murmured goodbyes. In truth, Carruthers still couldn't remember the other staffer's name. He was some ensign, somebody's nephew, and the beneficiary of nepotism and politics, like Trent.

Carruthers feared he was the exact opposite: a victim rather than a beneficiary.

Alone in his office, Carruthers returned to his letter. "Commodore Prescott," the text began, "I write to inquire about my requests for staffing and increased security force presence…"

All but growling, Carruthers blanked out the text to begin anew. "Dear Jean," he opened, "I'm writing to you via personal channels because I feel like we've known each other long enough to speak candidly. I was as thrilled as anyone when you made commodore, and I supported your candidacy from the beginning." That was a slight embellishment, but would she know better? "I have to come right out and ask: What did I ever do to deserve this terrible assignment?"

He stared at the words on the screen. Written words didn't always carry the correct tone. The general considered writing this out and then recording it as a video message. A letter might come off as whiny. If he recorded this in video, though, *Commodore* Jean Prescott would hear him speak, and then she would know he wasn't whining.

His holocom buzzed with an annoying alert and a high-priority call screen. Carruthers rolled his eyes, figuring it was Trent already. Fortunately, he looked at the screen before accepting the call. "Vassily," he said to the commander of the orbiting task force, "I just sent one of my staffers to contact you."

"Then I take it you see what I am seeing?" asked the grim captain.

Carruthers blinked. He walked out into the command center outside his office. "Sorry, one moment," he said to cover for his ignorance. His first thought was to find out what Sokolov saw. His second was that he could probably tell Sokolov that his staffers had him tied up in a meeting. Before that thought went any further, he found the command center full of concerned faces and alarming signs on large tactical screens and long-range scanner data.

"Oh shit," Carruthers murmured.

Suddenly the activity near Raphael didn't look like an exercise. Not with it barreling across the short distance separating Archangel's capitol from its occupied neighbor.

"Sir?" asked one of the technicians.

"General!" called out Martha from across the room.

"Why didn't you come get me?" he snapped.

"Sir, I was getting the report from CIC and activating the alert—"

"Put everyone on full alert!" Carruthers shouted before she could finish telling him she'd already done that. "Get the field commanders on the line. I want anti-orbital defenses going, and—oh shit." He turned back to the holo screen floating along with him. "Vassily, we're down two of our anti-orbital cannons outside of Geronimo."

"Yes, your aide told me. I have three ships ready to shift over to that sector. With your permission, I want to pull the task force in closer to the planet. The enemy will be more restrictive with their fire if there's a risk of collateral damage."

"Right, I agree," said Carruthers. Really, did Vassily need to explain simple fundamentals like that to him? Fleet commanders could be so pretentious.

"They're picking up speed, sir." reported Martha.

Carruthers noted the change. He also took note of the revised rundown of the ships arrayed against him. The armada seemed to be most of Archangel's navy, along with civilian ships from the AISG carrying landing troops. Yet it obviously wasn't the entire fleet. He saw *Hercules*—he refused to call NorthStar's captured ships by the names Archangel gave them—and *Los Angeles*, along with the stolen cruiser *Halley*, but he didn't see the other battleship. The destroyers didn't add up, either, or the corvettes.

This looked too much like an even fight. Hell, if one factored in Michael's anti-orbital defenses, NorthStar had a significant edge. They had to move in to exploit that gap near Geronimo, or else pound the hell out of their own soil to land anywhere else on the planet, and that was presuming they could fight their way through the task force at all. If they brought everything they had, Archangel could make a decent go of it, but without their full fleet…

The general watched the armada cross the halfway point between Raphael and Michael as it built up speed. Yeoh was too tricky for something this straightforward. She had to have something up her sleeve. She always did. Still, Michael's occupiers could see her coming. Apart from coordinating somehow with the insurgents here on the ground, how could she gain any element of surprise?

Then, as if in answer, the armada vanished. Carruthers looked to his command staff for answers that came immediately: "They've jumped into FTL! They're gone!"

NorthStar's forces on and above Michael remained on full alert for three days. No attack ever came. The enemy ships never came back, either.

Carruthers maintained the alert for another day longer.

Then he got really worried.

CHAPTER TEN

Never According to Plan

> *Reeling from the sudden withdrawal of all support from NorthStar, Prince Murtada's fortunes on the battlefield have quickly gone into reverse. Lai Wa has also ordered a pullout from the conflict. Prince Kaseem, the middle brother in the three-way war of succession, has quickly moved to exploit these new opportunities, though many observers believe he, too, has now overextended himself. Regardless, the pressure on Prince Khalil's loyalists seems to be off—and external aid from other Union states is said to be quietly flowing in.*
>
> --THE SOLAR HERALD, JULY 2279

Mansa Musa dropped out of FTL outside the Endeavor system's legal boundary. She found clear signals for navigation and traffic control and in return offered up her identification and flight plan. As her "light-bubble" expanded, adding active sensor information to passive signal reception, the yacht settled into a smooth cruising speed.

"You don't wanna look *too* casual," counseled Chief Everett from the captain's chair.

Both of the younger bo'suns seated at the front of the bridge turned to throw exasperated looks his way. "What the fuck is *too* casual?" asked Sanjay, while Mohamed complained, "You said not to come in too hot!"

The chief didn't try to hold back his amused grin. "You think VIP shareholders coming in on their own yacht go below the speed limit? We've got deals to make and resorts to enjoy."

Sanjay frowned. "They should've let me be the shareholder."

"You have to be the driver on the ground, remember?" asked Sinclair from the auxiliary systems chair.

"That only means I'd have to steal a car nice enough for a rich guy."

The yacht's small but comfortable bridge spoke to that same concern for wealth and image. The bridge crew's vac suits came from civilian manufacturers well outside Archangel, much like the rest of their gear. They'd all left behind their personal holocoms and anything else that would tie them to their real identities on *Beowulf*.

Every one of the twelve days spent in transit had been filled with whatever training and preparation the yacht allowed. That mostly came down to computer simulations, roleplaying exercises designed to cement everyone's cover, and mild close combat training. The activity helped distract those on board from the looming tension and stress of their mission. All of that tension rushed back as their arrival drew down to a matter of hours and minutes...provided they were allowed to land at all.

"Busy day out here," Mohamed observed as sensor readings stabilized and the picture of space all around them became clearer. Though they were several light-minutes away from any given contact, the yacht's instruments identified a great number of signals and objects well beyond the sensor bubble. The traffic outstripped anything that Archangel usually saw, even on a busy day before the war. No small number of their contacts were military vessels.

"It's about what I expected," said Everett. "This system hasn't been hit since the Expansion Wars. The most we've done here is long-distance recon. As far as these folks are concerned, it's all business as usual. Wars happen to *other* people."

"Traffic control acknowledges us," reported Sinclair. "Flight plan is approved pending security fleet checks. There's a message here about inspections and boardings. Looks like it's all pretty standard."

"Then we hold steady and keep moving," Everett replied. "No sense volunteering for a delay. They'll give us instructions to come in closer to one of their patrol ships. With any luck, we'll only get a routine scan."

Almost before the chief finished, Sinclair's console beeped loudly. He pressed the receive key to enable the audio. "Starship *Mansa Musa*, this is *NSS Doberman*. Please alter your course to rendezvous at coordinates transmitted along with this signal for security clearance. You have been randomly selected for boarding and inspection. We apologize for the delay. Please acknowledge."

"Aw, shit," grunted Everett.

Sanjay rolled his eyes. "That's on you, chief. You jinxed us."

"Yeah, yeah." Everett reached for the comms panel at his seat. "*Doberman*, this is *Mansa Musa*. Altering course now." Then he cut the channel. "Nothin' we can do but play through. Mohamed, head for the coordinates. Go ahead and drop our speed some."

"Is there a *casual* speed I should go?"

"Naw, not casual. We're getting pulled over. Slow down to passive-aggressive speed." The chief called up another comms channel, this one offering a view of Jacobson and several of the others in the yacht's passenger lounge. "Sir, we got tagged for boarding," Everett warned. "NorthStar corvette, so it shouldn't be a big crew, but we're gonna have company. ETA eight minutes."

Jacobson frowned. "Any idea why we got tagged?"

"They said it was random, sir. I'm inclined to I believe it. Seems pretty busy out here, no way are they boarding everyone. They even apologized."

"Right. Let's not take for granted that they'll be so cordial when we're face to face. Thanks." Jacobson cut the holo screen and turned to the others in the lounge. Unlike the men on the bridge, he wore expensive, slick civilian clothes rather than a vac suit. Most of those with him lacked such protective gear as well. "You heard the man. Let's find out if we're as prepared as we think."

Everyone stood from the couches and plush chairs. Ravenell and Alicia dressed in much the same just-shy-of-formal look as Jacobson. Fuller looked a touch more professional in her sharp businesswear. Baldwin wore a fine but understated black dress to suit her role as the ship's steward. Their sudden rise and serious expressions put a grin on Jacobson's face despite the pressure of the moment. "You realize you don't have anywhere to go, right?" He motioned for them all to settle back down. "We're passengers. Remember to act like it. The only one who has someplace to be is you," Jacobson added, turning to Tanner.

His all-too-recognizable face meant that he wouldn't have a part to play in this. It also kept him in a crewman's vac suit. "Yeah, I'm on my way, sir," he said.

"Let the gunny know?" Jacobson asked as Tanner stepped into the passageway outside. "Thanks. Good luck."

Tanner grimaced. Given his training and experience with boardings, he knew too many ways this could go wrong. The boarding team could have tech that they didn't expect. They might be running new protocols. NorthStar's security fleet might be all too aware of the risks created by this shareholders meeting and could have doubled down on searches.

The one aspect he didn't worry about was his team. All they had to do was stick to their story, volunteer minimal details, and act a little impatient. Everyone could hold a straight face.

He knocked on the door to the "ladies' room," which, he had to concede, was far too posh to be called a head as it would be on any other ship. "Gunny?" he asked.

The door snapped aside. He hardly recognized the knockout staring back at him. She had the dark brown skin tone and dark eyes of Gunny Janeka, but the rest didn't compute. Her hair was much longer, full, and stylish. Her lips seemed redder. And her eyes—was that *eyeshadow?*

"What is it?" asked the same flat, demanding voice he'd always known. But it didn't come from the right face. This couldn't be Gunny Janeka. She never wore civilian clothes, and surely not silk dresses. Or jewelry. How could a vac suit or a uniform hide a figure like—?

"*Malone!*"

"Boarding! Sorry. Um. We're being boarded. Right away. Sorry." Her annoyed glare banished his cognitive dissonance. *My mistake,* thought Tanner. *That's the gunny. That's the gunny out of uniform. Wow. Okay. Moving on.*

"Anything suspicious about it?" she asked.

"No. Sounds like it's ordinary bad luck. Jacobson says we stick with the plan."

"Understood. You'd better get to your station. Do you need help?"

"Think I've got it, gunny."

"It's Mrs. Rambeau," she reminded him sternly.

"Right. Gotcha. I'm on my way." Tanner quickly moved off, opening the hatch leading out of the passenger cabin. He looked back to add, "You look great today."

Her glare threatened to tear open his chest and rip out his soul. "*Are you saying I don't look good all the time?*" she roared, but he didn't hear the rest. The hatch slammed shut on her last word, preventing him from seeing her grin.

The passageway continued back toward the aft end of the ship, past a master bedroom and two guest bedrooms. Even the crew quarters on the lower deck were nicer than anything Tanner had seen on a warship. Tanner's destination was much more utilitarian: between the galley and dry stores, the ship carried isolated life support tanks for air and water as a back-up for the main tanks near engineering.

The ventilation and purifiers inside would eliminate the danger of being detected by a sniffer unit. The cold conditions would mask Tanner's heat signature, while his vac suit would keep him warm. If the boarders wanted to tear into the space, he'd be busted, but the boarding would turn into a battle before the others let that happen. Still, for the boarders to become suspicious in the first place, they would have to recognize the false panel in the bulkhead that Tanner knelt to open up…and found immobile.

He tugged. It held fast. He crammed his gloved fingers into the small groove between the bulkhead and the carpet on the deck and pulled. It wouldn't move.

"Oh shit," Tanner grunted, pulling again. And again. And again. On his final tug, he heard exactly the sort of metallic snap that the false panel wasn't supposed to make at all. "Aw, *shit!*"

His heart raced. The panel remained in place, but he could feel a little more open space with his fingertips. In his mind's eye he could see exactly which fitting broke and the pieces he'd find lying on the deck if he opened the panel the rest of the way.

"Sir, Chief," Tanner said with one finger on the holocom at his wrist. "We've got a problem. The false panel wouldn't open, and I heard something in there break."

"What?" Jacobson responded.

"Baljashanpreet's in engineering," Everett thought quickly. "He can help you."

"Chief, there's no point," countered Tanner. "Even if we get it open, it won't sit right. The break in the bulkhead will be visible and air will start whistling through it. If I leave it alone, it'll be fine, but if I fuck with it we're screwed."

"We're screwed if they see you, Tanner," said Jacobson. "We can't stuff you in a closet!"

"We might have to," said Sinclair, joining them on the comm. "It's better than nothing."

Staring at the bulkhead, Tanner's mind raced for a way through this. *Something will go wrong*, he heard Janeka say in his head. She'd been right about that, except apparently *he* was the thing that went wrong.

"No, it's worse than nothing," Everett replied. "Even if this is only a formality, they're bound to have somebody with a chem sniffer or a thermal reader. We can't hide a human being from that on the fly. Running him around the ship to avoid them is no good, either. I've seen people try that con. Too much can go wrong. Shit, they're already moving in for a link-up."

"Can we stall?" asked Jacobson.

"I don't think so."

Tanner felt an ugly pit in his stomach. Emotions he'd first felt back on *St. Jude* welled up in his gut as he imagined the approaching corvette, with its deck crewmen standing outside the hull. He'd done that job so many times, and fucked it up over and over…

"Put me outside!" Tanner snapped. He jumped up and ran for the ladder down to the ship's lower deck. The main airlock lay right outside the yacht's small cargo bay.

"What?" asked Everett.

With his feet and hands against the outside rails of the ladder, Tanner slid right down in the space between heartbeats. He tugged his helmet down from its shoulder mount. "Avery, have you sent them our manifest yet?"

"No, they haven't asked."

"Add me on as a crewman. Chief, sir, I'm going outside to help with the link-up and to make sure they don't scuff our paint or dent the ship."

"But we're connecting with *our* landing struts!" argued Everett. "They're the ones who have to put up the vestibule!"

Tanner kept moving. The airlock was barely more than a walk-in closet, the hatch at his feet just broad enough for two people to squeeze through shoulder to shoulder. Stepping inside, Tanner settled his helmet into place and hit the seals. He grabbed one of the spare oxygen tanks from the rack inside the airlock and attached it to his helmet.

"Chief, it's the only thing I can think of. Outside, I can at least keep my helmet on and nobody will recognize me. Hiding in plain sight seems like my only option."

"Link-up in one minute," warned Sanjay.

"Chief?" asked Jacobson, leaving the decision to the man at the wheel.

"Do it," said Everett. "Avery, tie him into the crew comm net. Tanner, try not to talk much."

Tanner closed the interior hatch behind him and keyed the controls to depressurize the small compartment. He felt the air rush out through the vents as he activated the magnetic grips in his vac suit and tried to steady his breath. The queasiness in his stomach intensified.

His gut remembered this sort of thing from *St. Jude* all too well.

With the status panel inside the airlock showing everything in order, Tanner threw the wheel on the hatch and pushed it open. The yacht's artificial gravity field made that tough, but he managed it in time to see the *Doberman* rotate into place a few dozen meters away.

NorthStar's Watchdog-class corvettes had broader, thicker wings and a shorter "nose" section than Archangel's. He'd seen them over Scheherazade, flying in the service of Murtada's invasion fleet. For all he knew, this was one of those same ships. Or maybe it had flown at Raphael or one of Tanner's other battles. He'd been through all too many by now. Any one of the three crewmen standing on *Doberman*'s hull might have taken shots at him. They might have killed people he knew.

With a groan, Tanner heaved himself through the airlock and the invisible, disorienting edge of the yacht's artificial gravity field. He climbed out onto the bottom of the hull and offered a nice, friendly wave.

"*Mansa Musa*, we see one of your people coming out onto your hull," announced a voice inside Tanner's helmet. "We've got the link under control."

"Copy that, *Doberman*," came Sinclair's calm response. "Be advised, our crewman is only out there for training and observational purposes." Sinclair paused. "He's new."

"Ah. Understood," replied the corvette's spokeswoman with a knowing tone.

The landing struts extended far enough to allow Tanner to stand upright without hitting his head, but he stayed low regardless. *Doberman*'s crewman stood clear on their end. He noted the silvery padding on *Doberman*'s hull that marked out the connection points. Chatter over the comm net held to a minimum as *Mansa Musa* drifted in. The landing struts connected all at once in the sort of fine maneuver Tanner would never be able to execute.

"Smooth hand at the helm there, *Doberman*," commented Everett.

Oh shut up, Tanner thought irritably.

The NorthStar crewmen came around to the bottom of *Doberman*'s hull. One of them opened up their airlock hatch, lined up perfectly with *Mansa Musa*'s, and started pulling out the transparent, flexible vestibule that would create a safe passageway between the two. Tanner stood, trying to take on an amiable posture around men who walked on a deck that loomed over Tanner's head. Everyone stayed out of each other's way, but Tanner reached out to help the first crewman with the slight jump over to *Mansa Musa*'s hull. The receiver in his helmet let out a longer beep than usual as it adjusted to a different brand of comms unit.

"Hi," grunted Tanner. "Can I help?"

"You might want to step back," suggested *Doberman*'s bo'sun. "We can get this."

"Mind the hull. We just had it waxed." The bo'sun turned to look at him quizzically. Tanner shrugged. "Or whatever."

• • •

"You said you're coming straight in from Arcadia?" asked *Doberman*'s XO. She stood with Everett at the open hatch into the passenger lounge while the members of her boarding party checked the identification of the passengers inside. "No stopovers, no detours?"

"Nope. Straight shot," Everett reiterated calmly. "Mrs. Rambeau didn't want any delays. I think she's a little concerned about this whole shareholder meeting thing."

"And she's the owner of the ship?" asked Lieutenant Banks. She gestured subtly toward Janeka, who sat with the other "passengers" inside the lounge.

"That's correct. Her and Mr. Rambeau, but honestly," he added under his breath, "it's mostly hers."

"She's the one I want to talk to?" Banks asked in a similarly low tone. Everett nodded. "Thanks," she said before stepping inside. "Mr. and Mrs. Rambeau, thank you so much for your patience," Banks began, making noticeably more eye contact with the latter of the two. "This is a routine security measure. I'm sure we'll have this wrapped up shortly."

"Of course," Jacobson replied.

"Isn't this a little far out to be stopping people for inspection?" asked Janeka in a light, cordial tone. She kept her eyes focused on the lieutenant, and therefore didn't see her younger companions all look up in surprise at the unfamiliar sound. "Is there a safety concern?"

"No, ma'am. At least, not in any specific sense. Boarding inspections are more common with the recent conflicts, of course, but you've got nothing to worry about. Security in the Endeavor system is solid. We've even got extra ships rotating through the area right now. You couldn't be safer. You'll get through to your destination faster if we take care of this out here. The queue stacks up fast closer to Fairhaven. Would you mind answering a few routine questions?"

"Not at all, go right ahead."

"Is this visit business or pleasure?"

"Business. The shareholders meeting."

"And I see we've got five passengers? Are you all together?"

"Yes. Myself, my husband here, our personal assistant," Janeka said with a polite gesture toward Fuller, "and our two children. We thought it was time they learned the ropes."

Banks glanced over to the other two couches, where Alicia and Ravenell sat side by side. The lieutenant blinked, clearly noting the ethnic disparity among the white man and black woman's children. Baldwin, playing the yacht's steward, managed to catch her gaze and warn her off from asking about it with a shake of her head.

The lieutenant took the hint. The last thing she wanted was to insult wealthy investors with personal questions. That sort of thing could haunt an officer's career. "And the crew?" Banks asked. "Are these all regular employees?"

"Yes," Janeka answered brightly. "Jessica over there has been our steward for a few years now, and Bill has run the ship almost as long as we've had it. Thomas is the only new hire, I think. Right, Bill?"

"Yes, ma'am," Everett confirmed.

"And you plan to remain on Fairhaven for the duration of the shareholders meeting?"

"However long it takes," Jacobson grumbled.

Janeka patted his hand. "We obviously didn't have time to make arrangements beyond that. With something this unexpected, it's hard to make solid plans."

"That's totally understandable, ma'am. I'm glad to see you care enough to come out here and make the commitment. A lot of other shareholders don't cast their votes at all. Thank you for your time. We'll get on with the rest of our inspection. Captain?" she said, turning to Everett. "I'm going to send three of my people around with our sniffer units. We'll need to see all of your crewmembers for a quick ID check. You'll have to bring in that other guy from outside, too."

"Oh." Everett shrugged. "I figured I'd just relay his ID info to you."

"No can do," Banks replied with a shake of her head. "It's more than a headcount. We need to match everyone visually." Her brow furrowed. "You weren't gonna leave him out there until we left, were you?"

"What? Naw! Naw, we wouldn't do that…"

• • •

He understood the fatal flaw in his plan once the boarding team had gone over. He'd done many of these boardings himself on *St. Jude* during the initial Hashemite refugee crisis, and then a handful more while still assigned to *Joan of Arc* after Scheherazade. He'd walked or climbed across a transparent vestibule like the one between *Mansa Musa* and *Doberman* plenty of times…and not once had there been anyone left standing around on the outside of the ship once the link-up was finished.

No one raised the issue once NorthStar's team had gone over. A couple of their deckhands remained outside, but they, too, seemed to have little to do other than watch him. Tanner, for his part, had nothing to do at all.

His presence grew more and more awkward with each passing second. The queasiness in his stomach grew, too, but at least he knew how to deal with that. He kept his eyes mostly on the deck of his own ship. When he had to look up, he immediately looked straight to the corvette above—or, technically, *beneath* his own ship, since Tanner was standing on the bottom of *Mansa Musa*. That was exactly the sort of perspective-bending problem that caused vertigo if he dwelt upon it too much. He shoved it out of his thoughts, kept his eyes mostly on the deck, and absolutely *did not* look at the spinning stars around the two ships.

He'd held it together for the jumps in Operation Beowulf by virtue of two weeks of training. He kept his lunch down during the *Polaris* incident mostly because panic and desperation had pushed any concern for his stomach far from his mind. Out here, waiting for one endless minute to pass after the next, he had far too much time to let nausea creep in.

A waving hand in front of his face caught his attention. Tanner moved over and took it in his own in a strange up-meets-down handshake. His comm unit interfaced with the other man's. "Hey," said the NorthStar crewman, "are you just gonna stay out here?"

"Uh…yeah," grunted Tanner.

"Why?"

Tanner didn't know. He honestly had no good reason at all. Caught in a bind, Tanner went with that honesty, or at least got as close to it as he could. "It's standard procedure for link-ups on this ship, I guess," he explained.

"You guess?"

"I'm new."

The NorthStar crewman snorted. He looked to his comrade, who also seemed to shake a bit with laughter. It seemed the new guy always got the raw end of things in their service, too. At least that made his awkward situation believable.

"I mean, I'm supposed to make sure the hull doesn't get marked up," Tanner elaborated. He felt bile well up in the back of his throat and swallowed hard to keep it down. *Yup*, he thought. *Just like old times back home.* He tried to keep his mind off of it, and that led him to another idea. It was best not to let these guys think too much of his situation, either. "What's it like in the NorthStar fleet? Do you guys, uh, get…do they treat you okay? Is it a cool job?"

He could see the NorthStar crewman's face through his transparent visor. It wasn't even partially tinted or altered by interior lighting the way Tanner's was, nor did any of the heads-up display info show for an outside viewer. That let Tanner see the hesitation in the crewman's eyes at his question. "Oh yeah, it's great," said the crewman. "The pay is top notch, the people are good, you can move up quick…"

His voice, surely being recorded by his own comms systems and the tie-in to his ship, told one story. His face told another. "You should think about joining," the crewman added with wide eyes and a "no way" hand gesture warning against doing any such thing.

"Yeah. I'll do that." Tanner swallowed hard again, both to control his stomach and to get a grip on his thoughts. These guys were the enemy. It did no good to dwell on the fact that most of them were ordinary people who'd signed up for a job with the best of intentions, only to get caught up in an ugly, awful machine. Madelyn had warned against it the day he crashed the Test. Her words came back to him now. The Archangel Navy wasn't ideal, but the corporate services were built as debt traps.

He knelt down near the edge of the vestibule. "Suppose I should check this over for scratches and such," he mumbled. "Helps my balance, too."

"Y'know, it's not like we're careless about this stuff," said the crewman.

"It's not you," Tanner explained. "My bosses are, uh, kind of demanding."

"You don't say."

"Hey, *Thomas*," broke in Sinclair's voice on Tanner's comm net. "Captain says come inside. He needs you to do an ID check with the boarding team."

Fuck, thought Tanner. This could turn out horribly. He looked up at the two crewmen again, felt fresh waves of queasiness rush through his brain and his stomach, and then hit on one last gambit. "Hey," he huffed, "I have to, uh, go back inside. Um…can you…help me with the vestibule?"

"Sure," said the crewman. "We've got it." He gestured to his comrade, who knelt at the panel outside Doberman's airlock and hit a couple of buttons. Tanner saw the vestibule contract slightly as the air within rushed out. The other crewman tugged the seams loose.

Tanner didn't watch the rest. Instead, he deliberately watched the stars.

"Slip inside, we'll put it back," the crewman instructed. "No scratches."

"Hey, thanks," Tanner mumbled before crawling inside. Again, he felt the unpleasant push and pull of *Mansa Musa*'s internal gravity. It only left his head spinning harder once he drew his legs in after him. He lay on the deck, wanting nothing more than to stay there until he got his bearings again, but that was the last thing he could do now. He keyed a button on the outside of his helmet to kill his person-to-person contact connections, leaving him speaking only on the ship's internal comm net. "Okay, I'm in," he groaned.

Tanner forced himself up. He looked back, saw the vestibule connection secure again, and returned the thumbs-up motion from the crewman on the other side of the transparent material. He then activated the airlock vents to flood the compartment and the vestibule with air again.

The all-clear beep from the airlock controls confirmed that the space was fully pressurized. He pulled his helmet free and spun the wheel on the interior hatch. By the time he stepped through, his control was all but gone.

Everett stood with several of the NorthStar boarders. "Hey, Thomas," he said, "the lieutenant needs you to show her your ID."

"Ohkhay," Tanner moaned, "I've got it right he*uurrgh*!" The rest of his response took full, revolting, visible form. His helmet fell from his hand as he bent over and heaved his guts out all over the deck. Everyone else instantly stepped back. Most looked away. They'd all seen spacesickness before, but it was never pleasant.

"Oh God, I'm sorry," Tanner said with exaggerated despair. "I'm sorry, sir."

Everett didn't miss a beat. "For fuck's sake, Thomas, *again*? Ugh. Hand over your ID and let 'em get it over with."

In truth, throwing up provided a rush of relief from Tanner's nausea. He actually felt better, but he didn't need to let anyone else see it. Tanner stood nearly upright, holding out his left arm with his holocom exposed while keeping his right hand over his mouth and nose. The disgusted NorthStar lieutenant waved to one of her subordinates and stepped around. "I think this wraps it up, captain," she told him as Tanner's fake ID holo screen popped up and went through the bo'sun's holo reader.

"Yeah, thanks, Lieutenant Banks. We've got a little cleaning up to do here now, obviously."

No warning lights flashed as the NorthStar bo'sun checked Tanner's ID. Nobody recognized him with his hand covering the lower half of his face. Tanner faked a gulp and a shudder to drive home the urgency of finishing the task. "We're clear," said the bo'sun.

"Sounds good," said Banks. She sent her men through the vestibule. "Captain."

"Ma'am," Everett replied.

"Miss—captain—I'm so sorry," Tanner reiterated as pathetically as he could.

"Don't apologize!" Everett barked. "Go get some rags and clean this up!"

Tanner ducked out of the airlock. He hustled around the corner and nearly collided with Alicia and Janeka, both lurking nearby with knives at the ready. They stepped back as soon as they saw him. The clank of the airlock hatch closing up once more rang clearly through the passageway.

For once, even Janeka looked surprised. Out of sight from the boarders, Tanner stood tall, took in a sharp, dignified breath, and breezed past them to open up the cleaning supply closet right behind Alicia. He nodded politely. "Ladies."

• • •

"We're not sure what the boarding team found or what set this off," explained Commodore Jean Prescott. "I'll send the video feed from their helmet cameras. It's ugly. The crew and passengers came at our people with knives and hand tools. Not the sort of weapons you pick up with a sniffer or a cursory energy scan."

The center screen showed the view from a destroyer's starboard side as a yacht broke from its gangway tube and mooring cables with a sudden burst of its thrusters. Someone in a NorthStar Security Fleet vac suit tumbled helplessly out of the tube into the void, blasted away by venting atmosphere that also trailed from the yacht in the first seconds of her flight. The cables pulled off mooring clamps and the gangway hatch didn't seal right away, leaving a trail of vented gas and debris in the yacht's wake, but then the chase was on.

"*Tethys* didn't open fire right away out of concern for her boarding team," Prescott continued. "Her comms officer confirmed three flatlined signals from the boarders' holocoms before she lost contact, and you can see what happened to the crewman on watch at the gangway. The others cried out as well. The comms officer made a snap judgment that they'd all been killed. After-analysis backs her up on that. Then the yacht escalated."

Following the commodore's narration, the view switched to the destroyer's main tactical screen. Secondary screens on one side provided ranges and other info in simple text. *Tethys* pursued while one of her signalmen demanded the yacht surrender. The yacht answered with a blast from her sole laser turret, followed by a couple of chaff missiles that detonated between hunter and prey.

"Was *Tethys* at least *trying* to disable rather than destroy?" asked Pedroso. She sat on a comfortable living room couch, watching the video with the windows tinted for privacy. On the screen, the destroyer fired back at the fleeing yacht, unable to keep up with the smaller craft's acceleration. Lasers from *Tethys*'s smaller turrets flashed across the empty space between the two, missing more often than not. The one that struck home caused a significant explosion. "I mean we're not taking someone's word for that, are we?"

"They tried. The logs and targeting data all check out," said Prescott. "When a ship flees like this, the only ways to bring them down are to target their engines or their bridge. Both options run this risk."

Seconds after the laser hit, a second explosion rocked the yacht's aft quarter. Then came a third explosion that destroyed the entire ship.

"And the crewman from—I'm sorry, Ms. Pedroso," said man seated beside her. His business casual clothing marginally softened the tough image presented by his size, physique, and dark, closely-cut hair. "If you don't mind?"

"No, go ahead."

"Commodore," he began again, "this is Jeff O'Neal. I'm the head of Mr. Brekhov's personal security detail. That crewman from the gangway—did he make it through this okay?"

"Yes. *Tethys* dispatched her shuttle to retrieve him. He didn't suffer any physical injuries, amazingly enough, but understandably the incident shook him up. The captain transferred him to temporary shore duty. He's been debriefed. He didn't see or hear anything that we don't already have recorded."

"And we didn't pick up any clues at all from the debris?" asked Pedroso.

"Unfortunately no," Prescott replied. "I've sent the full report with this call. What I can tell you is that their passengers carried legitimate gold-level shareholder ID numbers and related credentials. They claimed to be en route to the meeting. Their timing and logs all line up with that. If that's not true, they went to a lot of effort to establish their cover. As far as we can tell, the boarding team found no evidence of contraband, either."

"That's what has me concerned." Pedroso looked to O'Neal, hardly needing to ask out loud for his evaluation. They'd known one another for decades. Pedroso opted to leave field work years ago for the executive track while O'Neal remained an operative, but shared experience still resonated between them.

He watched the scenario play out again. "Cameras and sniffers don't pick up everything. It could've all come down to body language. Maybe they realized the boarding team leader was onto them."

Pedroso had already come to a similar conclusion. "Onto them for what?"

"Well, no contraband, nothing more than knives…we have to assume the passengers and crew were in on it together. They must have been smuggling themselves. If they had all the credentials they needed to get into the shareholder's meeting, we have to assume they meant to be there. Little too pricy to get all the way up to gold tier just as a distraction."

"Now you see why I wanted you here. It's publicly-traded stock. There are always unfriendly people in the crowd. We can count on spies from Lai Wa and Archangel and any number of others, but they usually don't send groups of people who'd take on a boarding team with knives and hammers."

O'Neal nodded. "We've got a solid security force on hand already. I'm more than happy if you want to beef it up."

"I do. Jean," said Pedroso, turning her attention back to the commodore on the holo screen, "I'd like to bolster our fleet readiness, too."

"We've already got the battle group around *Perseus* and two destroyer squadrons on hand," replied Prescott, "plus our own corvette squadron and another from Fairhaven's militia. Archangel couldn't match that even if they brought every ship they had. Two battleships to our one doesn't mean as much when you consider the escort total. But if you want, I can pull our patrols on the outer half of the system in closer. I can also look into getting *Taurus* ready for emergency deployment from her drydock on the moon. She's not ready for anything lengthy, but she could be good for combat within 24 hours."

"Do it. She won't have to go far or operate long. And Commodore—do it quietly. Keep all of this within the fleet and Risk Management. Send any updates or problems directly to me. I won't ask you to hide this from Anton, but he has enough on his plate with the meeting and the political bullshit. Let's only bother him with security concerns if we can't avoid it, agreed?"

Prescott's head tilted curiously. "Are things that bad?"

"He's pushing through. We all are. Still, the last few months have been the roughest since our last big blow-up with the Kroks. We were all younger then."

"I hear you. Let him know I've sent my proxy instructions already. He's got my votes."

Pedroso offered a tight smile. "He'll appreciate that, Jean. Thank you." She cut the channel and looked to her companion. "And you?"

"He'll ask when he sees the extra muscle," O'Neal pointed out. "Stressed out or not, he's observant. I haven't seen him skip a single beat in all of this."

"You haven't had to sit through as many meetings and conference calls as I have. The board is behind us, but they're still asking about as many questions as you'd expect before a revolt. The shareholder meeting will be the same, only worse. This is wearing him down, Jeff. I've never seen him look so tired. Let's not add this to the load. We're Risk Management. This part is our job."

The two stepped out of the living room—one of several in Brekhov's primary residence—and headed down the hall to his main study. Brekhov's estate offered more than enough space and comfort to host political functions and high-class social events, along with all the state of the art communications gear and every other requirement for running the most powerful corporation in the Union, with security to match. NorthStar's top leadership was every bit as effective here as it was in the main headquarters.

As it happened, the day's agenda made Brekhov's estate all the more attractive. Better to escape the distractions of headquarters to focus on the shareholder meeting. Everyone had enough on their minds. The change of scenery helped…or so Pedroso hoped.

Recent events cemented loyalties for some, but aggravated tensions between others.

"We'll have the expo center up and ready to open by morning," said Walters as Pedroso and O'Neal stepped into the main study. "Event Management came through for us on that end. Seventeen different product divisions have something to show for this. We're bound to see a few of them come up short of the projections they make, but they've all got something worth showing. They know we're in damage control mode."

"You're saying the whole expo will be a lot of promises we can't deliver?" grumbled Weir.

Walters threw him an irritated look without a verbal comeback. Almost any response would plunge Brekhov's comfortable study into more of the blame-shifting and sniping that had plagued the executive committee for weeks. Rather than retaliate, Walters moved on. "The real showcase stuff comes from a couple of our larger consumer goods divisions and from Stellar Horizons. The latter took some cajoling, but they'll do a reveal of the New Dawn exploratory project and the next-generation terraforming plans. We've even got some big names from the entertainment division to play host."

Seated behind his desk, Brekhov listened attentively. Grim amusement crept into his eyes at the last few details. "Bread and circuses never goes out of style, does it? Thank you, Christina. I'm glad to see this come together."

"How much is this going to cost?" asked Weir. "Do we think a speech from a favorite soccer player about the direction of the company will sway anyone's vote?"

"Jon, look outside that window, please," said Brekhov. He gestured toward the floor-to-ceiling glass that made up most of the south wall. In the foreground was Brekhov's broad, opulent pool and patio. Beyond that lay a spectacular hilltop view of Fairhaven City spreading out along the coast. Glittering towers reached for the sky in the distance. While one could not make out birds from such a range, the shuttles and the aircars that flitted back and forth and even up into the stratosphere made up for their absence.

"Every hour, more stockholders arrive in that city and others on Fairhaven," Brekhov explained. "We called them in on short notice. Anyone who can afford to drop everything and come look after their investment or hire someone for it has done so. This whole mess is urgent and unique.

"They're worried, Jon. Our shareholders are rightfully worried about their money and their futures. They're stressed from travel and inconvenience, especially the wealthy and connected shareholders. The first-class hotels are all filled up. Many of these people aren't accustomed to budget accommodations or sleeping on someone's couch.

"But they're connected, you see. They're out there talking to each other right now. They're talking to their friends, and their lawyers, and their friends who think they're lawyers. The longer they do that, the more they'll feed on each other's stress and anxiety and the more riled up they will become. So yes, bread and circuses are in order, if only to remind them that NorthStar has much more to offer than war and chaos. We must keep them *distracted* until we're ready for the vote."

Weir knew better than to argue further. "Fair enough," he said.

Brekhov turned to the others. "We've done all we can to keep our guests entertained until the main event," he said. "Let's talk about security. Any situation this critical can draw in worse disruptions than some 'shareholder activist' staging an idiotic protest."

"We have high security on-site already," Pedroso spoke up, "from uniformed troops to high-threat reaction teams. They were in place two days ago at Symphony Hall and the expo center. Local law enforcement is also ready to respond. They're still geared up and organized from the referendum rallies. As far as they're concerned, it's already show time. Nothing comes or goes without being scanned and checked. No one enters without credentials. Naturally a certain amount of infiltration for an event like this can't be helped, but they won't get in if they're armed. Disruptions will be handled quickly.

"I spoke with Commodore Prescott minutes ago about the broader perspective. We have more combat and support ships in the area than usual thanks to the pullback from Hashem. Physical inspections of incoming spacecraft are up 75% from our usual standard. We also have our drone net deployed and active to extend our area of control."

"That was Fairhaven's drone net once upon a time," noted Donaldson.

"Only when we needed to be polite about it," Pedroso scoffed. "On that note, Endeavor's system militia is fully integrated with our forces for the near-term. After we win the referendum, we'll have to integrate their rank and file into our own forces, but Fairhaven's militia is used to working with our fleet. It won't be a problem."

"Another change we'll have to put off for now," said Brekhov. "As long as they're ready to handle an emergency, I'm satisfied. We should break for lunch. I want to spend the rest of our time after that preparing for our meeting with the board."

The executives drifted out. Some partnered up for smaller conversations. Soon only Brekhov and Pedroso remained. Even the CEO's bodyguard stepped out after he saw the nod from his boss.

"You know the board will support you," Pedroso said once they were alone.

"I don't know that," Brekhov replied. He released a long sigh, finally allowing his weariness to show. "The board's approval is not something I take for granted."

"And yet they have granted you a rubber stamp for what? Thirty, forty years?"

"Do you know why?" asked Brekhov. "It's because I never plan on having that rubber stamp." He rose from his desk to walk pensively over to the broad window overlooking his pool and the great city beyond.

"They backed us when Aguirre dumped out our dirty laundry," Pedroso said as she stood to join him. "They stuck with us for the invasion, and the occupation, and all the hits their stock took along the way. They know what is good for the long term."

Brekhov snorted. "You know, back in business school, some professors said corporate boards should be made up of people who held no stock at all, like so many of them were before the Expansion Era. I've heard the arguments, but I never saw the sense in it. A company has to be steered by people with a stake in its future, like a family or…or a nation," he grumbled. "This is what it comes to, isn't it? Aguirre's best shot is to drag me down to his level. To make me just another damn politician. Like him."

"A few of our more prominent board members could take the role," Pedroso reminded him. "We have options. You could plead the truth—say that you never wanted such power—and then run things from behind the scenes while we give the public an actual politician as a figurehead."

"No." Brekhov shook his head. "It has to be me. No one else has my stature in the eyes of our shareholders or the public. I'm the wise paternal figure. I'm the 'old man.' I feel old, too." His voice carried no arrogance. If anything, Pedroso heard regret. "No one else has my credibility."

"If you know that, then you know that you don't need to worry about the board's support," Pedroso pointed out. "They've backed you as chairman and CEO for decades. They'll back you as a president. Or a governor or whatever we've settled on. I'll confess, I haven't kept up with the window-dressing on that issue."

Brekhov's eyebrow rose in slight amusement. "You know, a couple of Christina's PR people gave a pitch about all that yesterday. I've got the proposal sitting there somewhere on my desk. They want us to establish special legal and property rights for shareholders living on Fairhaven and to lock them in for direct descendants—all assuming one has *enough* shares, of course.

Barons and dukes in all but name. They had some cute modern language to dress it all up, but it's still a formal aristocracy. And you know what? They have a point. Other systems have done it. Hell, three of our directors have 'noble' titles in their home systems. Many of our wealthiest shareholders would be all too happy to buy titles and status. They'd buy up even more stock just to feel that much more special."

"It's a little too transparent," Pedroso said, though she could tell that Brekhov had already shot it down. "Our strategy is to show ourselves going forward. That sort of thinking is outdated. One would think the civil war in Hashem is enough of an example, even if we didn't have the rest of human history to look back upon."

"We're never as far from history as we like to believe." Brekhov's gaze drifted out to the view of the city again. "Do they still teach students that it's all 'land, labor and capital?' It never did sound right with 'entrepreneurship' at the end."

"I'm not *that* much younger than you," said Pedroso. "I think that's still the line, yes."

"Look back at any point in human history and you'll see the imbalances. We started with plenty of land and no capital, but enough labor could make up for that. All of that labor had to come from somewhere, so builders and leaders took slaves. Then they could build monuments. They built civilization. On and on, until slavery went out of style because we finally had real capital. We had machines. But even the Industrial Revolution only shifted the imbalance. Labor still had to feed the machines, except slavery was out of style, so we used other words. 'Colonialism' sounded good. It's easier to ignore when it's faraway people in faraway lands.

"We built and built until we ran out of land and the resources started to run dry. By then we had the technology to reach for the stars. We had the capital. Endless land if we looked and reached far enough. But bringing the labor out would cost so much…unless the labor paid their own way out, and so we had the Expansion Era.

"Now here we are again. Plenty of land, but the capital we need to build starships and terraform our worlds takes so much money… only now the labor is used to paying their own way. We've taught them that it's the way things are. It's not slavery. It's personal responsibility. It's what they *owe*. So, yes, let's call it debt. Debt for schools, debt for medicine and longevity, primary debt for building all these new worlds to conquer. Whatever it takes. As long as none of the laborers ask where their paycheck came from in the first place. As long as they accept their debts, we can keep growing and keep moving. It's only when people whine and scream 'slavery' to shirk their debts that we have a problem.

"Sometimes I look out this window and think to myself that debt built all of this," Brekhov mused.

Pedroso blinked. "The pool and the deck?"

"What? No!" Brekhov laughed. "No. Debt built that city out there, and this world. No, I paid for the pool with money *I earned*."

• • •

"This is a hell of a city," said Ravenell. "It makes Salvation look low-rent."

"Yeah," mumbled Tanner. "It's pretty." He hardly looked up from his holo screen in the back seat of the van. The text floating before him was dense and required heavy use of the accompanying glossary and his dictionary file. Besides, even with his face partly covered by dark sunglasses and a loosened breath mask, he figured he shouldn't look out the windows too much.

He'd expected his face to keep him restricted to the ship until it was time to roll, but too many jobs had to be done. Sanjay went with Janeka and Alicia to scope out routes to their target. Baldwin and Fuller had their own scouting orders. Mohamed and the Chief were the natural choices to stay with the ship. That left the others to help Jacobson.

Janeka made no secret of why she specifically wanted Ravenell and Tanner on this job. Both young men had past dealings with the sort of people on the other end.

Up in the front passenger seat, Ravenell's head swiveled constantly. A well-managed traffic system kept everything in motion, with a thin layer of air traffic floating a dozen meters or so above the ground. Most of it tended toward boxy working vehicles like their van, but nothing on or above the road looked ten years old, or even five. The streets were clean. Traffic never bogged down. Beyond the structures lining the broad streets, most of them only a few stories high, rose the gleaming towers that helped make the city so picturesque.

Tanner didn't pay much attention to them. The towers only reminded him of a city on Scheherazade that was almost as dazzling, and how it looked when he left. He kept his eyes on his holo screen. He'd wanted to read this stuff ever since Janeka first explained the mission, but with *Beowulf*'s quiet status and then the trip from Archangel, Tanner had no open market access. Besides, he couldn't buy this material anywhere in Archangel right now, anyway.

"The people are pretty, too," Ravenell observed. "All the people, it seems like."

"It's Fairhaven," noted Tanner. "They can afford to be pretty. Or they better figure out how, at least. Being pretty is a proven advantage. It's not a luxury here. It's about being competitive. You can see the same sort of thing in some places back home, too."

"Sure, but the guy driving the disposal trucks back home doesn't look half as sharp as the guy you see driving it here," put in Sinclair.

He sat at the driver's seat of their van, looking a little less like a tourist than Ravenell. "And I haven't seen a woman yet that didn't look like she could be a model."

Tanner looked up from his reading. His lips twisted into an evil grin. "You know how people here manage their weight so easily?"

"Well, yeah." Ravenell shrugged, looking back at him. "They're taking pills."

"You know what's in those pills?"

"Metabolic managers."

"Bacteria," Tanner corrected. "You take one pill in the morning to plant a bunch of bacteria in your gut. They spend all day eating and reproducing off of whatever you eat. Then at night, you take another full of more bacteria to hunt down and eat the batch from the first pill. It all makes your trips to the bathroom a little busier and less pleasant, but you can take a pill for that, too. If you miss one end of the regimen for a couple days in a row, though, you wind up with too much of one kind of bacteria or another, so they eat away at the insides of your guts. Next thing you know, you're throwing up blood. But you look good doing it, right?"

Ravenell looked back at him with a mixture of disgust and disbelief. "Who would do that?"

"See, here's the thing that gets me," Tanner continued. "We've all got bacteria in us all the time as it is, right? I mean, that's natural. You need that. It's healthy. But the people who make these pills, and the people who take 'em? They figure the problem is they don't have enough little guys in their gut to stay thin, so they put in *more* of 'em."

"Gross."

"They have flagella," Tanner added, wiggling his fingers to demonstrate. "Little tails that they can spin in a corkscrew motion so they can swim around eating your lunch. Or each other."

"Okay, how come we've never heard of all this?" Sinclair asked, providing Ravenell with some much-needed reassurance through skepticism.

"Marketing, obviously," replied Tanner. "That and Archangel has a ban on those pills. Too dangerous for mass consumption."

"But not here?" asked Ravenell.

"Naw, man. This is big business central. It's all 'buyer beware' here, where everyone figures they need every edge they can get."

"Tanner," Jacobson finally spoke up, "how do you know all this?"

"He reads a lot," Ravenell and Sinclair answered simultaneously.

Tanner grinned. "I was big on life sciences in school. I did a report on metabolic enhancers in my sophomore year, I think. Maybe freshman. Mostly I was an ecology guy."

"Is that what you want to do when you get out?"

He didn't answer right away. Tanner's gaze drifted out the window. For all Fairhaven's aggressive development and heavy industry, NorthStar and the local government were mindful of ecological concerns. Cities here held to strict zoning and borders. The planet needed minimal terraforming. Native flora and fauna still thrived despite all the invasive species brought in by the settlers.

They called it the Fairhaven Miracle. Anyone with even a passing interest in such issues knew about it. Tanner used to know the timeline and the process of introducing new plants and which trees adjusted well and which ones had to be banned. He used to know the chemistry.

Now he couldn't think of any of it, but he knew how to reassemble a pulse rifle and he could eyeball the blast radius of a thermal grenade. His recreational reading no longer included science or exploration. Mostly it focused on an investigation he couldn't talk about.

"I hope so," said Tanner. "Someday. Feels like I've forgotten a lot since I was in school."

"What's that you're reading now?" asked Jacobson.

"Shareholder's guide."

"Wait, what?" Sinclair blinked.

"It's a NorthStar shareholder's guide."

"How'd you get that?"

"I bought a share of common stock when we got here."

"You *what?*" burst Ravenell.

"I bought a share of stock."

"Why would you do that?"

"So I could get the shareholder's guide. And the prospectus, and the—"

"Yeah, but you gave them money?" Sinclair pressed.

"I'm pretty sure I've cost them more than the value of one share of stock in the last couple of years." Tanner noted Jacobson's amused grin and his silence. "I think I'm clear of providing aid to the enemy. It's expensive to you or me, but it's a drop in the bucket to them."

"Whatever happened to 'not a damn thing?'" asked Sinclair.

"I dunno, whatever happened to 'know your enemy?'"

Ravenell laughed. "You're weird, man."

"Boss, I think we're coming up on our spot now," announced Sinclair. Conversation in the van fell off as they rolled past the gates that brought them back into the spaceport. Tanner breathed a sigh of relief. No new guards or security procedures had cropped up since they landed. Ship inspections focused mostly on inbound traffic, not outbound.

Smaller landing areas and hangars lined the outer ring of the commercial zone. Eventually, the vehicle rolled into the broader, open landing zones used by larger ships. Towering vessels measuring three hundred meters or more in length rested on a mixture of anti-grav cushions and sturdy, powerful landing struts carefully engineered to distribute a ship's massive weight. Major spaceports like this one often lay right on a coastline for the benefit of large starships built to settle in water rather than on dry land.

The team's destination lay behind a simple concrete security wall around the landing zone. Many of the cargo ship spots had the same set-up. To Tanner's best guess, the ship inside stretched out for a good two hundred meters or more from bow to stern, with room for at least ten decks inside. Knowing who owned the ship, Tanner wondered how many careers it had enjoyed before becoming an "independent freighter." It looked to him like it could have been anything from a colony ship to a cruise liner.

Nah, no way in hell, thought Tanner. *What are the odds?*

No security guards stood watch at the gate. Sinclair dialed in a security code using the van's holocom. "We're here to pick up a custom food service order," he announced. The gate opened up without further challenge.

Crates and bits of mobile machinery sat underneath the long vessel. A ramp descended from a cargo bay in the ship's belly to the ground. A couple of men in working clothes stood at the bottom of the ramp, holding up their hands to bring Sinclair to a stop. "Might want to turn around and back to the edge," suggested one of the men. "We can't bring the van inside."

"Why not?" asked Sinclair.

"Ship's policy. Besides, the way things are set up in the cargo bay, you couldn't fit anyhow."

Tanner stared up at the ship as Sinclair adjusted. Everything about it looked new, or at least fresh out of a refit. He had no idea how many ships the Ministry controlled, but odds were that this was one of their own rather than a semi-independent ship like Captain Madinah's.

Everyone climbed out of the van to meet the two crewmen. Tanner took note of the closest crewman's beefy arms and short, almost military hair. He'd fit in fine with the marines on *Beowulf* except for the beard. His partner struck much the same image. Tanner also noted the unfastened flaps of the tool pouches on their hips, which hung at the right sort of comfortable spot for a holster.

"Any sign of being followed?" asked one crewman.

Jacobson shook his head. "Wouldn't be here if there was."

"Good answer. Let's go." He gestured for the others to walk with him up the ramp. Tanner kept track of both crewmen. They seemed to keep their guests within a safe field of fire.

The spacious cargo bay contained many crates and barrels made of plastic and metal, but it was hardly full. The lack of people made sense. They wouldn't need any help with this relatively small cargo pick-up. Of the other half-dozen or so members of the ship's crew present, most struck the same fit, hardened image as their escorts… including the tall and broad-shouldered man wearing an officer's shoulder boards as part of his vac suit.

"Christ, really?" Tanner grumbled.

"Uh-uh. No." The officer pointed at Tanner. "He doesn't stay. You've got to be fucking kidding me, bringing *him* on this mission, let alone to this ship. He puts this whole operation at risk just by being here."

"I'm sorry, who are you?" Jacobson replied with a stern tone.

"Yeah," Tanner echoed, "who are you today, Zeke?"

The bigger man's eyes flared. "I'm the agent in charge of this operation, poster boy, and I am not in any mood to play. You came in a vehicle? Go back down into it. Now. Or this whole deal is scrubbed."

"I'm not sure I like your attitude, agent," said Jacobson.

"That's really too bad. My decision stands. He goes or you all go."

Tanner considered his options. Neither Jacobson nor Zeke were the type to back down for anyone. Zeke's confrontation with Tanner on Station 46 only went Tanner's way by virtue of the pressure of the moment. The "crewmen" watched the situation tensely, while Rav and Sinclair slowly closed ranks.

This was absolutely insane. Zeke knew what was at stake. He couldn't be ready to throw the whole mission down the tubes on a personal grudge. The ship was supposed to be a Ministry vessel. What harm would it do for Tanner to be on board? How was he more of a problem here than out in the van? Who would freak out about Tanner being on the ship?

Or was there something he didn't want Tanner to see?

"Sir?" Tanner asked.

Jacobson broke from his staredown with Ezekiel to confer. "What the hell's the deal between you two?" he hissed.

"I stopped him from doing something shitty on a 'training mission.' Everything worked out. We've got a personality conflict, but I don't see how it could be this big a deal. Sir, our mission is more important than whatever this is about. I'll head back below. He'll probably calm down as soon as I'm out of eyesight."

Jacobson's scowl only darkened. "Must have been a hell of a mission."

"Yeah, I guess so," Tanner agreed.

"I don't like it. You're here for a reason."

"I know, but let's face it: your experience as an officer counts for way more than my few dealings with these guys, and you've got Rav and Avery with you." He paused. "One thing, though: when he eases off and you're down to business, ask to speak with the captain."

"About what? You think this guy isn't in charge?"

"I don't know," said Tanner. "Maybe he is, maybe he isn't. Either way, I'm betting he's not the captain of the ship."

"And if they don't let me see the captain?"

"I don't think they will, sir. But that'll tell us something about what's going on."

Though Jacobson's jaw clenched, he accepted Tanner's advice. In truth, Tanner didn't know what else his boss could do. Jacobson gave a curt nod and Tanner turned to go. "Let's get this done, 'Agent Zeke,'" said Jacobson—as an order rather than a reconciliation.

Tanner walked back down the loading ramp to the van. Once again, he carefully looked over the ship as he moved, this time watching for security systems and cameras. Two of Zeke's men followed him all the way down. With no place else to go, Tanner sat on the edge of the van's open back end. He stared back at his watchdogs as he considered his options.

Ezekiel's presence might be a coincidence. Tanner had to concede that. He was, as Vanessa herself said, one of the Ministry's top field agents. She also warned that he was a Kiribati loyalist. He'd keep the dirtiest secrets. It stood to reason, then, that this might also be one of the Ministry's top ships…and that something on board might be very dirty.

He stood no chance of uncovering that dirty secret now. Not with two agents watching him, Ezekiel on his guard, and a much larger and more vital mission at hand.

The mission had to take priority. As much as Tanner wanted to go snooping, and as justified as his suspicions might be, he had to set that aside for now. The entire war could come down to this mission, and he still felt unprepared.

Sighing, Tanner brought up his wrist to key in some commands on his holocom.

"The fuck do you think you're doing?" asked one of the agents.

"I'm reading a fucking book, asshole," Tanner shot back ferociously. "Come stop me if it bothers you."

The agents blinked in surprise. One of them laughed.

Tanner ignored them, again forcing himself to think instead about what he *could* do rather than what he couldn't. Sitting on the back of the van, waiting to load it full of contraband weapons, ammo, and armor while Tweedledum and Tweedlejackass watched, Tanner opened up the NorthStar Shareholder's Guide.

CHAPTER ELEVEN

Personal Initiative

> *"Critical points to emphasize for any written orders or verbal briefings:*
>
> 1. *All ships are weapons-free upon arrival in the system. If a military target appears before you receive orders or while you are separated, attack.*
> 2. *Both sides employ covert assets. Upon arrival, all ships will broadcast an open warning to any civilian ships instructing them to leave the area. Treat any ship that approaches yours with extreme prejudice. Do not pursue any ship that flees.*
> 3. *Our goal is the surrender or neutralization of enemy forces. If the enemy offers surrender, grant it. If the enemy flees, monitor but do not pursue. Until and unless this occurs, attack.*
>
> --MEMO TO COMMAND OFFICERS AND STAFF, ADMIRAL MEILING YEOH, JULY 2279

"Didn't all the planning memos say we'd be at Symphony Hall, Jeff?" Brekhov had his face turned to the window as he gently teased his personal security manager. "I might not do my own driving these days, but I still know find my way around this city."

"We're headed there, sir." O'Neal's sharp, well-tailored suit looked nothing at all like the body armor it was, nor did it show either of the weapons that he carried. "The plans haven't changed."

"The driver seems to have missed our turnoff," Brekhov pointed out. "And the two turnoffs after that. Once upon a time, I drove myself to meetings in this town. Even with all the changes since then, the streets are still the same. I'm not completely out of touch."

"Of course not, sir," O'Neal agreed with a humble grin. "We're parking under the Wandsworth Tower. It has a direct monorail tunnel to the Jackson Center. From there we take the access corridor running under the street to Symphony Hall."

Brekhov's eyebrows rose. "We're sneaking in through a tunnel?" he chided. "Goodness, won't we get dirty? Maria wore such a nice suit."

The woman seated beside Brekhov rolled her eyes. "The tunnel is five meters wide. It's how they get celebrity performers in without going through crowds. You've done this sort of thing before, Anton."

"Yes, but only to avoid trouble," noted Brekhov. "Protests and assassinations and the like. Is there something you two aren't telling me about today?"

"We picked up an uptick in chatter from some referendum protest groups overnight," Pedroso explained. "Jeff, Christina, and I decided the media doesn't need video of you coming and going. Not if it means sharing the cameras with some rally."

"The site itself is clear," O'Neal added, "but we've got crowds at all the intersections in the surrounding area. They've slowed down traffic. General harassment, that sort of thing."

Brekhov keyed up a screen from the personal holocom set into the jewel on his right ring finger. The media broadcast that appeared showed him exactly what O'Neal meant. "These are some well-dressed protesters," he observed. "Orderly, enthusiastic. Everyone seems on-point." His eyes turned over toward Pedroso. "Who hired them?"

She let out an irritated sigh. "Governor Heath's office, from the looks of it. Indirectly."

"Frank hired protesters to gum up a referendum that he endorsed?"

"I think he wants a better retirement package or a fancier replacement job title. Don't worry, I'll handle him during the shareholder meeting."

Brekhov's attention turned back to the protesters on his screen. He rolled his left shoulder and put a finger under his collar to relieve some irritable tension. "I could swear we have aircars and airvans to get around this sort of thing."

"We have them on hand at Symphony Hall, and the Jackson Center and Wandsworth, sir," assured O'Neal. "There are multiple options for exiting for both convenience and security. Nothing has been taken for granted. We've even got a plan in case the shareholders decide to throw their own riot."

"Oh, come on, Jeff. Wealthy people don't riot. They hire other people to do that sort of work."

• • •

"I'm surprised by all the greenery," Vanessa said to her handsome companion. She leaned on his arm as they walked across the open plaza in front of Symphony Hall. Tall trees and well-trimmed hedges helped to separate the site from its neighbors. "Everything else around here is glass and steel and marble. It's pretty, but this is a nice change of pace."

"I suppose it helps people get their minds off their daily lives outside and focus on whatever they're here to see inside," mused Brad. "Assuming it's a performance, at least."

The Hall's six-story front edifice rose at least six stories into the air, with its reflective walls broken up by tall marble columns. Behind Vanessa and her companion, a few curved steps led down into the spacious plaza, partly obscured by thick planters. "It does break up the sight lines," she murmured, though her true concerns were far more tactical than aesthetic.

Other late arrivals trickled in with Vanessa and Brad. Most of the people still outside the hall served to direct shareholders, control the crowd, or cover the event for the media. Uniformed NorthStar Security personnel, local police, and the site's regular staff all provided a visible sense of safety and a deterrent to trouble. No fences or gates blocked foot traffic into the plaza. No one challenged Vanessa or Brad, either, but they were clearly dressed for the event. Vanessa's dark suit and long black leather coat rode the line between business and casual wear. Brad had "executive" written all over him.

It was one of the reasons Vanessa picked him out of the crowd at the reception the night before. He belonged at events like this. He knew all the ins and outs. He had at least as much access as Vanessa by right of his shares and even more by virtue of personal connections. Yet with all that, his experience with intrigue and subterfuge began and ended with sales meetings and dinner parties.

"I'm actually glad for the short notice this time around," he said. "Usually these meetings are a much bigger production, with three days of seminars and five times as many attendees. Symphony Hall feels almost intimate by comparison."

"Is there always this much security?" Vanessa's gaze drifted up. She saw the glint of sunlight against helmets and armored shoulders on the roof of the Hall. It made sense to have people in powered armor up there. The rooftop offered a broad field of fire while keeping the heavy weapons out of public view where they might make people nervous.

"Oh, sure. A lighter presence would only encourage protesters or some other disruption. Don't worry," he said with a smile, "the guards aren't worried about *you*."

Vanessa's return grin didn't hold as her eyes continued to scan the crowd. "What about all these other people? The reporters, the valets...are they going to stay around out here?"

"Usually, yes. There'll be other media inside, but they can't broadcast. In the meantime, someone has to be 'live and on the scene.' Sometimes the ones on the inside slip out to relay updates. As for the valets and the rest, it's their job to stay outside."

The answer heightened her concerns, though no one would know it from her expression. She didn't find the security all that surprising. The rest represented a wrinkle nobody had included in their planning—or at least, not that they'd told her about. Armed professionals and their wealthy financiers were one thing, but ordinary working stiffs like the rest of these folks...

"You'll need to have your credentials ready," Brad reminded her as they came to the entrance. Two ushers stood at each open door with one security type or another nearby, all checking to ensure no one got in uninvited.

Vanessa offered up her certified identification card and the matching codes held in her personal holocom. She looked over the entryway as the guards verified her information. She could see now that the towering glass was only a thin decorative layer over much thicker concrete, or perhaps something stronger. Any number of scanners or sniffer receptors could be embedded in the doorway.

They passed through without trouble, coming into a wide foyer with a vaulted ceiling and several large crystal chandeliers that seemed to cascade downward like frozen waterfalls. At either end of the foyer, broad spiral staircases rose to meet an ornate balcony. The tables, chairs and couches in the various lounges all sat empty as they arrived, with only a handful of other attendees still lingering.

"Now I know why you wanted to wait until it was closer to show time to get here," Vanessa said as they moved across the foyer to the theater doors. "I can see how that sort of entrance check would slow things down. Glad we skipped the lines." Her eyes continued to scan her surroundings, taking note of exit points and sight lines. She felt a jolt of gratitude as she discovered a small vestibule separating the foyer from the main audience hall—and, especially, for the "staff only" door she saw to one side within that vestibule.

She didn't get a chance to examine it. "They've dimmed the lights," Brad pointed out. He picked up the pace, bringing her into an ornate audience hall packed with six thousand people dressed for business rather than music.

Vanessa whispered with a grin, "Is it snobby that I thought the platinum section would be closer to the stage?"

Brad grinned back. "It's a first-come, first-serve system within each section, and we are a bit late. The front rows at these things are always reserved for the board of directors and certain executives. They also have to make sure the media gets seated up close. From there, it's the platinum-plus shareholders that get first priority seating."

"Oh. I suppose that makes sense," Vanessa mused. "I never should have sold off so much of my stock when the scandals started coming, but my brokers were all so nervous. I'm so happy to find someone to show me the ropes. Like I said last night, I've leaned on my broker to do this stuff too long. For something this big, I want to take care of it myself. Er…" Vanessa looked over her limited choice of seats. Faces both old and artificially young looked back at her, some with annoyance as the two latecomers clearly wanted to squeeze through. Wealth didn't make theater seating any more spacious.

"Um, hi," she said with a nervous wave to the people near the aisle. "I don't suppose I could trouble anyone to maybe trade seats with me? I'm over there," she explained, pointing to an empty seat near the center, "and I might have to get up again in the middle of things." Her pained expression seemed to have no effect on the men and women before her until she added, "My doctor just started me on standard metabolic enhancers."

"Oh my god," blurted a suddenly sympathetic and particularly attractive blonde only two seats in from the aisle.

"Yeah. Allergies."

"Steven," said the blonde to the man seated beside her, "let's switch with them."

"But I thought—"

"Steven," she hissed, "show a little consideration. She'll have to get up for the bathroom five times before this is over, anyway." The blonde stood and smiled. "You can take our seats."

"Oh, thank you so much!" Vanessa smiled gratefully as the generous couple shuffled around her and Brad. Soon enough, she and her surprised escort settled into seats close to the aisle.

Brad glanced around at neighbors who were all either too polite or too passive-aggressive to acknowledge him and his rather forward companion. He leaned in and whispered, "Was that stuff true?"

"Far as you know," murmured Vanessa.

The lights dimmed a final time. The stage offered little of the great showmanship from past shareholder meetings. A mostly transparent podium stood to one side of a towering holographic NorthStar logo floating at the back of the stage. Anton Brekhov took the podium amid scant, faint applause that underscored the awkwardness of this event.

If he expected anything more, his demeanor did not show it. "Ladies and gentlemen," he began, "good morning and thank you all for coming, especially on such short notice. I know many of you accepted considerable stress and expense in making it here, so I wanted to begin by thanking you for that and for your diligence and dedication as owners of our company. I've been informed by our chief administrative officer, Jon Weir, that our audience today represents a quorum of shares. Everything we decide is binding per NorthStar's corporate bylaws."

As Brekhov went on to recognize corporate officers and directors present, Vanessa leaned in to whisper to Brad, "What are the odds that Brekhov carries enough shares in his own pocket to create a quorum?"

"Oh, it's not quite that bad," replied her companion. "Surely he needs at least two friends to make up that much voting power. It just doesn't matter which friends in particular. Probably any random waiter or sanitation worker in this city has enough shares to make up the difference."

Vanessa glanced up toward the balcony seats behind her. "I'm guessing we don't have any waiters or sanitation workers here."

"Oh, they usually invest through mutual and pension funds and such. But you're right to look up into the balcony, and in the back. That's where you'd find the fund representatives."

"You sound like you don't approve."

"Hey, I like being in front as much as the next rich snob. But I'm only looking after my own money. Those fund reps? Some of them are here for more than a hundred thousand people. It's a little unfair somehow that they're in the back, isn't it?"

"How egalitarian of you," murmured Vanessa.

Brekhov continued. "The matter at hand is not something that I, nor the board, nor anyone wanted, but we're stuck with it now. As difficult as it is to wrap our heads around the Assembly's decisions and its alleged reasoning, this is our reality. NorthStar has become a sovereign state, even without any such intent or desire.

"Naturally, that leaves you, our shareholders, wondering what that means for your stake in the company. To cut to the chase: NorthStar is still the single largest corporation in the Union. It will continue on as a publicly traded stock, regardless of borders or questions of citizenship. Our industries will continue. Our science, our research, our services in education and finance and medicine will continue. Our arts will continue. Our *growth* will continue. The Union will continue to need us—just as NorthStar still needs you.

"We are the leading institution in planetary exploration and settlement. NorthStar is one of the greatest powers in military and security services in the Union. Education, public works, diplomacy: we can do it all. And here we are, even now, gathered in a democratic manner to determine our future. There is no reason we cannot provide all the functions of government for ourselves—and no reason we cannot still profit as a company from them.

"Ladies and gentlemen: we have seen many cases in history stretching back to well before the Expansion era of nation-states seizing control of companies and corporations. 'Nationalization,' as we commonly call it, is not entirely uncommon. What we're experiencing is, in a way, a reversal of that process. Yet even in reverse, it provides us with a road map."

His voice strengthened as he spoke. Vanessa didn't think that Brekhov lacked for confidence when he first stepped up to the podium, but he had to begin by addressing NorthStar's current adversity. Now he was on a roll, reminding his investors of the company's strength—and, along the way, his personal charisma.

"Your shares still matter, my friends. Your investments in this company still matter. They matter more than ever."

Applause began and then swelled. Vanessa didn't hear enthusiastic or universal approval, but Brekhov and his people clearly understood how to perform damage control. It took him all of five minutes to get repairs well underway with his biggest investors.

• • •

"Engine two is fully evacuated," reported the deep, jarringly smooth voice of the destroyer's comms officer. He sounded more like a holoshow host or an advertising voiceover than a man conducting a serious operation, but the emergency was only simulated. "Damage control team two is assembled, suited up, and on scene in good order."

"Lieutenant," spoke up the captain, "could you try to make this feel a little more like a real situation and not like you're trying to pick up on your fellow bridge officers?"

"Yes, ma'am," he said in exactly the same all-too-charming tone, eliciting further chuckles.

Captain Hunsaker grinned rather than scold him a second time. One last joke aside, he would obey, and she knew the importance of humor for morale. She turned her attention to her ship's patrol path, outlined on the largest of the tactical screens looming at the front of the bridge. *Tethys* cruised along a course between Fairhaven and Tourmaline, where she could run combat maneuvers and emergency drills without disturbing anyone. She stood ready for boardings and other patrol functions, but for the last week she had focused on training in a run-up to deployment.

The last four months in home port had been good for the crew, particularly after their run in Hashem. The news that they wouldn't be headed back there anytime soon came as an added bonus. *Tethys* had performed even better there than in Archangel.

The only thing that made Hunsaker prouder than the ship's service record was the retention rate among her officers and crew. Two years of combat service left *Tethys* with little turnover. While NorthStar's attractive bonus pay programs and other incentives deserved some credit, the numbers strongly validated her leadership. The men and women on board *Tethys* not only served well in combat, but tended to sign on for more.

Hunsaker keyed up her personal holocom and waited for a response. "Baker here," came a voice, and then a man's face on the holo screen. Behind him, she could see crewmen in the heavy, protective vac suits of the damage control team as they went through the motions of entering a breached compartment.

"How are they looking, XO?" she asked.

"Pretty good, ma'am. The new guys have picked up on the mistakes from last time."

"Good. Listen, if this goes well enough, I think we should shift back to combat drills. The memos I've seen this morning suggest that we'll be doing plenty of interdiction and skirmishing in Archangel."

"They're assuming an awful lot about the future, aren't they, ma'am?"

Hunsaker shook her head. "No matter what the suits decide, we're still going to occupy Michael until they say 'uncle.' We haven't been in it this long to give up now. They can pull all the political shenanigans they want. This still comes down to which dog is bigger and meaner."

"Capt—*Captain!*" blurted out one officer, and then another. Hunsaker's eyes immediately went to the tactical screens, where she saw a pair of ships coming in off *Tethys*'s starboard side at high speed. The computer identified them as corvettes—and the ships that followed as destroyers. Only ships coming out of FTL could appear so suddenly. All four would pass by *Tethys* in seconds. Alarms screamed out warnings of active scans against her ship's hull, and that meant targeting computers.

Her hand slammed down on the general quarters alarm, which simultaneously activated the destroyer's electrostatic reinforcement generators and unlocked weapons systems. "Battle stations!" she shouted.

She didn't have time to repeat herself. The first laser cannon fire struck *Tethys* along her port side thrusters, setting off an explosion that shook the entire vessel. Hunsaker gripped the arms of her seat, pushing herself upright to look again at the tactical screen.

The captain tracked many more vessels than the four that had screamed past. Several of them were much larger. All of them approached at high speed, holding to a loose formation around a single huge ship headed straight for hers. The visuals made *Tethys* look like the world's most inadequate speed bump.

"Evasive action!" she cried out. "Chaff missiles! Curtain spread, now!"

Though her officers obeyed, she didn't get a chance to see her orders reflected on the tactical screens. The next blows to hit *Tethys* knocked Hunsaker from her chair before she'd strapped in. Lights flickered and crew cried out in surprise and bewilderment. For all the distance between her ship and the others, Hunsaker's first thought was that they'd been rammed and swatted aside like a bug.

• • •

Hundreds of kilometers separated *Tethys* from *Beowulf* and her escorts. An observer on *Tethys* would only barely see the battleship with the naked eye, and then only because of her many running lights—and, in this case, because of the laser beams and the pair of missiles that streaked out from the battleship's belly. A glittering cloud of chaff missiles exploded around *Tethys* to create a protective arc, but they did little good. *Beowulf*'s guns hit home again and again. Despite the disruptive effects and the shrapnel put out by the chaff, her missiles detonated well within range of their intended target.

Beowulf soared past as *Tethys* was blown off course, practically spinning away. Flying close by at starboard, the destroyer *Monaco* added to the punishment with a few blasts of her own, but likewise carried on without further engagement.

Tethys drifted off helplessly, trailing burning gases and debris without getting off a single retaliatory shot. *Beowulf* left her behind, leading an armada of destroyers, frigates, freighters, liners, and corvettes in a rapid dash for the system's capitol.

• • •

"They'll see us coming on Fairhaven in five minutes," reported a voice from across *Beowulf*'s command bridge.

"They'll need another minute to analyze and confirm and figure out how much to panic," said Admiral Branch. "Hope that works out for our people on the ground. At least we're only a couple minutes off schedule. How's it going with that destroyer back there?"

"*St. Bernadette* is breaking off to force disarmament and surrender," reported one officer.

"No battle damage reported here," confirmed another. "Everyone's fine."

"Captain," spoke up the officer training at comms, "she got off an emergency signal broadcast. It's still going."

"Don't call out to the captain directly," warned the other ensign quietly. She leaned in as much as the straps on her seat at the comms station would allow.

"I'm sorry?" said Ensign Spencer. Like the young woman beside him, he still had the faceplate of his helmet up. The manuals all said that the faceplates should drop as soon as the general quarters alarm rang, but he'd been privately warned off of that during his first drill. Officers, someone told him, needed to wait until the actual trouble started so they didn't come off as too jumpy. It was the first of many things that didn't go by the book. He correctly guessed he was about to hear another.

"Call out the report, but don't say 'captain' or 'admiral' or whichever," explained Ensign Perez. "He'll hear it. The old man has good ears for that sort of thing. Don't actually call out for him unless you need his undivided attention."

Nathan asked, "Any rules on when that's appropriate?"

"None that I've ever seen. I guess if the ship's about to explode. Even then, that's his call, not ours. Kind of an unwritten rule." She turned her attention away to the workstations of the enlisted techs to her right.

Nathan did the same to the left. The duty comms officer was supposed to keep track of the whole duty section in a battle. Allegedly, that meant never taking his eyes off the section and their status screens. At this point, though, Nathan was waiting for someone to give him the unwritten exception to that rule, too. The academy went by the book; the actual navy seemed to run on unwritten rules with unwritten exceptions.

He didn't mind that so much. Growing up as the son of two high-powered professionals, Nathan understood that every workplace had its own culture and practices, and that not everything made it into the manuals. Leaders had to set examples by going beyond the books. He also accepted that the next year and more of his life would involve a steep, demanding learning curve. He only wished he'd had more time to absorb it all and at least become fully proficient at one duty station or another before *Beowulf* launched into an invasion.

He'd just gotten the hang of running the helm before being shifted off to train with Perez as the comms officer. Nathan understood the reasoning. He wasn't experienced enough to be trusted with anything critical in a fight like this, particularly the wheel of the ship. Still, working comms had its drawbacks.

"I see what you meant about this being counterintuitive," said Nathan. "You're tied into every other ship, but you can't actually see what's going on."

Out of the corner of his eye, he saw Perez twist in her seat to look over her shoulder. Then she sat back and opened up a holo screen between them both to show the info and graphics streaming across the main tactical screens at the front of the bridge. "Something one of the signalmen showed me," she explained. "It helps to keep track of things. The books say you're not supposed to get distracted from your station, but the books are wrong."

Nathan smiled. "Good to know." His smile quickly faded, though, as he looked over the fleet's speed and position and did some quick math. "They're gonna see us coming with plenty of time to gear up. Not much of an element of surprise. And we're still not sure how many ships they've got ready to go."

Perez glanced down at Nathan's feet, or more accurately, his legs. His vac suit bore no bloodstripes. "This is your first fight?"

"Yeah. The academy assigned me to a combat ship during my one apprenticeship summer, but she took some hits in a skirmish right before I got there. I spent most of the time in the yards helping with repairs. It's not my first time under a gun, though…just my first chance to actually shoot back." He frowned then, gesturing to the workstations and harmless comms gear. "Metaphorically, I guess."

"Don't let the set-up fool you," Perez warned. "When the shooting starts, you'll have plenty to do."

Nathan glanced at their private tactical screen. If nothing stood in their way, they'd be at Fairhaven's drone net in a matter of minutes. Then the real shooting would start.

• • •

Vanessa ran her finger across the simple gold bracelet on her wrist. The local time appeared in soft, muted holographic numbers beside her hand. *The fleet might be here by now, or it may be a few minutes off.* Regardless, she hadn't received the signal to abort.

She couldn't wait any longer.

"I'm going to turn the podium over to Terry Donaldson for a brief report on our financials," Brekhov went on. "Yes, our stock prices have taken a hit in all of this. We also see some silver linings. From there, we'll hear from Christina Walters about our plans for moving forward into establishing a formal government and citizenship…"

"Already time to step out," Vanessa grumbled quietly to Brad. "Don't let them do anything fun without me." She rose, keeping low and hissing apologies to the people between her and the aisle. "Sorry. Altered nature calls."

"Point of order!" called out someone all too near Vanessa. She froze in her tracks and looked over to the suited man standing in the audience only a few seats away from hers, but soon realized he wasn't addressing her. She slipped the rest of the way out of the aisle. "Mr. Brekhov, I hate to interrupt, but I know I speak for a lot of people here. Can we skip to the biggest concern? If NorthStar is to become a sovereign state, do you plan to stay on as CEO? And does that mean you'll become the de facto head of state?"

Murmurs of agreement swept through the audience. Brekhov acknowledged the demand with an almost coy smile. "I suppose I can't blame you for your urgency on that point, Mr. Mikulski," he said.

Vanessa didn't worry about how Brekhov could recognize random people from the audience. For all she knew, this guy was planted to create a scene. She kept a low profile and moved out toward the door.

"I think it's important to understand that NorthStar will still handle selection of its leaders through the same process it uses now," said Brekhov. "I'll admit, I'm as surprised as anyone to learn that the Assembly can force sovereignty upon whomever they choose. That said, they cannot dictate our form of governance. They cannot force us to abandon our corporate identity. We will need to hold an election, yes…and I will of course accept a nomination if I'm offered such."

Vanessa heard applause as she reached the exit. A man in a suit smiled at her and pressed a key on the door panel. She noted the subtle bulge under his arm and the way he, in turn, made sure to establish eye contact as she passed through. Brekhov wasn't president of anything yet, but Risk Management and his personal security detail weren't waiting for an election. This man wasn't an usher.

"Can I help you, miss?" he asked as he stepped out behind her.

"Yes, actually." She swept the vestibule with a quick gaze to ensure they were alone as she turned to face him. Another step backward drew him in more. He let the door shut behind him. Vanessa then stepped toward him again with a casual, disarming smile that closed the gap between the two.

An untrained observer would have taken her attack for a slap. Even with the power added by her swiveling hips and the rapid, upward arc of her arm, she struck him across the face with an open hand. It was the heel of her palm that delivered the damage, though: solid bone against his jaw with all the force of a closed fist and the added disorientation of her fingers slapping against his ear and rupturing his eardrum. Her victim almost reacted in time to save himself, except that his first instinct had been to step backward away from the blow—only to bump into the closed door behind him.

He fell to his knees with one hand out to catch himself, not quite knocked out as she'd hoped but unable to react. Vanessa expended an extra second on winding up for a vicious kick that sent him sprawling backward, hitting the back of his head against the floor.

She didn't pause to see if anyone heard. Vanessa snatched his forearms and dragged him to the "staff only" exit to the vestibule's side. The controls bleeped plaintively at the touch of her finger, but let out a much more welcoming sound when she tried her unconscious burden's fingers instead. The door slid open to reveal a small landing in front of a staircase. Vanessa tugged her prisoner inside, grunting in gratitude when the door slid shut again.

The stairwell landing contained a handheld fire extinguisher and medical kit mounted on one wall, but no cameras or other dangers. She found gear of greater use on the unconscious man at her feet: a personal holocom, earpiece, restraints, and a stunner pistol, along with a smaller laser pistol in an ankle holster. Vanessa confiscated all of it, tucking the earpiece into place. Soon, she had the magnetic and biometric safeties on the guns deactivated. Security chatter over the earpiece confirmed that no one had noticed her victim's absence. The holocom was locked, of course, but at least it kept the earpiece tied into the right channels.

She had no more time to waste. Vanessa left the man on the floor as she launched herself up the stairs, taking two or three steps at a time. The restricted passageways didn't enjoy the décor of Symphony Hall's public spaces. They did, however, present a much easier route to her destination.

Five steep flights of stairs and two fortunately unguarded doors later, Vanessa came to the end of the line. This door, too, was marked "staff only," but the lone control button assured her this one would be unlocked. It also indicated that she'd found the business floor of the building. Offices and meeting rooms awaited on the other side. It would make a good spot for a command center.

Vanessa swiped her finger over the fake jewel on her ring to check the time. Then she brought up a muted media broadcast and found the world no different than when she arrived. All those reporters in the plaza outside babbled on while the other working stiffs served as background, just like Brad predicted.

She let out a silent curse. The operation stretched Ministry agents out all over Fairhaven. Too many vital points had to be covered. If any of the other agents had made it into the shareholder meeting, she hadn't identified them. Even if others were on site, they might be too close to exposure to slip away. Security here was tight. She'd only made it this far by taking a huge risk, and her trail could be uncovered at any second.

Her orders were clear. Somewhere on the other side of this door, maybe right nearby or maybe down a hall or two, Vanessa would find some office commandeered as a control center. She would find officers vital to any orderly response to an emergency. A few well-placed gunshots and some thrown switches could throw that response into chaos.

On her holocom screen, some stupid reporter yammered on with his stupid face about something or another while some dumbass innocent groundskeeper walked by to clear out the trash cans. To escape that, she closed her eyes—only to think of *Aphrodite*'s passengers floating helplessly around the ship as her pirate captors readied for their getaway.

Aphrodite wasn't her fault. She didn't blame herself. She'd done more than enough to make amends regardless, at least with herself. It had been beyond her control from the start. This wouldn't be her fault, either.

That didn't mean she had to let it happen.

Her holocom gave her a few minutes. She set an alarm and pulled the confiscated weapons from her pocket: laser in her right hand, stunner in her left. After one last breath, she stepped to one side of the door and opened it up for a look.

The hallway stretched out for thirty or so meters ahead. She saw closed office doors and darkened interior windows to either side. The hallway ended at a T-intersection, offering turns to the left and right.

She darted back into the stairway as she saw movement halfway along the hall ahead. Two figures in combat armor and helmets walked out of a side room, turning toward the end of the hall. Their better weaponry and relatively isolated position made them targets she couldn't pass up. By virtue of its location, the door behind presented a likely spot for a command center.

She didn't have much time. If anyone else lurked on either end of that intersection, she'd deal with it when she got there. Vanessa strode out into the hall, glad for the carpeting that muffled her long, rapid footsteps that soon broke into an all-out run. The trooper on Vanessa's left caught the sound only a heartbeat before her partner, turning to look back in time for Vanessa to tag her with an electric blast from the stunner.

"Shit!" the other trooper blurted out, but then he caught Vanessa's right elbow across his cheek. She managed to pivot on the first foot that got past him as he buckled, twisting to throw her other leg against the side of his knee to bring him down along with her. This put all three of them on the floor, though Vanessa managed to control her fall and quickly regained her footing. She plugged the other woman with her stunner again for good measure before kicking the rifle away from her remaining opponent's hands.

The move cost her the initiative. He was considerably bigger than Vanessa and able to shrug off more than a blow to the cheek. The trooper retaliated with a meaty fist, tagging Vanessa in the face to give himself a little room before launching into a tackle. Vanessa fell onto her back to get under him before he could really connect. The close contact put her at as much risk of the stunner's electrical charge as for him. She dropped the stunner and grabbed at his jaw, knowing she needed to keep his mouth shut for what came next.

If the trooper felt the other pistol against his hip, he didn't do anything about it in time. Vanessa's hand over his mouth smothered his cry when she pulled the trigger, burning a thin but crippling streak through his side and leaving a scorched line in the wall and floor. He gurgled, then slumped over.

"Who was that?" demanded someone over Vanessa's earpiece.

"Guys?" asked a voice from inside the office nearby.

She snatched the headset microphone from the fallen guard's face and blurted, "I just fell on my fucking knee!" before throwing it away.

Ignoring the voice in her ear that demanded further detail or identification, Vanessa sprang to her feet. The hallway remained clear. A voice from the other side of the office door called out, "Chuck? Angie? You okay?"

She spared only a second to ensure that the pulse rifle dropped by her enemy had no magnetic or biometric lock.

The office door opened up in front of her as she got to her feet. Another security trooper looked back at her with undisguised shock. She seized the moment without hesitation. Vanessa put the butt of her rifle right into his nose, knocking him backward against a desk. Her first glance into the office revealed several more uniformed troopers in the room. None of the rest wore armor. They all looked up in surprise.

Vanessa opened up as they drew their sidearms, immediately establishing fire superiority with her heavier weapon. The desk and the trooper with the smashed nose laying on top of it offered some cover. Her opponents fired back, blasting debris off the furniture and walls all around her. She saw considerable computer tech here, along with holographic "posters" and office knickknacks to remind her that this was not ordinarily a military site. That also meant that the chairs and desks offered much weaker cover than she enjoyed by virtue of the armored trooper still reeling in front of her. For all their efforts to aim and spare their comrade, more than one laser struck his stunned body. Vanessa swept the room with deadly pulses of light, bringing down men, women, and office equipment.

The exchange lasted only seconds and ended with only one woman left alive. More demands for reports and security status came over her earpiece. Vanessa disregarded the voices in favor of locating a functioning computer or even an open holocom on one of the bodies. Her heart pounded in her chest. *Dammit, this isn't what I wanted*, she thought. *I've got bigger problems than the fucking mission now and time is running—there!*

She knew NorthStar's security practices well enough to recognize the command layout on their control screens. The holographic site map, now floating on the floor beside their dead owner, told her where she needed to go. It was just around the hallway corner.

Her holocom buzzed and pinged with an alarm. She'd run out of time.

Vanessa spared only one last moment to input a single command in the security station: Lockdown.

"Ritter!" snapped someone over Vanessa's earpiece as she darted back out into the hallway and down the adjacent passage. "Get someone into the command room now!"

The door at the end of the hallway offered the words "Roof Access" in plain, big letters. She hurtled toward the door, hearing the banging of heavy boots on the other side until she opened fire on the door with her pulse rifle. A second, more careful blast at point blank burned through the control panel, forcing it open to reveal the smoking bodies of the men she'd cut down on the other side. She leaped over them, running up the last flight of stairs and through the doorway above into the open air.

Symphony Hall's rooftop looked much like the courtyards on the ground. Bushes and small trees in marble planters joined a couple of fountains and statues to provide a welcoming setting, along with tables and chairs for receptions. A raised platform at the rooftop's center held three airvans with NorthStar Security markings. Security troopers stood in almost every direction—several of them in the black powered armor of NorthStar Rangers.

Vanessa ran for the rooftop's edge. She fired away with her rifle, bringing down one trooper and then another in her wild dash before the enemy shook off their surprise. Most troopers dove for the nearest cover as their training dictated. Several of the Rangers opened up on her with their weapons, most of them heavier and more powerful than an ordinary person could effectively wield. The rooftop décor and the presence of friendly troops nearby limited their fire. Vanessa's training and experience took her through a zigzagging motion that bought her a few more meters.

It was all she needed. Lasers, bullets, and even plasma bursts flew past her in several directions, flying off the rooftop with noisy flashes that ultimately aided in her objective. A waist-high planter that anchored a line of cherry blossom trees near the edge of the roof took her out of the line of fire, if only for a breath or two. Vanessa leaned over the crenellations to shoot at the open ground below.

She didn't target anyone in particular. To the contrary, she aimed to ensure she didn't hurt anyone at all. Frightened pedestrians and reporters below couldn't tell the difference, of course. She counted on that.

"Run!" Vanessa roared as she fired. "Run, you stupid assholes! Get out of here!"

People screamed and scattered for cover. They ran away from the plaza, offering Vanessa a glimmer of hope that she'd pulled this one off.

Something slammed against her from behind, striking all over her back and knocking her off balance. She slumped to the floor, fighting for breath that wouldn't come. A pair of NorthStar security troopers approached with their assault rifles up, smoke floating from the muzzles of their weapons. Several Rangers joined them, keeping their weapons trained on her.

She couldn't tell if her thin layers of armor-weave had stopped the bullet. Vanessa couldn't breathe. Air wouldn't move into her mouth. The spasms wouldn't stop. Her gun had fallen out of reach. She barely managed to curl into a ball behind the marble planter full of those pretty trees in one last defiant attempt to escape.

One Ranger in powered armor came forward to stand directly over her. She wasn't sure if he planned to restrain her or shoot her until he brought his weapon to bear, and then her vision was filled with a blinding light.

• • •

Argent's launch bays opened and turrets extended without warning or preamble. Birds flew from her hull and fled the spaceport as the weapons fired, all of them pointed skyward along well-planned paths.

Red beams of light connected with satellites far above the clouds. Most of the missiles arced downward almost as soon as they reached the sky, exploding against military ships in their hangars and NorthStar security fleet buildings all around the spaceport district. Others flew out farther, demolishing anti-orbital weapons emplacements outside the city limits. Still more flew straight up and burst only a few kilometers from the surface, creating a broad cloud of burning chaff to disrupt any view of the spaceport grounds from above the atmosphere.

Another series of chaff missiles streaked toward a building only a hundred kilometers away. They detonated well within reach of Symphony Hall's rooftop, engulfing the structure with a crown of fire that burned everything and everyone that stood.

CHAPTER TWELVE

How to Make an Entrance

"After reviewing intercepted signal evidence of Bravo Team's interdiction and/or elimination, Alpha Team's leader decided to continue with the mission as planned. He declined my offer of reinforcements from the ship's security contingent. I believe the questionable selection of personnel for his team has created considerable mistrust. Regardless, Alpha Team has decided to carry on at half the strength originally planned for its objectives."

--Agent Ezekiel Barnes, Mission Log, July, 2279

"Three minutes. Weapons, everyone."

In the back of the rover, Alicia, Baldwin, and Tanner pulled rifles and sidearms out from under the seats in compliance with Jacobson's order. The rifles had collapsible stocks and shortened barrels for the sake of concealment. Ideally, they wouldn't need to do much shooting at range, anyway. Everyone took up a stunner and grenades in a second round of preparations. Three minutes gave them enough time to fix last-second problems with gear. The civilian cut and style of their clothes was good enough to fool most observers at a glance, but a trained eye with a close look would recognize the armor-weave fabrics for what they were. A tailor could do only so much to hide a knee guard or a back plate.

Sitting up front, Janeka took care of her own weapons and Sanjay's to let the young bo'sun focus on driving. They would pass along an avenue with a view of their destination in a couple more blocks. For now they stayed clear with good reason.

"Y'know," said Sanjay, "the last time I did something like this, Tanner cut off my left arm."

Tanner looked up from the back seat with wide eyes, only to see everyone but Sanjay looking back at him in shock. No one spoke. He had to break the silence somehow. "Guess you shouldn't have made fun of my PTSD."

The wide eyes remained. So did the silence, until Sanjay couldn't hold back anymore and let out a snort. Then Tanner grinned, allowing the rest to release their laughter.

"Jesus, Tanner," said Baldwin.

"I know, right?" Alicia agreed. "And you keep saying *marines* are jerks."

"You are," argued Tanner. He caught a minor scowl from Janeka. "What? Gunny, am I wrong? You went to all that trouble to desensitize me during basic training, and look at me now. Listen to the awful things I say. I'm a monster. Who's responsible for that?"

Jacobson passed on the jokes. "Sanjay, are you ready for this?" he asked. "There's still time to switch out if we do it right now. Someone else can drive."

"What? No sir, it's fine," said Sanjay. "I'll be okay."

Janeka, too, took things seriously. "You didn't mention this until now," she pressed without anger or frustration. "I know about Scheherazade. No one will hold it against you if this is a problem."

Tanner didn't take his eyes off Sanjay, either. He remembered all too well how shaken up the young bo'sun had been by the injury. For all their joking, the incident had scarred both of them. Since that day, however, Sanjay seemed fine...but no one had asked him to be groundside in advance of another planetary invasion.

"Gunny, you brought me in to drive, right?" Sanjay asked. "I'm good for it."

"I brought you in because Admiral Yeoh recommended you. And not just for your driving."

They came to a stop at a corner. Sanjay's eyes flicked up to look in the old fashioned rear view mirror, catching Tanner's gaze. Tanner nodded in silent confirmation. A vote of confidence from Admiral Yeoh bolstered one's spirit far more than any tasteless humor ever could.

"I'm good, gunny," repeated Sanjay. "Don't worry about me." He gestured at the crowd outside the vehicle. "I'm more worried about all these stupid protesters."

"They'll go to ground as soon as the warning sirens go off and they see alert flashes on their holocoms," Janeka assured him. "We can't let that distract us. This will be ugly." She looked back at the others to make sure they listened. "I've warned you about that all along. I brought you in because I knew you wouldn't let it get any uglier than necessary, but do not get distracted. This is war. The only way to keep it from being ugly is to keep it from happening at all, and it's too late for—"

"Aw shit!" Alicia called out, pointing down the corner toward their destination. "Weapons fire on the rooftop!"

"What?" Tanner looked up from his weapons prep to see protesters and other pedestrians also craning their heads to look down the street.

"Shit, what happened?" Sanjay burst.

"Why are there so many people still in that plaza?" Tanner asked in alarm. "I thought—"

"Doesn't matter!" barked Jacobson. "Go, Sanjay, go!"

While the rover sat in front of an intersection with a clear, slightly downhill view, it wasn't the route they wanted. Sanjay hit the accelerator and turned straight into oncoming traffic, aiming for the space between lanes but still swatting aside one lighter vehicle and then another with the rover's bulk.

Aircar traffic had been restricted for a two-block radius around Symphony Hall for the day, providing an unobstructed view of the flashes of energy weapons that zipped off of the roof. Some of those blasts continued on toward buildings across the street. Green bolts of plasma, at least, couldn't hold together over such a distance, but lasers and bullets were a different matter. Glass and debris fell into the street, causing drivers to swerve erratically even before Sanjay's wrong-way driving could scare anyone.

One other factor added to the disorder: pulse weapons fire from the rooftop coming down at the plaza in front of the hall. Pedestrians scattered, with the vast majority opting to put distance between themselves and the danger rather than getting under the nearest available cover. Uniformed and plainclothes security did the opposite, taking up positions and training their weapons on the roof.

The shooting stopped only a heartbeat before Sanjay passed the final intersection. His engine roared and other vehicles struck one another to get out of his way, drawing attention from all around. Then a third surprise took precedence over guns or crazy drivers.

The sky over Symphony Hall exploded in flames.

• • •

O'Neal's first warning of trouble came over his earpiece in the form of a few urgent, quickly silenced words. His earpiece kept him tied in with the NorthStar Security captain in the control room, the team leader on the rooftop, and a few others, but not every single member of the security force. O'Neal trusted the others to do their jobs and report concerns as necessary. He, in turn, focused on his own job.

He stood in the shadows only a few meters from the podium as Brekhov spoke. While he kept a constant vigil, O'Neal saw little to worry about. After ten years in executive personal security, along with thirty and change as a field operative, O'Neal understood that some risks had to be accepted.

He couldn't have Brekhov deliver the speech via hologram from some secure, undisclosed location. Nor did he want any such thing. Brekhov needed to be visible and accessible, or at least to convey such an impression. O'Neal respected him, even liked him as a person and certainly cared about his safety, but paranoia and overwrought emotional attachments did no one any good.

Thus when those first concerning sounds came over the comms net, O'Neal held his position. Others on the net asked about the noise. Seconds ticked by without a response, which naturally raised concern, yet O'Neal did not leap into dramatic action. Instead, he slipped past a few others in the crowd backstage toward Pedroso without taking his eyes off Brekhov for more than a heartbeat.

Pedroso had her own concerns. She busily typed away at a holo screen. The posture of her assistants made it clear she didn't want to be bothered. O'Neal didn't wait on them. He reached past and put one firm hand around her wrist and squeezed. Pedroso caught the concerned look on O'Neal's face and immediately activated her earpiece.

A second later, they heard the automated lockdown warning. So did everyone else on the security comms net. "Top floor!" someone shouted on the command channel. "Shooter on the top floor! Control room is hit!"

Pedroso reflexively looked up to O'Neal, but he was already in motion. The big man roughly pushed through the others in the shadows as she asked, "Confirm that! Rostov, can you confirm—"

"Confirmed!" answered the rooftop security lead. "Female, dark hair, armed and firing!" The sound of Rostov's own pulse rifle underscored the seriousness of his words. "She's moving for the edge! We're on it, stand by!"

O'Neal didn't obey that order. He stepped out onto the stage, leaning close to speak in Brekhov's ear. "We have a situation," he warned quietly.

Thankfully, Brekhov held a neutral expression. His outward calm held off any concerned murmuring from the audience. "What is it?"

"Shooter's down! Shooter's down!" reported Rostov. "Franks, move in and check her."

"Shooter on the roof," O'Neal explained. "Security has her down now. No other alerts, but it sounds like she took out the control room, so—"

The entire building shook with the detonation overhead. People screamed, both in the audience and offstage. O'Neal pulled Brekhov into the wings, holding him against the tall corner wall that offered the greatest structural support nearby. Nothing fell from the ceiling as the reverberations subsided, but that didn't make anyone feel better.

• • •

Windows shattered everywhere, from the towers surrounding the plaza to vehicles on the street. All of the rover's side windows burst as well, covering its passengers with chunks of safety glass. The much thicker windshield held firm, though numerous cracks appeared and quickly spread.

Screaming in terror and defiance, Sanjay drove straight into the firestorm. Chaff rained down all around, setting every tree and bush alight and brightening their surroundings so much it was difficult to see. His visual memory of his last glances at the plaza dictated his path. He brought the rover into a hard right turn and felt the bumpy drop of the vehicle rolling down the plaza's steps.

Like the rest of the passengers, Tanner kept his head down as Sanjay cleared the rest of the distance to the Hall's entrance. It seemed the entire world outside the rover burned. He knew better, but only on an intellectual level. Briefing details like the remarkably low yield and accelerated burn time of the chaff missiles intended for the hall meant little at the center of the destruction and chaos.

No. Not the center, he reminded himself. *It went off over the roof. Way over the roof. All the way up there*, he thought, though without looking up. *If it was a regular chaff missile, we'd be dead. The building would be incinerated.*

Instead, the building still stood. Sanjay pulled up alongside it and stopped the rover.

"Out!" ordered Janeka. "Everyone out!"

Tanner obeyed. He threw the door open and rolled out, finding himself in between the vehicle and the tall, formerly shining walls of Symphony Hall, now cracked and shattered to reveal the grey masonry underneath. Baldwin came out after him, taking up the same crouching position with her rifle covering their open flank.

Alicia went straight for the door rather than pause as she came out, but it held firm. "Locked!" she declared.

"Good," said Jacobson. "Hopefully everyone's still inside." He stepped to the left of the door with his plasma carbine pointed low and fired. The bright green ball of energy from his weapon blasted straight through, destroying the magnetic locks and burning a small crater into the floor on the other side.

The doorframe offered him partial cover. He wore the same protective clothing as everyone else on the team, kept his cool, and made no rash moves.

None of it saved him. As soon as the door flew open with sparks and smoke all around, multiple red flashes of laser fire from within burned through Jacobson's chest.

• • •

"Rostov, report!" barked Pedroso.

"What the hell was that?" Brekhov asked. All around him he saw bodyguards and security agents with weapons drawn.

"Rostov!" Pedroso tried again. She grabbed another nearby Risk Management agent. "Taggart, take charge here. We're in lockdown. Nobody gets in or out. The danger is outside. They're all safer in here!" With that, she looked to O'Neal and came to a silent, instant agreement: they needed to leave, lockdown or no.

"Perimeter breach!" yelled a new voice on the security net. O'Neal didn't recognize this one, but he heard plenty of gunfire to go with it. "Rover at the front entrance. Rover at—urgh!"

• • •

"Boss!" Tanner shouted.

"No!" yelled Baldwin. She reached out for him, only for Alicia to grab her and pull her back before more laser fire cut her down, too.

Janeka threw herself up against the doorframe, held her rifle around the side without looking and opened up with a burst of pulse lasers. "Check him! Malone, help me out!"

Alicia dragged Jacobson clear of the doorway. Tanner and Janeka fired more or less blindly into the hall at first, then with a little more direction once they had a sense of where the shots came from. Though he could risk only a couple of glances, Tanner quickly realized the enemy included much more than a handful of security guards. "Christ," he grunted, "half of these guys look like regular infantry!"

"We knew security would be heavy," said Janeka.

Loud bangs and high-pitched humming from behind caught Tanner's attention. Sanjay leaned over the hood of the rover, firing off his pulse rifle. "We're taking fire from the street!" he warned.

"Jacobson's gone," declared Alicia. "There's nothing we can do."

Behind her, Baldwin crouched under the rover and fired at targets farther back. "We can't stay here! Where's our back-up?"

"They get here when they get here," said Janeka. "Malone, I need the plasma carbine."

The weapon lay just inside the door. Reaching in for it would be suicidal, but he was closest to it or Janeka wouldn't have said anything. Tanner pulled back, drew one of his two chaff grenades and hooked it around the doorframe. The smoke and flashing lights alone wouldn't be enough, though. Not considering the disciplined marksmanship that brought down Jacobson and kept the team pinned in the doorway. As soon as he let go of the grenade, Tanner aimed high with his pulse rifle and fired.

The red light of a laser flashed so closely in front of Tanner's eyes that it left a bright glare on his vision, but not before he hit his target. His short burst struck the outer edges of the grand chandelier, burning through crystal and mountings. The massive piece fell straight down to the floor with a tremendous crash, sending pieces everywhere and forcing the briefest pause in opposing gunfire. Tanner nearly dropped face first onto the floor in a mad lunge for the plasma carbine. Bullets and laser flashes chased him out again. He propped himself up against the wall outside, blinking hard to clear the glare from his eyes.

Janeka brought her weapon around the doorframe to fire off another blind burst while the chaff grenade inside popped and screamed. The enemy fire from within picked up again, though a bit wilder than before. "You okay?" asked Janeka.

"Think so. Just need a second."

"Good idea with the chandelier."

He kept blinking. "I always wanted to see one of those fall," he confessed.

"Wong," said Janeka, "do you see any cover from your angle?"

Crouched beside Tanner, Alicia craned her head around the corner for a quick look and then pulled back. "There's a bar about twenty meters in. Looks solid."

"That's weak cover against bullets or lasers," Janeka warned. "A bar won't last long in this."

Alicia almost grinned. "Will it have to?"

"Okay," agreed Janeka. "You're faster than I am. You wait for suppressing fire before you pop up again, then focus on taking out shooters, understand?"

"Got it."

"Malone, you ready?" asked Janeka.

The worst of the glare had cleared from Tanner's eyes. He nodded and tossed the plasma carbine to her, but she tucked it into one of the deep pockets of her longcoat rather than make immediate use of it. "We need to cover Wong," she explained.

"Gunny!" warned Sanjay. He and Baldwin continued to return fire from opposite sides of the rover, which rattled and even began to sag under the punishing blasts from out beyond the plaza. "I think the bad guys' back-up is here!"

"Working on it. Wong, Malone, chaff grenades. I'll fire high. Ready? Go!"

Once again, Tanner threw a grenade around the door frame, joined this time by Alicia while Janeka sprayed in a wide arc with her rifle. As soon as the grenades blew, Janeka blasted the next closest chandelier. Tanner laid down with his rifle and pulled the trigger. Alicia leapt over him and sprinted for the bar.

She only needed a few seconds to cover the distance. Tanner's suppressive fire, the distractions of more chaff, and another crashing chandelier made her tough to track. Shooters on both the balcony and the ground floor noticed their new target a second too late. Alicia leapt over the bar as she drew the first direct fire.

The sudden spread of threats split the enemy's attention, pulling the aim of many away from the door. Janeka made them pay for it, bringing down two of the balcony shooters with short, precise bursts from her pulse rifle. Tanner managed to tag another enemy on the opposite end of the lobby, though he doubted the man would stay down. NorthStar didn't skimp on body armor for a detail like this.

Janeka's prediction about the bar proved true. Bullets and lasers punched and burned through the painted wood to send splinters flying. Bottles, glasses, and other supplies burst. Still, the barrier hid and protected the younger marine long enough for her to pitch her remaining chaff grenade up over the side.

Alicia then rose with her pulse rifle in her left hand and a pistol in her right. The rifle served only to spit out suppressive fire to her vulnerable left side. She hardly even looked down its barrel, reserving her aim instead for the pistol in her other hand as she put down one of the plainclothes security guards shooting from behind an overturned table. Then she dropped down behind the bar again, quickly rolling away from her initial spot as return fire threatened to cut her to pieces. The bar suffered terrible damage. Alicia rose, fired, fell, and relocated once more.

Tanner moved to capitalize on Alicia's offense, but as soon as one of the troopers on the balcony left himself open, Tanner's rifle cut out. He cursed and he twisted back around the doorframe to replace the overheated power magazine. "Piece of shit!" he growled.

He heard the familiar hum and whoosh of a plasma carbine to his side. Janeka took out the balcony trooper with a blast that tested the carbine's longest effective range. Though the ball of plasma had begun to dissipate as it reached him, its heat and coherency still blew straight through the balcony railing and the trooper's armor. He fell straight through the breach in the rails, leaving a trail of smoke on his way to the ground floor.

The roar of engines overhead drew Tanner's attention, initially giving him a scare followed by hope. *Mansa Musa* floated by overhead, landing gear already extended with rapid laser fire streaming down onto the plaza from her open cargo bay. "About fucking time!" shouted Sanjay.

• • •

A pair of small missiles struck *Mansa Musa* so close together their impacts were almost indistinguishable. They both flew in from the rooftops of the tall offices and residential towers surrounding Symphony Hall. Neither were enough to bring the yacht down while her ES systems ran, but they rocked the ship and set off complaining alarms on her bridge.

"Shit, we don't even get a warning?" asked Mohamed.

"Ain't like we didn't know better," said Everett, seated beside him at the helm. "No time for warning messages, anyway." Everett cut off several systems before the damage got worse. *Mansa Musa* no longer needed anything in her oxygen tanks, nor would her main thrusters see further use. Better to vent compressed gasses and neutralize powerful engines than to have them explode.

He also had to cut off the ES system as Mohamed swung the ship around the front of Symphony Hall so he could drop the gangway. That at least gave Ravenell a chance to shoot at the gathering enemies on the ground during their final approach. "Okay, that's it," Everett announced. "Everybody off the boat as soon as we land."

"Chief," spoke up Sinclair at the ops station, "the fleet's still got five minutes before they get to the drone net." He pulled the release on his safety restraints and rose from his seat, grabbing his rifle and comms unit backpack on his way out.

"Then let's hope our back-up gets here in six minutes," said Everett, vacating the bridge right behind him. He paused only to let Mohamed out before pulling the hatch shut.

A much rougher and louder series of blows shook the yacht as several more infantry-scale missiles blasted through the bridge canopy. *Mansa Musa* was no longer a moving target, nor was her hull enhanced by the defensive systems. The force of the explosion blew the hatch open and nearly took the whole thing off its hinges. It also sent Everett falling against Mohamed, bringing both men to the deck.

Sinclair stumbled, but kept to his feet. His ears rang and his head hurt like hell despite the noise baffles and other protections of his helmet. He saw his comrades on the deck through the smoke and went back for them. Mohamed picked himself up and joined Sinclair in hauling Everett away before anything else hit the bridge.

"I'm okay," said Everett. "Get moving!"

Despite the chief's order, Sinclair hesitated long enough to look Everett over. He saw plenty of frayed fabric and burn marks along the back of the chief's combat jacket and the legs of his vac suit, along with a small dent in the back of his helmet, but no blood or punctures. Rising up onto one knee, Everett repeated, "Go! I'm behind you! Move!"

Sinclair obeyed. The gangway wasn't far. He heard the noises of combat as he reached the exit, saw a bullet ricochet off the scorched surface of Symphony Hall's roof, and knew he had to take his chances on the way out. He sprinted down the gangway to join up with Ravenell, who fired his big repeating laser over the edge of the roof.

Ravenell occupied a good spot. A concrete planter holding a still-burning tree trunk shielded him on one side. The armored body of a NorthStar Ranger lay propped up against the rooftop crenellation in front of him for added protection. Lasers streaked past from below. Most either burned against the edge of the roof or flew high over their heads. It was the bullet ricochets that concerned him. They didn't come from ground level.

God damn it, Sinclair thought, his eyes sweeping the towers looming all around them while Ravenell fired over the edge of the roof with his repeater. *Snipers everywhere*. Smoke from *Mansa Musa*'s wounds and the destroyed aircars on the landing platform at the rooftop's center obscured much of the skyline on their rear. The aftereffects of the chaff strike over the roof would still interfere with most targeting systems. Even so, Ravenell seemed awfully exposed. "How are you not dead already?" he asked.

"Fuller!" Ravenell answered.

"What?" Then the distinct *whump* of an infantry missile clarified Ravenell's answer. A streak of orange light flew up from the nearest corner of the roof to the top of another nearby building. As soon as it registered in Sinclair's mind, the missile exploded, blasting two bodies off the building's edge. Sinclair back-traced the missile's trail to see Fuller roll out from behind the smoking wreckage of an aircar. She held the collapsible, magazine-fed launcher against her chest rather than resting on her shoulder for firing.

"How many more?" she called to Ravenell.

"Don't worry about it!" he yelled back. "I've got Avery. Bal's on the other side. Go help him." Fuller didn't stop to nod, instead rushing off to join Baljashanpreet on the other side of the roof.

Though he wanted to help Ravenell pin down the enemy in the plaza below, Sinclair had other priorities. He tapped a couple of keys on the holocom on his wrist to bring up a screen from the comms unit on his back. Civilian media channels sent out only emergency warnings. Sinclair also heard the recognizable screech of military scramblers, meaning he'd found NorthStar's frequencies but couldn't get anything useful out of them. Most importantly, he picked up nothing from the ground team's comms net. The check only took a few seconds and a couple of holographic keystrokes. With another command, Sinclair prioritized an automatic search for anything from the ground team. Then he turned back to the battle.

Looking over the edge, Sinclair found plenty to shoot at. A battered and burned rover sat directly below. NorthStar Security troops moved in around the edges of the plaza beyond the rover, clearly reluctant to charge out into the open where Ravenell might bring them down. More than a few uniformed bodies lay in the plaza, but they didn't catch his attention as much as the group of live troopers bunched up off to his left. He focused his fire on them. "Looks like the others made it inside," he said hopefully. "I guess the bad guys aren't holding off to hear our demands."

"Get on the comm and tell 'em I want my money back!" suggested Ravenell.

Sinclair almost laughed, but he knew how grim their situation was. Unlike the others, he'd seen the skies on the yacht's sensors. Help had to get through a fleet that controlled space around Fairhaven.

More armed troops poured in on the ground below. On the bright side, the local police kept busy evacuating nearby buildings and cordoning off the area rather than joining the fight. Unfortunately, that also meant every one of those buildings might soon become a giant sniper nest. "We can't stay up here long," Sinclair thought aloud.

"No, we can't," agreed Ravenell. "We gotta know—"

"How are we doing?" asked Everett as he arrived. His tattered clothing still gave the impression of serious injury, but he sounded fine.

"Stretched thin," Ravenell explained. "I've got Fuller and Bal covering the south side and we're holding here for now. Need someone on the south and west."

"Mohamed's on the south," said Everett. "Sinclair, you hear anything from inside? I've got nothing."

"Not yet. I think the hall has privacy bafflers or something. I might be able to talk to our guys if I can move inside."

"Well, nobody's coming up from inside, so—shit, Sinclair, are you hurt? Ravenell?" The chief looked from one to the other with sudden urgency and then down at the rooftop surface between them.

"No, I'm okay," said Ravenell.

"I'm fine," Sinclair answered, looking down to follow Everett's gaze. He realized that he and Ravenell occupied a spot slightly bare of the soot and ash that covered much of the rest of their surroundings.

Blood filled some of that gap. He also noted a trail leading back toward the center of the rooftop.

"Ravenell, you have this covered?" Everett asked.

His first answer was another long burst from his repeater, momentarily quelling the laser fire from one corner of the plaza. "Long as they're out of missiles," Ravenell noted. "Once they get heavier back-up, we're in real trouble."

"Okay, I'm gonna go cover the east," said Everett. "Sinclair, I don't like sending anyone alone, but we gotta find out what's going on downstairs."

• • •

Security agents rushed to guard the doors to the audience hall. One of Pedroso's men stepped up to the podium, warning the audience with his natural commanding voice to stay put where it was safe.

O'Neal, Pedroso, Brekhov, and a pack of bodyguards did the exact opposite. They made it to the backstage stairwell entrance as the guards in the lobby reported fighting. The doors remained on lockdown, but O'Neal's team carried all the override codes they needed and bumper units in case codes weren't good enough. As soon as the entourage started up the stairs, though, they heard the news: "Rooftop detail is down. I say again, Rooftop detail is down!"

"What the hell happened up there?" demanded Pedroso.

O'Neal's personal holocom buzzed with an alarm. So did everyone else's. For those who hadn't carefully managed every detail of their audio settings, the alarm came with a spoken warning: "Civil defense alert! Civil defense alert! Please shelter in place!"

"Is the whole planet under attack?" someone asked incredulously.

"They couldn't be hitting the surface already!" another agent countered. "Not without—"

"It's a coordinated attack," Pedroso snapped as if it should be obvious to all. "We can't get out in the air, anyway. It's too vulnerable."

"Out the way we came, then," decided O'Neal. "Across the street and then we hit the rail car. Move! Let's go!"

• • •

With his gun cleared and ready, Tanner rolled back into the doorway to rejoin the fight inside. More gunfire from above rained down on the street behind him. Ravenell, Sinclair, and the rest brought larger and heavier weapons than the ground team. Tanner heard the boom of grenades and worse in the plaza as he focused on the lobby.

Janeka had shifted back from the plasma carbine to her rifle for its faster rate of fire and longer range. She covered Alicia's spot, making sure that no harm could come to her without significant risk. Alicia, in turn, brought down another of the troopers by the landing of the stairway to Tanner's far right with a burst from her rifle. The bar was a shambles. She wouldn't be able to stay there much longer.

"Gunny," he began, but she was well ahead of him.

"We're moving in!" Janeka declared. She slung her rifle over her shoulder, switching back to the plasma carbine now that Tanner could cover Alicia. Fire support from the rooftop meant they could push in with their backs covered. "Baldwin! Bhatia! Pull in!"

The pair abandoned their spots at either end of the rover. Sanjay slipped up behind Janeka. Baldwin stood over Tanner. "What's the plan?" asked Baldwin.

"Most of 'em are on our left," said Janeka. "The audience hall will be straight through those doors across the lobby, probably with a small room in between. Still a bunch of guards in there. Wong's got the right mostly anchored. You move in to the right, fire to left and center. Don't get bogged down. We need to push through and take over. Malone, you hear all that?"

Tanner fired a burst into an overturned table and thought he saw an arm flail around on the other side. "Yeah, something about shooting everyone and not dying?"

The gunny rolled her eyes. "Yes."

"On it!"

"You two," said Janeka, "go!"

They made their move. Sanjay and Baldwin rushed in while Tanner held back to pin down the men on the other side of the vestibule doors up ahead. The other two fired away at the remaining opposition as they moved, most of it to the left of the entrance as Janeka warned. The wreck of the chandelier in the center of the room provided a halfway marker and an attractive bit of cover. They'd almost made it there when Sanjay let out a cry and tumbled forward, clutching his abdomen.

"Damn!" grunted Baldwin. She practically jumped on top of him in a protective crouch as another trooper leaned around the vestibule doors to finish them both off. Baldwin put him down with a frantic burst from her rifle, but she couldn't do much about the others.

A loud, fearsome roar and a dark longcoat swept by them both to handle that problem. Janeka ran headlong for the doors up ahead, blowing a hole straight through one of them and the man behind it before she crashed into the wreckage. Baldwin couldn't see her after that, though she heard screams and more gunfire. Aware of the other threats in the lobby, Baldwin looked out to the left flank. She saw that Tanner hadn't quite followed the gunny's instructions to the letter, either.

He ran directly along the inside of the wall facing the plaza, moving around the cover provided by the lobby's sculptures, indoor plants and overturned furniture to fire at the men and women lurking behind it all. Tanner took out two of them in his rush before the rest even spotted the threat. More fell before they could pin him down. By the time Tanner reached the far corner, putting himself behind their remaining foes, Baldwin took advantage of his distraction to bring more down with her rifle. The crossfire lasted only seconds. Tanner crouched in the corner, blasting away until he had no one left to shoot through the hazy smoke of burnt bodies and scorched carpeting.

His heart pounded hard. He hadn't fully expected to pull that off. Tanner's eyes swept the lobby. He saw Baldwin crouched over Sanjay, Alicia slipping out from the wrecked bar but still firing at the last of the bad guys on the far right, and no Janeka at all—just a breached door and flashes of red and orange light on the other side that suddenly stopped.

Tanner bolted for the open door.

"Sanjay?" Baldwin nudged the tall young man lying on the ground in front of her, hunched over with his arms tucked under his torso. She got her hands around his sides and rolled him over. His groan gave her hope. "Sanjay!"

"Hurts," he groaned.

"Oh thank God, you're still alive." She saw a gash in his sleeve and blood flowing from his wrist and suspected his arms covered something worse. "Let me see," she said, taking hold of both wrists.

"Ow, Jesus," he winced at her less than gentle treatment.

Baldwin sniffled. "Shut up and let me…" She patted his heavy shirt and felt the stiff material of the body armor underneath, finding creases and seeing holes in the fabric, but little blood. It seemed the only bleeding came from his forearm. "I think you're okay," she assured him, touching his face.

"Why are you so upset?"

"Oh for—how fucking obvious do I have to get? I like you, jerk!" she snapped, dropping his wounded arm. "I think you're hot."

Sanjay winced. "Ow! Wait, really?"

"Yes! Jesus, do I have to wear a sign? You never had women flirt with you?"

"Sure, but…I thought maybe you were cozying up so you could bust me or something."

Baldwin's jaw dropped. "Wait, what the hell would I be trying to bust you for?"

"I dunno. Stuff."

"Is he okay?" Alicia shouted from the bar between rifle bursts. "We've still got a fight here!"

Baldwin grabbed his shoulder and tugged him up. "No time for arguing. We're going out later," she warned.

"Uh…you're buying, right? You make more money than me."

Passing the conversation behind before it even began, Tanner burst through the vestibule doors with his rifle at the ready. The space was considerably darker than the lobby and just as hazy with smoke rising from the bodies that littered the floor. Tanner spun in an arc from one side to the other, finding no standing targets until he brought his weapon almost all the way around. Someone grabbed his rifle by the barrel and tugged it aside.

Janeka's firm demeanor seemed strained for the first time. "Breathe," she counseled, and then coughed and stumbled forward into him.

Tanner caught her. She was wet with blood. "Gunny?"

"'m fine," she said, though she clearly wasn't. Tanner felt the hole in her upper sleeve and saw a gash under her collarbone. "Just breathe."

"The air in here's terrible," he replied.

"Oh." She straightened up and stood on her own, though Tanner suspected it took more than a little willpower. "That's the problem." He could see her resolve return, even if the power in her voice didn't. "Couple shots to the ribs, too. I'll be alright."

Another vestibule door flew open behind Tanner. He realized Janeka had it covered, her plasma carbine up and level around his hip, but it was unnecessary. Alicia wasn't a threat.

Janeka glanced from one to the other, tilted her head toward the next set of doors, and stepped aside. "The place is on lockdown," she grunted.

Alicia stepped up, blasted downward against a locking panel much as Jacobson had at the entrance, and kicked the door. She dropped back and crouched, bringing her rifle up again to meet any threat while Tanner covered the other side. They heard only the frightened yelps and commotion of a broad, deep, crowded hall where thousands of unarmed civilians hid behind their seats.

No shots came their way, but that assured them of nothing. "Big room," said Alicia. "I dunno how we can manage a crowd like that without more people."

"I do," said Janeka. "Malone."

He took a breath, kept his weapon at the ready, and walked out into the back of the audience hall. Gasps and even whimpers came from the closest rows. He saw frightened faces and even some tearful eyes.

These people watched the news, or at least got the company shareholder letters. They'd seen all the PR stuff and heard the propaganda.

No one had any trouble recognizing him.

"Everyone," called out the man at the podium, "stay in your seats and remain calm." He held up his empty hands as he gave his instructions, watching Tanner and Alicia move together down one aisle while Janeka, Sanjay, and Baldwin split off to walk down the other.

The audience followed the first order. The second was a little unrealistic.

"This is crazy, they're all crazy—"

"Can't believe this is happening."

"It'll be alright, just stay behind me."

Tanner rolled his eyes as he walked down the aisle. "Get over yourselves," he grumbled. None of the audience members looked ready to make any trouble. He noted as he scanned the room that some seemed more collected and protective than the chivalrous guy to his left, but less showy about it. Naval intelligence warned that some of these people would bring professional bodyguards. Still, a bodyguard would protect his or her client above all else. In a situation like this, fading into the crowd and being just another face was the best defense.

One man who fit the bodyguard image rose with his hands up as Tanner and Alicia came near his aisle. "Can I go home if I ask nicely?"

Tanner blinked before he remembered the countersign: "Not without a note from your mother."

"Funny you should say so," the man replied. He clenched one hand, activating a screen from the holocom in the ring on his finger. Tanner naturally recognized the flag of Michael. He reached behind his back, produced a spare laser pistol and handed it off to the intelligence ministry agent. "What do we call you?"

"I'm Paul," said the man, checking the weapon's power settings as he stepped out into the aisle. "There's one other with me. Julia, right over there," he added, gesturing to another agent stepping out into the open. "Not sure if there are any others."

"Got at least one more back there," said Alicia. She gestured to what looked like the same conversation between another suited man and Janeka, Baldwin, and Sanjay farther back along the opposite aisle. Unsurprisingly, the gunny declined when he offered his hand to help her walk. "Where's Brekhov?" Alicia asked.

"They pulled him off the stage as soon as the first boom hit. I think they got a few seconds' warning before that. Something went wrong."

• • •

Sinclair headed straight for the access door in the middle of the battered roof. Taking the corner carefully, Sinclair found only an open door and stairs leading down. Dead troopers lay atop one another along the last few steps. Several holes burned through the door explained their presence. Sinclair wondered if the top floor had already been cleared from within.

A trail of blood ran along the stairs. Whether it led up or down, he couldn't tell.

The hallway at the bottom showed few signs of combat aside from the door. Sinclair moved steadily on through, grateful for the carpet that muffled his steps and the plentiful office windows—some demolished and providing good sight lines, others holding firm and offering reflective views around the corners. Seeing no danger, nor hearing anything other than the sounds of gunfire outside, Sinclair pressed on until he found the body of a NorthStar trooper around the next corner.

The dead man lay near an open office door. That trail of blood from the rooftop seemed to end here, though he didn't find a body to match. It didn't seem to belong to the dead NorthStar trooper.

Broken words crackled into his ear from the receiver inside his helmet. He'd been right about the privacy bafflers, though the lingering effects of the chaff explosions outside likely made it all worse. He needed to push farther into the building.

Sinclair moved into the office, curious about the flickering lights inside and not wanting to leave any surviving enemies behind to sneak up on him. He immediately understood what happened within: someone took out everyone in the office from inside the doorway. Holocom screens and hardware terminals still glowed, though their owners lay dead beside them.

Recognizing some of the gear, Sinclair rushed in to sort out what he could still work with. Not all of the security cameras still fed into this room, but he could see the audience hall and the lobby on a couple surviving screens. He saw his friends move in through the aisles while the shareholders huddled in their seats. An overturned security monitor provided a full building layout complete with color-coded lights showing breached and secured doors.

Someone had set the building into lockdown. Every entrance remained sealed apart from the doors blown open in the lobby and the rooftop...and a door backstage leading to an access corridor nearby. Sinclair quickly found an appropriate security camera to see a pack of men and women in suits rushing down the hall.

One of them had an instantly recognizable face.

Sinclair switched over to his own holocom, maximizing the broadcast strength of his comms unit. "Ground team, this is Sinclair!" he said, frantically looking around for whatever might manage the Hall's privacy bafflers. It had to be up here somewhere. "Ground team, Sinclair! I have eyes on the primary! He went out the south backstage door! Do you read?"

He kicked debris out of his way and checked every live terminal and holo screen he could find. Some were locked. Others were useless.

He didn't notice the reflective flash in the window across the street from the office.

"Ground team, Sinclair!" He repeated, and then finally spotted what he needed. The monitor teetered on the edge of its desk. Sinclair straightened it and keyed up the menu to kill the baffles. "Ground team, Sinclair! If you hear me, wave a hand! I see you on the security cameras!" On the other monitor across the room, he saw Tanner and Janeka respond. He didn't wait for them to speak.

"Brekhov went out a backstage door! South side! There's a hall, he's headed for a tunnel to the building across the street!"

On the security monitor, he saw Tanner and Alicia take off running for the stage. Sinclair continued. "He's got a bunch of bodyguards with him, and—"

The rifle that killed him from the building across the street benefited from a full optic suite. The gun automatically accounted for the resistance of two thick windows along with the distance from barrel to target. Its user had hit harder targets than this on his own, but the computer helped him bring Sinclair down with a single shot. The bullet caught him in the side, tearing a fatal hole through Sinclair's right arm, ribcage, and both lungs.

Sinclair collapsed on top of a desk, unable to catch enough breath to call for help as the world went black.

• • •

"Shit," Alicia hissed, then gave Tanner a nod. "C'mon, let's—"

"Ground team, Sinclair," called a voice over their earpieces. "If you hear me, wave a hand! I see you on camera!"

Tanner looked up reflexively, waving one arm at nothing in particular. Janeka seemed to do the same. "Brekhov went out a backstage door!" Sinclair shouted urgently. "South side! There's a hall, he's headed for a tunnel to the building across the street!"

"Go!" ordered Janeka from the back of the audience. "Wong, Malone, go! We'll keep this under control! Go!"

They took off running. Tanner hauled himself onto the stage, pausing only to shout out one thought: "Put Baldwin on crowd control!" With that, he and Alicia were gone.

Accompanied by one of the Ministry's undercover agents, Baldwin walked down the opposite aisle with a fierce scowl. The petite young woman met every gaze with a dark glare as she got to the stage, rising up the steps on its left side. "What's your name?" she asked of the suited man at the podium.

"Taggart," he answered readily. "Miles Taggart."

"Are you in charge?"

"More or less. At least of security."

Baldwin's expression darkened further. She looked out at the audience. "Do I even need to make a speech?" she asked loudly.

No one responded. No one even moved.

"Do I?" she repeated, somehow even louder than before.

Thousands of heads shook back and forth. Several people murmured "No." She might possibly have even heard one or two people call her "ma'am."

Toward the back of the audience, Janeka let out a quiet grunt. "She's talented."

CHAPTER THIRTEEN

Sacrifice

"Having successfully completed all the requirements of references (a), (b), and (c), you are hereby designated as a qualified Duty Helmsman of ANS Beowulf. This marks the first step in full qualification as an Officer of the Deck (OOD). Remaining steps include qualification as Communications Watch Officer, Operations Watch Officer, Fire Control Officer, and In-Port Officer of the Deck before your final board examination as OOD. While this process may seem long and arduous, take heart in the knowledge that you are now proficient in skills vital to any bridge officer."

--Personal Training Record,
Ensign Nathan Spencer, July 2279

"Archangel Fleet, this is Commodore Prescott. I don't think I need to point out that you are outnumbered and heavily outgunned. Unless you're here to return that battleship and the other vessels you've stolen, I suggest you turn around. Threat gestures do not amuse us. If you come within range, we will fire."

"She sounds cranky," observed Booker once the broadcast cut out. He sat strapped into the starboard side command chair on *Joan of Arc*'s bridge opposite Kelly to port, with Montes in the fold-out battle stations seat at the helm in between them. It had taken until after the Battle of Raphael for someone to decide a corvette's bridge needed more chairs during combat. The "seats" were little more than collapsible armatures that folded into the nearest consoles, but they were better than nothing.

"Yeoh will shut her down," replied Kelly. She watched the tactical screens at her chair. One showed a head-on view. The other displayed an "overhead" extrapolation of the same. In under two minutes, the attack fleet would hit Fairhaven's first line of defense: a drone net twice as big as anything Archangel could manage even before the war. Though the drones' light armaments presented a minor threat to a warship, they extended the danger zone created by Fairhaven's natural gravity well for anything traveling faster than light.

The real threat came from the ships waiting on the other side of that line. The battleship *Perseus* and her escorts lay dead ahead of *Beowulf* and her fleet. As the commodore warned, NorthStar's forces were indeed bigger and more numerous. *Perseus* lay at the center of a large formation of ships: a cruiser to her left and right, one destroyer above her and another below, with a third destroyer and a couple of frigates out in front. A second similar formation waited nearby with the cruiser *McNaught* at its center for lack of another battleship. Even with all of that, still more ships lay nearby, with corvettes littered around both formations and several combat-converted liners waiting in the rear.

"They're holding tight on their side of the line," said Kelly. "They've gotta expect some sort of trick if we're coming at them with half their number of ships."

"They aren't wrong," pointed out Booker.

"Look how much they've stacked up their backfield. That's a whole destroyer squadron and three loose frigates, too. They see us all clear as day, but they're still holding a big reserve. It's like they *expect* us to sucker them somehow, so they're keeping a safety net ready."

"You think they know our plan? Even if the main body is distracted, that second line is gonna be a big problem for us if they stay put."

Kelly shook her head. "I think they know Yeoh is in command again and they don't want a repeat of Raphael…and we should use that." She reached for her personal comms panel and hit a button. "Miguel, you there?" she called out to the captain of *St. George* just off *Joan*'s starboard wing.

"What do you think, Lyn?" came Lieutenant Duran's voice before another transmission caught both his attention and that of *Joan*'s bridge.

"Commodore Prescott, I believe you know who I am," said Admiral Yeoh. "Your employers have had two years to come to their senses. It's too late to talk your way out of this now."

Kelly couldn't hold back her grin, but she stayed on the task at hand. "I think we can't shoot straight through as planned. Even if *St. Nicholas* and the others on the far wings draw off some trouble, it's not gonna be enough. We won't get through to the surface until they commit more of that second line."

She could almost hear Duran wince. "You want to get stuck in with everyone else?"

"For a minute at least, yeah."

"Alright, what do we do?"

"I'll tie you into my tactical here and you'll see. Montes," she said, leaving the channel open for her sister ship's benefit, "we're going high on this plane, then we dive in at *Perseus*, okay?"

"Ma'am?" Montes blinked.

"Straight down on 'em. Evasive speed."

"Holy shit," hissed Montes.

"Yup," Booker grunted, calling up options on his controls he knew he'd need soon. "Command," he said on another channel, "this is Airborne One. We are joining Paranoia Pass for our initial run. I say again, we are joining Paranoia Pass."

"Guns, you there?" asked Kelly.

"I'm here, ma'am," said Ordoñez, sounding considerably more intrigued by this plan than everyone else.

"Get the cannon ready for rapid cycles. Sometimes direct shots, sometimes wide to clear us a path. I trust you to decide. We may burn the gun out but not before we deliver some pain. You'll know your targets when you see 'em, understood?"

"Aye aye, ma'am!" Ordoñez all but cheered.

Booker shook his head. "She's really not right," he muttered.

"XO—" Kelly began.

"I'm ready," he assured her, pulling down his faceplate. "Turrets," he said to *Joan*'s three other gunners, "I'm feeding you priorities. You are weapons free."

"Montes," said Kelly, "I'm gonna draw lines on the tactical screen, but you're the driver. Use your own judgment, okay? Don't wait on me to tell you to dodge and don't feel like you have to follow my course exactly. If you get us there, that's all that matters. I trust you."

The younger woman hesitated. "Yes, ma'am."

"Montes. If I thought I was the better helmsman, I'd take over."

"Yes, ma'am."

Kelly and Montes dropped the faceplates of their helmets. The captain drew a course for her helmsman before taking control of *Joan*'s offensive missile targeting system. Booker had control of the chaff launchers, while the senior ops specialist watched the big picture. *Joan*'s remaining crew stood by in engineering, turrets, or the cargo bay.

"Ten seconds to break," warned Booker.

"Montes?"

"I'm ready, ma'am," Montes replied with resolve, if not confidence.

"Five…four…three…"

• • •

NorthStar's formations held firm as Archangel's armada approached. While the defenders kept their biggest ships at the center of spherical formations, *Beowulf* came in as the front of a wedge. Archangel's battleship headed straight in for a confrontation with *Perseus*. With less than a minute before contact, *Los Angeles* swung around from *Beowulf*'s right to join the cruiser *Halley* on her left, creating a stronger line against NorthStar's second big formation as the two largest ships on the field faced off.

Gambling that the enemy would not break from their course, NorthStar's larger ships turned their sides to the attackers, allowing each to bring the greatest number of weapons to bear. Yeoh chose that moment to release half of her corvettes in a wild spread around the defending formations. The smaller ships kicked into rapid acceleration, pairing off and flying high, low, and to the extreme left and right of the enemy.

The shooting began as soon as the corvettes came within range of NorthStar's drone net. Lasers flashed and missiles flew. Though the drones had little hope of bringing down any of the corvettes, fleet engagements always came down to a struggle of attrition. Even small threats couldn't be ignored. Several drones landed early hits, but then the main body of Archangel's fleet opened fire at long distance and easily tore a hole through the net. The corvettes did their part to widen that gap, then turned inward on the defending fleet.

• • •

Lasers flashed at the corvette as soon as she came within range, but *Joan* accelerated and spiraled upward from her initial course before her bridge crew saw the lights. *St. George* followed close behind. Their sudden maneuver mirrored that of the other lead corvettes of the armada. While the larger ships punched holes in the drone net from tens of thousands of kilometers away, the corvettes broke off, went into evasive, and curved halfway around the enemy fleet before turning back in on *Perseus* and her closer allies.

The initial hits to *Joan* inflicted little more than cosmetic damage. Her reflective hull and ES systems could withstand worse. The corvette flew in a steep arc that brought her away from the main battle as the two fleets opened up on one another. Two of NorthStar's corvettes broke away from the rest to chase *Joan* and *St. George*. Fire from both the new pursuers and the drone net intensified until Kelly barked, "Now!"

Nothing could turn on a dime while traveling at such a speed, but *Joan* came surprisingly close. *Shepherd* and *Chinook*, the two NorthStar corvettes, now spat out chaff missiles in a panicked attempt to ward off a counterattack that never came. *Joan of Arc* shot right between them both.

St. George followed right behind, catching *Shepherd* with a solid blast of her main gun that tore the enemy corvette's port wing from her hull. *Chinook* turned to starboard to avoid a similar fate. *St. George*'s secondary turret gunners fired more parting shots. *Shepherd* soon suffered a pair of explosions that broke her into a dozen pieces.

"There!" counseled Kelly, drawing a new line for Montes on her display. "Go there—" she urged until *Joan of Arc* shuddered from a detonation right along the course that Montes plainly ignored. "Or do what you want," Kelly offered and turned back to her targeting screen.

Up ahead, the destroyer *Callisto* floated hundreds of kilometers above *Perseus*. The screens made the ships look much closer together than they really were. Like the rest of the battle group, the ships had turned to present their sides to the oncoming Archangel forces.

Joan and *St. George* dove straight down on them. The battleship concentrated most of her fire on *Beowulf* and her escorts. The destroyer's job was to act as a screen against threats to the battleship. *Callisto* shifted her focus from the Archangel fleet to the approaching corvettes, surrounding both with a spray of lasers and explosive shells from her defense turrets. *St. George* veered off. *Joan* twisted, sporadically accelerated, and continued on.

"Guns! Hit it!" Kelly ordered. A broad flash of red light shot from *Joan* against *Callisto*, doing little harm to the destroyer itself but vaporizing much of the clutter of explosive shells and chaff debris from *Callisto*'s defenses. "Again!" Kelly shouted. This time Ordoñez fired a tighter beam, though she only tagged *Callisto*'s edge as the ship maneuvered clear. *Joan*'s turrets joined in, raining more fire down on the enemy, but ultimately doing little harm. Even a big ship could be a hard target at such speeds.

Callisto's weapons managed to tag *Joan* as the ships passed one another by. A laser flashed across *Joan*'s underside, causing an explosion that rattled the ship. Everyone heard the brief, panicked scream that cut short with a second jolt as air and metal burst from *Joan*'s belly turret, along with its gunner.

"Gene!" cried Montes in shock.

"Stay on it!" Kelly urged her. "We can't go back! You've gotta stay in this!"

"Oh god, I should've—"

"You're doing all you can!" Kelly shared a knowing glance with Booker. Losing the turret was bad. Losing the crewman running it *hurt*. Still, the blast had only grazed Joan's underside. Had it struck the cargo bay directly, it could have been catastrophic. Both officers knew they were lucky to have Montes at the helm.

A second later, *Joan* rushed past *Callisto* to continue on straight for *Perseus*. Booker madly fired off chaff missiles behind *Joan* to cover her back from the destroyer. Once again, defensive clutter intensified as *Joan* drew close. She became an even harder target when Kelly unexpectedly ordered, "Montes, slow it down hard!"

Maneuvering jets embedded all along *Joan*'s bow and the fronts of her wings fired while her main thrusters dropped out. The sudden drop in speed saved *Joan* from a great blast of missiles and lasers from *Perseus* timed to catch her. For a brief instant, the void of space in front of *Joan* turned red and orange with explosions. She couldn't remotely come to a halt, though—something her skipper counted on.

"Guns!" called Kelly. Another broad flash of cannon fire cleared the way. "Attack speed!" Kelly ordered, and an instant later *Joan* accelerated once more. "Get in close enough to board. Ordoñez, hit 'em again. Montes, slow a little, enough to make 'em blink—yes! Now burn! Burn!"

The big ship's defensive guns contracted their fields of fire. She spat out more chaff missiles that detonated less than a hundred kilometers from her hull, creating an almost impenetrable blanket of white hot debris. That wasn't all *Perseus* did to protect herself, though. Fearing a boarding action, *Perseus* rolled off of her course, throwing her out of synch with her escorts.

"Suckers!" Kelly declared. *Joan* blew straight past. Her real target now lay dead ahead. *Ganymede*, the battleship's other escort destroyer, had almost no time to react to the unexpected threat. *Joan*'s main gun blazed a trail, cutting into the destroyer's hull and incinerating launchers and defense turrets. The decisive blows came from her missile tubes, though, as Kelly fired off two shots and then two more in quick succession.

The first two may have been enough for the job. *Ganymede*'s guns didn't catch either in time. The blasts rocked the destroyer mercilessly and tore gaps in her defenses. The second pair made it all the way through to strike against *Ganymede*'s hull.

Montes pulled away as soon as she saw the first blast, though at such a speed and short range, the corvette couldn't escape everything. A frightening shudder overtook the entire ship, cutting out holo screens and overwhelming sensors while debris struck against the hull. Someone screamed in pain over the ship's internal comms net. "Engineering! Report!" shouted Booker.

For a heartbeat, then another, *Joan* flew on with her bridge almost completely dark. Then the tactical and enhanced-visual screens projected against her canopy returned and other systems came back to life. Fairhaven lay dead ahead. None of NorthStar's reserve ships stood in the way.

A quick look at the rest of the battle revealed exactly the tangled mess Yeoh wanted. The enemy was so concerned about losing battleships and cruisers to boarding actions that they jumped as soon as they saw the threat. Yeoh knew she couldn't get away with the same trick twice. Paranoia Pass only intended to take advantage of the fear. The enemy had broken formation to prevent feigned boarding attempts by numerous corvettes, *Joan of Arc* included. Thinking Yeoh had revealed her hand, the reserves joined the battle.

Now it only fell to *Beowulf* and the larger ships to make the most of the disruption. *Joan of Arc* had other priorities.

"XO, it's Baker," answered a woman's voice. "The chief's down. I don't know how bad yet. We're working on a hull puncture. I think the engines are fine. Hunk of something went straight between 'em."

Kelly hit a button on her control console. "*Beowulf*, this is *Joan of Arc*. We made a hole for you. Good luck." She sat back against her seat to allow herself a single breath.

"We keep going, Montes," counseled Booker. The XO's reach extended far enough to get his hand on the helmsman's shoulder. "No time for it now. Don't think about who you lost. Concentrate on who you can still save. We aren't done yet."

Montes nodded. "Yeah. Okay."

"Let's get to it," said Kelly. "Take us into the atmosphere."

• • •

The last six minutes until contact felt endless. Then the shooting started, and Nathan wondered how six minutes could have passed so quickly.

The gap created by the destruction of *Ganymede* made *Beowulf*'s path an obvious choice. She came low against her foe, trusting her escorts to deal with their counterparts while *Beowulf* accepted the greater threat of *Perseus* and the cruisers to either side of her.

One of those cruisers shook off her fear of the corvettes faster than the other. *Donati* and *Beowulf* threw missiles and heavy laser beams at one another. Nearby frigates on both sides sent in even more ordnance to protect their respective allies, creating a tremendous spread of explosions and light. Missiles burst before striking their targets. Lasers flashed past their mark. Distance, speed, and the havoc created by one explosion after another threw off dozens of targeting systems.

The comms station was promptly swamped with alerts, calls for damage control, casualty reports, and more. Nothing came in as clearly as it should, speaking to both the powerful interference put out by the enemy's signal jammers and the chaos of combat. Nathan soon understood why *Beowulf* needed such a large comms watch. The ship required this many people to make sure nothing got missed.

The jolts and tremors that passed through the ship challenged Nathan's nerves as well as his hearing. He remembered the pirate attack on the *Pride of Polaris* all too well, but that had been only one ship against another. *Beowulf* took fire from more ships than she could accurately count, thanks to all the chaff and other disruptions. Interceptions and deflections made for a constant rumble punctuated by the occasional solid hit.

Nathan wondered if this was what earthquakes were like. *Except earthquakes don't deliberately try to kill people.*

"Shuttle bay is breached!" called out one of the signalmen at his post. "Compartment vented. We've got casualties. DC team two en route."

"Defense turret five is jammed. They're clearing."

"Fire on deck seven, starboard—it's the enlisted rec room."

"Tell 'em to seal it off and leave it," said Perez. "It'll choke itself out. We've got bigger problems. Spencer," she said, turning briefly to him, "work with Rogozinski there on the Oscar channels."

"Oscar?" Nathan blinked, and then felt an all new stone in his gut. *Oh holy shit*, he thought. He turned to the enlisted signalman on his left and touched his sleeve to establish a direct comms channel between them. He discovered that Rogozinski was busy already.

"—got your frequency and your position, okay? Hang tight. There's nothing else you can do right now anyway. We'll get to you. *Beowulf* out." Rogozinski looked up. "Sir?"

"How can I help?"

The signalman's second class insignia and bloodstripes suggested that he had plenty of experience. He certainly knew not to assume too much about an ensign's training. "Sir, you know the drill for going 'overboard.' We're the other end of it. This band is for anyone stranded or overboard," he said, gesturing to his screen. A duplicate appeared at Nathan's station. "We respond as soon as we see a new signal. The computer logs the connection so we don't lose it, but they need to hear a human voice. Get their ID and status and say we'll get to 'em when we can. If you've got the time, talk 'em through the standard safety check. There's a cheat sheet right here if you forget. Don't stay on too long with any one person, though. The board might get crowded."

Nathan looked over the status screen as Rogozinski explained. "We've already got three guys overboard?"

"We're looking after more than our own boat. *St. Andrew*'s gone, sir. Three survivors is a fucking miracle."

That drew Nathan's eyes to the tactical board floating between himself and Perez as a sharp, serious jolt hit the ship. *Donati* and *Perseus* held their positions and kept firing. The disruptive mess of debris and signal jamming between combatants mattered less with each passing moment. Another missile broke through the cloud of fire and lasers to blow up near *Beowulf*'s port side on the aft quarter, shaking the whole ship yet again. The comms section erupted once more with damage warnings and new calls for aid.

"Pick a signal, sir!" Rogozinski urged, and then hit an indicator on his own screen to do the same. "This is *Beowulf*. I've got you. Who am I talking to?"

Swallowing hard, Nathan reached out to touch another of the four flashing indicators on his screen. He heard a panicked voice: "—oh God help please I fell please help me!"

"Crewman Wyatt, this is *Beowulf*," said Nathan, reading the text that appeared on his screen. "We've got you. Can you hear me?"

"Yes! I'm outside the ship! I got blown outside! I'm all alone!"

"You're not alone. I've got your signal locked in. The fight's already moving clear of you. We'll pick you up as soon as we can. Are you hurt?"

"I don't...I don't know!"

"Pat yourself down," Nathan instructed, trying hard not to let the fear in Wyatt's voice affect his own. "Remember your training. You've done this before. Check yourself and your suit."

"Okay...okay, I'm doing...oh god, I'm gonna be sick."

"Don't worry about that," said Nathan. "Concentrate on your suit."

"That's easy for you to say! You're not out here!"

Nathan swallowed hard. The other guy wasn't wrong, and he had every reason to be afraid. Another hard blow rattled the bridge as if someone hit the overhead with a giant hammer. Nathan wondered how long Wyatt's point would hold true. "Wyatt, it's what you need to do! Check your suit!"

"I'm okay. I'm okay, I think—wait, I've got a puncture near my boot, but I can take care of it. Ugh, God, I'll go back to church every fuckin' week if you let me live through this, I swear to fuckin' Christ..."

Nathan felt a hand on his shoulder. "Sir," said Rogozinski, "we can't stay with anyone long. You need to move to the next signal." Then the older man turned back to his own work.

"Wyatt, I've gotta move on. Hang in there."

"What? No, don't leave me!"

"We're not leaving you, I've just gotta get to other people."

"Don't leave me!"

Wincing, Nathan cut the audio connection and hit another signal indicator. This time he heard nothing. "Donnington, this is *Beowulf*, do you read?" he asked. "EM1 Donnington. This is *Beowulf*. We've got you on the Oscar board." The next hit against the ship scared Nathan less than the others. The job kept his mind off his fear. "This is *Beowulf*, do you read?"

He heard nothing but the same hiss that seemed to accompany every other signal. Nathan adjusted the balance and then opened a second link to the same channel to see if he might get something clearer with a fresh start. Nothing came. He looked to his newfound mentor. "Rogozinski, I can't hear anything on this signal."

The signalman barely looked at the young ensign as he reached past to hit something else on the control panel. "That means she's dead. Log it here and move on."

Nathan blinked. "Are you kidding? It's been five seconds, we can't—"

"I'm sorry, sir. That's how it is. We've gotta triage. When this is over, we'll pick up everybody we can find, alive or dead. Until then we help who we can reach."

• • •

The *ANS Devout* pulled more than her weight in a fight. Her missiles, though few in number, were no weaker than any other ship's. Her guns did not punch as hard as a destroyer's, but they reached just as far. At 60,000 kilometers behind *Beowulf*, the frigate was small enough and far enough away that the enemy's big ships were reluctant to expend serious firepower on her. The reverse was not the same.

She drove off the destroyer *Callisto*, already damaged by *Joan of Arc*, before the other ship knew who'd shot her full of holes. She crippled the corvette *Greyhound*. Her missiles briefly forced *Donati* off-course to give *Beowulf* a critical break in the fight.

By then, the enemy had realized the damage *Devout* inflicted. *Hanneken*, one of NorthStar's frigates, broke from formation to engage *Devout* head-on. The challenge distracted *Devout* from the real threat. As the frigate turned her guns on *Hanneken* and released a full salvo of missiles, the battleship *Perseus* trained her main guns on *Devout* and fired.

Devout exploded in a single flash before her last missiles reached *Hanneken* to deliver her final blow, so far from her nearest friends that the naked eye would only have seen a brief glimmer of light.

Admiral Yeoh saw *Devout's* last moments from *Beowulf's* flag bridge almost as a matter of luck. With her attention focused mostly on directing *Los Angeles* and *Halley's* standoff against the enemy's second battlegroup, she'd had to leave *Beowulf's* struggle to Admiral Branch and her subordinates. She would not have missed the loss of the frigate, as *Devout's* name remained on her tactical boards as a grey and lifeless reminder, but she could not let the gap in the formation remain. Nor could she let *Devout's* loss go unanswered.

"Commander Beacham," she called out as *Beowulf* trembled from another detonation too close to her hull, "pull *St. Elizabeth* and *St. Joseph* to our rear. Tell them to get rid of that frigate and hold back any other attempts to get around us."

"Aye aye, ma'am," he responded. "They're both damaged, ma'am."

"I know. We'll have to have faith." Yeoh shifted over to another tactical table—gripping it with both hands and grateful for her magnetic boots as the deck trembled—to look over *Beowulf's* struggle. Almost immediately, she saw an opportunity and hit the comm switch that put her in direct contact with *Beowulf's* skipper.

"Admiral," she said once Branch came on the line, "*Devout* put a hole in *Donati*'s defenses. I think *Donati* lost turrets. She's backing off to hide it. A stronger salvo might get through."

"I see what you're saying," replied Branch. "Guns! Put a full-strength missile salvo on *Donati* on my mark! Hook 'em around to her port side. They'll get through."

"As soon as they hit, I want to move straight into *Perseus*," Yeoh explained. "We stay low from their line and give them everything we've got with the main cannons. Can we do it?"

"That other damn cruiser's gonna focus on us as soon as *Donati* is out of the picture. That's still the same problem we've got now."

Yeoh nodded. "I'll have *Resolute* and *Belfast* ready to run interference. They'll give us the time we need to deal with *Perseus*." She looked up to Commander Beacham again, relaying instructions to him as Branch readied his bridge officers for their move.

"On your mark, Admiral," said Yeoh.

On her viewscreen showing the command bridge, Yeoh saw Branch turn to one side. "Guns! Missiles on *Donati*! Fire!" Then she saw him look back to his own tactical screens and heard him blurt out, "Hard to port! Hard to—"

A bright red flash of light cut through the command bridge. Yeoh's compartment lay three decks below and a hundred meters back, but she felt *Beowulf* shake as *Perseus*'s main guns burned through the battleship's hull to wipe away everything on her screen.

The missiles struck *Donati*, evading her weakened defenses to set off a series of explosions that would prove fatal. *Beowulf* could not capitalize on the achievement. Without her captain or anyone at her helm, Archangel's flagship reeled.

• • •

Kelly took for granted that *Joan of Arc* would have a rough ride to Fairhaven's surface. She knew the atmosphere would shake up her ship. Ground-based defenses would do their best to shoot her down. Aside from all that, there would be a wide, lingering spread of sensor-disrupting chaff across the skies to make her descent all the more challenging…if all went well.

She didn't count on being chased.

Montes brought the ship in an arc through the atmosphere over her destination, mostly to bleed off speed. *Joan* looked more like a fireball than a corvette as she streaked across Fairhaven's sky. Her hull was more than up to the challenge of withstanding the heat and friction of high-speed entry. ES systems and reflective metallurgy designed to stand up to heavy lasers provided more than enough protection for such a job. Everyone on board knew that, though any who tried to tell themselves such reassuring facts had trouble hearing it over all the noise. The ship shook with frightening intensity all the way down.

"We're taking fire from below," warned Booker, gripping the ends of his control station.

"How can you tell?" Kelly shouted back. Much of the ground imaging still suffered from chaff interference and battle damage to their sensors. The ship's computer reverted to archival records rather than sort through the mess. Yet despite her dark humor, Kelly saw the trails of missiles shooting up into the sky on *Joan*'s canopy projections.

She also saw the tactical screen displaying the battle beyond Fairhaven's atmosphere. The vast majority of threats lay well outside weapons range—with one exception. The destroyer *Metis* slowed in her pursuit, but she didn't need speed now. Her missiles could easily follow *Joan* all around the globe, though they were no more optimized for flight through air than the destroyer herself. Instead, she availed herself of other options. Lasers flashed to the left and right of the corvette as *Metis* tried to tag her with her light turrets. One successful shot tore open a nine-meter line on *Joan*'s portside wing.

"Shit! Change of plans, Montes," said Kelly. She'd wanted *Joan* to spiral down a little more and then drop in under the edge of the chaff cloud, giving herself a clear look at the scene below before moving in for their final approach. *Metis* revoked that option. Aerodynamics weren't much of a problem for a corvette, but hull integrity was a critical concern during high-speed atmospheric entry. "Take us straight in, right through the chaff cloud. Shortest line you can draw."

"Ma'am, we're not even sure which site to go to!"

"Either we'll spot a mess on the ground or this whole mission is fucked, anyway. Head for the capital and start looking."

"Skipper," said Booker, "that destroyer isn't gonna give us any breaks. Or the ground defenses."

None of her crew could see her frown. "You're right." She then threw a couple of switches on her comms panel. "Lieutenant Thompson. Get your people ready for a rough drop. All hands, prepare to abandon ship. XO, take remote control of the turrets. Ordoñez: looks like you might get to do some more shooting after all."

• • •

"I didn't think we'd be shooting this long," admitted Ravenell. "Shouldn't they have disengaged by now?"

The mission planners had hoped the enemy would adopt a hostage situation response and hold off attempts to take the building by force. That hope had clearly been in vain. NorthStar security troopers took the lead in the battle while the police established a perimeter. Civilians in the vicinity still streamed out of their offices and apartments while more troops flowed in. The latter got better about cover and overwatch with every passing minute.

Ravenell's situation, in contrast, deteriorated. He was now on his third firing position after the first two had crumbled under continual punishment. The thought that he didn't share on the comms net was how surprised he was that they were all still alive. Then again, nobody had heard from Sinclair since his last call.

More of the masonry crumbled around him, forcing Ravenell to pull off from his current spot to shift to a new position. "Moving down the line!" Ravenell warned. "Chief, that gap between us is getting bigger!"

"Understood," came Everett's voice over Ravenell's earpiece. Ravenell heard the chief's weapon fire off a short burst before Everett asked, "Mohamed, how are you and Fuller doing?"

"Can't break away, Chief," Mohamed called back. "Fuller needs me to spot for her and to cover! The street here is getting kinda busy!"

As if to add her own input, Fuller's missile launcher let out another whistle, followed almost instantly by the boom of an explosion. "On the bright side," she said, "they're gonna have to fly up that street, 'cause driving isn't an option anymore."

"Bill," said Janeka over the comm, "I've only got Baldwin and Bhatia down here with a couple agents and Bhatia's wounded. I can come up there, but—"

"There's something like six thousand people down there!" Everett pointed out. "You don't have nearly enough eyes on 'em as it is!"

Ravenell grimaced as he listened, lighting up the remains of a charred tree in the plaza below to send the security troopers behind it running. He swept to the left with his weapon to chase away anyone who thought he was distracted. His vigilance put down another two troopers. "We gotta think of something," said Ravenell. "They're getting brave."

A larger, closer explosion than the last cut him off. It came from the same direction, accompanied by a man's scream over Ravenell's earpiece and a vibration that ran the full course of the roof. "Oh shit, guys!" Ravenell blurted, thinking immediately of his comrades—friends since basic—on the other end of the building.

"Bal, go check on 'em!" Everett ordered. "Ravenell, stay put! Don't let 'em break us up!"

Though he gritted his teeth in frustration, the young marine understood Everett's decision. The roof wouldn't hold without active defenders, and Ravenell anchored the widest avenue of approach.

Besides, Baljashanpreet was a survivalman and therefore a far better-trained medic. He could also keep a level head under pressure. "Aw, no," Baljashanpreet lamented over the comms net, followed by the sounds of his rifle. "They're gone. They're both gone. There isn't enough left of either—Chief, they're unloading armored troopers over here!"

Ravenell's eyes widened as large armored hovercars dropped into the street up ahead. Both of them opened up their side doors to reveal the same threat Baljashanpreet reported. "Fuck, I got 'em here, too!" warned Ravenell.

"Okay," said Everett, "we're gonna pull back while they know we're still here. They'd have dropped in right on top of us if they were willing to risk a close-quarters fight, but they must not want to—ahg!" Everett yelled in tandem with another boom that shook the rooftop.

"Chief?" Ravenell asked, and then called, "Bal! Check on him!"

"Way ahead of you," Baljashanpreet replied as he ran. Everett let out a pained growl, giving both of the younger men a glimmer of hope but no details to work with.

Ravenell tilted his repeater to open up on the armored troopers across the street. Their suits could deflect most laser blasts, but his repeater put out more power than ordinary pistols or rifles. They wouldn't stand up to a solid hit. Ultimately, though, he wanted to delay them from moving in. Most jumped for cover, knowing better than to trust in their armor alone when there was a perfectly decent vehicle to hide behind.

His delaying tactic worked for about ten seconds. Then they returned fire. Ravenell jumped back and rolled away from the rooftop's edge as the crenellations disintegrated under a barrage of bullets and lasers from weapons much heavier than his. Everett's plans made sense: the enemy didn't want a close-quarters fight on the rooftop lest a stray downward shot go straight through the building into some hapless civilian inside. On the other hand, a well-orchestrated crossfire could chew up the whole rooftop without risking those on the lower floors.

Ravenell rolled farther from the edge, surprised at how aggressive the armored troopers were with this tactic. "Bal, we gotta go!" he shouted. "How's he doing?"

"Shitty!" snapped Everett.

"I've got him," answered Baljashanpreet. His voice offered enough strain to tell Ravenell that he was probably carrying the chief. "He'll be okay, but I can't wait to patch him up. He's out of this fight."

"Alright, take him downstairs. I'll see if I can find a choke point on the top floor inside. It's all we can do now. Gunny! We're comin' in!"

"Understood," said Janeka.

Ravenell winced. He spotted Baljashanpreet running for the nearest door with the chief over his shoulders. Everett bled from awful wounds on his right arm and leg and probably more. He looked lucky to be alive.

He had orders to hold the rooftop until reinforcements arrived. The fact that the enemy was chewing up the rooftop all around him didn't make him feel any better. Deadly red flashes and whizzing bullets flew all around, threatening to cut him down at any second, yet he thought only about not letting down his mentors and his friends.

Resolving to give his comrades time to get inside safely, Ravenell sank to one knee and looked around for any threats. Movement on a nearby rooftop caught his eye. He brought up his weapon and fired again, forcing the enemy to drop out of sight.

"Ravenell, you've done all you can!" barked Janeka. "You made the right call, now follow up on it and get your ass inside! This isn't on you!"

Cursing, Ravenell took one last look to make sure he wouldn't expose himself to any other threat in his run for the door, rose to his feet...and heard an overwhelming boom unlike any of the others from the field so far.

The corvette's engines roared as she dropped out of the sky. She came almost to a halt directly over Symphony Hall with her bow pointed toward the plaza. *Joan of Arc* looked like hell, with burns running from bow to stern and a smashed wreck where her underside turret used to be. Almost immediately, the enemy all around Ravenell shifted their fire to target the ship. *Joan* retaliated with her remaining laser turrets as she sank closer to the rooftop. Ravenell dropped back down to his knees, wondering how low she'd get. He didn't see any landing struts.

Her cargo bay ramp, on the other hand, was fully extended. That detail almost escaped his notice until a cylindrical white anti-grav field generator tumbled out of the ramp. Marines in combat jackets and helmets followed it. The field only took the edge off of a fall such as this; each of the marines still had to drop and roll to mitigate the impact. He saw a number of grey navy vac suits, too, though they landed without as much grace. As soon as they were on their feet, they ran for the door leading inside the building. All except for one.

Despite the faceplate and the armor, Ravenell recognized Collins. The two had served and trained together long enough to identify one another even in the dark. Ravenell looked up with surprise as Collins recovered from his safety roll and promptly rushed at him while all the others ran away.

"What the—" Ravenell began.

"Down! Get the fuck down!" Collins yelled. He tackled Ravenell.

The sky above them turned red and *Joan of Arc* jerked to one side as a wide laser blast destroyed her main thrusters.

• • •

Alarms screamed. Control panels sparked. The main tactical displays not only blinked out but turned red as the retractable armor plates over the bridge canopy absorbed the last thermal stress they could handle. Montes let out a yelp when the helm all but blew up on her, reflexively throwing her arms up over her helmeted face to protect herself.

Kelly reached for the emergency helm transfer button as soon as the first sparks flew from the main controls. She had only the few seconds *Joan* spent dropping the marines—and most of her own crew—to get a sense of the warzone in front of her. Even that image was marred by the chaos sown by the corvette's remaining turrets unloading on the troops below.

Still, it was enough. It had to be. She had enough space in front of her, unless she didn't, in which case they were all just as screwed as if she did nothing. "Impact!" yelled Kelly.

Booker dropped his control of the turrets to throw the alarm per Kelly's order and hung on. Kelly hoped two seconds was enough. She blindly nudged the ship forward, gave *Joan's* maneuvering jets one last touch to spin her around 180 degrees, and then brought her down with only the barest aid from her anti-grav generators—and entirely without her landing struts.

The loudest and roughest jolt any of the crew ever experienced ran through the ship as *Joan* collided with the concrete below. Artificial gravity could do only so much to lessen the impact. Everyone bounced roughly in their seats. Systems went into automatic emergency shutdowns as Kelly, Booker, and Montes regained their bearings.

"Are we all okay?" Booker asked, pulling himself out of his seat.

"Yeah," coughed Montes. "Yeah, I think…yeah."

Kelly unlatched her harness and fell straight to her hands and knees on the deck. She shook her head again, trying to clear it enough to move while Booker helped Montes. "How are you so steady?" she asked.

"I didn't have to drive," Booker replied, hauling Kelly up by her shoulders. "Think I might lose a couple teeth, though. You good?"

"I'd better be. Montes?" she asked, and waited only to see the younger woman nod. "Are we all that's left?"

"The roster says we've got one more still on board," answered Booker. "Guess who."

Kelly didn't bother. "Let's go." She threw the wheel on the exit hatch and staggered into a slow run down the passageway.

Had they been unfamiliar with the ship, they could still have found their way out by following the sounds of gunfire. One last crewmember remained at the portside exit, slinging bullets outside the ship from an assault rifle. A pile of other weapons laid at her feet.

"Ordoñez!" said Kelly. "What's it look like out there?"

"Still a mess!" replied the petite gunner's mate. "Think we can make it inside the building, though. It's right around that way. You dropped us on top of a rover parked in front of the door, though," she added.

Kelly glanced down the length of the ship and saw the remains of a vehicle crushed by the tip of Joan's bow. Then Ordoñez nudged the pile of guns on the deck with her foot without turning away from her field of fire. "I brought everyone a keepsake."

"Captain Kelly!" called a voice over her earpiece. "This is Sergeant Collins. Are you okay?"

"Sergeant, it's just four of us now," said Kelly as she grabbed and checked a pulse rifle. "We're about to make a break for the entrance. Can you let 'em know we're coming?"

"Yes, ma'am! We'll cover you from the roof and the top floor, but make it fast. Bad guys are getting their act together again and that destroyer's coming in overhead!"

"They *can't* fire on us down here," said Montes. "What are they gonna use?"

"Yeah, well, I didn't think they'd shoot at us over the hall, either, but they took that risk," Kelly grumbled. "XO? Guns?"

"Got your backs, ma'am," Ordoñez declared. Booker nodded. So did Montes.

Kelly knew better than to argue with her gunner's mate about who would go last. The other two were a different matter. "You two up front. We'll bring up the rear. Okay, go!"

Laser fire rained down on enemy lines that still hadn't recovered from *Joan*'s lasers or the shock of her crash landing. Kelly and her remaining crew came out shooting, pinning down the troops to their left flank as they ran for the building. Only a few of the enemy managed to get off any shots. Thankfully, none of them hit.

At the corner of the wrecked rover crouched a black woman in a bloodied longcoat. Like the marines up on the top floor, she provided covering fire for the crew's escape. Booker and Montes hustled over to her and then around her side. Kelly and Ordoñez followed, chased by gunfire from several directions. The other woman lingered long enough for the last of *Joan*'s crew to make it past the rover before joining them.

"Captain Kelly?" she asked as they made it into the lobby.

"Yes," Kelly huffed. "Gunnery Sergeant Janeka, right? I've heard a lot about you." She gave the other woman a quick looking over. The blood was likely hers given the tears and punctures in her clothes, but either she had already received first aid or she was somehow immune to pain. The latter seemed more likely, given the letters Kelly had read. "Sorry we couldn't manage a smoother arrival."

"I'm glad you made it at all." The weary shake of Janeka's head hinted at fatigue, but she was clearly still up for a fight. "Captain, you're the senior officer on site."

Kelly winced. That wasn't good news. "Understood. I'm told this is your show regardless."

"Good." The two stayed near the cover of the hall's concrete entrance, much of which now lay blocked by Joan and the rover. "We've had too much on our hands in holding the building to open any sort of dialogue with our prisoners, let alone the opposition."

"The bad guys don't want to give us time to consolidate."

"No, ma'am."

"Well, what are your…" Kelly's voice dropped off as a shadow spread over the entrance. Despite *Joan of Arc* lying just meters away from the front of the doorway, both women could easily see the destroyer that loomed in overhead. It blocked out much of the sky. "Oh shit," she murmured. "I don't know what the hell we're gonna do against that. If they drop troops or—"

A loud explosion overhead cut her off. Then came a second and third as missiles streaked across the sky to slam into *Metis* with thunderous bursts of fire and light.

• • •

"Casey, what the fuck are you doing?" roared Ezekiel as *Argent* lurched into the sky. He tore off his safety harness to step out of his seat, ready to kill the captain.

"Winning this thing!" Casey answered. The main tactical screen was almost filled with the image of *Metis*, now covered in the burning effects of a low-yield chaff missile. She was only a few dozen kilometers away—essentially no distance at all to a starship. "Guns, put every defensive turret that'll manage the angle on that bastard. Helm, keep moving us in slow and steady. Ground vehicle speed, low as you can get us without hitting any buildings. No evasives. We'll have to suck up whatever they throw at us."

"We can't suck that up!" Ezekiel countered. "Helm, belay that order!"

"Oh, it's too late for that, buddy," replied Casey. To Schlensker's credit, he concentrated on his job rather than letting the argument distract him. *Argent* drifted slowly toward *Metis* over the city's skyline, throwing out laser blasts and explosive shells all the while. "We're in it now. They'd have seen us soon enough, anyway. Guns! Main cannon on my command."

"This ship has *half* the cannons it used to," Ezekiel reminded Casey, standing right next to him now and ready to take his head off. He pointed at the big warship dead ahead. "We can't stand up to that!"

"Why not? What're they gonna do, throw missiles back at us? Blow us up with their cannons? They'd hurt their nice little city. 'Course, I don't have that same problem."

Argent shook as *Metis* opened fire with a spread of her smaller turrets. Though the destroyer boasted considerably more firepower than the defanged *Argent*, the immediate results backed up Casey's point. The destroyer couldn't use her biggest guns, nor even half of her lighter weapons. *Argent* absorbed the damage and kept slowly approaching.

Metis held her ground. She remained in place, unable to dodge or deflect anything *Argent* threw at her. Chaff missiles would lay waste to the city below. Defensive guns, normally good only for shooting down incoming missiles, now turned to holding off the approaching enemy.

The narrow gap of sky between the two ships quickly darkened with smoke, highlighted by streaks of lasers and the bursts of explosive shells against the hulls of the two ships. *Metis* turned to bring more of her weapons into the line of fire, giving Casey the opening he needed.

"Guns! Now!" demanded Casey.

The brilliant flash of *Argent*'s cannons seemed to ignite the air like a lightning bolt and traveled just as fast. Though the lasers carried no kinetic impact, *Metis* reeled as if struck by a huge rock. Flame and debris burst all along her hull as internal explosions rocked the big destroyer. She listed sideways, yielding ground to *Argent* to get away.

"Renaldo! Send a message!" said Casey. "Give 'em a chance to turn around and run away or we'll drop 'em right where they are!"

"Aye, aye," acknowledged his comms officer. She threw a switch on her panel to carry out the order.

"What if they call in reinforcements?" Ezekiel pressed.

"Then we take 'em on," Casey answered. "Right here. Helm, put us over Symphony Hall and hold us in place. Don't move for shit, you got me?" With that handled, Casey turned his attention back to Ezekiel. "Anything they can drop on us hurts their people, too," he snapped as Renaldo repeated his demands. "Even if they get us sidelong, we could crash right into their building full of rich fuckers. You wanted to know why your boss put me in charge of this ship? Here's your answer!"

The shaking stopped. "*Metis* is moving off," reported Schlensker.

"Hold fire!" Casey ordered. He watched the destroyer slink away, picking up only a little altitude while trailing smoke from a dozen breaches in her hull. "That's right, put her over the water, asshole," the captain growled. "Give all the rats a chance to swim for their lives."

Ezekiel fumed, but didn't follow his urge to throw Casey into his quarters and weld the hatch shut…or worse. "So we stay here? And then what?"

"Then we hope your fleet and your people on the ground can get their shit together." Casey turned his attention to the main tactical screens. The chaff in the upper atmosphere had largely dispersed. He could see garbled data from the battle overhead. "Come and get us, assholes," he grumbled.

• • •

He couldn't believe he was still alive. For an instant, he considered that maybe he wasn't, and that this was how the afterlife began.

What if it picked up right where life ended, and a person had to wander around to find heaven or hell or whatever came next?

Only a steady hiss came through the earpiece in his helmet. The lack of pretty much every other sound told him that the compartment had vented out into space. Screens and indicators fluttered back to life as surviving systems rebooted. For all the lack of air, he could feel the downward pull of the ship's artificial gravity field. The ship wasn't completely demolished.

He considered what that could mean about everything else. The internal comms relay might have failed. He'd studied the diagrams as part of his qualifications process. Secondaries and work-arounds could restore basic functions, but after a catastrophic failure some channels might not return automatically.

Nathan looked to his left for his new mentor and realized that Rogozinski hadn't survived. Nor had most of the comms section. The enlisted signalmen all slumped forward or back in their chairs. On one side, Nathan saw a bent support beam that had crushed people and equipment alike. On another, he saw the ugly aftermath of an exploded power relay and its bloodied victims.

It seemed to Nathan that he'd been spared purely as a matter of luck—along with one other officer slumped against her control panel. Nathan reached out to reconnect their person-to-person comms channel. "Perez! Hey, are you okay?"

"Unh, I think…yeah…oh my god," she said as she sat up and looked around. "Oh no!"

The ship rocked again with another hit. "Hey, there's no time for that," Nathan warned. He repeated the first appropriate thing that came to mind: "We've gotta triage, right? Find out who and what we can save."

Nathan hit the release on his harness and hauled himself out of his seat. The sight of the rest of *Beowulf*'s command bridge threatened to steal whatever courage he had left. Much of the compartment had been burned to a cinder. The weapons consoles, astrogation table, and other workstations now looked like furniture after a house fire. Few of the men and women of the command bridge remained. Most of them either sat dead in their chairs or lay under fallen debris from the overhead and racks of equipment that had come loose in the blast.

His eyes swept the silent compartment for any survivors. The nature of the devastation made it easy enough to write off most as dead. He spotted one officer, however, who might yet go either way. "Admiral!" he yelled out.

The man slumped over in the captain's chair couldn't hear him, of course. Nathan climbed through the debris with urgency, slipping and nearly tearing his vac suit on jagged metal as *Beowulf* suffered another frightening jolt. Nathan shoved those worries aside. *Beowulf*'s flag bridge could run the ship, and even after that she had auxiliary helm controls down in engineering. Someone else ran the ship now.

Nathan's gloved hand came down on the admiral's. "Sir, are you okay?" he asked. Debris suggested that he might have been struck by flying metal, but Nathan saw no punctures in Branch's vac suit. The admiral's holocom automatically showed his vitals upon activation. He wasn't dead, but he wasn't conscious, either.

"Admiral, can you hear me?" Nathan tried again. "Sir, you've gotta wake up!"

The other man didn't stir. Nathan thought he heard some sort of echo on the line. Then he heard a new voice: "Hello? Can you hear me?"

"Yes! This is Nath—Ensign Spencer!"

"You're on the bridge with Admiral Branch? Is he okay? We can't get visuals."

"He's alive and in one piece, but he's out cold. Most of the bridge is destroyed." Nathan looked around again. Perez was helping someone else out from under a fallen equipment rack. "There's only a few of us left."

"Ensign, is the helm intact?" broke in a new voice. It didn't matter that they'd never met. He recognized her voice instantly. "Or any of the other stations that can assume control?"

Nathan looked around again. The ugly scar burned through the bridge seemed to have fallen short of the forward control stations. A couple of them even hosted active lights and holo screens. He touched a couple of buttons on his holocom to tie his helmet camera in with his audio feed. "I think so, ma'am. I'm sending you video so you can see for yourself." Something ignited in the overhead, briefly showering the space between Nathan and the controls with sparks that soon died for lack of air.

"I need you there immediately, Ensign," said Admiral Yeoh. "We're unable to shift helm control."

His eyes widened. That wasn't good at all. "Perez!" he called out as he picked his way through the debris and *Beowulf* rocked yet again. "Help Admiral Branch! We need to get him out of here!"

"What are you do—?"

"This is the only thing I know how to do!" Nathan interrupted. "I haven't had time to learn anything else. I can do this."

"Okay," Perez said without further argument. She grabbed the other crewman's arm. "Come on."

Given the enormity of his situation, Nathan was glad there was someone else to tell him what to do. He quickly confirmed the helmsman's death. The solid display screen above her station showed no sign of life, either, but with the touch of a couple of buttons Nathan had the tactical feed overlaid onto it via holo projection.

Unsurprisingly, things looked bad. *Beowulf* drifted forward with *Perseus* right behind her while the cruiser *Coggia* moved in to port. Both the battleship and the cruiser fired on *Beowulf*, but the ship's defenses seemed to work fine even if the command bridge no longer coordinated them. *Beowulf*'s escorts also followed closely to provide extra cover. It wouldn't last—none of those nearby allies could match a cruiser, let alone a battleship like *Perseus*—but it explained her continued survival.

Opting to try the first productive thing that came to mind, Nathan reached forward and keyed the accelerator. The helm responded, putting some extra distance between *Beowulf* and her pursuers. He adjusted the heading to turn her slightly to starboard and found success with that as well. "The helm works, Admiral!" he declared.

"Take control, Ensign," she replied, though Nathan was way ahead of her. He hit the release on the helmsman's harness and pulled her out of the seat as Yeoh continued. "Bring us about. One-eighty by zero-one-zero and roll forty-five degrees to port. We don't want to make it easy to target that hole in our bow."

"One-eighty by zero-one-zero and roll forty-five, aye aye," said Nathan as he carried out the order. The simple act of turning the ship around brought instant results. The shaking caused by nearby detonations ended, if only for the moment, while the hail of lasers beating down on *Beowulf*'s hull fell away. Even a few seconds of rest could revitalize strained ES systems fighting to bind the hull together.

"Ma'am, I don't think I have anything other than helm here," Nathan warned, looking at other stations nearby once again. "Weapons is smashed, and—"

"We only need you to steer, Ensign," Yeoh cut him off. "Everything else is under our control. We're working on transferring the helm and a damage control team is on its way to you. In the meantime, I need you to stay at your post."

Nathan looked back toward the captain's chair and found it empty. Perez and the crewman were near the exit hatch, dragging Admiral Branch between them. He also noticed the gaping hole in the overhead. Something burst outside the hull, causing a brief flash of orange light that he would have missed if he'd blinked. It illustrated how vulnerable the compartment was.

NorthStar had built this ship. For all the adjustments and refits Archangel had put in, it wasn't like the enemy didn't know how and where to hit.

"I know what I'm asking, Ensign," said Yeoh. "We'll get you out as soon as we can."

Funny, thought Nathan, *that's what I told those guys floating around all alone in space. Guess I still have less to complain about than they do.* "It's alright, ma'am. What do I do now?"

"Get us into spitting distance of *Perseus*. We have to get in so close that any missile fired at us will catch her in the blast, too. It's the only way to counter her remaining escorts. Keep that gap in the hull turned away from the enemy. Understood?"

"Yes, ma'am. I'm on it."

"Execute," she said.

He brought the ship around again, evading fire for another critical few seconds but soon bringing *Beowulf* closer to danger rather than escape.

"On my mark," Yeoh continued, "we'll make a sudden roll to bring both of the topside cannons around at *Perseus*. I'll need you to keep her in our line of fire to give our gunners as many shots as possible. She's going to fire back," the admiral warned, "but we'll have our best shot at bringing her down. *Coggia* will try to stop us, too. I'll make sure our escorts take advantage of the distraction."

Nathan glanced at the broader tactical screen and nodded. Though NorthStar still outnumbered Archangel's fleet, knocking out *Perseus*—even at the expense of *Beowulf*—would leave both sides evenly matched in cruisers. By now, everyone was hurt. The fight could go either way as long as *Beowulf* managed one last kill.

Another frightening jolt almost knocked Nathan out of his chair. He grabbed the harness to make sure that wouldn't happen again. "I'm good, ma'am. Say the word."

"Stand by," said Yeoh.

The storm of enemy fire resumed. *Perseus* seemed to realize the danger. She began to back away, while *Coggia* found herself stymied by interference from *Belfast* and *Resolute*. Nathan glanced at a second tactical screen showing the action beyond his ship's immediate area. *St. Nicholas* held her position near a wrecked NorthStar frigate and offered what help she could at a distance. Nathan almost grinned. *At least Santa Claus is looking out for me.*

Another topside blow hammered *Beowulf*, this time accompanied by a flash of light that seemed to engulf the entire compartment behind Nathan. He cringed reflexively, but it was over before he could register an appropriate level of terror. A yellow flash on his holocom warned of radioactive contamination. *Oh sure*, he thought. *Like I'm gonna live long enough to worry about that.*

"We're ready to go as soon as we close," Yeoh spoke up again. "Twenty seconds. Are you ready?"

"Yes, ma'am!" He watched the tactical screens carefully. *Perseus* increased speed and turned to pull away in another direction. Nathan accelerated and turned to match her. The enemy battleship fired off her main guns, missing with one cannon but wiping away a defense turret with another. Nathan held his course. She wouldn't get away from him.

"Your file says you're new to the ship?"

Nathan's breath came out hard. He wondered if his voice shook. "Yes, ma'am."

"People shouldn't pick fights with kids from Geronimo."

That made him grin. "No, ma'am. No, they shouldn't."

Beowulf threw missiles at *Perseus* as she came alongside the rival battleship. As the admiral instructed, Nathan steered in close enough that both vessels felt the heat of each explosion. The two ships tore into one another with everything they had, including defense guns meant for very different work. In the airless flag bridge, Nathan heard none of it, but he felt *Beowulf* shudder and shake and saw the flashes of debris from explosive shells ricocheting around behind him.

He pulled in ever tighter, practically matching *Perseus* for speed as he came within sixty kilometers and kept closing.

"On my mark," said Yeoh, and then paused. "Now!"

Nathan threw *Beowulf* into a half-spin and then held her steady. Cannons built to annihilate warships a hundred thousand kilometers out opened up on a target close enough to spot with the naked eye. With no loss of power or concentration over distance, wide red beams tore into *Perseus*. Reinforced armor plates disintegrated while others peeled away. Explosions rocked the enemy battleship from bow to stern. Magazines ignited and gun emplacements broke apart.

The final explosions engulfed *Beowulf* with burning gases and debris. Nathan felt the bridge shake all around him, and then screamed as hot shrapnel ricocheted through the bridge and his body.

CHAPTER FOURTEEN

Dirty Enough to be True

"All warfare is based on deception."

--SUN TZU, THE ART OF WAR,
CIRCA 6TH CENTURY BCE

"We all go only as fast as you can, sir," O'Neal assured his boss. "I'm not an invalid, damn it!" huffed Brekhov. "That pool at my house isn't for show!" He ran at the center of a pack of men and women in suits, Pedroso and Donaldson included, though the latter was the only one besides Brekhov without a gun. The rest of them weren't executives at all. They'd left the rest of the executive committee back with the board of directors and their shareholders. Almost every other body in the tunnel was a highly-trained professional thug.

The tunnel offered little variety. Simple, glossy white tiles lined the walls. No one used it for storage space or other practical purposes. Brekhov didn't even see decorations. Uniform lights and tiles made it impossible to tell how far they'd gotten. Only the occasional maintenance access doors broke the monotony. His security team treated the doors as possible threats every time they appeared, but no door attacked them.

Brekhov figured it was the claustrophobic feeling of so many people around him in an enclosed space that left him short of breath and sweating. He felt dizzy. It was almost embarrassing.

A short run like this shouldn't have presented a problem. He jogged and swam regularly. He worked out at home. Brekhov didn't fall prey to ego or laziness. When his doctors told him after his last longevity treatment that he needed to be more active, he took it to heart and followed their instructions.

Perhaps, he told himself as looked from one grim bodyguard to another, he saw here the difference between amateur fitness and professional training. Was the short run back to the Jackson Center really enough to expose that gap? Donaldson seemed okay—frightened, of course, but he kept up.

Brekhov rolled his left arm to relieve the tension and pain he felt along his shoulder and kept going.

Gunshots echoed behind them. They heard the rapid popping sounds of an automatic, the somewhat softer whistles of pulse rifles, and a yelp of pain.

"What do you mean, the rail car isn't there yet?" Pedroso snapped suddenly. Brekhov glanced at her and realized then that she was using her earpiece to talk with the rest of the team. "Who the hell ever let it leave in the first place?"

"Angie, Mikhail, Brandon," said O'Neal. "Secure that door, then set up at this corner." The three Risk Management agents stayed behind as the pack took the left turn of a T-intersection. Brekhov looked over his shoulder to see them take up firing positions. Then he looked forward again. From what he remembered, they were almost at their destination.

"Like they'll do any better than the others?" gasped Donaldson. "I thought you people were the best in the Union!"

"Those people on our tail have been actively at war for over two years," Maria snapped. "That tends to even things out."

"Steven," Brekhov slurred, "shut…shut up about the people…people protecting you."

"Sir?" O'Neal broke in. "Sir, are you alright?"

Brekhov swallowed. In truth, he felt like he might throw up, but they were almost there. No sense in worrying his bodyguards about a little nausea. "I'm fine."

For the first time Brekhov could name, his head bodyguard ignored his words. O'Neal put a hand on his boss's shoulder, bringing Brekhov and the rest of the group to a halt. He looked at the older man with a new urgency. "Oh my god," he murmured.

"What?" demanded Pedroso.

"Pick him up!" O'Neal ordered two of the bodyguards, then keyed his earpiece again. "Medical emergency! Get a kit ready *now*!"

• • •

Alicia's idea of a distraction scared the hell out of Tanner. He figured she would toss a spare power cell or some other random object down the staircase to make the bad guys around the corner at the bottom step think twice before shooting. Instead, she threw *herself* down the stairs with her guns blazing.

Thankfully, Alicia scared the hell out of the enemy, too. She rolled on her shoulder with her finger on the trigger as she landed. The wild move sent laser pulses flying everywhere, including one back up toward Tanner. He focused on his aim, though, clipping the enemy agent in the shoulder as he fell out of cover to dodge Alicia's fire. Then all Tanner could do to back Alicia up was to leap down the flight of stairs to join her while she blasted their remaining foes at point blank range.

He landed on his feet and managed not to clobber Alicia, but he still tumbled bodily into the wall behind her. Luckily, he turned as he landed, keeping his back to the wall. It gave him a chance to fire back at the last remaining agent. His pulse blasts hit the third man at about the same time as Alicia's cut him down.

Four men lay on the floor, with two at the edge of the corner and two a little farther back. Even pulling a wild-assed stunt like that, Alicia somehow took down her targets. "Ow," she grunted, conceding her move hadn't been entirely flawless.

"Fucking crazy."

"No time for a shootout."

"Can you run?" Tanner asked, and found himself trying to keep up with her before the last word left his mouth. They saw no other targets down the next leg of the access corridor.

"I'm more worried about bombs or grenades," she said.

"Bodyguards aren't gonna carry explosives," Tanner replied—knowing he spoke from no real authority on the matter. It made sense to him, though. "The whole job is to keep their principal safe."

"What do you think they pay these guys to make 'em stay behind like the ones back there?"

"Couldn't pay me enough." That led to a sobering thought. "Must not be money."

Desperation played against deeply-ingrained training and practical experience. The tunnel offered essentially no cover. Tanner and Alicia took for granted that any bodyguard at this level of employment was likely an expert shot. Their last encounter was more about aggression and luck than marksmanship. Yet they kept running, compelled to take the risks by the value of the man at the end of the chase and the unknown length of his head start.

A sense of dread welled up within Tanner as they took on one last all-too-open and brightly lit leg of the tunnel. He saw the corner up ahead, but the tunnel also continued past it. He cursed inwardly, seeing no clue of whether they should continue on or take the corner—and then the threat appeared.

"Down!" Tanner and Alicia yelled simultaneously. They even pushed one another to either side as the guns at the corner opened up. Something solid clipped his left shoulder as he belly-flopped to the floor. He didn't see what happened to Alicia. He had no time. Tanner stayed flat on the floor, rising only enough to point his rifle in the right direction and fire. He hardly aimed before he pulled the trigger.

His left shoulder took another hit, this one from a laser pistol, but his jacket seemed to absorb the worst of it. He couldn't check. He kept firing. More than one foe waited around that corner, unafraid of Tanner's and Alicia's weapons as the young marine opened up from the other side of the hallway. Another shot from the corner struck the center of Tanner's rifle, sending sparks flying up in front of his eyes and rendering his weapon useless.

Then a series of laser blasts lit up the hallway—almost straight from the wall, Tanner first thought—to strike the group of agents at the corner. Rather than look a gift horse in the mouth, he drew his sidearm and aimed it at the enemy. By then, there was no one left to shoot. The hallway was quiet again.

He looked to his left. Alicia remained where she'd fallen, unhurt but surprised. "Holy shit," she breathed, "did that just happen?"

"Now you know how it feels when *you* do it," Tanner replied. Only then did he spot the maintenance access door that lay across from the T-intersection. A woman in black stepped out with a smoking pulse rifle in her hand.

Tanner's jaw dropped. "Vanessa?"

The dark-haired woman gestured down the corner passage with a weary hand. "Thataway."

"You know her?" asked Alicia as she and Tanner quickly got to their feet.

Tanner left his rifle behind. He didn't have time to fix it even if it would ever work again. "Yeah, she's a friend," he explained. "Vanessa, are you okay?"

"Hi," she huffed. "Hey, you're Alicia Wong, right?"

Alicia blinked. "You know who I am?"

"Well, yeah. We all know who you are."

The older woman was barely on her feet. Her tattered clothes, matted hair and blackened face made her look like she'd crawled out of a car crash. "Are you okay?" he asked, reaching out to steady her.

"Yeah," she answered, and then sniffed. "Drugs are kicking in."

"You're hurt."

"Nah," she plainly lied, "my armor's better than yours."

"You've been here all along?"

"Sort of. Did you see a bunch of dead civilians when you pulled up to the hall?"

Tanner blinked. "No."

"You're welcome. Anyway, sorry about the gunfight." She gestured to the maintenance door. "I was gonna shoot 'em all, but I passed out—Brekhov!" Vanessa blurted suddenly, grabbing Tanner's arm. "That way! They said something about a mag-rail car! Go!"

He ran. He had no time for his shoulder. If it moved, he'd worry about it later and trust adrenaline and self-delusion to carry him through for now. Tanner paused only long enough to scoop up one of the pistols from the fallen agents, though he soon realized it was keyed to its dead owner. Alicia ran beside him while Vanessa followed behind as fast as she could.

• • •

The technicians reported recovery of helm control twenty seconds after *Beowulf*'s ride through the debris field. Yeoh saw it happen as the techs yelled out their achievement. They pulled *Beowulf* back to a steady course as a final check. So many systems fell into failsafe protocols and emergency reboots as *Beowulf* plowed through the wreckage of her enemy that it wasn't clear what had corrected the problem, but it made Yeoh want to howl or throw something.

She didn't. She held it in, and thanks to the faceplate of her helmet, no one saw her expression. The technicians worked as fast as they could. None of them enjoyed their predicament, or wanted to leave a young shipmate on the bridge alone and exposed, or wanted to hear his screams as Yeoh had. No one acted carelessly.

Awful things happened in war. Yeoh moved on.

"Helm, bring us about," she ordered. Battle damage and the disruptions from *Perseus*'s demise disrupted *Beowulf*'s sensors. While Yeoh's staff called out damage reports and casualties, the battleship's crew received a full breath without another blow, and then a second.

Then the tactical screens cleared to reveal another battleship dead ahead.

The destruction of *Perseus* seemed to have brought the battle to a pause. Irrationally or not, most ships in the vicinity broke off and held their fire to form up with their nearest allies. Some of the fighting farther out continued: *St. Nicholas* was now engaged with another NorthStar corvette, while *Monaco* barely fended off a pair of frigates. Yet the second battle group seemed to have stalled in its push toward *Beowulf*, held off effectively by a battered *Los Angeles* and *Halley*. The remaining cruiser from *Perseus*'s escorts, in turn, now fell back to join the newcomer to the fight.

Yeoh could almost feel the sinking hearts of her shipmates on the flag bridge. After such a close fight that finally evened the odds,

Beowulf didn't have the strength to defeat another battleship—especially one coming in fresh and prepared.

Her eyes narrowed. *Taurus*, as the tactical screens identified her, had been reported in drydock before the invasion fleet departed for Fairhaven. NorthStar wouldn't risk another battleship on a bluff, but the fact that she approached without firing left her readiness open to question.

"Admiral," called out one of her bridge officers, "we're receiving a call from the enemy battleship."

She glanced at the clock, and again at the tactical screens. One of them showed Fairhaven, where the cloud of chaff in the lower atmosphere over the capital still lingered. Every second gave her crew time to repair and reload, however little that meant in the face of a new threat such as this.

That time, however, could mean anything or nothing at all on the ground.

"Let's talk." Yeoh slid her faceplate back and removed her helmet, but kept it ready in her hand. She activated a new holo screen at her chair. "Put them through."

The face that greeted her was partially obscured by a helmet with a transparent visor. Yeoh allowed herself the slightest grin at the sight. The man on the screen either refused to acknowledge his lack of nerve or completely missed it. The hints of stubble and the bushy look of his eyebrows made Yeoh wonder if he'd been pulled into work on his day off.

"Admiral Yeoh," he began, "I'm Captain Mayfair. Obviously I'm a little late getting here, but I wanted to give you one last chance to end this insanity. No one else has to die. Stand down. You know you can't win this fight."

"That's quite gracious of you, Captain," Yeoh said without emotion. Her words came with deliberate care—or, more accurately, deliberate slowness. "I share your concern for the needless loss of life. Tell me, out of curiosity, what are your terms?"

His face twitched as if he almost snapped at her, but held back. That increased her interest, and her hopes. "No terms. Unconditional surrender."

Yeoh's response came to mind immediately. She waited a few beats anyway. "We would not be talking if you could force such a thing, Captain. Your fleet has suffered significant losses, as has mine. Understandably, you wish to salvage the rest without further loss. How much is such a victory worth to you? We have come this far, Captain. We have risked and lost this much. Do not think we will falter now. If you wish to avoid further bloodshed, you will have to make it worth our while."

• • •

Worst-case scenarios filled his mind: the mag-rail could already be gone; the place could be full of innocent civilians seeking shelter; they could come headlong into a hundred police and security troopers, or any combination of all three. His only consolation was that if this was a public mag-rail line, the tunnels seemed awfully clear of people for some reason.

The group didn't have far to run. Solid, painted signs along the walls guided them straight to their destination. "Wandsworth Tower," Vanessa huffed. "It may be a dedicated line."

"Good. Fewer civil—shit!" Tanner yelped. The group came to a new T-intersection breaking off to their right—only this time Tanner saw trouble whip around the corner before the enemy could shoot. Tanner dropped to one knee, aimed, and fired in the same second as the opposing shooter pulled his trigger. Pressed for time and aiming urgently, both of them missed.

Alicia didn't. Nor did she slow down. With her rifle on full power, she practically put out a single unbroken beam of searing light that swept along the wall and through the man leaning around the corner while continuing to run at full tilt. The shooter fell back behind the corner with a scream.

No one else appeared before Alicia made it to the intersection. She took the opposite corner while Tanner hustled to catch up. Vanessa trailed behind. Laser blasts erupted from the adjoining tunnel, preventing Alicia from pushing on. Tanner noted the upward tilt to the enemy fire as he came to the corner. The adjoining passage sloped downward, with a short flight of steps replacing the smooth floors that made up the path until now.

"Hold them!" someone shouted on the other side of the passage. "Just a minute more!"

Tanner glanced at Alicia, who growled as she hooked her rifle around the corner and fired without placing her head or shoulders in danger. "It must be right down there," she told him. "You can see the terminal station!"

He risked a glance. She was right. The tunnel wasn't that large at all. It couldn't be designed for public access. That meant the tunnel probably held fewer civilians. Still, the agents on the other side of the short stairway put out more than enough fire to drop anyone who gave them even a half-decent shot.

So close, Tanner thought. *It's not even half the distance of the stairway that Alicia took...* yet the same trick wouldn't work against an enemy that saw trouble coming. At least, not the same *exact* trick.

He pulled the pistol he'd grabbed from the dead agents back at the last exchange from his belt. "Fuck it," he grunted, and then warned Alicia: "Grenade!"

"What?" Alicia blinked, but the gamble was already underway.

Tanner threw the pistol down the passage and immediately jumped down after it. No one cut him down as the enemy understandably flinched in fear of an impending explosion.

Landing on his feet, he found his targets so close that he hardly had to aim. Tanner jammed his pistol into the gut of the agent on his right and pulled the trigger, then slammed his left forearm against the uniformed security trooper on his other side to prevent him from bringing up his weapon.

By the time he'd done that, he realized he faced much more than an agent to his either side. He saw suits and uniforms, guns and angry faces. Beyond them, hardly even shouting distance away, a mag-rail car came to rest at the end of its line. More people in suits stood waiting for its arrival.

Tanner needed only the blink of an eye to recognize three of them.

Swamped with enemies, Tanner could spare no more than that blink. His right hand was already coming back around to fire on the trooper still tangled up with his left forearm. Tanner got a single shot off, tagging the beleaguered agent but losing his pistol to the other man's thrashing hands. Pulling backward, Tanner saved himself from the worst of the incoming fire from those farther ahead. Several of the agents fired, taking the risk of hitting the trooper for the sake of bringing down a foe with him.

The risk didn't pay off. The trooper absorbed most of the shots. Tanner held the trooper up as protection and dropped to his knee. He heard rapid fire laser blasts to one side and saw Alicia with him at the bottom of the stairwell, finishing off the opponents that Tanner had left behind him. "What is this? Copy Alicia Day?" she snapped.

"Cover me!" Tanner yelled. He recovered his pistol as Alicia fired over him, bringing down one more enemy and dispersing the rest.

Twenty meters. Hardly any appreciable distance at all. Tanner sprang out from behind the dead trooper and bolted forward, firing all the way.

A larger man in a suit pushed Brekhov into the mag-rail car. Tanner pulled his trigger again and again as he closed the distance, putting two beams through another of the suits. Alicia's lasers forced the larger man back from the car as Tanner closed the distance.

The clutter of suits and uniforms with guns fell away. Tanner barreled through them all as the mag-rail car's automated warning systems advised people to step back. Someone knocked the pistol out of his hand again in an attempt to tackle him, but he slipped free and kept moving.

The big guy remained. Tanner was on him before he could bring his weapon to bear. He got in under the bodyguard's reach, delivering the same open-palm uppercut that had worked so well in other fights. He didn't press the attack, fixating angrily instead on the mag-rail car.

Its doors were still open. Brekhov was in there, stepping backward into the car with his eyes wide in fright and his hand over his chest. Roaring with fury, Tanner threw a single punch at the man responsible for so much loss.

It never landed. Someone's foot drove into Tanner's gut, stopping him cold. Another blow came in as Maria Pedroso emerged from the rail car to put herself between Brekhov and Tanner. He grabbed her wrist before she could shoot him, brought his other elbow down on her arm and then pulled and twisted to yank her around him and out of the car, all of it too late.

Brekhov wasn't alone in the car. Tanner saw someone come to the older man's aid as he fell back onto the floor. The doors slammed shut.

"No!" Tanner yelled.

All at once, a thick arm came around his throat and a hand gripped his belt right through his coat. The big bodyguard lifted Tanner up into the air and threw him down onto his back against the concrete. "Fucking savage!" he growled, slamming his foot down on Tanner's chest while he pulled a second pistol from under his jacket.

Tanner knew this dance. He swung a brutal right hook directly into the bodyguard's knee, bringing the man down to his level. His hands seized the bigger man's ears. Tanner pulled hard while bringing his forehead up into the bodyguard's nose.

Pedroso recovered almost as quickly as Tanner, but found herself in no position to help once Alicia collided with her. The young marine drove the butt of her rifle into Pedroso's side. The rifle's barrel came up against Pedroso's cheek an instant later, pushing her back and keeping her off-balance. Pedroso managed to block the third blow from the rifle, grabbing and twisting to rob Alicia of her control of the weapon. Alicia let her have it in favor of delivering a vicious punch to the throat. The older woman staggered back, losing her hold on the rifle, and found herself too shaken by the relentless punishment to block or dodge the boot heel that came up into her face.

Laser fire continued. So did screams of pain. Tanner had no time for any of it. The bodyguard reeled without falling, still between Tanner and the mag-rail as it jerked forward from its cradle. "No!" Tanner shouted again. He elbowed the bodyguard in the side of his head to shove him out of the way and rose up off the concrete.

The mag-rail car slipped away. Tanner jumped at the car, lacking any weapon but bringing his gloved fist down hard enough against the window to put a spider's web of cracks into the glass. The car offered nothing to grab onto. No handrails, no corners.

Tanner got only the one blow against the window before it slipped away and accelerated faster than anyone could run.

Tanner grabbed the bodyguard's gun off the floor, aimed and pulled the trigger. The weapon merely beeped. He threw it down the tunnel, falling well short of the car that was already half a football field away and picking up speed.

"*Fuck!*"

Something let out a loud thump. Tanner glanced over to see Alicia kick the big bodyguard in the head, putting him down for good. The laser blasts had ended. Tanner and Alicia stood alone on the platform with ten or more bodies around them. Vanessa limped up from the corner of the passageway, smoke trailing from her laser rifle as she watched for any further movement from the enemies on the deck.

"Tanner," Alicia began.

"The rail!" Tanner blurted, pointing to it. "Shoot the—damn it!" he shouted again as he realized the futility of the idea.

"We can keep running," Alicia suggested. "Maybe he's not going…damn," she said, finally seeing the map on the wall. The rail's destination lay six kilometers away. They'd never catch up in time.

Tanner turned to follow her gaze, rushed over to the map, and then understood the pointlessness of that, too. He swore again, turning and looking to the bodies on the platform for something, anything he could use.

The only thing that stood out to him as different from the rest was the body of Steven Donaldson staring up at him with lifeless eyes. In his rush, he'd shot down an unarmed noncombatant. Tanner gave it little weight compared to the rest of his overwhelming frustration, but the implications still hit home. He'd missed the CEO, and all he'd managed instead was to bring down a couple of bodyguards and the VP of Finance.

"Maria Pedroso," Vanessa grunted as she came over to the other fallen VP. "Always wanted to meet her. Just like this, too."

"I don't think she's getting up," observed Alicia. The pool of blood around Pedroso's head backed up her prediction.

"Yeah," said Vanessa. "Kind of what I mean."

Tanner barely registered it. Even his usual relief at seeing friends survive a battle with him didn't break through his frustration at their failure. Brekhov had escaped. He left on his back, clutching his chest and looking terrified, but even if… "Brekhov looked bad," Tanner mumbled.

"I saw that," Alicia agreed. "I only caught a glimpse. Did you tag him, at least?"

"No. No, I didn't." He looked over the platform again. This time he saw the discarded bits from someone's medical kit. He saw torn sterile wrappers and disposable hypo shots. Nothing suggested an open wound. Sterilizing sponges and clotting gel applicators lay unused in the open kit.

"He was having a heart attack," Tanner guessed.

"That'll put him down for a little bit," said Vanessa. "Nothing that'll kill him if he's got someone to take care of him. Nice to know he's hurting, though."

Tanner shook his head. "It doesn't matter. Brekhov is still the boss. We could've ended it all today if we'd grabbed him. Maybe we've got some major shareholders and some other executives, but every NorthStar holding in the Union knows he's still the boss. The fleet reports directly to him, just like Risk Management and all the security forces," he explained bitterly. "They have protocols. The CEO holds all the emergency authority. Brekhov can still order his people to fight, and they still hold Michael. Any override of his authority will take time that his people will spend shooting at us."

"How do you know that?" asked Alicia.

"I read the prospectus and the shareholder…" He stopped. "I read the shareholder voting guide…"

Tanner started walking back and then broke into a run. "Come on!"

• • •

"Can't believe he *left* us here. He left *us*!"

"Jon, shut up," hissed Walters. "I'm trying to hear what they're saying." Sitting in the front row to the left of the stage with many of her fellow executives, Walters leaned forward to listen to their captors. Several of them stood on the retractable flooring that covered the orchestra pit. They seemed to be the leaders.

Walters hardly knew one military rank insignia from another. Still, her career hinged on understanding social dynamics and body language. Their captors seemed to report to the pretty redhead in the uniform, but she wasn't exactly the one in charge. A couple of others in different uniforms—marines, Walters gathered—also appeared to hold some authority. Yet the longer the whole drama played out, the more Walters believed that everyone deferred to the tall black woman in civilian clothes.

Most of the people around Walters ignored details like their captors' organizational setup. Faced with armed men and women and stuck in theater seats while things exploded right outside, the audience tended more toward terror than analysis. The last word any of them received on their holocoms was a garbled civil defense alert saying the planet was under attack. Their captors had even made a point of letting everyone know they'd brought along their psychotic mascot, and that was before the crash of whatever meteor had landed out front.

Still, someone from the executive committee or the board of directors needed to show some leadership. Instead, they cringed in their seats.

"When are they going to talk to us? Or start…doing something?" Weir wondered out loud.

"Either they'll go for the board or the highest-ranking VP," said Walters, "which is you."

Weir's eyes widened. "You think they know that?"

"I think they can look it up," she grumbled. Though she didn't activate the holocom mounted on her ring, she noted the slight change in color that indicated weak reception. Even "weak" translated to an improvement over the last few minutes. Their captors noticed, too. Several of them looked to their own holocoms, bringing up holo screens and listening to reports.

Walters saw surprise but also grim expressions in the enemy leadership. The snippets she heard didn't please her. "Shit," she muttered.

"Did they say we lost *Perseus*?" asked Weir.

"You got that, too?"

"But we've still got other ships out there. They had *Taurus* on standby, and—"

"And I'd have heard what they just said about *Taurus* if you'd *shut up!*"

"Something about a standoff," put in another executive nearby.

"How much of their fleet did they bring in?" Walters frowned. Military matters weren't her strong point, but she read the memos. The whole strategy with Archangel was to ensure they would have to expend so much of their strength in liberating Michael that they'd be vulnerable to a follow-up attack. If that was the case, though, how could they afford to strike all the way out here? How badly had Pedroso and the fleet officers miscalculated?

Moreover, if Archangel held all the major shareholders hostage, how much did that calculation even matter anymore?

The longer she sat and waited, the angrier she was that the whole conflict had been allowed to come to this. Bad enough that the company had to shift into statehood.

The two women in charge conferred with others in hushed tones. Someone gestured to the center front row containing the board of directors and then to the section on the left where Walters sat with the executive committee. The redhead nodded, came to a decision, and walked with the other woman toward the executives.

"Stand up," Walters whispered.

"What? Why?"

"Because you're the highest in rank!" Fuming, Walters stood as the leaders approached. Weir rose with reluctance. She wished he'd let her handle this, but the odds of that were slim.

"You're Jon Weir?" asked the redhead. "Chief Administrative Officer?"

"Yes," Weir confirmed.

"And you're Christina Walters? Public relations?"

"I am."

"I don't recognize the rest. Mr. Weir, are you the ranking executive here?"

"Yes, I am," said Weir, his confidence taking another step forward. Walters understood that. Simple questions gave him a chance to find his footing.

"My name is Lieutenant Kelly. I'm the officer in charge. This is Gunnery Sergeant Janeka. We've secured the site and we have a warship directly overhead. Shooting could start back up at any second. In the meantime—"

"Lieutenant," said Janeka, turning her attention away.

Three battered and bloodied figures emerged from one side of the stage. Someone Walters pegged as a medic rushed up to aid of one of the women at the behest of the other.

The third figure, whom Walters easily recognized, walked down the steps on the left of the stage and turned toward the group.

Blood marred his forehead, his jacket, and his hands. He looked weary but alert. Walters realized that she could probably hear a pin drop in the tense, crowded hall.

She stood her ground as he approached. She'd only spoken with him once and didn't like the memory of it. She had no intention of repeating the experience.

"Ma'am," he said to Kelly, and then to Janeka, "Gunny."

The redhead looked relieved to see him. "Malone," said the other woman.

Tanner glanced at Weir and Walters with something between contempt and indifference. "You're gonna need a new CEO."

Walters inhaled sharply. A few others nearby cried out in shock. Malone continued on into the aisle and walked toward the exit.

Weir fainted into his seat.

The lieutenant looked down at the unconscious executive with a frown. "Okay, then."

Walters swallowed her aggravation. In truth, she knew she should probably be grateful to have him out of the way. "Lieutenant," she said, "what are Archangel's terms?"

As Walters expected, Kelly glanced to the other woman before answering. "Same as they've been," said Janeka.

"You want an end to combat," Walters recited, "the release of all Archangel prisoners, an immediate withdrawal from Archangel space, and forgiveness of all primary, educational, security, and medical debts held against Archangel's government and its citizens?"

Kelly keyed up a screen from her holocom for the executive's benefit. "That's the bottom line, yes. We have it in diplomatic language here if it matters. There might be a detail or two."

"No indemnities or punitive claims?" Walters asked as she waved her hand in front of the screen so the holocom in her jewelry could copy the text. She didn't bother to look at it.

"None," said Kelly. "We want to finish this and leave. As soon as we see our conditions met, we send all of your captured personnel back here."

"Everyone here stays under guard until we see our conditions met," said Janeka. "We'll move them to some of the hotels nearby. They can live it up all they want as long as they don't go anywhere."

"And the captured warships?"

"We're keeping them."

"I suppose that's not worth arguing over. May I address the audience?" Walters asked. Kelly and Janeka naturally hesitated. "I think it's time to resolve all this," she added.

Slowly, after once again consulting Janeka with a glance, Kelly nodded. "Very well."

"Thank you." The vice president of public relations stepped around the two military women and walked up the steps to the stage. She paused at the podium to instruct its directional microphone to follow her and then stepped away, looking out over her literally captive audience. The only person that moved in the entire hall kept walking for the door without looking back.

"Ladies and gentlemen," Walters began, "despite this disruption of our schedule, I can assure you that we still have a quorum. I have been informed that we require a new chief executive officer. Immediately." She paused for the shocked gasps and worried murmurs that she knew would follow, then held her hands out to quiet the crowd. "Given the urgency of our current situation, I hereby step forward for the position. Are there any other candidates?"

No one spoke. The door at the back of the audience hall closed.

Two minutes later, Christina Walters became the first CEO of NorthStar Corporation to be elected by a unanimous vote of the shareholders. She issued her first executive order within sixty seconds of taking office, though she had to borrow communications equipment from her enemies to do it.

• • •

"Do you think I can't tell that you're dragging this out to buy time?" Mayfair scowled. "Whatever your crews get fixed up while we talk, it won't make any difference when the shooting starts."

"And yet here we are," observed Yeoh. She watched him carefully. He had to know what was happening on the ground. NorthStar wouldn't risk a battleship in the field against her if it wasn't ready for combat, but here he was letting her stall against his own best interests.

"I'm not out here to play games with you," Mayfair growled. "You're flying around in stolen property that NorthStar wants back. If I can't recover it, I'm perfectly happy to blow you out of the sky."

"It's your decision, Captain," said Admiral Yeoh. "That's a lovely battleship you have there. It would be a shame if something bad happened to it."

Activity outside of Yeoh's view drew Mayfair's attention. Yeoh carefully lifted one hand, ensuring her movement would not show up within the frame. Commander Beacham had already issued quiet instructions to the other ships in the armada while her other staffers selected targets and drew up new courses. They might not be exactly what Yeoh would want, but she trusted her staff's judgment. The fleet would spring into action again at the drop of her hand.

"Confirm that!" Mayfair demanded of his subordinates.

Yeoh risked a glance to her staff. Beacham looked surprised as well. An officer at the comms station stood and waved with eyes wide. Yeoh hit the mute button on her controls. "What is it?"

The comms officer hit a button at his station to play back the message.

"All NorthStar Security Forces: by executive order, you are to withdraw from combat. Cease fire and withdraw to await further instructions. Please acknowledge."

"That's a clear transmission, ma'am," said the comms officer. "It's in tandem with an encrypted signal on their naval channels. Probably the same message."

Yeoh's eyes turned back to her screen. Mayfair seemed to be at a loss for words. She offered him a crisp smile. "It seems that pausing to talk was a good decision, Captain."

• • •

"You gonna live?" Janeka asked.

She found Everett slumped into a plush chair in a backstage dressing room, claimed as an aid station by Corpsman Matuskey when he arrived with Thompson's marines. Baljashanpreet and Matuskey both had their heads down as they worked to wrap the burned shoulder and arm of another marine on a nearby table, but they'd finished up with the chief already.

Almost half of his face was covered with a self-adhering bandage pad. His blood-soaked right sleeve and pant leg had both been cut open to dress other wounds. Everett opened his good eye to look at her. "I might need some tough love to make sure I don't drown in self-pity," he replied wearily. "So thank God you're around to get me through. Or did you come back here looking for a place to slack off?"

Janeka took up the chair beside him, letting out a tired breath. "Nothing gets by you."

"Not on this side, anyway," Everett agreed, raising his left hand and then letting it drop back onto the arm of the chair. "Gonna have a blind spot on the right until they grow me a new eye. And an ear, I guess. Can't really tell. The guys are bullshitting me, so I imagine it's pretty bad."

Janeka glanced over to Matuskey and Baljashanpreet. Matuskey gave an apologetic shrug. She waved it off.

"So we've got everything under control?" asked Everett.

"It's moving along. The shooting's mostly stopped."

"We lost Mohamed and Fuller upstairs. Don't know what happened to Sinclair. Can't be anything good."

"No. Jacobson didn't make it, either."

"That's too bad. He was pretty decent as officers go."

"Yeah."

Janeka turned her head to look at him. "We did good with these kids, Bill. I still don't know how you sold the navy on the whole 'new guard' approach in the first place."

He nodded, then winced at the pain it caused his neck. "I put your name on all the paperwork and told everybody it was your idea."

"Oh."

The pair stared off into space, and then said in unison, "Your husband's gonna kill me."

• • •

He'd kept the encounter short to make sure Walters and all the other professional people-readers didn't get a chance to study his eyes or his voice. He sold the lie the best way he could think of: he made himself believe it.

If the war wouldn't end until Brekhov lay dead, Tanner decided, he'd make it happen. Whatever that took, he'd do it. In that sense, he told himself, what he said to the suits was true enough. He took care to extract himself from the conversation before anyone had a chance to parse the statement.

Technically, he should have reported to someone for orders. Even with Janeka busy with Kelly—and thank God she was okay— other ranking officers and NCOs were on hand. Instead, he kept walking to the lobby to sell his bluff to the NorthStar suits. On the other side of the vestibule, he found Archangel marines and a couple of people from *Joan of Arc* arranging sturdier cover from the debris to guard the entrance. Booker stood among them. So did Ordoñez.

He let out a tense breath. Kelly was alive. Alicia was fine. Baldwin stood guard on the stage, where she'd probably been all along. Janeka would be okay. On the way through the backstage area, Tanner had seen Sanjay and a wounded marine propped up along some storage boxes to cover the exits. Everett and Sanjay were hurt, but they'd recover, just like Vanessa.

Somewhere nearby, Jacobson lay dead. If he hadn't been retrieved from outside already, any attempt to get him now might set off another exchange of fire. Tanner didn't like it, but he accepted the logic.

The vestibule remained littered with dead NorthStar security and plainclothes agents. One looked like he had been pulled halfway through a doorway to keep it from closing. Past the body, Tanner saw a staircase leading up. It looked like some staff area.

He'd only glanced up at the balcony, where he saw a handful of marines and a couple of apparent agents from the Ministry standing guard over the audience there, but he didn't recognize any of them. They didn't check off any of the names on his mental list. He took the stairs.

Symphony Hall's upper floor offices looked almost as bad as the lobby. Bits of the ceiling now lay on the floor. Glancing up through the gaps that had been burned or smashed through the roof, Tanner saw only the looming grey underside of a ship hovering directly overhead. The occasional crack of a rifle or boom of an explosion echoed through the halls, but none of it seemed to come from close by. He turned back to his search.

Marines held several offices with exterior windows. Most of them stayed under cover, using relay cameras from their holocoms laid on the windowsills to watch the streets below.

Chatter on the comms net grew clearer as he picked his way through the wreckage and the bodies in the halls. Residual interference from all the chaff bursts and whatever jamming the enemy had tried seemed to fall away. He heard Collins relay a couple of orders, and then he heard Ravenell. Two more names on his list. At least one other name remained conspicuously absent, especially given the talk on the net.

He found Sinclair on the floor of another office amid destroyed furniture and fallen enemies. Half of the exterior wall had caved in, leaving the room open to the air outside. The buildings across the street and the starship overhead blocked out most of the direct light. Tanner swallowed hard, knelt at Sinclair's side, and went through the usual checks.

It was long past too late.

Tanner shut his eyes tight and gripped his roommate's arm. His breath shook. He stayed there until he felt his eyes water, and felt grateful for it, and then worse for needing to be hit so close to draw out that kind of reaction.

His eyes eventually opened again. He couldn't stay with Sinclair long. Tanner looked through the gaping hole in the wall and the corner of the roof. In the distance, past the starship and the nearby skyline of office towers, fireballs of debris burned their way through the upper atmosphere.

He heard explosions here and there. They didn't sound like a threat. They sounded like something ending.

Tanner turned back to his dead friend. He had responsibilities to any fallen comrade, including cold considerations like equipment recovery. Any serviceman would be expected to take the whole field comms unit off the dead man's back, but like Sinclair, Tanner held Epsilon security clearance. He had options beyond simply stripping the pack off Sinclair's body.

The unit remained undamaged. Lights and indicators worked properly. The unit continued to receive, decrypt and record.

A shadow spread over the room, steadily enough that it didn't startle Tanner, but he looked up for its source. *Argent* turned in place overhead, watching over the wrecked streets and battered ruins below.

Tanner locked in the decryption, removed the unit's memory chip and put it in his pocket. Then he picked up a fallen chunk of concrete and smashed it into the comms unit.

CHAPTER FIFTEEN

Rollercoasters

"To: General M. Carruthers, Commander, NorthStar Asset Recovery Task Force Michael; Captain V. Sokolov, Commander, NorthStar Security Fleet Task Force 19.

From: Acting Commodore T. Mayfair, NorthStar Security Fleet.

Subject: PRIORITY ORDERS – READ IMMEDIATELY

"Per attached executive order, all NorthStar operations, personnel, and assets will leave Michael and the system of Archangel within 24 hours of receipt of this message. All individuals detained by NorthStar Security for any reason and any confiscated property will be released to local authorities. NorthStar personnel will retrieve only personal and company property. No exceptions or cause for delay will be accepted. Property that cannot be retrieved in time to meet this deadline is to be abandoned.

"Arrangements for the location and return of NorthStar employees missing or captured in the theater of operations will follow at a later date. No such

concern is acceptable cause for delay in the execution of these orders.

"All personnel are to return directly to Fairhaven for further orders."

--NorthStar Security Fleet Order #CW2278.08.01, July 2279

"So you didn't consult with anyone before lying about Brekhov's death?"

"Only Agent Rios and Sergeant Wong on our way back."

"You decided the advice of an Intelligence Ministry agent loaded up on painkillers and a marine infantry sergeant was all the preparation you needed to intervene in discussions with the enemy's high command?"

Tanner's dry gaze shifted over to Commander Beacham. "It seemed rude not to include them, sir."

Sitting at the head of the wardroom table, Admiral Yeoh promptly cut off Beacham's understandably irritated response to Tanner's answer—and his tone. "I believe we can accept Malone's haste. However, some reflection on how this may have been handled differently is more than reasonable," she added with a glance toward Tanner.

Vanessa picked her head up off the back of her comfortable chair beside Tanner's. Unlike the others, she made no effort to conceal her exhaustion. If Tanner's military bearing and sense of etiquette had faltered, Vanessa's complete lack of either made him look good by comparison. "We didn't call ahead for the same reason we had to come straight up here to deliver the news face-to-face," she pointed out. "Something this sensitive shouldn't go out over a signal. I don't care how good your encryption is. If it takes 'em a year to crack the code, that's still too soon."

"We informed Gunny Janeka and Lieutenant Kelly right away," added Wong. "Afterward."

"Look," grumbled Vanessa, "you guys know the value of a good lie. I *know* you do, Admiral," she said with a pointed if weary look. "We had to sell it. The fewer people in on the lie, the better. Tanner was the perfect guy to deliver it. If *he* told anyone in that audience he'd murdered their grandmother, they wouldn't doubt it for a second."

Tanner frowned. "Thanks for that."

"Anytime," Vanessa replied with a woozy brush of her hand.

Beacham sighed and looked to the Admiral. "I can't argue that," he admitted.

"No," said Yeoh. "To be blunt, I completely approve. I am only concerned with going forward. We must expect Brekhov to recover. Lieutenant Torres, assuming a worst case scenario, how long do we have before he can take charge again?"

"I'm sorry, ma'am?" The nurse sitting beside Beacham paid more attention to his holocom screens than to the people around him for most of the debriefing. Though the last shots of the battle landed three hours ago, *Beowulf*'s medical staff would be in crisis mode for hours to come. In any other circumstance, the chief medical officer would have been the one to attend this meeting. As it happened, Torres was spared only because of injuries sustained in the fight. Even with both hands wrapped in medical gel packs, he still did what he could via computer interface.

"What's the soonest we can expect Brekhov to recover and take action?" Yeoh asked patiently.

"Not knowing his medical history and assuming this is his first heart attack—if that's what it was—he could be awake and aware even now. First-time heart attacks usually don't kill if aid is rendered right away. But he must be on his second or third course of longevity treatments." Torres shook his head. "Those first-generation procedures weren't perfect. If he had a heart attack, it could've been bad. They would want to put him to sleep for at least a night, and that's if they didn't have to operate."

"That's what I'm asking, Lieutenant," said Yeoh. "If it's his first and he has no complications and luck is on his side, could he be active again already?"

"It's possible," the nurse confirmed. "Or he could've been stabilized long enough to issue orders or whatever before they put him down. But if we haven't heard anything from him yet, I'd give it at least twelve hours."

"So even though Walters sent the order to withdraw from Archangel," Beacham considered, "he may get another ship to carry another order to cancel it? Or maybe he already has?"

Yeoh nodded. "For all we know, the ships that left with the orders to retreat may have received contradictory instructions before departing."

"If we think he's dead, we're not gonna look for him," Tanner spoke up. "That's the way they'll have to look at things. They need to hide him and help him recover. Letting us believe our own bullshit is in their best interests."

"And you know this how?" Beacham asked.

"It's what I would do if I was his bodyguard and Brekhov's safety was my top priority, sir."

"He's got a point," said Vanessa. "Brekhov's people may be more loyal to the company than they are to him personally, but even so, I don't think they'll pipe up about his survival yet. Not even internally. It's the same risk we had to weigh. The fewer people there are who know the truth, the better. He doesn't want to have to fight for control of his company and dodge us at the same time."

"You believe Walters will resist if he attempts to regain control?" asked Yeoh.

"To stay on as CEO of NorthStar? Bet your ass," Vanessa scoffed. "Even after all this shit, they're still at least the second biggest company in the Union."

"And you think she can hold it against Brekhov?"

"Listen, Brekhov made a lot of money for all those shareholders over a long period of time, but now he's the guy who ran out on them when Walters *didn't*. That's a hell of a card she can play for the rest of her life. And this war cost NorthStar big time, with no end in sight. Those shareholders and the board won't think of Walters as the one who surrendered. They'll think of her as the one who stopped the bleeding. She's the voice of sanity. She knows how to work that angle. You could hear it in what she said at the hall."

"Then we play the hand we've been dealt," decided Yeoh. "Brekhov is dead until he decides to show the world otherwise. The matter is *beyond* Epsilon clearance, understood?" She paused until she heard confirmation and saw heads nod. "If he's smart, he'll lie low until we're long gone, and then NorthStar's internal struggles will be their concern. We stick with the original plan: secure the hotels closest to the meeting hall, move the shareholders over there, and hold them politely but firmly until this is over. We'll look for Brekhov quietly, but if we don't find him, we may well not need him. Ultimately, these actions have my endorsement."

Vanessa leaned back and nudged Tanner. "Told you."

"Told me what?"

"Any level you want." Then she shrugged. "You'll remember later."

"Agent Rios, thank you for your help…and your candor," said Yeoh. "Our medical staff is strained at the moment, but I'm sure we can at least find you a place to rest."

Vanessa let out a tired laugh. "I'll sleep in the corner over there if you need the table."

"I'm sure we can do better than that. Lieutenant Torres, you're dismissed. With my thanks. Good luck out there."

"Ma'am," Torres said, leaving immediately.

"Sergeant, Master-at-Arms," Yeoh said, "we'll have you back on the surface as soon as we can. I want you to relay what you've heard here to Captain Kelly and Gunnery Sergeant Janeka, and only to them."

"Aye aye, ma'am," Tanner replied.

"Ma'am," Alicia spoke up, "is there anything we should be doing here in the meantime? It looks pretty bad."

Yeoh shook her head. "Any available window for sending you back to the surface may be brief. I understand your desire to help, but as soon as you get involved with something, you may have to leave it. Your mobility is priority."

"Yes, ma'am."

"We're sending more marines down as fast as we can," said Beacham, checking one of his holo screens. "The next drop won't be for another twenty minutes at least. I'll let them know you're coming."

"Malone," added Yeoh quietly, "I suggest you visit the infirmary before you go."

Tanner opened his mouth to say he was uninjured, but then stopped. Yeoh said nothing more. He bolted from his seat.

"Hey. Alicia," said Vanessa, rising slowly as Alicia got up to follow Tanner. "Hold on a second." She took the younger woman's offered hand in getting out of the chair, then walked out of the room on her own power. "Oof. Painkillers are really kicking in now."

"You gonna be okay?"

"Oh yeah. Just have to hold the wall while I walk. Listen. You're overdue for discharge, right?"

Alicia gave her a suspicious look. "Why do you know so much about me?"

"This wasn't your first covert op." Vanessa grinned. "It's not that I know 'so much' about you, but I know enough. What are your plans after they lift the exit hold? Have you reenlisted already?"

"Not yet, no," Alicia answered. "I've got an application in for the Academy on Uriel. Figured I'd give it a shot. Don't know if I'll get accepted."

"They'll take you. Hell, after this, they'd take Sanjay if he applied. This is good. You'd need a university degree anyway, but we could still make that work."

"For what?"

"Have you ever considered an exciting career in interstellar espionage?"

• • •

No one had time to explain a patient's condition to a visitor. Tanner didn't even ask. Every doctor, nurse, and corpsman had their hands full. A pair of third-class yeomen filled in at the front desk to free up better-trained hands for actual medical work. As soon as he identified himself as a master-at-arms, they let him straight through without further questions. Tanner let the misrepresentation slide. If someone wanted to yell at him for unintentionally abusing his authority, they could do it later.

Men and women lined the deck of the passageways outside, most of them lying down or sitting with bloody bandages or burn-care gel packs holding them over until someone could get to them.

The scene left him wondering how many people didn't make it even this far. He felt ghoulish for simply passing the wounded by, but if they'd been left on the infirmary floor, they had received about as much care as he could give them already.

The critical care ward ran out of beds, so more were brought in from other rooms until the ward offered just enough room to move them around. Tanner recognized a couple of patients. Admiral Branch was laid out next to some crewman apprentice from engineering. Everyone in the ward seemed to be out cold. The only sounds he heard were from oxygen pumps and other automated systems.

He found his friend's bed easily enough, though he wished it was the wrong one as soon as he saw it. The blue fluids in the flexible tubes running beneath the blanket suggested far worse burns than a simple bandage could handle. Seals put in place at the edges of the bedding indicated radiation exposure. Other colored tubing indicated graver internal concerns.

The shifting display on the holo screen over the bed told Tanner the full story. Memories of the infirmary at Fort Stalwart came back to him, though his fight with Janeka hadn't left him nearly this hurt. Images of Nathan's body revealed ugly areas of tissue all up and down his torso and arms that had been destroyed by a combination of burns and exposure to the void, along with the internal damage done by the shrapnel that pierced his vac suit in the first place. How they'd ever gotten Nathan off the bridge in time to save him was beyond Tanner.

Nathan's helmet was obviously a critical factor in his survival. His face looked fine aside from a simple bandage on the side of his head and an oxygen lead under his nose. He'd been able to breathe. His heart and his brain escaped damage. The rest of him, though… "Jesus, Nathan," said Tanner.

"Yeah, I know, right?" spoke a soft voice. Tanner almost jumped out of his skin at the sound and the sight of Nathan's lips moving. The voice didn't come directly from Nathan, Tanner realized. He'd seen voice-assist systems before, but the fact that Nathan was conscious at all shocked him. Nathan's eyes slowly opened. He didn't move his head. "So I guess we both made it?"

Tanner nodded. "We did," he said. "We pulled it off."

"That's good," replied Nathan's soft, largely artificial voice.

"How the hell are you even awake?"

"I dunno. Science, I guess? That's supposed to be your gig. You tell me." His words came slowly and with almost no inflection or emotion.

"I'm way out of practice."

The voice assist registered a nonverbal response. Words seemed to work fine. Grunts and groans only confused the vocabulary identifiers. "Problem is I'm not really tired. Slept pretty well right before the fight. I guess they can't give me anything to put me to sleep now. Interacts bad with all the other stuff. They explained it, but you know me. I only listened to the bottom line."

"What's that?" Tanner asked.

"Guess I'm gonna spend most of my term in a hospital bed," said Nathan. "They gotta rebuild or regrow a lot of stuff."

Tanner winced. Sanjay's arm had been a relatively clean loss of a limb, and that was rough enough to fix. Nathan needed all kinds of work from shoulder to waist. Even his feet looked bad. The surgeries and regrowth periods could take a couple of years, as he stated, not to mention months of physical therapy. "Yeah, I guess so," said Tanner, fighting back his emotions. "You were up and moving for the bit of your term that counted, though. I hear you're the big hero this time."

"All I did was drive for a couple minutes," Nathan replied.

Tanner grinned in spite of the tears trying to escape. "Uh-huh. You really do have that false modesty thing down, don't you?"

"It's important when you're rich and good-looking. Why do you think I never got beat up in school?" Nathan's bed beeped. Tanner heard a series of mechanical noises in a matching sequence as drugs flooded the patient's body. "Oh. I guess laughing is bad. No more of that."

"I'll try not to be funny."

"Yeah. Wouldn't want to start now."

Tanner chuckled. "Asshole."

"Y'know the crazy part?" said Nathan. "All through the fight, I kept thinking about your mom. Do you remember bringing her to class that time when we were little?"

"Sure."

"My mom got all bent out of shape. She got over it once we became friends and she got to know her better, but…I think she felt like your mom showed her up."

Tanner frowned. "Wasn't your mom already the chief general counsel of the biggest firm on Michael by then?"

"How many kids knew what that meant besides you and Heather Verde? Lawyers are boring. Your mom pulled people out of car crashes for a living, and she was a veteran. That's cool."

"She'd be proud of you, Nathan. Your own mom, too. NorthStar's gonna pull out of Michael and your family will know you're the reason why."

Nathan didn't say anything. His eyes closed. Tanner wondered if he drifted off to sleep. Then Nathan said, "So what did you do today?"

Tanner glanced over his shoulder. "Not much. Gave some nice old man a heart attack."

"Did you at least get shot?"

"A little, but not like you. You know they only give you one Purple Heart at a time, right? Extra credit doesn't count."

"You and Madelyn made me all self-conscious that night at dinner. I had to catch up somehow. Guess I screwed myself."

"Nah, you did fine. Nobody's gonna notice your screw-ups now."

Nathan's eyes opened again. "What is it?"

"Nothing," Tanner replied. Nathan didn't speak, and then Tanner realized his friend would wait him out. "I shot a non-combatant. He wasn't a threat, just some guy in a suit, but he was in the wrong place and I lit him up."

"Didn't you blow up a whole assault carrier?" Nathan asked. "Something like forty-whatever thousand people? You don't think there was at least some civilian journalist or a couple of observers or something on that boat?"

The question made him blink. Even Tanner's therapists hadn't opened that line of discussion. "I'd thought of it, yeah. I figure anyone on that boat knew they were walking onto a military ship going into combat, y'know? It was out of my hands."

"You don't think the same thing happened with whoever you shot? I mean, you'd take it back if you could, but you can't. Obviously you care that it happened. Who's to say he wasn't there for a reason?"

Then it was Tanner's turn to fall silent. "You're better at this officer thing than I expected."

"Privileged guys aren't *all* assholes."

"I know." Tanner smiled. "I've always known."

His holocom beeped. Tanner hit the answer key on his wrist. "Malone," he said.

"We're riding back on *St. George*," came Alicia's voice. "Main hangar. They're here in four minutes and they aren't waiting around."

"I'm on my way." He killed the connection and turned back to Nathan. "I gotta go."

"I heard."

"Listen, they're probably gonna have me on the ground for a long while. Once they put me back up here, whatever the visiting hours are—"

"I know. Do your thing."

"Okay."

"Tanner," said Nathan, his eyes opening again. His natural voice, though still raw and faded, came through clearly along with the bed's vocal assistance program. "I'm gonna be okay. Someday. It's more than others can say."

"You will," Tanner confirmed. "You're gonna be fine."

Nathan shook his head—barely, but enough that Tanner saw it. "I wanted to be here for the big show. I chose this. I'm gonna get better. So don't be a mopey asshole about me, okay?"

Tanner let out a laugh, though a couple of tears escaped along with it. "Aye aye, sir."

"You're right," Nathan replied, his eyes closing once more. "That sounds goofy out of you."

• • •

St. George looked worse for wear as Tanner arrived in the hangar bay, but Tanner felt glad to see her nonetheless. The hangar bay itself had seen better days, too. At least one of *Beowulf*'s shuttles sat in pieces in its cradle. Bulkheads were left blackened by explosions. Any hull breaches had been sealed, though, and people could work freely in the big space again.

The remainder of a marine platoon stood under the corvette's wing with their gear all collected and ready to load up. Tanner helped a pair of marines carry a field generator on the way in, then turned to find himself a spot inside *St. George*'s cargo bay. Alicia waved to him from one corner, seated on the deck beside a gear bag. He made his way over and collapsed into the open spot on the deck beside hers.

"You okay?" she asked.

"Yeah. Why?"

"You don't look like it."

Tanner sniffed. He realized then that his eyes were probably completely red. "Yeah, I just…I was thinking that I'd gotten off really lucky in all this, all things considered. And then I thought about how 'really lucky' is still, uh…" he sniffed again. "It's still pretty shitty."

Alicia leaned against him shoulder to shoulder. "You're supposed to get de-sensitized to all this."

"I know," he said, and then shrugged. "I don't wanna."

She smiled a little. "I guess you picked the right things to hold onto."

Tanner reached one arm around her to give her a hug. Their position made it difficult for her to return the gesture, but she didn't resist. He glanced at her gear bag. "What's in there?" he asked as he let her up.

"Couple of vac suits." She pointedly looked his battle-worn civilian clothes up and down. "Can't help but notice that you magically didn't have time to grab any of your own."

"Nope," Tanner replied. "Can't say I mind, though. I'm tired of wearing 'em."

Alicia smiled thoughtfully. "Yeah. Maybe I am, too."

• • •

> "Current operations on Fairhaven are no exception to standard rules of conduct and military justice. All personnel will immediately report any use of physical force. Civilian complaints of harassment, violence, theft, or other misconduct will be fully investigated. Goods or services acquired from local sources must be paid for. Looting is prohibited. Personnel can expect to have their gear searched for contraband upon return to their ships.
>
> "Some degree of hostility or resentment from the population is to be expected. All personnel will behave honorably. The safety of navy personnel takes priority, but if in doubt, withdraw and report. Do not violate the Rules of Engagement.
>
> "Remember at all times that our goal is to end the current conflict, not to continue it. Revenge is not within the Archangel Navy creed."
>
> --MESSAGE TO OCCUPYING FORCES, AUGUST 2278

"This shit is gonna explode in your fuckin' face," Casey warned with casual disdain. He walked beside Ezekiel to *Argent*'s cargo bay while the ship's PA system repeated the call for the impending all-hands meeting. "Four days of busting ass on repairs, less than a day after the service for all their dead shipmates, and you wanna drop this on 'em."

"What I want is irrelevant," snapped Ezekiel. He came to a halt, looking up and down the corridor before saying more. Even now, he maintained the illusion of deference to the captain's authority while others were watching. When they were alone, though, he didn't need to keep up with the act. "I've got my orders."

"Everyone on a ship gets orders. You're acting like this is a military boat all of the sudden."

"It's more military than pirate. Everyone knows who they work for on this ship. Everyone knows where we get our orders."

"Oh, get off it. They're the crew of a Ministry ship. That doesn't make 'em Ministry agents. You know better than to expect these people to salute and say 'thank you, sir,' when you're screwing 'em. A little sacrifice here and there is fine, but dropping bad news like this and then telling 'em all to suck it up isn't gonna go over well at all."

"I've got my orders," Ezekiel repeated.

"You've got weeks-old contingency orders drawn up by assholes who drive desks back on Raphael. It ain't like you can't use your own judgment to soften the blow."

"What do you want from me?" the bigger man fumed.

"I think you'd better figure out a way to make it up to the crew *before* you deliver the bad news," Casey replied evenly. "And you'd better make it good."

"Or what?"

"Or we're gonna have a serious morale problem. I don't know if you remember, Zeke, but this boat used to have shit like swimming pools and a fuckin' casino. They took out all that fun shit right after you came on. Ring any bells? Everyone having a room to themselves? All that gone. Then a couple months without liberty, a fight where some of their friends died and then all the repair work—"

"Since when do you care?" Ezekiel scowled.

"I care about *crew morale*. I gotta depend on 'em in an emergency, buddies or not. Shit gets dodgy real fast when your whole crew is pissed off and tired. They've been on a downhill slide for months, but they held it together. Now the war's over, or close enough. They expect some sort of payoff. You gotta throw 'em a cookie or two, not kick 'em in the ass."

"I think you're forgetting the sort of incentives they've got waiting for them at the end of this job. It's not that far off now."

"You hope," Casey corrected. "We've got more than three weeks to wait before we get anything out of the rest of the corporate assholes back in Archangel, whether it's a white flag or a 'fuck you.' A lot can happen in three weeks."

"I'm done," Ezekiel declared. "We're following orders. Will there be a problem?"

"I'm not the one you need to worry about," the captain replied mildly.

Ezekiel didn't dignify that with anything more than a brief glare. Casey would always be Ezekiel's biggest concern on the ship, and they both knew it. The XO turned and continued on to the main cargo bay with the bemused captain at his side.

With the exception of those standing watch at critical stations, Ezekiel and Casey found *Argent*'s full crew gathered and waiting. Most of the 342 remaining crewmembers found boxes or machinery to sit on. About the only ones who didn't take a completely informal approach to the meeting were the security officers—all of whom reported directly to Ezekiel—and even they adopted a casual stance.

Argent's CO and XO entered at the second level of the wide, mostly open compartment, coming to a spot on the catwalk around the edges of the bay where they could address everyone at once. "Everyone present and accounted for," reported one of the security officers.

"Sure you don't want me to do the talking?" Casey taunted. Ezekiel turned slightly toward him to sneer without everyone seeing it. Casey shrugged. "Wouldn't want to shirk my duties. But go ahead," he added, gesturing to the spot closest to the rail.

Ezekiel turned to the crowd. "Ladies and gentlemen, the captain and I want to express our gratitude and pride once again for your performance. You got us through the battle and you worked hard to get us back into shape right afterward. The ship might not look as pretty as she did when we got here, but she's ready to roll.

"Our orders are to remain in place and be ready to provide assistance for occupation forces. If there's a sudden need for evacuation or other unexpected development, it's best to start out here below most of the ground defenses. When the fleet pulls out, we'll pull out."

The crew watched and listened without interruption. The longer he spoke and watched their faces, though, the more Ezekiel detected signs of skepticism and impatience. He wondered if there might be more to Casey's warnings than the pirate's usual grumbling.

"Now we know a lot of you have been expecting liberty calls since we arrived," Ezekiel continued. "It obviously wouldn't have been a good idea to let you all off the ship before the battle. I think you can all see that now."

"Oh, sure," Casey muttered under his breath. "Patronizing them will win 'em over."

"Unfortunately, we're still in the same situation," said Ezekiel. Disgusted looks and groans scattered throughout the crowd provided the first confirmation of how unpopular this would be. They only grew as he continued. "The navy will occupy only a few small zones and specific sites, and they're under strict rules. They can't provide security across the planet or even throughout this city."

"We can't go anywhere?" yelled one crewman.

"You gotta be kidding us!" called out another.

Ezekiel held up his hands in a vain effort to quiet the crowd. "We don't like it any more than you do, folks. Orders are orders. Again, we have to be ready to move—"

"Yeah, in a couple of weeks!"

"We're cooped up in here until we leave? And then until we get back to Archangel? Or will we even get to leave then?"

"Alright, that's enough!" Ezekiel snapped. The crowd quieted, but the sullen and resentful looks held on. "Like I said, the navy can't provide security. The locals obviously aren't happy to see Archangel faces, so it's not like there's anywhere to go, regardless."

"Half of us aren't even from Archangel! What about us?"

"That doesn't make any difference. You think the whole spaceport isn't under surveillance? Even with the navy in control? They know we're here and they know what to look for. It's too big a risk. End of story. This isn't up for debate."

"Okay," spoke up Schlensker, "but when are we gonna have a port call ever again? Or are we all stuck on this ship until our contracts are up?"

"Yeah, is this a ship or a jail?" someone else asked.

Casey snorted. He saw Ezekiel twitch, not quite looking back but hesitating before he spoke again. It looked like an opportunity. "You need to make it up to 'em," Casey reiterated quietly.

"How?" Ezekiel grumbled, finally turning back. "I'm not letting people off this ship. We've got sixteen felons in the crew workin' on amnesty deals, not to mention the other sensitive cases. It's a matter of operational security."

"Okay. Pay 'em."

"What?"

"This is a Ministry ship. You've got discretionary funds, right? Couple million, at least? Start coughing up. Do it fast and it'll look like you planned it." He saw Ezekiel hesitate again. "I'd make it generous, though. They risked a lot. Their buddies died."

"People," Ezekiel said, turning to the crowd, but his hesitation remained. The crew seemed almost oblivious to his attempt to regain their attention as they complained amongst themselves. "How much?" he hissed back to Casey.

"Oh, five grand ought'a do it."

"Five thousand?" the other man protested. "That's—"

"A little over a million-seven. You've got the money. But don't dangle it like a carrot. Give it to 'em right away or they'll smell bullshit and get madder."

Ezekiel turned back. He knew the crew was impatient for some time off, but this reaction was worse than he'd expected. Doubt crept into his mind. For all his frustrations with Casey, the man knew how to run a ship. He'd shown that during the battle, and the insertion, and before that. He'd held together the worst pack of criminals on this side of the Union for years before the war, too. He knew how to motivate people. Ezekiel's leadership experience came from a very different setting. To have things go wrong now…

"Folks, hold on a second!" he bellowed, quieting much of the crowd. "People! Calm down! Nobody wants to see you all get screwed over. Command anticipated this. We'll get some drinks and fresh food and all that and we'll relax the schedule so everyone will get some free time, but we're stuck with the rules as they are.

"On the other hand," he said, "you'll all be getting a bonus for combat and hardship. Five thousand credits, transferred to your personal accounts by the end of the day."

Grumbles turned to cheers. Ezekiel didn't know whether to be relieved at their shift in attitude or angry that he'd allowed himself to be backed into a corner…until he happened to look down into the crowd. Standing amid the rest of the crew, Schlensker looked up toward Casey and winked.

Ezekiel gripped the handrail of the catwalk. Suddenly the crew's widespread irritation made much more sense.

The war was nearly over. *Argent* would soon return to Archangel. Ezekiel would give his report, along with his recommendations for what to do with the ship and its crew. Though Kiribati placed great value on assets like *Argent*, he also understood the need to tie up loose ends.

• • •

Task Force Fairhaven took over only a handful of areas on the planet. NorthStar forces remained in an "alert stand down," which amounted to most of their ships remaining on or near their moon bases and lots of rhetoric about being ready to move back into combat should the situation change.

Archangel's forces never found Anton Brekhov.

The occupiers took up positions to deny him optimal refuge. Though they could not cover every hospital across the planet, Brekhov could not use those within the capital. Even if he could safely make it to one of his private starships, he had no hope of escaping Archangel's blockade. He could not return to NorthStar's main headquarters, nor their top-tier facilities, nor any of Fairhaven's militia facilities without running the risk of discovery by Archangel's "monitors."

He could not go home, either. Not while the Archangel Navy used his estate as a secondary field headquarters for its occupation of the planet…or, on a couple of days during the fourth week of the occupation, as the site for some loud and necessary parties.

As it turned out, the Archangel Navy greatly enjoyed his pool. And his kitchen. And his wine cellar. And his living room, game room, state-of-the-art theater, golf course, tennis court, personal gym, sauna, secondary indoor pool, and whatever else they found in his home.

"Wow! Do you keep that bikini in your bags, or did you pick it up here?" asked Ordoñez as Alicia stepped out onto the pool deck. The gunner's mate lounged at the side of the pool, half-submerged with her arms propped up against the edge where she could reach her drink.

Alicia wanted to be nonchalant about it, but the instant attention she received from several of her comrades—all of whom were polite enough not to say anything, though she saw plenty of double-takes—left her grinning from ear to ear under her big sunglasses. It felt good to wear something attractive and get a reaction again.

Nobody gave a damn about her scars. Almost everyone had their own.

"I found it in a dresser," Alicia said as people went back to their conversations, games, and other distractions. "It wasn't the only one. Different sizes, smartweave stuff. Lots of choices. All high-end labels, too."

"Shit, really? I've had this ugly thing since basic." Ordoñez hauled herself out of the pool, then froze. "Waitasec," she said, sinking back in with a suspicious frown. "This fucker's got a room full of sexy bikinis and dresses in different sizes? Does he even have a wife or a girlfriend? Or do you think he keeps it all on hand in case he's 'entertaining' or somethin'?"

Alicia shrugged. "Hey, it's all clean. Besides, I figure after everything I've done in the last few years, something like this isn't remotely scandalous. Gonna burn it when I'm done using it, anyway."

"Good point," Ordoñez decided, climbing out of the pool. "Which way?"

"Down the stairs, hallway to the left, second room on your right. Probably others."

"Thanks!" Ordoñez replied. "Hey, Montes!" she called over to the impromptu water polo game that had broken out on the other side of the pool. "Shopping trip! C'mon!" Then she walked inside, leaving her towel behind. A trail of water from the pool across the carpets would be the least of the damage inflicted on the home before the day was over.

After a quick look around to consider her options, Alicia spotted the red stubble of her boyfriend's scalp among the two water polo teams. Neither side looked all that serious about the game. On her way to join them, she came across Tanner sitting in a deck chair with a pair of holo screens floating in front of him. He wore only shorts and a pair of dark sunglasses, with his towel and other belongings piled beside him on the chair.

"You're reading? Seriously?"

"Not since you walked out here. Damn."

Alicia rolled her eyes. "Uh-huh. I thought you'd be in the pool."

"Taking a break. Anyway, you don't have to burn the bikini. Keep it if you want it."

"What about all the contraband rules? It's not like I have a receipt. This costs more than I make in a month."

"The rules are there to keep assholes from looting random stores and homes," he explained with a dismissive wave. "It's not like we're strip-searching people. Wear it under your uniform on the way back to the ship. No one's gonna care."

"Seems like a double-standard is all," Alicia teased. "Didn't you start out fighting pirates?"

Tanner smirked. "How many people have you put on report in the last three weeks?"

"Four. One for assaulting a civilian, two for harassment, one for vandalism. You?"

"Not much more than that," he replied. "Soldiers have looted since the job was invented. I think you'll find that this is one of the gentlest and most conscientious occupations in human history. So no," Tanner said with a smile, "I don't feel the least bit bad about trashing the rich bad guy's house and swiping some random clothes. It's not like we're pillaging the city."

"Seems a little unfair that it's only us from the initial landing at this party and nobody else gets a crack at it," Alicia pointed out.

"Yeah, that's an ugly double-standard, Sergeant. You should do something about it."

"Just giving you a hard time. What are you reading? More college application stuff?"

"User manual for a toy I found inside. I'm saving the applications for the trip home."

"Alicia!" someone called out. "C'mere!"

"I'm coming! Catch you later, Tanner."

"Stuff one on Ravenell for me, okay?" Tanner asked, and then let out an annoyed yelp when Alicia deliberately dragged her hand through his holo screens on her way by to snuff them out. He craned his head around to watch her go, then settled back in and reactivated the screens.

The instructions seemed clear enough. Tanner reached under his towel to pull out the personal entertainment player he'd found inside the house and activated its user interface screen, then readied the earpieces. He looked around to ensure that nobody looked ready to interrupt him before he fished the memory chip out of his duffle bag.

The lack of opportunity to review the chip after the battle made the whole thing irrelevant until now. For all the "understandings" and "subsections" about rules for the occupation and personal property, Tanner didn't want to wind up explaining why he had certain military electronics in his pockets when he went back up to *Beowulf*. He likely wouldn't have a less conspicuous chance to check it out than here and now in plain sight.

He already knew the right timespan. The chip identified each individual broadcaster picked up during the allotted times, making it easy for Tanner to sort them out. He only needed to find one. The earpieces filtered out most of the noise of the party. The channel that interested him the most contained no visuals, so he only had to listen to a few minutes of audio.

He listened through once before turning up the volume and filtering out a few obvious bits of clutter. In truth, he felt about ready to give up on this in favor of returning to the party. Dead ends never surprised him anymore. He set the player for the run through, hit play—and then jerked with surprise as a familiar face came right through the holo screen displaying the user manual. "*Tanner!*" yelled Ravenell.

"Woah! Jesus!" Tanner blurted, then pulled out his earpieces.

Music and laughter flooded back into his ears as Ravenell stood upright again. He, too, wore only swimming trunks and a towel over his shoulders, though he was dryer than most. "They're calling for you downstairs," he explained. "Is your holocom dead or something?"

Tanner blinked. "Uh, no. Sorry, I took it off. What's up?" He realized then that his holocom was indeed beeping and buzzing away on top of his towel.

"The duty watch guys are calling for you downstairs. They buzzed me to get you."

"Gotcha. Sorry. Has it been long?"

"Only a minute or two," said Ravenell. "Somebody here to see you, I guess. Didn't want to keep 'em waiting. You okay?"

"Yeah, I'm fine, sorry." Tanner killed the playback. "Studying for a thing."

"You know it's a party, right? You've been to them before."

"It was only for a minute," Tanner grumbled. He waited until Ravenell turned away before he popped the memory chip out of the player, pocketed it, and then put the player in his duffle bag. With his thoughts back on the world around him, Tanner threw on the loose shirt and sandals he'd liberated from the poolhouse and headed inside.

A fierce computer game raged between a group of marines and crewmen in the living room as he passed by. More laughter and music came from the kitchen and study. Things didn't get quieter until he rounded the staircase leading to the main level and then the next flight of steps to the entry floor.

The "watch station" amounted to a desk hauled down from the study to the foyer. The guys on duty seemed relaxed enough, though Tanner didn't see any feet kicked up or food out in the open. That brought the formality up a half-notch, at least. "What's up?" Tanner asked.

"You've got a visitor," one of the marine corporals answered, though as the words came out of her mouth, Tanner made it far enough down the staircase that he could see for himself.

"Malone," said Lieutenant Kelly. Like the watchstanders, Kelly wore a standard duty vac suit. She stood patiently by the desk, apparently keeping herself occupied with something on her holocom until he arrived.

"Oh. I'm sorry to keep you waiting, Captain," said Tanner. "I was—is it Captain here, or Lieutenant? I can never keep it straight."

She shook her head. "It's Lieutenant today, and I'm sorry to drag you out. That's one of the reasons I waited here, actually," she said, stepping forward. "Enlisted party."

"Aw, nobody'd care about that, Lieutenant," Tanner replied. "You were there for the landings like the rest of us."

"The officers' party was here last night," Kelly added with a smirk. "It's not like I didn't get my turn. Anyway, I'm doing reports on the landings. Figured I should come talk to you in person."

"Yeah, that was a hell of a mess you all left for us to straighten up this morning, ma'am," said Tanner. He gestured for her to follow him back up the stairs. "Thanks, guys," he added for the watch section.

"Is your holocom back on, Malone?" one of them called after him.

"Yeah, I'm good now. Sorry!"

"I take it you're all on a tight leash even for your day off?" Kelly asked quietly as they came to the second floor.

"Not that tight," he answered. "If there's trouble, we're supposed to get ourselves together fast. Mostly that means nobody can get roaring drunk."

Kelly chuckled. "Someone should've told that to Lieutenant Duran last night."

"I'd love to see how the officers act at their parties," said Tanner. He paused as they came off the staircase. The second floor held far fewer people than the first and third, but even so, his voice fell a notch. "So is this about something sensitive?"

"Potentially. You're a sensitive guy." A sly, tight smile spread across her lips. "Granted, you've been mindful of what you've said in writing and all, but I like to think I can read between lines. Of course, I haven't seen any such letters since the landing. Or since the fleet went quiet, or…well, for a while, actually."

His eyebrow rose. Once again, Tanner glanced up and down the hallway before speaking. "Given all the security concerns after the landing, I didn't want to do anything that could raise any flags," he explained, though he didn't quite apologize. She didn't seem upset. "Hell, I didn't even get time to say more than hello at Symphony Hall, and that was three weeks ago."

"Sure was."

"Three weeks and you don't have that report finished yet?"

"I broke my ship coming to your rescue, you jerk!" Kelly laughed.

"I can't tell you how glad I was to see you."

"Can't? Or couldn't?"

"There were a lot of people there watching," he conceded.

"I remember. But I *thought* you looked glad to see me. And then you completely cut me out on your clever little plan," she added with mock indignation.

"One more thing I couldn't say out in the open."

"Too many people."

"Yeah."

"Okay, now you're just dragging this out."

"Whatever I can do to keep you smiling," Tanner confessed.

That smile brightened further. "Now that sounds like the sort of thing you couldn't say at the hall. Or in a letter to an officer."

"No, ma'am."

"Nobody's watching now, *Tanner*."

"I like 'Lynette' a lot better than 'ma'am,'" he said.

"So do I," she agreed. "We've put on a lot of the same miles since then, I guess. Anything else you haven't been able to tell me?"

"Lots of things. Didn't want to risk getting you into any trouble."

"But no concern for what trouble *you* might get into for it?"

"I'm not bucking for any promotions. Worst the navy could do to me is assign me to combat duty and oh, look, here I am." He grinned. "As long as I'm not in trouble with you, I don't care."

"Yeah. Funny thing is, I'm not bucking for anymore promotions, either."

Tanner nodded. "You didn't re-up when your term expired, did you?"

"You remembered when it expired," noted Lynette. "You remember those little things. I like that. And you're considerate about stuff that might embarrass me. No grand gestures, no dumb stunts to get my attention. I've never worried about you doing anything stupid."

"Oh, I can be stupid. Like I said, I figured that would probably cause you problems."

"You never gave up, either."

"I would if you told me."

Her grin brightened. "See, and I like *that* a lot, too."

"Lotta guys can't take no for an answer?"

"I've had that problem before, yes."

Again, Tanner glanced up and down the hallway. "I'm guessing you didn't come out here to tell me to go away, did you?" He noticed a new glint in her eye. "What?"

"What I *really* like is the way you look at me when you think nobody's watching."

The hallway lay deserted but for the two of them. He knew it, and so did she.

Tanner stepped closer, slipped one hand around her waist, and kissed her.

They didn't stay together long. The hallway was clear, and neither of them hesitated. Both could feel the electricity. The kiss grew awkward for an entirely unexpected reason: Lynette couldn't control her grin.

"Okay, that's never happened before," she admitted, covering her mouth.

"I'll take that as a compliment," said Tanner as he stepped back.

"Bit of a complaint, too," she chuckled, poking him.

"Would practice help?"

"It might." For the first time, Lynette looked up and down the hallway instead of Tanner. "Shouldn't we find someplace safer, though?"

Tanner's smile turned sly. "How much trouble are you willing to risk?"

"All of it."

He suggested a direction with a tilt of his head. As they walked past a few rooms with closed doors, Tanner explained, "Pretty much everything but the bedrooms and the main study was left open for the party. A couple of the bedrooms are open so people can use them to change or whatever. The rest are all locked up." He paused at a pair of double doors, looked down the hall and quietly added, "The locks aren't on the security grid. Most of the watch section doesn't know the entry codes."

"I assume they trusted the MAs with the codes?"

"Well, yeah." Tanner keyed in the entry commands. "It's not like MAs ever abuse their authority or anything."

They heard a low, male groan as the door opened. Tanner's eyes went wide. Baldwin peeked out from the bed sheets and then hurled a pillow at the door. "Dammit, Tanner, get out!" she roared.

Tanner immediately slammed the door shut, then stared at it for a second as the lock reset. He turned to Lynette and jerked his thumb at the door. "Hey, did you want to say hi to Sanjay while you're here?"

Her forehead wound up leaning against his shoulder as she tried to stifle her laugh. "I still can't believe he got off my ship without ever facing a captain's mast."

"He hasn't mustered out from *Beowulf* yet, so there's still time," Tanner muttered. "On the bright side, that accounts for half of the remaining people who know the entry codes." He tried the door on the opposite side of the hallway. The guest bedroom was smaller, but at least it was empty.

"Is the other person the Officer of the Watch?"

"Yeah. I'm not too worried about him. He's—"

Lynette shoved Tanner into the room and stepped inside after him. "Whatever. Shut up and kiss me."

• • •

"Wow. I needed that," said Lynette.

"Me, too," agreed Tanner.

Her body stirred against his in the tangle of sheets on the bed. She turned her head a little to nuzzle against his shoulder. "I couldn't tell."

Tanner laughed. "Thank you."

He felt her head shift against his neck again. The room wasn't all that dark, though the sun began to set outside the sole window. "Never heard that before," she mused. She kissed his neck. "Thank you." Lynette rose onto one elbow when he said nothing else. "What's on your mind?"

"More things than I'd want at a time like this."

"Show me yours and I'll show you mine. Again."

He smiled, but it quickly faded. "What's next? What happens after this? Or does asking spoil it?"

"Nah," said Lynette. "Better to talk about it than not." A self-deprecating grin moved across her face as she added, "Might've talked that out before we got this far, though."

"Like you said, you needed this."

"Oh, was it obvious?"

"Not at all," Tanner answered innocently. "I'm not throwing stones."

Lynette chuckled. "No, this isn't a one-time fling, if that's what you're asking. Not if you don't want it to be, anyway. Takes two to decide that."

"You've got my vote."

"Then that's settled."

"But…?"

She sighed. "I think it might be a while yet before we see a lot of follow-through. You've got plans for college, for one thing. Had 'em way longer than you've known me. You can't give all that up," Lynette told him soberly. "Sooner or later, it'd eat at you. And it'd spoil us…whatever 'us' turns out to be."

"Can't really argue that," Tanner admitted. "My plans are pretty malleable, though. Hell, I still have to go through the whole application process again. Lots of options there. In the meantime I'm gonna be kicking around a bit. I need to visit my family on Arcadia. Other than that…" He shrugged. "You said you pulled the trigger on getting out. You still haven't told me what you plan to do."

"Wondered when you'd ask," she teased.

"We've been a bit busy."

"Fair. I volunteered to stay on for a few weeks after we get back. That's assuming NorthStar really is done, but I guess everything assumes that. Anyway, it's not like I'll have any time to see you even if you hang around on Raphael. We're probably going to be underway for most of the time while the navy and Civil Defense get sorted out again. And I'll be prepping Booker to take command, since he's staying in."

"They're gonna give him *Joan of Arc*?" asked Tanner.

"That's what it looks like. Plus if anyone else steps up for the job, I'll run them over on the flight line. They gave me a command after only one term, and he's been through more crazy shit at this point than I had in the same amount of time. He's ready. He'll get it."

"Good," Tanner agreed. "So you're on for a few more weeks, and then…?"

"Probably about five or six, give or take a few days. I figured the extra money would help." Lynette rolled over to reach for something on the floor beside the bed. Tanner's gaze followed as much out of admiration as curiosity. Soon enough she was laying against his side again with her holocom in her hand. "You've got to go do college, and I've got to do this."

A holographic ship appeared. The yacht floated in the air over Tanner and Lynette with its landing struts down. Tanner saw some battle damage, but it wasn't anything that couldn't be repaired. He looked from the hologram to Lynette.

"I've been saving for my own ship since my first term," she explained. "Didn't expect to get offered a command so soon, but once they floated the possibility…" Lynette sniffed and shook her head. "People in the navy say they're gonna buy their own ships someday like high school jocks talk about going pro. Most of 'em never make it happen. I knew I could do it."

"How could you save enough for your own ship in two terms?"

"It's only enough for a down payment and starting expenses. Navy command experience makes it a hell of a lot easier to get loan approvals for something like this. Domestic bank, obviously."

"Enough for *that*?"

"She's more than most people can swing starting out, sure, but she's also seen better days. The thing is, she's up on the block at the end of the quarter and there are rules to favor small business buyer types like me. It's not exactly good pillow talk," Lynette finished, shaking her head. "I've done my homework. If I can't swing this, I have back-up choices. I'll have a lot in my favor. And I won't be entirely alone," she added with a grin. "I'm not the only one about to be discharged."

"You got some of *Joan*'s crew to sign on?"

"Cervantes is on board, yeah," said Lynette. "So that's some expert engineering help. I've also got a great gunner's mate all ready to go…and a bo'sun with some extracurricular talents."

Tanner's eyes widened. "That son of a bitch. He never said anything!"

"I'm sorry. I asked him to keep it quiet." She killed the holo projection and looked in Tanner's eyes. "But that's what's next for me. You've got college. I've got this. Can't give either of 'em up."

He let out a slow breath. "No. No, I guess not."

"I'd ask you to come with me. Thing is, getting between you and your dreams sounds like a great way to make sure we burn out fast."

Tanner stared at the mangled sheets. "I've lost track of most of those dreams. Y'know, I was talking about that right before the landings with…anyway." His eyes came back to hers. "What if you're a part of my dreams now?"

"Two years of writing letters, visiting me every day in *Beowulf*'s infirmary, and now we're risking a misconduct charge? I'd *better* be part of them," Lynette joked, drawing a laugh from him. "I don't know how long it'll take us to figure out what we are, but I'll be mobile. You'll be free to do what you want. Whatever that is, I think you'll be a lot happier once you're making your own choices. Might be a whole different guy. I'm looking forward to seeing it."

"A lot could happen between now and then," he pointed out.

"Yeah."

"What do we look like in the meantime?"

"Hm. You're gonna be at some university and I'm gonna be roaming around the Union. How does committed non-monogamy and a promise to see each other at least a few times a year until you're done with college sound?"

Again, Tanner laughed. "What does 'committed non-monogamy' mean?"

"It means we can see other people and still be whatever we are, but we don't get serious about anything until we figure *us* out first. I don't think we need to pine away for each other across the stars. Maybe I'll meet other guys and maybe I'll give 'em a chance. Same for you with the girls wherever you go to school." Lynette's grin became more enthralling than ever. "But given the competition, I don't like their odds."

• • •

"What the hell was that, you ass?" hissed Baldwin.

Tanner looked up from the spread of food on the tables in bewilderment. "What is it with all my favorite people calling me names today?" he asked no one in particular. "Did everyone take a vote and pick a spot on the calendar?"

"No, it's an ordinary Tuesday," joked the young man gathering food on the opposite side of the table. "Whiner."

"I said 'favorite people,' Other Gomez!" said Tanner.

"Oh, that is—I'm the *only* Gomez! The other Gomez isn't even in the navy anymore! *He's* the other Gomez now! Do you even know my first name?"

"Nobody cares," Baldwin shot back. "And don't try to dodge this," she continued, jabbing her elbow into Tanner's side and almost causing him to drop his plate. "What was the big idea earlier?"

Tanner gauged the sincerity of her anger with a quick glance before pushing any further. "Well, I suppose we should get it all out into the open. See—"

"No, not in the open! You know what I mean."

"Okay, okay," he relented. With his plate in hand, Tanner fell out of the informal line to walk with her to a couple of chairs at a less populated corner of the pool deck. He let his duffel bag and towel slump to the ground and set his plate on the table before leaning in to match Baldwin's conspiratorial pose. "So. How'd it go?" he teased.

"It went *great* until you scared the hell out of us," Baldwin pouted. "Real funny."

"Did I ruin it?" Tanner asked, his expression finally turning apologetic.

"No," Baldwin admitted, glancing away at the ground. "I just got a little shaken up wondering how to explain getting busted to my mother."

Tanner laughed. "You know I'd never say anything!"

"I know, but still! Anyway, what the hell were you doing opening those doors? I was afraid you were called up by the duty watch to…I dunno, do something, and…are you blushing?"

"Only a little."

She nudged him hard. "Tell me!"

"You'll figure it out soon enough anyway," he grumbled, rolling his eyes. "Lieutenant Kelly."

"You did *not!*"

"Fine, I didn't."

Baldwin gasped. "You did?"

"No, I've shifted over to denying everything now."

She let out exactly the sort of squeal he never thought he'd hear from her. "I can't wait to…*not* tell anyone at all! I promise. Got your back. Even though you almost completely derailed my moment of triumph."

"Yeah, well, sneaking her out of here turned into a heart-stopping slapstick fiasco, so your revenge is already taken care of.

Seriously, I thought she'd have to climb out a window. Anyway. Are you two a thing now?"

"Eh, he's got a little more time on his enlistment and then he's already signed on for a civilian job. We'll see. So that really wasn't a prank? Nobody knows we were in there?"

"Nope. Hilarious accident. Nothing more."

"It wasn't funny," Baldwin grumbled as she stood to leave.

"I thought it was hysterical." He gladly accepted the gentle kick she planted in his thigh as she stepped over him to return to the chow line. He watched her go, then realized he was alone in his particular corner. He'd chosen an empty spot to talk with Baldwin, and now she was gone. He looked down to pick up his belongings and rejoin the party, only to remember what sat inside the duffel bag.

His schedule and duties after the party remained vague. He couldn't take the entertainment player back to *Beowulf* with him, nor did he want anyone to find the memory chip. No one seemed to be headed his way, at least not yet. Tanner pulled out the player and fished the chip out of his pocket. The settings remained unchanged from where he'd left off. He put the chip in its slot, inserted the earpieces, and hit play.

The audio ran. Tanner heard the demands of NorthStar port control and security services broadcast on open channels and dialed them down, waiting for the voice of *Argent*'s apparent comms officer.

On the other side of the pool, Baldwin joined Alicia, Collins, and Ravenell at their table long enough to whisper something in Alicia's ear. The other young woman's surprised and amused reaction left Tanner wondering whose gossip Baldwin was spreading now. Alicia looked around, waved a taunting hand toward another table—where Tanner finally saw Sanjay sitting with some others—and laughed openly. Sanjay threw up his hands in a "what the hell?" gesture as Baldwin headed over to him with a wide grin.

None of the sound came through the noise dampeners of his earpieces. Some of that made it all the more entertaining. The pantomime across the pool held more of his attention than this second play of the audio…until he heard a snippet of a gravelly voice he'd remember for the rest of his life.

Tanner paused the recording, swallowed hard, and pulled it back a few seconds before playing it again. He heard the strong female voice of the ship's communications officer loud and clear. With a minute to reference the user manual and play with the filtering options, Tanner managed to eliminate that. He quieted the rumbling of all the background noise, too, until he could isolate that one familiar voice that spoke in the background.

"… we could crash right into their building full of rich fuckers. You wanted to know why your boss put me in charge of this ship? Here's your answer!"

His heart began to beat harder. His jaw set. One of his hands clenched into a fist over and over.

He ran the audio three more times.

The party carried on around him. Baldwin playfully sat in Sanjay's lap and smeared icing from a cake around his mouth. Ravenell somehow got his arms around both Collins and Alicia and hauled them both into the pool. Water splashed all the way over to hit Tanner's feet.

He stared off into space, playing the audio again. "…rich fuckers. You wanted to know why your boss put me in charge of this ship? Here's your answer!"

• • •

"Real brave of 'em to show up three and a half weeks after the shooting stopped," grumbled Admiral Branch.

Yeoh turned from the list of daily condition reports to look up at the battleship on the main tactical screen. The *UFS Fletcher* and her battle group loomed between Fairhaven and its moon, effectively staying interposed between NorthStar's fleet and Archangel's armada over the planet. "I'm only sorry you weren't well enough to join in our conference with *Fletcher*'s captain when they arrived," said Yeoh. "Between Acting Commodore Mayfair and a bunch of Union fleet brass, I thought the one thing that would truly improve the collegial atmosphere in the room would be your rosy personality."

"Yeah, I'm sure," replied Branch. At Yeoh's insistence, he sat in what was ordinarily her chair on the flag bridge. The ship's doctor only allowed him to return to work the day before, and even then restricted him to light duty. The activity would help, but too much tissue had to mend in his legs to leave him standing all day. "What you'd need in that room is my sense of tact."

"Indeed. The Union officers kept pointing out how they'd turn their guns on whichever side tried to make the first move against the other, and I said to myself, 'Admiral Branch would have the perfect response for this.'"

"Did you tell 'em we're so scared of their battleship group that we'd go hide behind the pieces of the even bigger battleship group we already smashed to bits?" asked Branch.

"No, but I'm sure that would have relaxed tensions nicely."

"Well, I'm up and around for next time."

"Multiple ship contacts outside the bubble!" announced a crewman at the lookout station. "Four, no, make that five vessels at 330 million kilometers at heading—wait, make that six—"

Branch didn't wait for the complete report, nor for the OOD to interrupt. He reached out to his control panel to put the long range chart onto the main tactical screens. The vessels appeared far out beyond the next planet's orbital path, all converging at a decent pace in sublight speed. Soon enough, more contacts appeared. Some of them were huge, especially the handful of assault carriers.

A couple of other contacts registered as quite small. "Captain," spoke up the OOD with an excited voice, "I have *St. Nicholas* and *St. Bernadette* identified and confirmed. Both are transmitting Mike Alpha on coded channels!"

"Mission accomplished," Yeoh translated softly, though hardly anyone heard her. Most of the bridge officers and crew cheered much too loudly for that.

"Can't complain about their punctuality," said Branch. "Or maybe the door hit 'em on the ass on their way out."

"We can only hope," Yeoh agreed. More contacts appeared. The approaching group quickly outnumbered her armada. "This isn't just their Archangel task force. They've pulled in ships from other areas."

"Probably to make sure we don't hang around?"

"Probably," said Yeoh. "Although they won't make it here for another three or four hours at that speed. I'm surprised they've given us that much time. Comms!" she called out over the din, silencing the impromptu celebration. "Signal our people on the ground. Tell them to pack up immediately. We're going home."

• • •

Someone called it "Evacuating to Victory" over the comms net, and the phrase quickly stuck. The pullout had been planned well in advance. Everyone knew their responsibilities, from the equipment they had to pack up to their pick-up locations and timelines.

Archangel's marines, navy ratings, and certain civil defense force units had spent almost a month on Fairhaven. The withdrawal took less than two hours. The last units to leave guarded the pair of hotels holding NorthStar's shareholders. Under the watchful eyes of orbiting warships, the marines of Bravo Company and the rest of *Beowulf*'s detached personnel boarded *St. George, St. Catherine,* and *St. Patrick* on the rooftops of the hotel towers with neither ceremony nor delay.

On board *Beowulf*, Tanner was pressed into service to search for contraband. The process took some of the wind out of everyone's sails as jovial enlisted men and women eventually grew cranky about the wait in *Beowulf*'s battle-scarred hangar bay. Masters-at-Arms and senior NCOs stood behind tables as their shipmates grudgingly opened their bags and other gear for an honesty check.

After two hours, the worst thing Tanner discovered was a bottle of wine.

Released from that chore, Tanner hesitated to return to his quarters. He hauled his personal gear to the MA office rather than his berth, where he checked his messages, talked with the other MAs about watch schedules, and heard whatever else people had to say.

He checked in on Nathan, only to find him asleep. He took advantage of a late chow call and hung around in the enlisted lounge until he found himself nodding off in his chair. Then, and only then, did he return to the MA office, pick up his gear, and head for his berth.

His deck, or at least this portion of it, suffered no damage during the battle. Passageways lay deserted. He found no "enter quietly" warning on the outside of the room. Apparently no one inside was asleep. Reluctantly, Tanner opened the hatch.

His rack lay undisturbed. The other three held only bare mattresses.

He saw no name placards on the lockers. No towels hung inside the head. Tanner found no sign that anyone lived in this room except some tidy guy named MA2 Malone.

No evidence of Avery Sinclair remained. Nothing of Juan Domingo lingered. Tanner couldn't even remember the newest guy's name. They'd barely met before Tanner and Avery headed out on their covert mission. Any sign of Pedro had long been scrubbed away.

The hatch fell shut as Tanner's breath shook. He backed away from the entrance until he bumped up against the opposite bulkhead. He slid down until he sat on the deck.

Pedro Guzman owed one hundred forty-eight thousand credits.

Avery Sinclair owed one hundred seventy-two thousand.

Sanjay owed fifty-one thousand, nine hundred seventeen. His left arm had to be grown from cloned tissue to replace the original and would likely feel odd the rest of his life.

Nathan Spencer came out of The Test owing twenty-eight thousand credits. His family paid it all off that same day and sent him on a gap year. He turned from his comfortable university life to liberate his world and to free others from the burdens of unfair debt that he never shared. Now he would likely spend years lying in one hospital bed or another while they rebuilt his body.

Trevor Jacobson never spoke to Tanner of his debts. Nor had Lieutenant Breckenridge, Stan Grzeskiewicz, George Romita, Hyun Jun, or Antonio Rivera.

Cassandra Fuller owed thirty-seven thousand credits.

Abdul Mohamed owed forty-six thousand.

Joseph Fitz owed fifty-one thousand.

Gavin Foster never said how much he owed, but his burdens killed him.

Tanner had already paid out sixteen and a half thousand credits. They still wanted fifty-three thousand, nine hundred seventy-four. He would never have to pay them again, nor would any citizen of Archangel. Their individual debt was gone. Archangel's primary debt was gone.

So many people who'd owed that money were gone, too.

Tears fell down his face.

How could that money have been worth all of this?

He stayed seated on the deck, directly across from the spot where he and Avery drank their roommate's whiskey in memory of his loss.

The passageway lay deserted. No one came by. No one saw Tanner's tears.

• • •

"Woah, slow down there, buddy," counseled Yeoman First Class Ocampo. He held up his hands in a cautioning motion, seated behind his desk with a mug of coffee and a spread of holo screens. "You know how many people I've had to talk off this ledge in the last two days? Listen, this is serious business. You have to take it slow and think it through. As soon as you sign those discharge papers, that's it. There's no turning back. You're on the way out."

Tanner leaned forward in his seat on the other side of the yeoman's desk, his eyes alight with energy. "I know!" he hissed. "And I get more excited every time somebody tells me that!"

Ocampo groaned, leaning back in his chair. The damage and debris from the battle over Fairhaven had been cleaned up weeks ago. With the ship now underway, *Beowulf*'s personnel office was back to business. Throughout the big compartment, men and women diligently worked to process the endless reports, requests, and records for the battleship's thousands of officers, crew, and marines. As a fairly new 1st Class, Ocampo tended to get the silly stuff. Since the first morning of *Beowulf*'s return journey to Archangel, it had been this.

"Okay. First off, the authorization only applies to personnel at least three months overdue for discharge—"

"Like me."

"—and who have completed any additional time in service obligations due to training agreements, leaves of absence—"

"I read the whole message seven times and checked every detail. I'm qualified."

"—and the policy still holds personnel to a further four week extension upon our arrival back in home territory. You're jumping the gun here, buddy."

"I'm past my discharge date even if we didn't count the six weeks of unused time on leave I have coming to me. I'm spending it all as terminal leave. Per regulations, that qualifies me for full discharge as of our next port call with my department head's approval. I can quote the reg if you want."

The yeoman sighed. "And have you got approval from your department—?" Tanner slapped it down onto the desk. Ocampo's head twitched. "You printed it out on *paper*?"

"I printed out ten of them. I'm thinking of having one framed."

"Okay. Fine. We'll go with that. Let's take a step back and consider all the things you didn't think about. For one, there are bound to be reenlistment incentives once we get home."

"I don't care," said Tanner, a grin playing at his lips.

"You don't care now because you haven't heard them."

"They won't be good enough."

"You don't know that! You could be pissing away a ton of money!"

"It won't be enough."

"How do you know until you see how much money it is?"

"There *isn't* enough money," said Tanner. "Not anywhere. Not *everywhere*. I'm out."

"Have you got a job lined up on the outside? School? Is it all legally binding? You know how many guys I've seen get out thinking they had something waiting for them, only for it to fall through and then they're out in the cold? Do you know what the economy is like right now?"

"The first form is the AN-214," said Tanner, undeterred by Ocampo's scary questions. "I've got one already filled out if you want it."

"You've got…? You can't fill out forms like that on your own! They're complicated records!"

"They come with step by step instructions. I can read."

"Why the hell would you dig up personnel paperwork and fill it out on your own?"

Tanner's eyes and his smile glowed. "The last time I talked to a therapist, he said when I was feeling down I should 'visualize my better tomorrow.' So I did. I called up the forms and filled them all out so I'd see what my better tomorrow looks like on paper."

"Oh my god. Are you serious, or are you fucking with me?"

"*Yes!*"

Ocampo leaned forward on his desk to bury his face in his hands. "Why the hell did I get this stupid job? I could be doing payroll reconciliations right now."

"AN-214," repeated Tanner. "It's under 'personnel,' subheading 'separations.' Or I can copy you on the one I filled out."

"Don't," Ocampo cut him off. "We're not using paperwork you did yourself." He sat up again with a distinct rumble in his breath as he opened up the personnel matrix on his desktop terminal. "Maybe as we go through this, you'll slow down and think twice about…huh. Hold on." He keyed the screen lock on his terminal and stood. "I'll be back."

"What's wrong?" asked Tanner.

"Flag on your file." Ocampo headed off around the partitions that separated the main offices from the chiefs' and officers' compartments.

Flag? thought Tanner. He opened up his holocom screen to see for himself. No flags were on his personnel file when he looked at it yesterday. Even now, he didn't see one, but that only meant that whatever flag the yeoman saw carried restrictions. *Of course there's a flag,* Tanner decided. *Why wouldn't I have a flag? What possible reason would there be for anyone to let this be simple?*

He waited several minutes, and then much longer than that. He called up the ship's status boards on his holocom screen, dreading a shipwide drill that would take him from Ocampo's desk and cost his place in line. Fortunately all the current drills were limited to specific stations. The rest of *Beowulf* observed an ordinary work day schedule. Tanner had spent the last two work day shifts on watch in the brig or in department meetings and patrols. This was his first chance to handle discharge paperwork…or, at least, his first chance to find out about his flagged file.

Someone above Ocampo's level had to come explain it, most likely. Ocampo probably had to get one of the chiefs out of a meeting, or maybe one of the officers. For all Tanner knew, he'd be here a while yet.

"Malone," said Ocampo from behind him. "Come with me." The yeoman then walked off, leading Tanner out of the office and into the nearest lift. Wordlessly, Ocampo hit the button for deck three. He eventually brought Tanner directly to the command offices adjacent to *Beowulf*'s flag bridge.

"Reporting as ordered," said Ocampo as the hatch opened in answer to his arrival.

A lieutenant Tanner didn't know appeared. "Thank you, Yeoman Ocampo," he said. "You're dismissed. Master-at-Arms Malone, at ease. Take a seat."

Tanner walked in as the hatch shut behind him. He'd only seen these offices while making his patrol rounds, by and large caring only that the hatch was shut. He found a conference room table inside, with hard screen charts of Archangel, Fairhaven, Hashem, and the Union along the bulkheads. Most of the chairs along the table were unoccupied. At the far end of the table, busy with several holo screens, sat Admiral Yeoh and Commander Beacham.

The lieutenant walked over to her, gestured for Tanner to take the seat nearest Yeoh, and then sat down beside him. "Master-at-Arms Malone," Beacham greeted him.

"Sir," said Tanner. "Ma'am."

"Tanner," Yeoh murmured, then killed her holo screen. Beacham did the same. Yeoh looked him squarely in the eye. "How are you feeling?"

"Doing good, ma'am. Yourself?"

"I'm pleased to be going home, but concerned for the future. Tanner, I ordered the release on discharges out of a concern for transparency. Yeoman Ocampo tells us he reminded you that the Senate and the defense minister will surely enact reenlistment incentives by the time we get home, but that's outside my purview as Chief of Naval Operations.

"I don't imagine it will shock to you to hear that the navy places a high priority on retention of experienced personnel, and particularly the new guard."

"No, ma'am."

"And given your rather unique service record, it shouldn't come as a surprise that you, specifically, are one of the people the navy—and that I—want to keep with us."

Aw man, thought Tanner. *I could laugh in almost anyone else's face…* "It does, ma'am."

"I've always enjoyed your humility," she quipped, but didn't give him a chance to wonder if that was a joke. "I imagine you have plans for college. Given your academic scores and your service record, I could guarantee you a spot in the next class at the academy right now." One of her faint smiles crossed her lips as Tanner blinked. "You wear an Archangel Star. It would be worth it to me just to watch the commandant of the academy twist himself into knots over having to salute a first-year cadet."

"No thank you, ma'am," said Tanner. "It sounds like good comedy, but I'm still not interested in a commission."

"Nor any imaginable reenlistment incentive?"

"I'm sorry, ma'am, but no." He paused. "This isn't where I belong."

"The last five years would suggest otherwise," said Commander Beacham. "You've made it through the worst times I've ever seen. It's not all crises and catastrophe, you know."

Tell that to Gavin Foster, Tanner thought, but he held it back. No one here shared any blame in that. He had plenty of other complaints, anyway. "Sir, Master Chief Floyd put out a *flow chart* today to remind everyone who on the ship they're allowed to date and who they're not. This isn't where I belong."

Beacham barely covered his groan. Yeoh sighed. "We do live in a different world," she admitted. "It gets easier to navigate as you go along, but I can appreciate your perspective. However, there is another concern I wanted to bring up.

"This war is over. NorthStar sees no benefit in pursuing the conflict further. Even if Brekhov returns to power, he's not fool enough to return to the battlefield now. *St. Nicholas* and the others brought back word from Archangel that Prince Khalil's faction in Hashem has new momentum. Yet for all that, you know the instability on the rise across the Union. Smaller conflicts have broken out. For all their faults, the Big Three provided a significant portion of the Union's military strength and security coverage. All of that is now greatly diminished. Piracy and other rogue elements are on the rise. I fear we are in for a dangerous peace.

"You have been at the center of so much of this, Tanner. Brekhov will remember you, as will Prince Murtada. NorthStar maintains its Risk Management division, and they have already made one attempt on your freedom, if not your life. Those shareholders on Fairhaven were all wealthy, powerful people. Every one of them will remember you as one of their captors.

"If you leave the navy, Tanner, we cannot keep you safe."

Admiral Yeoh held Tanner's greatest respect. That she'd taken such a personal interest in him meant more than he could say. Her grave tone gave him pause for three entire seconds.

Then he exploded into loud, uncontrollable laughter.

"Malone," Beacham snapped, "this isn't a joke!"

"Bwahaha!" Tanner responded, pointing at Beacham and then at Yeoh's placid face. "Yes it is!" He wrapped his other arm around his stomach. "It's 'cause…she said…ahah…" He tried to explain again, snorted as he inhaled, and then leaned forward to catch his breath but smacked his forehead into the table. "Oh god it hurts!" Tanner laughed.

Yeoh held up a hand to stop Beacham from ordering Tanner to attention. She gave the slightest shake of her head, watching Tanner's meltdown with a quiet grin.

Tanner looked up in time to see her face. It only made things worse. "Gaahh stop," he wailed. "Stop, it hurts…oh God, I'm dying."

"That's enough, Malone," said Beacham.

"You don't understand," Tanner managed as he sat up. "It's funny 'cause she said…she said I'd be *safe*…in the *navy*! Oh God," he choked, looking at Yeoh through teary eyes. "You weren't kidding that time on the shuttle. You really are hysterical."

"If you've gathered your wits, at least...?" Yeoh asked.

"I dunno," Tanner admitted with a high-pitched voice. "I'm trying. Ma'am."

"Good enough," she said patiently. "The gentleman on your left is Lieutenant Da Costa. He's part of Beowulf's counterintelligence section."

Tanner sniffed hard. "Sir," he said as politely as he could.

"Malone," replied Da Costa with a brief nod and a partial smile.

"We will be home in roughly two weeks," Yeoh continued. "For the remainder of our journey, you will split your time between your duties as an MA and working with the lieutenant and our counter-intel specialists."

That brought Tanner's giggles to an end. "Ma'am?"

"As I said, your time in service has earned you more than your fair share of enemies. At the very least, we should teach you how to spot trouble coming and how to avoid it before sending you out into the civilian world. A two week crash course on board a ship might not amount to much, but it's what I have to offer."

Tanner blinked. "I don't know what to say, ma'am. Thank you."

"You're welcome. I'll clear the flag on your file. Head back to Yeoman Ocampo, and be nice to him. He's under a lot of pressure to stem the tide of discharges. And Tanner, if I don't get a chance to say it before you're off to future plans: thank you. For everything."

•   •   •

In the end, Tanner barely remembered any of the words spoken during the homecoming ceremony. *Beowulf*'s hangar bay turned out to be the only place large enough to host it, and even then only after it was emptied of almost everything to accommodate hundreds of family and friends and the bleachers they sat on.

The Vice President and the Governor of Raphael attended, but in all the ceremony was kept mercifully short. Many of the distinguished guests had to get to later, somewhat smaller ceremonies for the other ships arriving at Apostle's Station. Admirals Yeoh and Branch spoke briefly in a display of empathy that surprised many. Branch may have only said ten words in all. Tanner forgot even that much once it was over.

He remembered Baldwin tightly holding his hand until the dismissal from formation, and the flood of bodies as people rushed to their loved ones. Baldwin gave him one last fierce hug and said something about writing soon before she disappeared into the crowd. He saw Ravenell enveloped by his large family. Chief Everett hobbled around the edge of the crowd on a cane with his leg still in a therapy brace. He met a similarly tall, wiry man for a kiss that didn't look like it would end anytime soon. Alicia came past, tugging Brent along with her, and paused only to throw her arms around Tanner, kiss him on the cheek and say, "My parents are here. Gotta go. Keep in touch or I'll hunt you down!" Then they were gone. He didn't see Sanjay at all.

No one came to meet Tanner. The delays for news and travel between Arcadia and Archangel made that a foregone conclusion. Even if they'd known when *Beowulf* would be back, his parents couldn't have made the trip. Tanner could have paid their way. He'd saved much of his pay since Archangel forsook its debts to the Big Three. Unfortunately, travel costs were one thing and having a job that would allow that kind of time off was another.

As much as the mass of reunions all around him made him feel otherwise, Tanner reminded himself that it was for the best. He slipped out of the crowd not long after the chaos began and wasted little time in his trip back to his berth.

He'd already been through his check-outs and goodbyes. Even his rack looked like the others: stripped bare of everything but a mattress. Tanner opened up his locker for the last time to change out of his vac suit in favor of simple black civilian pants and a casual blue shirt before unceremoniously stuffing the vac suit into one of his bags. He would have preferred to burn the thing, but he had to admit that he might have use for it someday. He zipped up his bags, threw on his jacket, and left the crew berth behind.

He had nowhere else to stop on his way off the ship. Nathan had been transferred off along with the other severely injured personnel before the ceremony. Everyone else had run off with family. Tanner went straight for the hangar bay and its connections to Apostle's Station, where he found a much thinner crowd. He paused for only one last look for anyone he should wish farewell, but saw no one. Then he headed for the large open bay doors and the station on the other side.

"Tanner," said a familiar voice that stopped him in his tracks.

His head turned. At first, he saw only civilians and other servicemen he didn't know, but as soon as they cleared out on their way he found her waiting patiently. "Is it okay to call you Tanner?"

"Yeah, Gunny," he replied. "Sure. I'm sorry, I figured you were already…gone."

A young boy in an Archangel marines t-shirt came up beside her. He had so many of her features: her cheeks, her skin, her eyes. He couldn't be more than nine years old. "Mom," he said, "Dad's helping Angelo get Bill's stuff 'cause of Bill's arm and leg."

"Okay," said Janeka with a tone Tanner had never heard from her. "We'll go catch up with them in a second, honey. I wanted to say goodbye here."

"Hey." The boy pointed at Tanner. "I've seen you on the news."

"This is my son, Andrew," she explained, and then turned to the boy. "Andrew, this is Tanner. He's one of my friends."

The lump that grew in Tanner's throat when she said those words seemed likely to kill him. "I'm…hi, Andrew," he managed. "It's nice to meet you."

"Nice to meet you, too," Andrew replied.

"You're on your way?" asked Janeka.

"Pretty much, Gunny. I'm glad you caught me, though. I wanted to say thank you. For everything."

"My name is Michelle. You don't have to call me gunny anymore. I hope to hear from you once in a while."

Tanner swallowed hard. "I think you'll always be the gunny. Even if they promote you."

"This is too good a day to suggest awful things like that," she told him, frowning a little.

"Do you work for my mom?" asked Andrew.

"Sort of," answered Tanner. "Sometimes. Your mom is my hero."

Andrew smiled, obviously recognizing the opportunity. "She's my hero, too."

"Damn straight," said Tanner.

Janeka openly laughed for the first time in Tanner's memory, rubbing her son's head. "Yeah, you're learning to lay it on thick like your dad."

"We missed you!"

"Well, I'm home for a while." She turned back to Tanner. "I'm glad you were with us."

"Same."

"Keep in touch?" Janeka stepped forward and hugged him. Tanner dropped his bags and hugged her back, first out of wide-eyed shock and reflex, and then with genuine warmth.

As it turned out, the scariest person he'd ever met also gave the best hugs.

A minute later, he reached the final checkpoint for outgoing personnel headed into Apostle's Station. A pair of uniformed marines from Bravo Company awaited him with wide eyes. "Bravest fucking thing I ever saw," one of them declared.

Tanner blinked, then realized they'd watched the whole scene. "What was I gonna do?" he hissed in feigned terror. "Tell her no?"

Hundreds more civilians awaited in the wide, open receiving bay on the other side of the checkpoint. Tanner spotted reporters and station police here and there, but the majority of the crowd seemed to be ordinary, cheering well-wishers come to show their appreciation for their returning troops. In principle, Tanner thought the whole thing was great. His comrades deserved to see and hear that appreciation.

On a personal and practical level, the crowd presented an obstacle. Tanner didn't need a parade. He wanted a clean, quiet getaway. As the marines finished the last check of his bags for contraband, he threw on a simple Archangel Navy ballcap and scooped up one of the many Archangel flags that littered the deck.

His first instinct would have been to duck his head and hustle through the crowd. Everything he'd learned from *Beowulf*'s intel specialists said to do the opposite. He had to blend in with the crowd, and this one was loud and cheerful. Freed from the marines at the checkpoint, Tanner strode across the gap between *Beowulf* and the civilian world with bags in hand and a constant look over his shoulder as if waiting for someone else to come off the ship. Rather than crossing the rest of the open space leading off into the station's main concourse, he moved into the crowd on his right.

The transition took only a few seconds. At first he felt a pat on the back, then another, and someone tugged on his arm and kissed his cheek. People who correctly guessed he was an off-going serviceman told him "thank you" and "we love you guys." Soon, though, Tanner adopted the same smile and called out the same cheers, turning to face the mostly open pathway left for other people coming off *Beowulf* like any other well-wisher. He shuffled farther from the ship. Soon, he slipped away from anyone who'd seen his departure. Once at the back end of the crowd, Tanner dropped the flag and the act.

Even beyond the crowd, Tanner found a much happier Apostle's Station than he'd ever seen. Banners and holographic "welcome home" signs were everywhere. He saw more uniforms than normal, but also far more smiles. The bars and restaurants all along the main concourse looked stuffed with people. Stores offered specials for anyone with a military ID. On the large screens that loomed over the broad passages, Tanner saw video of the arrivals of *Beowulf* and other ships and the smiling faces of the station's news anchors.

He also found the normal signs and status boards. Civilian traffic seemed undisturbed by the naval homecoming. Shuttle services to Raphael and other points nearby continued. Schedules to Gabriel and Uriel directed travelers to different wings of the station, as did flights headed for Michael—an option Tanner hadn't seen on the boards in the last few times he'd been on the station. He moved out of the way of foot traffic to look over the lists.

"Good job of blending in with the crowd," said a woman beside him. Tanner saw a familiar grin. Vanessa looked at the same directory screens as she spoke. "No flashy clothing, ballcap to cover up that military regulation haircut—and it makes it a little harder to recognize that face of yours." She gave up the show of looking the other way as he set down his bag. "I suppose most people would associate you with the uniform, though. Throw on a coat and hat and you're halfway to obscurity. The important thing is to look like you belong."

Her appearance shocked him. Glad as he was to see her, Tanner suddenly didn't know what to say. He didn't know what he *could* say—or more accurately what she could hear. "Where the hell have you been?" he asked with a smile he only half felt.

"I came back on *Beowulf*, same as you. They kept me busy on Fairhaven during the occupation, but your bosses didn't mind a hitchhiker. I didn't even sneak on board. I asked nicely for permission and everything."

"And you didn't say hi?"

"Well, I might've spent the first day or two sleeping off a hangover," Vanessa admitted. "They gave me a spot in an officer's berth. Mostly I kept to myself. Part of my line of work. Anyway, they had you in the spooky side of the boat for the trip back. That's the last place I wanted to be seen talking to you. '*Hey, Tanner, who's your amazingly gorgeous friend?*' they'd say, and you'd stammer and I'd try to cover and then we get more questions, you know?"

"Yeah, I guess that makes sense," said Tanner. "I'm glad to see you. Where you headed?"

"Down to Raphael. I've got endless debriefings and probably a couple of days behind a desk revising my reports ahead of me. Oh, I wrote everything up on the way back, sure, but they'll tell me to re-write it at the office. They always do. It makes the bureaucrats feel like they have a purpose.

"Anyway, I wanted to tell you there's no way in hell anyone tries to take you out here and now," she said. "If you're feeling shy, keep doing what you're doing. If not, there's no reason why you should have to pay for your own drinks or your own meals today, y'know. This station is crawling with people who'd love to pick up your tab."

"Nah, I'm good," Tanner replied. "It's nice to know it, but I'm not hiding out from danger. Just felt like having a smooth exit."

Vanessa nodded. "Fair enough. You're a hero, though. It's okay to swagger a little."

"Yeah. I guess."

"You okay?"

"I'm gonna miss you, Vanessa," Tanner confessed. "I mean, it's not like we've worked together all that much, but still."

"Eh. No point in long goodbyes. You aren't gonna live a quiet life. We'll bump into each other again. This transitional stuff is hard, but you'll be fine." She winked, then hugged him. "See you whenever you pull another stunt that gets you on the news."

"See you whenever you let me."

"Got that right." She gave him a final wave as she moved back toward the crowd. Tanner picked up his bags again and watched her.

She'd only been with him in a couple of tight spots, and yet she'd been through all this from the beginning, just like him. Hell, even longer than him. She'd been fighting the same war before it began…and some of the same demons.

Fuck it, he decided. "Vanessa!" He worried for a second that he'd lost her already, but as the swarm of people continued to crisscross in front of him, he saw her stopped in the middle of the concourse, looking back curiously. "Do you—" he began, then frowned and walked over to join her. "Do you have time to talk a little more?"

She shrugged. "Sure. About what?"

"About things I can't tell anyone else."

"Okay," she answered, waiting for elaboration. "You're not gonna make everything weird, are you?" she teased when he hesitated.

"No. It's serious."

"Lead the way."

Tanner started walking. Vanessa stayed at his side. "Hey, Tanner," she spoke up, "this isn't the way to the terminal for Michael."

"Yeah. I know," he said as they passed under the signs leading to flights to Uriel.

CHAPTER SIXTEEN

It's Not About You

"I'll come out to Arcadia as soon as I can. Believe me, I'd be on the next liner if I could, but I have things I need to do before I leave. I hope you understand. It's nothing I can explain in a letter.
"I love and miss you both."

--Tanner Malone, personal letter,
August 2279

"I only regret that we can't give you and yours the day in the sun that you all deserve," said Aguirre. He smiled broadly as he shook the big man's hand. "The Ministry of Intelligence and covert operations like yours played a tremendous role in our victory. *Especially* your covert ops. The people of Archangel owe you a debt they may never know."

"Thank you, Mr. President," replied Ezekiel. "We don't need a day in the sun, though. That's not what we do."

Aguirre nodded to concede the point. "As long as you all know who I'm thanking when I'm out there at that podium." Through the tinted security glass, they could all see the gathered employees of the Ministry—or at least those who didn't live under secret identities and strict anonymity—gathered for the president's speech. "I appreciate all the analysts and staffers, too, of course, but...well, you get my point. Hell of a job you did out there."

"On that note, Mr. President," said his chief of staff, "we should get going."

"Absolutely," said Aguirre. "I only wanted to come shake your hand as long as you're here. David?" he asked, looking to the man standing behind the desk.

"We're finishing up," Kiribati replied. "I won't keep you waiting."

"You'd better not," noted Aguirre. "You're introducing me."

Ezekiel and Kiribati remained standing as Aguirre and Hickman left. The agent turned to his boss with a curious frown. "I'm surprised you still wanted me here today. Don't you have a speech to give, too?"

Kiribati shrugged. "He wanted to meet you. I couldn't exactly bring you to Ascension Hall. We could keep you out of sight from the media and all, sure, but some conversations don't belong in the president's office."

"Then does he know—I'm sorry, I shouldn't ask," Ezekiel corrected with a grunt. "It's been a long mission and a long trip back."

"He knows plenty," answered Kiribati. "Enough that he didn't want to have this meeting in his own office, either. Regardless, your timing worked out fine. Arriving three days after Yeoh's task force gave the media plenty of time to get fixated on the troops. Even if someone recognizes your ship as the one from the attack on Fairhaven, they'll have an uphill battle getting any attention for it. By the time that happens, you'll be back on Uriel."

"So about that...?" reminded Ezekiel.

"Yes. About that." Kiribati chuckled. "Five thousand apiece, hm? Oh, don't take it the wrong way. I'm impressed that you managed to get through this whole mess with everyone still alive and the ship still under control. I half expected an escape attempt or a mutiny by now."

"If I hadn't coughed up the money, we very well may have had that mutiny," warned Ezekiel.

"Yes. As I said, I'm not mocking you. Well, if the writing is on the wall, there's no reason to hold off on our clean-up plans." Kiribati glanced at the monitor on his desk. "The sooner we wrap this up, the better. Don't take any chances. Play it cool until you're back on Uriel and the ship is completely powered down. Let me know when it's done."

"I might need some extra help," said Ezekiel. "My security team on the boat is solid, but some of them have been with this crew for a couple of years now. They may hesitate."

"I can see how that could complicate things," Kiribati agreed. "We have a security team on Uriel you can borrow. You can brief them when you get there. The less put into writing or recorded on a signal, the better."

"Understood," said Ezekiel.

Kiribati rose from his chair and buttoned his coat. "And just to echo the president: you have the thanks of a grateful people. You should pass that along to your captain and crew."

• • •

He could get out of bed whenever he felt like it.

He didn't sleep all day, or even come close to sleeping through the mornings, but the opportunity alone made an incredible difference. The bed was big enough that Tanner could roll over—actually roll over and not twist in place—without falling out or bumping against a bulkhead. He even had more than one pillow. He had no watch rotation, no work shift, no tight schedule for chow. He could sleep until he was done sleeping.

It was the greatest. Or at least the second. Maybe the third or fourth, if he was fair, but the second and third greatest had both broken up with him and the greatest was still in the navy, so it was best not to dwell on any of them. Sleeping on an unrestricted schedule was amazing regardless…especially given how hard it was to get to sleep and stay there.

Falling asleep at all could be difficult, no matter how tired he might feel. No drills or alarms screamed in the middle of the night, but that didn't keep him from waking up with a start three or four times. Though the hotel room offered near-complete silence, that "near" bit still mattered. He slept like a log the first night. On the second and third, he found it difficult to hold an uninterrupted stretch for long. The faintest chime of the elevator down the hall or some bump in the night outside his door could wake him up and send his heartbeat into overdrive.

Last night, set off by God only knew what, he leapt out of bed and almost panicked when he couldn't find his helmet and then realized he wasn't in a vac suit, either.

White noises from his holocom like rolling waves or desert winds helped, but he longed to sleep in actual silence like a normal person again. The trouble was that actual silence had become completely, depressingly unnatural to him. So had safety. He wondered if freedom had become unnatural, too. He seemed to do okay with that so far, yet it had only been four days. Maybe freedom would creep up on him and become a problem, too.

God, that was an awful thought.

The first few days brought incredible ups and downs. He knew he needed help readjusting. Unfortunately, he couldn't go looking for that sort of help yet.

Tanner checked the clock. He'd somehow managed to doze all the way to the start of a normal person's workday this time. Sitting up in the bed, Tanner called out, "Hospitality. Easy lights. Morning news, Raphael Public Media."

The hotel room brightened. The holo system embedded in the wall provided a pair of news anchors who offered the standard intro for a time-delayed broadcast, along with a holographic icon reminding Tanner of the option to skip forward to the current feed. He listened absently as he shuffled over to the tinted balcony door.

People who knew better would have called his lodgings a "business class" hotel room. To Tanner, it felt pretty luxurious. He'd almost decided to spring for one of the rooms actually listed as a luxury suite at first, if only for one night, but then figured he'd sleep through most of whatever extravagance that bought, anyway. Besides, for all the money he'd saved by hardly being able to spend his pay on a battleship, he wasn't exactly rich. This detour from the rest of his life wasn't cheap, either.

He'd resolved to move on to that ordinary life within five days of his exit from the navy. Three of those days had already passed.

In that time, he shopped, he slept, he took advantage of the hotel's gym and its pool, and he put in fifteen college applications. Those cost money, too, but nothing felt silly about that—nothing except the possibility of doing something so rash and stupid that he'd never get to make good on any acceptance letters.

Five days. Five days, and then he would let it all go and get on with his life. Maybe he'd write a letter or three about what he knew and what he suspected, and then it'd be someone else's problem. He'd have to get on with his life.

Tanner opened up the balcony doors overlooking Uriel Shipyards, took down the pocket-sized camera he'd mounted on the railing and shuffled back inside. The holographic Bob Norris continued on about the outlook of the post-war economy and interstellar trade. Only half listening, Tanner sat down on the bed, opened up a holographic playback screen on the camera, and activated the identifier program to skip to scenes of air traffic over the shipyard.

He saw plenty of shuttles every night. None of that interested him. A freighter took off in the early evening, but he quickly dismissed the image. He knew he wouldn't see much. For the sake of noise management, big ships generally took off or landed during daylight hours. The arrivals of *Virtuous* and *Devout* both happened in the late afternoon when everyone could make a big deal of them. Both frigates remained in the yards, with most of their crews scattered on well-deserved liberty. For the rest of the shipyards, things seemed to be business as usual. Tanner had three nights of video to prove he hadn't missed anything while he slept, along with daytime video to show he didn't miss anything while he was out. Hours and hours of fruitless surveillance made him feel silly about even trying.

On the fourth morning, his camera showed him *Argent*'s steady, quiet descent into the shipyards shortly before sunrise.

"Media player: Off," he said. Bob Norris and his co-anchor vanished. Tanner replayed *Argent*'s arrival. The big ship settled into the same restricted bay he'd seen in his first tour of the shipyards. The bay's gigantic rooftop doors closed up around the ship in a far more welcoming gesture than his insides could muster for his emotions.

All of the ease of the last few days evaporated. He'd prepared for this, sure: he bought gear, set up the camera, carefully watched the news, and did his recon work. Even with all that, he spent most of his time decompressing. The relatively easygoing journey home on *Beowulf* was regimented and stiff compared to a long weekend at a nice hotel in a major city.

Now he had to make a decision. His stay and his preparations no longer represented an effort in good faith before moving on to "normalcy," whatever that might be. His personal holocom held copies of nine university application receipts. The chair and the table held gear for a ridiculous stunt that could put him in prison forever, assuming he survived it, all in the pursuit of answers he might not find even if he pulled this off.

He looked at the video again, and then stared out the balcony doors.

A minute later, Tanner stood before another hotel room door in a loose shirt and the same pants he'd worn yesterday. It didn't open after he knocked, but he waited patiently—or at least pensively—until Vanessa answered, wrapped in a hotel bathrobe and with her hair as unkempt as his. Rather than speak, she stepped aside and let him in, closing the door behind him.

"Sorry if I woke you up," said Tanner.

"It's fine," she replied. "I told you to."

He activated his camera's playback settings to explain his arrival.

She knew what she would see. It was the only reason he would have knocked this early. "Yeah." She moved to one of the nicely-upholstered chairs by her small table. Tanner took the other. "You're still up for this?"

"I think I gotta," Tanner answered.

"It's a huge risk. And I'm not even talking about what happens if you get caught. You could pull this off and it might be all for nothing."

Tanner nodded soberly. "I know. We talked about that. Still think I have to try."

"Yeah, I figured," said Vanessa. "I shouldn't let you do this alone. Christ, it's the *worst* way to handle this sort of job. This business is about finding the right people on the inside who already have the access and know the secrets. You don't walk into the line of fire. You work through people who won't draw any fire at all."

"Haven't you been in the line of fire pretty much every time we've met?"

"None of those times were ordinary circumstances," she replied. A frown of confession appeared on her face. "And I've never liked sending other people to do my dirty work. Not without at least sharing the risk. It's the shittiest part of the job. I shouldn't let you go alone. I should go with you."

"We talked about that, too," Tanner reminded her. "You've got your role to play. I can't handle that part at all. And you've already done more than enough."

"More than enough for prison," the spy grumbled. She pulled over a handbag sitting on the end of the table. "Only they won't catch me if they don't catch you. So don't get caught." She produced a small box from the bag and opened its magnetically-latched flap. The device inside could fit in the palm of a hand. "Here. Bumper unit."

Tanner blinked. "That's a bumper? The navy's are bigger than a shoebox."

"The navy's also last longer. This will wear out faster. You could probably open up half the rooms in this hotel before it wears out, but the stuff you're gonna deal with? It'll get you past two, maybe three doors. Still, it's a little more subtle than the regular units, and the box will get it past most scanners." She deposited the bumper back in its case. "Risk Management issue," she added with a wink. "Anyone asks, tell 'em you picked it up on Fairhaven."

"Will do," Tanner answered. He let the rest go unsaid: if anyone had a chance to ask him that, they were both screwed anyway. Neither of them had any illusions about holding up under interrogation.

She set an even smaller box from the bag on the table. "Null gel. Use it sparingly. It's not cheap and it doesn't last."

"Creeps me out how that shit even exists," said Tanner. "And how I'd never heard of it."

"Eh. Secret tech like that never stays secret long. We're not the only intel group that uses it. Hell, we stole it from Lai Wa. Figure it'll be the next security industry boogeyman in about ten years, and then it'll be on the open market in another five. The arms race never ends. Build a better shield, somebody builds a better spear. That's why human interaction will always be the biggest challenge." She retrieved a data chip from one of the bag's side pockets. "Last thing. Give me your holocom."

"Okay." He pulled his sturdy but otherwise completely ordinary civilian holocom from his wrist and handed it over with a curious look.

Vanessa placed the data chip in the holocom's slot reader and ran through a series of commands on its interface screen. "I'm adding some security codes and an authorization signal," she explained. "Every holocom in the facility needs to have this signal. They won't use it to track you physically. There are too many of them on site to sort through, unless things get really crazy. If that happens, drop your piece and run. Until then, this will make the computers think you're one of the guys."

"How'd you get the codes?" asked Tanner.

"I had a late night," she answered, shrugging once more. "Little bar-hopping, little socializing. Little pickpocketing. Don't worry, the guy got it back before he knew it was missing."

Tanner shook his head. "I don't know how you…I don't even know where to begin."

"Flexible morals make for a good place to start. If it makes you feel better, the guy was a real jerk. Didn't even tip the bartender."

She handed his holocom back. "That's the simple stuff. The rest is up to you."

"Thank you, Vanessa. For everything."

"Thanks for trusting me. Remember: the biggest tool you've got is confidence. Don't *act* like you belong there. *Decide* you belong there. Because you do. They just don't know it yet. Or why. But they will.

"Now get outta here. I have to get dressed and catch a flight."

Tanner smiled as she leaned forward and kissed his cheek. "Nice not seeing you again," he said.

• • •

"Nobody except security leaves the ship until I get back," said Ezekiel. "Orders from on high. We make like we're still in deep space until everyone goes through their debriefings."

Seated with his feet up on the desk in the captain's office, Casey rubbed his face and looked at Ezekiel with undisguised annoyance. "You couldn't fucking tell me that before we got here?" he snapped. "The whole crew has been waiting to blow off steam for months! They're in home port, the war's over, and they've got money to spend. You want 'em to sit around here while you're off fucking around doing whatever it is you do?"

"I'm going out to meet the debriefing team and escort them here," Ezekiel said, completely unbothered. "The sooner that's done, the sooner we can release the crew. Half of these people aren't coming back once they're gone. The rest of them still need to know what they can and can't talk about in public. I'll be back in a couple of hours."

"A couple hours of all these assholes bouncing off the walls," grumbled Casey. "Whatever. I'm not the one doing the debriefings. You get back here and find a cranky crew, it's your problem."

"True," Ezekiel agreed. "It's not like you're going anywhere."

"Oh, fuck off." Casey's holocom beeped. "What is it?" he answered.

"Engine shutdown is complete," came the report. "Munitions and fuel cells secured, water tanks are recycling on shipyard pumps, and system-specific generators are spun down. The ship is set for a nice nap, skipper."

"Thanks." Casey killed the connection and looked at Ezekiel with renewed annoyance. "Guess they can all knock off work and sit on their hands until you get back, huh?"

Ezekiel shrugged. "I don't care anymore than you do. Nobody leaves the ship. Past that, it's up to you how much of a captain you want to be." He left without another word.

Casey stared at the closed hatch. Given another month or two of time underway, he could've turned enough of the crew around for a bloody mutiny. He already had enough influence to pull off little things like extorting bonus pay. They obeyed his commands in combat without question. Things were moving along.

The end of the war took all the wind out of those sails. As Ezekiel said, most of the crew were at the end of their contracts. People had sweet rewards awaiting like citizenship or amnesty. The rest planned to stay on for the sake of steady jobs if nothing else, and the ship wouldn't go out again for weeks. Current plans listed half-day schedules and long weekends. None of that would build the sort of friction and pressure that got people to go rogue.

In the meantime, Casey would be stuck on his prison with even less to do than usual. Maybe that was why Ezekiel seemed so cheery—or at least what passed for cheer for him.

Grumbling, Casey slipped out of his chair and headed toward the hatch. He held no hopes of turning the crew into good pirates now, but he could at least find ways to blame any delays and frustration on their asshole XO and the Ministry of Intelligence.

• • •

He'd taken the public tour twice since arriving, first with Vanessa and then without. The advice from the counterintelligence people on *Beowulf* paid off right from the start. Nobody recognized him. Even with all the media coverage of his moment in the Union Assembly and his fight with the spies right in this very city only a few months ago, no one spotted Tanner Malone on the tour. A different hairstyle, a touch of old fashioned make-up here and there, a bright red shirt, and a small change of demeanor—meaning, in his case, the sort of smile he usually didn't have for the media—and he hardly looked like himself at all.

With the war over, everyone seemed brighter and more relaxed, from the tourists to the shipyard staff. People came now to bask in pride rather than looking for hope.

Tanner saw a little less vigilance and a little more cheer in the guards, too. They still ran bag checks. They kept the chem sniffers and other scanners running. They collected personal holocoms and maintained a visible presence as a deterrent to trouble. But they didn't look over every attendee quite so closely. Nor did they count up everyone in each tour group. And no one paid attention to who went into or out of the bathrooms.

On Tanner's first trip, he'd only gotten a brief look at the shipyards' layout and restrictions. The sheer size and scale of the facility made everything difficult to absorb. He caught more on the next two trips, though, and Vanessa's professional eye provided a great deal of perspective. With her guidance, some tourist maps, a hotel room with a view, and a day to chew on things, he felt much better about his grasp of the layout. He knew now what to look for: bathrooms, employee access areas, and spots where tourist and worker traffic overlapped.

He also knew exactly what to wear under his civilian clothes.

Safely hidden away in a bathroom stall, Tanner swiftly pulled off his simple trousers and loose, roomy shirt, revealing the same dark blue work coveralls worn by most of the shipyard's civilian techs. He rolled down the sleeves of his coveralls and pulled the hems of his pant legs out from his boots. Once he pulled away the thin layers of plastic that coated the leather boots, they looked believably scuffed and old like a shipyard worker's should.

It wasn't difficult to wear a second layer of clothing and change hairstyles. A quick change like that could fool most casual observers. It wasn't so easy to hide a second pair of shoes, though, and so professionals paid attention to footwear. Tanner learned that early on in his training for the honor guard and again during MA school.

You've only worked security on a cruiser, a battleship and Ascension Hall, *for Christ's sake*, Tanner reminded himself silently as he balled up his discarded clothing inside the bathroom stall. *It's not like you don't know anything about this. All you've gotta do is think in reverse.*

The bathroom was empty. Tanner stuffed his previous outfit into a waste basket and moved over to the sink. He'd walked in with his hair neatly combed to one side. A little water, a dissolvable coloring tab the size of a pill and ten seconds with a comb gave him a slicked-back hairstyle with highlights that would fade out again as soon as his hair was dry. By then, he'd be far away from anyone who'd seen him arrive. His earring had to go, too. The little gold ball wasn't exactly expensive. He dropped it down the sink without a second thought.

Tanner pulled the holocom from the shielding pouch inside the chest pocket of his coveralls, put it on his wrist, and checked the time. His scheduled tour group had left almost a full minute ago. Hopefully, the memories of it were already fading in security's minds as the next group shuffled in.

No one in the lobby looked askance at a tech walking through the crowd of tour guests. Nobody stopped him. As he crossed over toward a door marked "Employee Access," Tanner even made eye contact with a guard and gave a quick, friendly nod. Nothing happened. The door slid open for Tanner as it did for every other shipyard worker. Apart from some cleaning supplies and a rack of safety gear, the hallway was deserted.

He reminded himself of everything Vanessa told him: *Walk with purpose. You work there like everyone else. Even the high security stuff is mostly ordinary people working an ordinary, everyday job. No way does security know everybody by name and face. It's too big. Make like a native and you'll be fine.*

Tanner started walking. He reached out to one of the racks along the walls to pick up a pair of tinted safety goggles and miniature baffles for his ears. The glasses went around his neck, hanging by a lanyard. The baffles went into place. By the time he came out into the open air once more, he felt confident in his disguise.

That confidence built as he strode through the facility, moving unchallenged past workshops, offices, and hangars. Occasionally, he received a friendly nod from strangers. Most people completely ignored him. Not a single guard screamed in alarm or drew a weapon.

He followed the lines along the pavement. Even with all of the other towering structures and cradles big enough to hold starships—which some currently did—Tanner had no problem locating the massive hangar bay that marked his destination.

He knew right where to go. He belonged here. He could do this.

He came around the last corner leading to his destination, spotted the two burly uniformed men at the sealed entrance with pulse carbines and scowls, and kept walking right on to the next corner as his heart climbed up into his throat. *No fucking way am I pulling this off.*

Every other entrance to the gigantic hangar held the same obstacle: double guards, a sealed door, and no traffic moving in or out. He should have seen some movement of technicians and other workers by the time he completed a full circuit. He found none. Any hopes of walking in under the cover of a group of people who actually belonged vanished.

Not far away, Tanner found a small automated dining kiosk. It offered him a place to stop and regain his nerves without drawing attention. He stood in front of a beverage dispenser and stared at the holographic options with a completely genuine sense of indecision.

The guards didn't scare him anymore than the countless other fights he'd faced. Granted, they had him dramatically outgunned, but he'd been there before. Unfortunately, he couldn't bash his way through them. He took a deep breath and told himself to start with the positives: *It's only two guys. They haven't seen me yet. No reason to be scared of them. You know how to handle that kind of trouble.*

Use what you know, said Vanessa, Janeka, and pretty much every other mentor in his life. He knew what it was like to stand guard. One had to deal with people all the time. People were fallible, frustrating, and forgetful.

A facility like that hosting a ship as large as *Argent* would need hundreds of techs. Maybe they were all inside. Maybe they'd been sent packing for some reason. Regardless, there had to have been a good number on hand for her arrival before dawn.

He took the series of deep breaths Janeka taught Oscar Company. Suddenly he felt like that was only yesterday. Maybe it was the memory of being so far out of his depth.

Tanner started walking. He had one shot at this. He put his right hand in his pocket, crushed the null gel capsule inside and ran the barely moist contents over his fingers and palm. As he crossed the blue line on the pavement around the hangar, Tanner withdrew his hand so as not to arouse any suspicion from the guards. They didn't return his smile.

One of the guards held up his left hand to stop Tanner, and suddenly the younger man came up with a better cover story. "Nobody goes back in," said the guard, confirming one of Tanner's suspicions. "You know better."

"Look, I know, I'm sorry," Tanner complained. "I forgot something and I didn't even realize it until a few minutes ago."

"Too bad. Get it when your work crew is called back."

"It's really too late already? Seriously?" pleaded Tanner.

"What's your name?" asked the other guard.

Tanner sighed. Either this would bust him or it was just an intimidation check. "Rick. Rick Curbelo," he said.

"ID," the guard replied.

Tanner raised his holocom and activated the identification screen Vanessa put together for him the night before. They had no way of knowing if workers assigned to this particular hangar received a special code, but it seemed unlikely. ID checks happened all the time. "Look, I'm in and I'm out," Tanner tried again.

"What'd you forget?"

"My engagement ring," he grumbled. The guards blinked. "I have to take it off for work. It's a safety thing. My boss is all over my ass about safety standards, so it has to go. But if I go home and my fiancée notices it's gone…y'know?"

"What's her name?"

"Madelyn," Tanner answered readily. He knew this game.

"What do you do that you have to take off your ring for safety?"

"Electronics. Lots of tech shops have the same rule, even if it's obviously not a danger. Some people are old-fashioned, I guess." He turned off his ID screen. "C'mon, man. You guys married? Or engaged? You know how people can get about this shit?"

"Yeah, actually, I do," answered the first guard in an almost scolding tone. "Where's your work station?"

"Halfway across the building."

"Not on board the ship, then?"

"No."

"And your fiancée, Megan, she's gonna kill you if you come home without it?"

And there's the other half of the game, thought Tanner. "Madelyn," he corrected. "She won't kill me so much as cry. You want to hear how ridiculous it is to plan a wedding?"

"No," said the guard. "Look, you're in and you're out, and if anyone asks us about it, we'll tell 'em you said your supervisor cleared it and you can answer to him."

"Thank you," said Tanner, stepping forward.

"Hey." The other guard stopped Tanner with a palm on his chest. "*Do not go near the ship.* You got me?"

"I know how it is. You guys are lifesavers." He offered his hand. The married guard accepted the handshake if only to get Tanner to go away. The other guard spurned it.

Tanner stepped forward and put his hand in the biometric reader built into the doorframe. The system paused only long enough to give Tanner a heart attack before the null gel on his hand fooled the reader into accepting the DNA stolen from the guard. Tanner heard a warm welcome as the door opened. He stepped inside without looking back, thankful the door didn't greet him by name.

He didn't know what to expect on the inside. He knew only that he'd have to act like he'd seen it a thousand times before. That wasn't too difficult in the small vestibule built to channel foot traffic through the hangar's thick walls. It felt almost impossible as he came through the other side and found himself looking up at the awe-inspiring sight of a starship the size of *Argent*—and the interior of a building large enough to contain her.

Los Angeles was bigger, *Beowulf* larger still, and this wasn't his first up-close encounter with this particular vessel. Even so, Tanner rarely saw such huge ships up close. The bow of the ship loomed directly above. Though its very tip likely had a good twenty or thirty meters of clearance from the wall of the hangar bay, it hardly seemed like enough room. Tanner swallowed hard as he took in the sight. He needed no visual reminder of the enormity of this challenge, but he found it anyway.

Cables, pipelines, and walkways stretched from the ship to the catwalks all along the towering walls. Men and women with guns patrolled the hangar bay floor. They didn't wear uniforms like the guards outside. They wore vac suits and combat jackets. So far, Tanner saw no technicians or other yard personnel at all.

A series of offices and workshops stood to his left. Windows and sliding doors revealed plenty of shadows in another sign that most if not all of the workers had apparently been dismissed. That little wrinkle meant that his disguise wouldn't do him much good from here on out. Finding the idea of a dark office perfectly attractive, Tanner headed for the nearest door.

The portal slid open without trouble, giving Tanner exactly a half-second of relief before the lights came on automatically. "Aw,

God damn it," he muttered, but kept walking now that he was committed. "What the hell ever happened to light switches?"

The door slid shut behind him. Tanner continued on through the office, casting his gaze sideways at the patrols under *Argent*'s massive bulk. The closest guards seemed to look his way, but none approached to investigate. He realized in this second look that their numbers weren't all that great. If they were spread out for more or less even coverage, he doubted he'd find more than twenty of them in total. More probably patrolled the upper levels of the hangar and the catwalks. Yet without maintenance and repair work going on, why the need for so many guards? Why not lock down the whole facility along with the ship?

Or was this what such a lockdown looked like?

The office held only ordinary desks and workstations. Monitors sat dormant, but they did him no good regardless. He didn't know the first thing about breaking into a computer system. A few signs on the walls offered standard management stuff like safety reminders and a map of the shipyards. Nothing seemed useful.

From there, Tanner moved through an adjoining door to a workshop that promptly lit up as if to join in on the office's joke—which got even more aggravating when lights in the office behind him snapped off as soon as he was out. Thankfully, the next room didn't have any windows to the hangar floor. He continued on, leaving the workshop behind until its lights went out, and then doubled back.

"Lights off," he said before crossing into the workshop. The voice-controlled system obeyed his command, leaving him in shadow as he returned to the dark office where he repeated the order. He slipped inside, glad for the shadows as he looked out over the hangar bay floor to confirm that nobody had done more than look his way.

Tanner took advantage of the darkness to observe the guards. The longer he considered the situation, the more it appeared likely that *Argent* was in some kind of lockdown. All the activity he saw—and lack thereof—fit his training and experience with in-port security work as an MA. *Argent* lay quiet. The cables and pipelines suggested replenishment services, but he saw no other maintenance work, nor anyone in crew uniforms or vac suits.

Where the hell is everybody? Tanner wondered. Frowning, he decided on two possibilities: either the crew left shortly after arrival, or they were all still on the ship. He wouldn't know unless he got on board to look.

The main cargo bay ramp lay open. He'd never get to it. Too many eyes and guns covered that route. While he may not have aroused suspicion as a lone tech moving straight into the offices on the far end of the building, he plainly wouldn't get away with pushing forward. Disguises and subterfuge seemed to have run their course. All he had left now was stealth.

Argent had more than one entrance. The connections to her upper decks offered other routes inside the ship. He might well encounter a guard or two there, but probably not ten. Tanner looked around the office for a minute longer until he found a binder marked "Facility Emergencies." He snatched it up and flipped through the pages with interest, finding nothing about *Argent* but grateful to discover some usable maps.

He had locked doors ahead of him, along with open catwalks, automated lights, and an awful lot of stairs. The locks, at least, he could handle with the tools in his pockets. The rest he'd have to take on one problem at a time. Another look through the window revealed two guards finally walking his way, telling him in no uncertain terms that he'd better get on with it.

Tanner stuffed the maps into his pockets, put the binder back, and got on his way.

• • •

"Okay, that's fifteen minutes. Maybe more. Szweda?"

"I've got nothin'. Still hasn't turned up on any of the cameras," came Szweda's voice over the net.

"Shit. McLeod? Brewer?"

"No sign of him," Brewer answered. "He definitely went through the hallway coming out of the workshop by the floor manager's office. Past that, he could've gone in three directions, including up to the next level."

"*Shit*," Grosser fumed. She stayed by *Argent*'s main cargo ramp, flexing her fingers around the grip of her rifle. Her eyes turned toward the catwalks rising up along the ship's starboard side, but she doubted she'd see anything. Some spaces had lights, others did not, and they were all more than a football field away from her spot on the floor—not to mention how much of it all was blocked from her line of sight by the ship itself. "Zeke's gonna kill us."

"Us? He ought to kill those two dumbass security guys at the front door. Engagement ring my ass."

"I still think it's sketchy that the door system registered one of those idiots when it opened up," said McLeod.

"Oh, now you think that's sketchy?" snapped Grosser. "You don't think that's a minor computer glitch anymore?"

"Well, to be fair, I don't think that reader has been cleaned in—"

"Shut up, McLeod. Okay, people, take this seriously. You see anyone who doesn't identify themselves on the first challenge, you open fire. Do not leave your post. We'd spread ourselves out too thin if anyone else went looking. Zeke is due back real soon. Until then, I want verbal call-ins every ten minutes. Don't rely on the net for vitals. Start now: Grosser. Clear."

"Szweda: Clear," said the agent in the hangar's security control room.

"McLeod: Clear."

"Brewer: spotted one complete moron. Looks like McLeod."

"Hey!" McLeod protested.

"That's enough!" barked Grosser. "No joking around! Continue the call-in."

"Ortiz: Clear."

"Reynolds: Clear."

• • •

"Overton: Clear," he reported, then let his thumb fall away from his holocom. He turned around to walk back across the ramp to *Argent*'s deck three airlock only a heartbeat before the crescent wrench flew into the back of his head. Overton and the wrench fell to the deck together.

Tanner darted out from hiding to drag Overton into the shadows, grateful his desperate tactic not only worked, but also didn't outright kill the guy. Working quickly, Tanner stripped Overton of his weapons, gloves, and combat jacket before binding and gagging him. One of the benefits of moving through a repair facility was the ubiquity of tools. He'd had no trouble finding plenty of tape.

He didn't feel good about this part, but now it seemed inevitable. At least, Tanner figured, it was one of the jackasses from Fairhaven and not some complete stranger who'd never said a cross word to him. "Don't worry, buddy," Tanner murmured. "This'll add at least another five years to my sentence."

Overton groaned and drifted out again. Tanner quickly donned the man's coat and headset and slung the pulse carbine over his shoulder. The carbine didn't beep in response to the touch of Overton's gloves, suggesting its safeties responded to something other than the magnetic grips. Tanner gave it little concern. He needed the weapon as a prop. Actually using it would cross a line that he'd already touched by knocking Overton out. No matter what secrets or scandals he might uncover, no one would feel they justified killing Ministry agents.

The entry hatch on the other side of the walkway remained shut, but the external access controls offered some hope. Most of the other airlocks and access points had no external controls at all. Tanner strode across the walkway, flexing his fingers in Overton's glove and hoping the magnetic grips would be all he needed to use the hatch. If that didn't work, he'd have to hope Vanessa's bumper would do the job.

Far below, Tanner saw patrols on the hangar bay floor. Nobody seemed to look his way. Tanner activated the control panel and opened up the hatch. No one waited on the other side. He spotted the usual lights, computer buttons, and manual controls of a ship's airlock. He took the presence of active cameras for granted, too, even if he couldn't see them.

Déjà vu much? wondered Tanner.

The airlock's interior hatch opened up with no trouble. The external hatch closed behind him. With a few more steps, Tanner came into a deserted passageway. As with most civilian ships, he found helpful signs and arrows pointing him in the right direction. Locating the bridge wouldn't be difficult.

Taking it over would be a different story. That seemed like a bad idea. He'd have to settle for something short of that.

• • •

"Sure is taking the XO a long fuckin' time to get back," complained Schlensker. "Seriously, what's the hold-up? They knew we were coming in today, right? He checked in with the bosses on Raphael as soon as we got back. You'd think he could've called ahead."

"Hell if I know." Casey sat in the captain's chair staring at a pair of holo screens, one offering a map of the ship and another displaying the last recorded images of Uriel Shipyards as *Argent* landed. It helped Casey's spirits to keep looking for an escape route. So far, he had a few crazy options he would only take if his life was already in danger. Sooner or later, though, a more practical option had to come up. That meant keeping an eye on things like activity outside the ship while in port.

Unfortunately, the most exciting thing to happen in the last few minutes was that one of the guards came inside, probably to use the head. The guy didn't exactly call in his plans. Ezekiel's security team used comms channels that the bridge couldn't monitor.

"What do you think they're gonna tell us, anyway?" Schlensker spoke up again. "We all know the score. Never talk about the ship. Never mention who we've worked with or where we've been. All that. It's the same as all our port liberties, right? We all knew when we signed up that we wouldn't be able to talk about this for years."

"Maybe they want to make one last big impression before you go out," mused Casey. "How many of you guys are gonna get shit-faced drunk as soon as you're cut loose?"

"Damn sure I am," vowed the helmsman. "Doesn't mean I'll talk, though. And who's gonna believe a story like this from a drunk, anyway? I mean would I really tell anyone that I served with a—I mean…well." He shrugged awkwardly.

Casey's eyes slowly turned from the holo screens. "Why Schlensker. You clever boy."

"Hey, all this time, I thought…that is…hell, it's none of my business, right?"

"You figure it out all on your own, or did somebody tell you?"

The helmsman shrugged again. "There's always been rumors. You look a little different and all, plus it's not like the news ever showed much of you speaking or, uh…shit, boss, how many other guys on this ship are working for an amnesty deal or something, right?"

"Right." Casey stood from his chair, killing his two holo screens as he stepped through them. "Guess I ought to go review the terms of my deal."

He left the bridge without another word. Schlensker could leave thinking his former captain was the greatest or he could walk off the boat carrying an armload of hurt feelings. He'd make no further difference in Casey's life either way.

Vigilant as Casey might be for a chance to escape, the captain had few prospects of leaving anytime soon. The last thing he wanted was to sit around with excited jackasses as they ran out their last few minutes before release while he stayed locked away. Fed up with his options for company, Casey decided to wait out the whole thing in his quarters. As far as he cared, the Ministry could line the whole crew up and shoot—

Casey stopped outside the hatch to his cabin. That made entirely too much sense. *Argent* performed more than a few covert ops, including raids in sovereign territories. While none of her crew approached Casey's degree of notoriety, more than a few still had considerable criminal records. Others represented varying compromises of standards, brought on because the Ministry could not supply a full, competent crew of vetted and fully trained agents. Yet the ship held secrets that the Ministry would only trust with its own people—Casey himself being the greatest such secret.

The prospect of letting the crew loose with those secrets in their head never made much sense, but it hadn't been Casey's problem. He had only himself to look after, and the Ministry needed him for the war...which was now over.

Many things made sense if the Ministry planned to clean house: the full engine shutdown, the departure of the ground crew, the security team spreading out to cover the exits, and most especially Ezekiel's smug attitude. The "debriefing team" might well be a kill team. "Son of a bitch," Casey murmured. He threw the wheel on the hatch to his cabin. Those crazier ideas for a desperate escape came to the forefront of his mind once more. The Ministry wouldn't take him down without a fight.

Holding to well-ingrained habits, Casey paused to look inside before stepping through the hatch. The precaution looked completely natural thanks to years of practice. An observer might hardly notice any hesitation at all. Casey immediately spotted the footprint in the traces of powder he left on the deck inside the hatch. He could see from the reflections on the computer monitor that no one awaited on either side of the entrance. If anyone hid inside, it had to be in the bathroom.

His assessment took only a couple of seconds, along with his decision. If Ezekiel planned to eliminate the crew, he'd want to start with Casey. To the captain's benefit, an isolated fight offered a better chance at both survival and acquiring a weapon. He closed the hatch behind himself, locked it for what little good it might do, and calmly walked toward the open door to his bathroom. He pulled the shiv from his sleeve with his left hand, then filled his right with the neck of a bottle of cheap wine kept on top of his dresser for just such an occasion.

Casey swung the bottle up and around the side of the bathroom door, clubbing the intruder right in the head. He stepped in and reversed the arc of the bottle as the intruder jerked away, bringing it down on the back of the other man's head. This time it smashed open in the sort of disorienting mess that made bottles useful weapons. The intruder's pulse carbine clattered to the deck as he reeled. Given half a second to evaluate his foe, even if only from behind, Casey decided that the guy's combat jacket posed too much of a risk of damaging his other weapon. The pirate aimed below the jacket, plunging his shiv into the back of his opponent's thigh with a vicious underhanded lunge.

The other man yelped and reflexively spun around. Knowing that would be coming, Casey ducked the retaliatory blow and brought his shoulder into the intruder's side to push him into the shower. The violent motion helped Casey tear his shiv back out of his opponent's leg. He dropped the remnants of his bottle in favor of grabbing a handful of that combat jacket to pull his enemy off-balance. The shiv came in again, this time going for the neck.

A brutal elbow dropped into Casey's shoulder in time to spoil the lunge of his blade. The pair fell into a tangle that quickly went wrong for the captain, who soon found both of his arms behind his back. The intruder maintained his hold long enough to swing Casey face-first into the side of the bathroom sink. He followed up with a nasty kidney punch that drove Casey to his hands and knees.

One of those hands found a new weapon. Casey snatched up the fallen pulse carbine and thrust low with it to strike his opponent's groin. "Gah! Shit!" the other man grunted as he staggered, bumping against the nearby wall.

Casey pulled away. He needed only a second to verify that the fucking gun had been built with a personalizing lock before he looked back to his opponent.

"Mother*fucker!*" Casey spat in recognition right before Tanner planted a field goal kick straight into his chest. The pirate tumbled back up against the bulkhead as Tanner staggered in pain from the wound to his leg.

The younger man recovered fast. He came at Casey with a left hook into the pirate's side. The blow took almost all of the air out of him. Tanner grabbed hold of Casey's collar and threw him roughly to the deck outside the bathroom door. The pulse carbine fell from Casey's grasp. He hit the back of his head on the deck beside his bunk.

By the time Casey shook off his momentary disorientation, Tanner stood in the bathroom door, training the pulse carbine on his foe with his left hand. He couldn't afford a proper two-handed grip; he needed the other hand to open the first aid kit mounted on the bulkhead inside the bathroom door and pull out the auto-suture. Still, even with Tanner's ragged breath and slight preoccupation, Casey didn't look interested in trying to outrun the pull of the trigger.

Tanner leaned on the doorway and glanced at the auto-suture for only a second to make sure he had it activated and turned right side up. Then he bent a bit at the waist, still keeping the gun pointed at Casey, and reached around to the back of his right leg with the small rectangular device. "Auto-suture: zero anesthetic," Tanner instructed before he put the thing against the stab wound in his thigh.

Tiny arms extended from the auto-suture with blades and needles to cut away the fabric of his pant leg and then set to closing up his wound. Tanner's eyes bulged as the device performed its painful work. Through gritted teeth, he let out a stifled growl. "God, I hate you *so fucking much*," he snarled at Casey.

"Cry harder about it, you little shit," the pirate seethed. His gravelly voice hinted at fatigue. The brawl had taken something out of both of them. Casey stayed on his back, propped up by his elbows as he caught his breath. He knew when to play for time to regain his strength. "So what's the deal? You move over to the Ministry and get a hit job as a sign-up bonus? Or is this an audition?"

Tanner held his tongue. He concentrated on keeping his eyes open and his weapon steady as the auto-suture finished up. The bloody stab wound in his thigh couldn't go untreated, but the need to keep his wits about him overrode the need for painkillers. Though the device felt like it was only making things worse, he had to trust it to do its job. His breath came in and out forcefully.

Casey's eyes narrowed as he thought things through. "No. They wouldn't take you. You're the one who fucked everything up from the beginning. Kiribati almost…" He stopped.

"Ngh!" Tanner grunted. He wasn't sure he should speak while the damn auto-suture did its business. His leg still wouldn't be in good shape when it was done, not to mention the rest of him, but he couldn't exactly take the rest of the day off now. In the meantime, this level of pain didn't make for witty conversation.

The murderer on the floor wasn't at his best, either, Tanner realized. Casey took a blow to each side of his head in the fight. He faced the same risks of saying too much while disoriented and hurt. *Hell,* Tanner thought, *maybe he already has. Gotta keep him talking.* "Fucked up your ship and your buddies pretty good," he huffed.

Casey sneered. "Real proud of yourself, too, aren't you? For all the good it did you and your little planet. No," he thought aloud, "you're not here for Kiribati. What happened? Who sent you? Did Yeoh find out about all this?"

That question made Tanner feel a little better. It *proved* nothing, but it suggested that Yeoh was still in the dark about this ship, as she'd been after Scheherazade. "What makes you think I didn't find out for myself?" asked Tanner.

"Yeah, right. That sounds likely."

The auto-suture beeped to signal completion of its work. Its computerized voice said, "The wound is now sealed. Swelling and bruising is likely. Keep the site clean and—"

Relieved at the noise despite the continued pain, Tanner dropped the device on the deck. "I'm a pretty smart guy."

"You're a fucking idiot," Casey replied. "And a tool."

"Says somebody I've beaten twice now. By myself." Gloating didn't come naturally. Tanner was usually too self-conscious. It seemed to hit a sore spot for Casey, though. Given the way the pirate's eyes flared, he figured he should best continue. "Christ, you even turned the element of surprise around on me in here and you still couldn't win."

"Oh, you want another big, shiny medal for that? Everyone patting you on the back? See yourself on the news where you can wave hi to mom and dad back on your home planet? Lot of good you did them."

"You keep bringing up Michael," Tanner observed. "Is there something you wanna tell me?"

"I've lost count of the things I'd love to say."

"So what's stopping you?" Tanner tried to consider what he'd heard so far: Yeoh wasn't involved, and might even intervene if she knew the truth. Casey said Tanner fucked something up "from the beginning," whatever that meant. And he brought up Kiribati, but cut himself off. "Have you got somebody to protect? Buddies in the Ministry who set you up with this ship? I don't see them protecting you here now."

"They're gonna kill you," said the pirate. "Whatever else happens, they're gonna kill you for this." His eyes narrowed. "Especially if you really do know too much."

"I know they lied about you being in prison and then faked your death. I know they gave you command of this ship. They did it before the war, didn't they? Far back as Scheherazade at least. How long have you been working for them?"

"Only about as long as your fucking president has been in office."

The younger man blinked. "What?"

"You know who I'm talking about. That suited asshole who put that big stupid fucking medal around your neck. *'We know the truth, and the truth has set us free.'* Ring any bells?" Casey's sneer grew darker. "If your people knew the truth, they'd all shoot themselves out of Catholic guilt. And if the Hashemites knew, they'd come shoot anyone who was left."

• • •

"Remember: nobody pulls a trigger until we have accounted for the entire crew *and* until I give the order." Ezekiel stood at the head of the shuttle, looking back at its thirty passengers. "We don't want one of them getting loose in time to cause a fiasco."

The shuttle settled onto the pavement. Ezekiel came out first, followed by a couple squads of men and women in the same business casual clothes common at the Ministry's central offices. The outfits limited the sort of weapons they could carry for the task at hand. Organization and ruthless planning would have to compensate for that.

The pair of uniformed guards at the main entrance allowed Ezekiel and his large entourage to pass by. They both wore uncomfortable expressions. Rather than ask if something was wrong, he waited until he could talk to one of his own people inside. As it happened, the answer came before he could bring up the question.

"Zeke, we've got a problem," reported Brewer as Ezekiel stepped into the hangar. "Those idiots outside let somebody in and we don't know where he is. He went through the front office over here and disappeared. The guy's dressed in a tech's outfit—"

"How long?" snapped Ezekiel.

"Just about twenty-five minutes now," said Brewer. "We couldn't call you—"

"I know you couldn't call! That's why I left—damn it!" He started jogging toward the ship, keying up his holocom. "Grosser! What are you doing about the intruder?"

"We didn't have the manpower to sweep, so we're keeping the ship sealed up," Grosser reported. "We've got every entrance guarded, but we started a call-in check and Overton isn't responding."

Ezekiel broke into a full run. "Damn it! Stay outside! Stick to your stations!" He looked back over his shoulder to see his entire "debriefing" team now running with him. "Sweep the ship and round up the crew, but *wait* for my order! Diego, Sandoval, you're with me!"

He hit the base of the cargo bay ramp a second later with his pistol in hand.

• • •

Tanner didn't try to hide his reactions. His discomfort seemed to loosen Casey's tongue.

"Did you ever consider how convenient it was that you had a civil war next door to keep the Big Three distracted when Aguirre started provoking them? Or that you had so many good reasons for a military build-up? You think this wasn't all planned out well in advance?

"The only thing that went wrong was *you*, asshole. *You* forced Aguirre's hand. Kiribati's guys bought up every ship my people captured and stashed 'em away. If we'd had time to do more of that, maybe Michael wouldn't have been left so fucking defenseless when the Big Three finally got fed up with Aguirre."

"You were working for them all along?" asked Tanner.

"Working for them or working with them. Take your pick. The only snag in the whole plan came from you being such a go-getter. Next time you go home, take a look at the craters and the tombstones, 'cause that's all on you." Casey's lips spread into a grim smile. "Still glad you came in here to find me?"

Tanner took in a long, deep breath. "Sure." He limped around to Casey's right. His leg hurt like hell, but it worked…more or less. At least the auto-suture did its job well. Gingerly, Tanner hooked one foot under the dresser by Casey's bunk to roll the video capture capsule tied to his holocom out into plain view.

"Much as some video might help," Tanner explained, "this is gonna work better if you explain it all in person."

"What?" Casey blinked.

"You're leaving here with me." Tanner produced a roll of electrostatic tape from one pocket of his combat jacket. "One way or another."

"The fuck makes you think I'd do that?" snapped the indignant captain.

"Because if they'll kill me for knowing all this, they'll damn sure kill you for telling. And you know it."

Something thumped outside the hatch leading to the passageway. Tanner looked up in time to see the lock on the hatch disengage and the wheel turn. "Aw, shit," he grumbled.

His foe swept one leg under Tanner's to bring the younger man down on his back. Neither of them pressed their fight further with new arrivals imminent. Tanner rolled back into the bathroom while Casey pulled open a small, loose deck panel under his bunk. Lasers flashed into the captain's quarters from the open hatch before the new intruders bothered to identify themselves. With both men inside now on the deck, the blasts only tore up the furniture and drew ugly black lines on the bulkheads.

Casey pulled the exposed wires in the deck panel. The lights died in the compartment and the passageway outside while the overhead fire retardant dispensers blasted the cabin with freezing spray.

The sudden chaos created a completely unexpected environment for the shooters. The first of them, his laser pistol emitting a bright white light he could see by, rounded Casey's bunk with an unsure step. He didn't know this place. His intended target knew it all too well. One second, the intruder had his weapon trained on the deck; the next, he felt someone pull his wrist down while a steel pipe jabbed him in the stomach.

The intruder's closest back-up missed it, keeping watch instead on the open bathroom door as they entered. He saw movement, fired his laser pistol through the doorway, and only caught onto the danger to his partner when the first man jerked forward and grunted. "Zeke!" the second intruder shouted at the first.

Tanner saw little more than blurred silhouettes against the dim lighting from the darkened passageway outside, but he recognized the opportunity. He launched himself out of the bathroom to slam the butt of his rifle into the second intruder's head. His target collapsed while the pirate captain struggled with Ezekiel. In the darkness and spray, Tanner couldn't make out much of their fight.

As his target dropped, a third intruder rushed in and tackled Tanner. The impact sent him bouncing against Casey's bunk. Before he knew it, he and his attacker were on the deck, struggling violently like Casey and Ezekiel beside them. For a brief second, Tanner considered himself lucky that his new opponent opted to brawl rather than shooting into such a mess where he might hit the wrong target. Then he took a punch to the ribs. Casey or Ezekiel—he had no idea which—stomped on his wrist. Tanner's foe brought an elbow down on the back of his head. Circumstances no longer seemed so beneficial.

Casey abandoned his pipe to wrest away Ezekiel's pistol. The agent drove his knee into the pirate's gut, but slipped on the wet deck before he could follow up with more. That left the two men on their sides, each grappling with one arm and attacking with the other. Casey pistol-whipped almost blindly, hitting Ezekiel's hip at first, then his arm, until a lucky swing struck Ezekiel's jaw that left the agent stunned. Freed from their struggle, Casey scrambled away only to crash headlong into the other tangled fighters nearby.

All three men wound up on the slippery deck. Casey kept on rushing for the exit. Tanner rolled up from his side to follow, pausing only to stomp his other opponent back down before giving chase. Once again, the fire retardant got the better of Tanner, sending him sliding toward the open portal and falling forward mere inches short of Casey's fleeing boots. To make matters worse, as he rose up once more, someone collided with him from behind. Both men tumbled out into the passageway.

The pirate kept running. Tanner pushed himself up again. So did the other man. "You!" Ezekiel snarled in recognition. He glanced inside the captain's quarters and pointed at Tanner. "Sandoval! Kill him, too!" he ordered, right before Tanner's heel slammed into his face.

This time, Tanner knew another tackle was coming. He bent forward as Sandoval collided with his back, throwing Ezekiel's buddy over his shoulder before taking off after Casey.

As bad as his leg hurt during the fight, the first steps of his run painfully emphasized the damage done by Casey's shiv. It couldn't be helped. Tanner ran awkwardly, his barely-corrected injury making for a wobbly, limping stride.

Up ahead, Tanner saw Casey round a corner into another passageway. He also caught sight of the gun in the pirate's hand. Behind him, he heard bigger problems. "Sandoval!" Ezekiel shouted. "Shoot the bastard!"

"Shit," Tanner grunted, ducking low and jerking to the left to make himself a harder target before he dove headlong around the corner after Casey. Lasers flashed all too close, one of them even tagging his coat as it hung below his backside.

Coming out of the line of fire, Tanner found a ladder well leading to the next deck below. He heard more laser fire in this direction, too, along with a howl from whomever wound up on the wrong side of it. *Tell me Casey didn't get that gun working already*, he thought. He didn't bother with the steps, instead grabbing onto the railing and sliding straight down.

He saw nothing at end of the adjoining passageway. Along the other, Tanner spotted a body lying in front of an open hatch. The smoldering man didn't look much like a ship's crewman. He wore a business suit. Ezekiel's buddy, Sandoval, seemed to be wearing the same thing. That didn't bother him as much as the other development: *Yep. Casey's got a working gun. Guess I'm the only guy who can't beat a biometric lock.*

The hatch beyond the body slammed shut while Tanner limped along. The sign above the hatch marked the compartment as Defense Gunnery Three. He had no time to consider Casey's path or his plans. Sandoval landed at the bottom of the ladder well behind him, with a re-armed Ezekiel trailing right behind.

Tanner threw the wheel on the hatch and pulled it open to block the lasers he knew would come from his pursuers. Instead, the first shots came from Casey's weapon. Tanner practically rolled over the bottom lip of the hatch to get into the gunnery compartment. *This is great. Everybody's got a gun here but me.*

A tall cabinet and workstation stood nearby. Tanner didn't think twice. He left the open hatch behind in a mad dash for cover. Casey's laser beams chased him, but the pirate soon gave up on shooting. At least one or two of his shots had gone through the open entrance to give the two agents pause, or so Tanner hoped. He risked a peek around the workstation to get a sense of Casey's intentions.

The orientation of the gunnery space suggested that the weapon pointed out horizontally along the ship's starboard side. The gun itself lay on the other side of the hull. Within the compartment, Tanner saw the usual access hatches, secondary machinery, and ammunition loaders. Most of the systems seemed to be powered down. Tanner saw lights and holo screens at only one station farther into the compartment. He didn't see Casey anywhere.

Instead, he saw the machinery spring to life as the curved housing of the ammunition loader engaged with the receiver mount up against the hull. Red lights flashed a warning throughout the compartment. Tanner's eyes bulged. *No*, Tanner thought, and then yelled out as he leapt from his hiding space, "No!"

Lasers shot past him from two directions as the defense gun finished its prep sequence. Casey lurked behind the lit-up console, shooting first at Tanner and then at the two agents who appeared at the entry hatch. Tanner rolled off to one side to avoid the gunfire while Casey tried to deal with the new threat. Sandoval cried out as red beams of light burned fatal holes through his shoulder and upper chest. Rather than press his luck in a shooting match with Ezekiel, Casey ducked back around the console again.

The console offered no protection from Tanner's new position. He rushed forward to grab hold of Casey's wrist and neutralize his weapon before thrusting one elbow into the pirate's face. The violent struggle pushed both men out from their cover.

An awful, searing pain engulfed Tanner's right side. The heat forced a scream from his lungs, completely distracting him from the other three shots Ezekiel took at him as he collapsed. He fought the urge to grab at his side with his left hand, working instead to unclasp and unzip the combat jacket to get at the wound.

More laser blasts came in. Casey crouched back behind the console and returned fire. Both pirate and agent benefited from solid cover and the rushed, desperate aim of an opponent more concerned with survival than marksmanship.

On the deck and now half forgotten by Casey, Tanner pulled his combat jacket away from his right side and saw what he'd desperately hoped to find: the flexible heat sink that lined the inside of the material gave off a faint red glow as it spread the energy out, saving Tanner's life but still much too painful to the touch. He probably had a nasty burn under his shirt—painful, but not crippling.

He gathered his wits, got his feet under himself once again, and tensed before striking. His recovery came a second too late. As Tanner drew back one fist to deliver an ugly shot to Casey's kidney, the pirate leaned over the top of the console to slap a button.

Argent's starboard defense gun fired a single shell into the hangar bay wall less than twenty meters away. The shells became armed only after flying clear of the guns; such a short distance from launch to impact prevented a vastly larger blast. Even without its warhead armed, the shell carried enough explosive power to shake *Argent* violently and inflict catastrophic damage to her surroundings. Alarms still blared and lights flickered amid the thunder of debris striking against the hull.

"You son of a bitch!" Tanner shouted. He had no way of knowing how bad the damage might be. The gunnery compartment offered no windows and almost all of the computers and screens remained dark. He knew only that Casey set off a ship's gun inside a hangar, and inside a shipyard. Tanner finally delivered that kidney punch as viciously as he could. Then he grabbed Casey's collar and flung him onto his back, moving in time to avoid yet another shot from Ezekiel's pistol.

They struggled on the deck once more. Tanner fought to control Casey's gun hand. Casey slammed a brutal punch into Tanner's burned side. Growling in pain and anger, Tanner thrust his forehead down on Casey's face, missing his nose but catching the pirate's cheek. The weapon in Casey's hand went off, though Tanner's grip kept the barrel turned up toward the overhead.

"Let go!" Casey demanded with a snarl, shoving hard but unable to escape Tanner's grip. Tanner brought his free hand down in a hammering blow against Casey, catching only shoulder instead of collarbone. Casey shoved once again, this time causing Tanner to slip and fall onto one knee.

The gap between them opened up right in time to let both men see Ezekiel come around the control console with his weapon level and ready to fire. Tanner kicked hard, knocking the weapon from Ezekiel's hand. Casey gave up on his pistol, relinquishing it to throw a jarring right cross into Tanner's cheek before trying to blow past both of his enemies. He didn't get far. Tanner tripped him. Ezekiel slugged him in the side and caught hold of Casey's arm. It brought all three of them into another violent tangle.

They all suffered from the previous brawl. As the trio fought, throwing punches and elbows and doing their best to block or evade the same, Tanner thought he might be at one other disadvantage: each man carried an intense hatred for the other two, but Tanner's didn't quite stretch into anything murderous. Since his first sparring sessions in Oscar Company, Tanner had been taught to fight dirty.

That training continued in MA school and even on *Beowulf*. Now Tanner found himself against two opponents he absolutely could not allow to die.

Ezekiel brought a right hook against Tanner's cheek that sent him turning up against the console, bumping into the metal with his hips hard enough to fall halfway over. Tanner felt Casey's elbow come in at his back to return the favor of the earlier kidney punch. Again, Casey tried to break free. Again, one of his opponents stopped him—Ezekiel this time, with a low stomp on the pirate's leg, followed by another stomp on his side. Casey went down with a gasp. Tanner turned around in time to catch Ezekiel's heavy fist with his stomach. The bigger man grabbed Tanner's left forearm and twisted hard.

"You came alone, didn't you?" Ezekiel huffed. "Yeoh would've sent in a full team to shut this down. How did you find out?"

Another confirmation. Now Tanner really regretted not trusting her. "You suck at your job," he growled.

"Got that right," croaked Casey, earning himself another stomp from Ezekiel.

Ezekiel's arm lock wasn't complete. He didn't want to tie himself up with one opponent and leave the other an escape route. It still hurt like hell. "What did you think you would accomplish, anyway? Did you come to take this asshole out yourself?" he asked, kicking Casey once more.

Tanner winced in pain, but crushed out any other sign of weakness. "It's not about him."

The agent drew a knife from his belt with his free hand. "Last chance before I get mean. How much do you know about this ship? About Casey?"

"I know he owes a lot of people answers. And so does your boss."

"Guess we do this the hard way, then," said Ezekiel. He raised his foot for another blow against Casey to keep the pirate captain down. This time he paid for it. Casey caught Ezekiel's booted foot, twisted, and shoved backward. Ezekiel stumbled, taking Tanner with him and dragging yet another involuntary cry of pain from the younger man as Casey took off.

The fall broke Ezekiel's hold—thankfully without breaking Tanner's arm. Seizing the opening against his enemy, Tanner planted a snap kick under Ezekiel's chin, catching him squarely in the neck and sending him onto his back.

As he turned to track Casey's flight, Tanner discovered yet another surprise he couldn't see until now: right across the compartment sat an escape hatch built into the deck. An arrow and red and white letters read, "Gunnery Evacuation Route."

"Aw, you're fucking kidding me," he complained. Casey threw open the hatch and swung both legs over the side. Tanner limped after him, leaving a staggered and choking Ezekiel behind. He refused to let Casey get away now. Not after all this. Bad enough that he'd lost Brekhov. As far as Tanner was concerned, Casey represented something far worse.

The guns no longer complicated things. Ezekiel might pick one up before pursuing, but maybe not. Either way, Casey carried no such threat. Tanner barely glanced down the escape hatch before jumping through.

He found storage racks in the compartment below. The lights remained on thanks to motion sensors or timers. Casey had already made it out. Tanner swept the room with his gaze twice when he saw the exit fully closed on the other side of the compartment, then rushed for it and threw the wheel. As he came through to the next passageway, he looked right and left and almost immediately saw Casey's most likely destination. Suddenly, the bit with the defense gun made sense. *Oh, that's bad*, thought Tanner—and then, *no wait, that's really good.*

For all the retrofitting and modifications performed on *Argent* since her original capture, the ship's lifeboats remained largely untouched. Superficial changes to their identifying marks and internal amenities covered up any relation to the ship's past, but even hyper-efficient corporate freighters often held larger lifeboats than strictly necessary.

If military hardware was often designed for easy operation under fire, emergency survival options like lifeboats were made to be idiot-proof. Tanner needed no code or key to open up the vestibule leading inside. Large, helpful signs painted onto the bulkheads and the deck outlined the way to the helm.

Once upon a time—a lifetime ago for Tanner, it seemed—Casey and his buddies managed to stuff this ship's original crew onto three of these lifeboats, minus those they'd already murdered. This one looked completely unused until now. Three columns of spotless bench seats consumed almost all of the space in the main cabin, with the rows in the center being the widest. The aisles separating each column looked equally clean except for the trail of blood along the starboard aisle leading toward the forward cabin.

Tanner ran as best he could. He didn't worry about any more ambushes. Casey couldn't afford to lie in wait now. Escape was too near. A move like this showed Casey's desperation. He would still have to evade a huge police manhunt and more even if the lifeboat made it out of the shipyards. On the other hand, Casey didn't seem to have better options. He might actually get lucky and slip away. Tanner couldn't have that. Nor could he stick around on *Argent*.

That last thought made him pause outside the hatch leading into the forward cabin. Casey might know he'd been followed. Like any small ship, the lifeboat's helm probably showed opened entrances and such.

Tanner didn't want him to get away. He also didn't want to interrupt yet.

"Launch in ten seconds…nine…" announced a computerized voice over the lifeboat's PA. *Okay then*, thought Tanner. He got his arm around one of the many handholds built into the bulkheads.

"Aft entrance opened," said the voice.

Tanner's shoulders sagged. "Aw, Christ."

"Helm override. Aft entrance closed. Resuming launch."

Ezekiel came through the aft hatch to the cabin. His eyes flared as he saw at least one of his prey out in the open. He raised his pistol.

Without any further hesitation, Tanner threw the wheel on the hatch and leapt into the forward cabin. "Launch!" he yelled.

"What?" Casey blinked, looking back from the controls. A laser beam split the air between the two, striking the main view screen that made up the lifeboat's false windshield.

"Launch now!"

Casey hit the override button, abandoning the last few seconds of warm-up time that would give the thrusters more power. Tanner looked up at the damaged view screen in time to catch a glimpse of the giant hole Casey had blown through the hangar bay's wall. Other than the rubble in the avenue below, the damage seemed limited to the bay itself. He got no more than that glance before the lifeboat launched.

Even with the ship's artificial gravity systems, Tanner still found himself thrown against the back wall of the cabin. He pushed himself up again, looked back the way he'd come and saw no sign of Ezekiel.

Casey rose from his seat to deal with Tanner. "Fucking kill you—"

The younger man waved him off. "Just fly this thing!" he said. "I've got Ezekiel!"

Casey blinked. "What?"

More shots came through the open hatch. Tanner made a quick judgment based on the path of the beams and rolled forward into the main cabin again. He'd only barely survived one three-way brawl. If he wanted to get control of this situation, he had to divide and conquer. Tanner crawled under the first rows of seats, twisted to gather himself up between the second and third rows, and waited for his chance.

Casey naturally piloted the lifeboat without any regard for his passengers. In fact, as far as Tanner could tell, the pirate deliberately took hard turns for no other reason than to make life difficult. Tanner hung on and waited, unsure if he had picked the best place to ambush Ezekiel or the worst.

His eyes fell on the back of the chair in front of him. Each seat held several modular survival kits: one filled with water, another with food, and a third with medical supplies. He unlatched the bottom module, filling his other hand with a kilo and a half of first aid.

Ezekiel emerged on the wrong side of the center row. Tanner threw the medical kit right at Ezekiel's head as the agent spotted the danger in the corner of his eye. Ezekiel jerked back. His gun went off accidentally, blasting a hole in the seats while Tanner jumped at him. The pair fell against the next row.

Tanner got his hands over the barrel of the laser pistol and twisted it away. Ezekiel drove his other hand into Tanner's face. The weapon went off wildly, and then the automated voice of the lifeboat announced a bigger problem: "Warning: Safety settings deactivated. Artificial gravity deactivated."

The lifeboat promptly lurched almost ninety degrees to one side. Tanner and Ezekiel flew across the cabin and hit the opposite bulkhead hard. *Oh you son of a bitch*, thought Tanner as he held onto a seat for dear life.

The bright side of Casey's dirty move was that it cost Ezekiel his weapon. The pistol and the smashed-open first aid kit clattered around the cabin wildly as the lifeboat lurched from side to side. The open hatch banged away, too, making a terrible racket. Tanner ignored all that in favor of climbing from one seat to the next toward the forward cabin.

He saw Ezekiel doing much the same thing. Tanner seemed to have the lead in the hard path toward their mutual enemy, but he had no idea how he'd get around that slamming hatch without it smashing him, let alone how to get control of the whole situation. "Damn it," he spat as the lifeboat tilted sharply again. He looked at Ezekiel until he saw the other man's eyes. "Okay, fine!" Tanner snapped. "Casey first!"

Ezekiel might have nodded. Tanner couldn't tell. Regardless, they made it to the front rows. Tanner reached out to grab a handhold on the forward bulkhead in one hand and the unfastened hatch with his other. Ezekiel gave him a wary look. Then, as the lifeboat steadied out between lurching turns, the agent jumped through the open portal.

Tanner heard thumps and grunts inside, but he focused on the hatch. Securing it in the open position took only a moment of relatively steady flight, which Ezekiel seemed to provide. With the hatch settled, Tanner flung himself inside, fighting vertigo and fatigue along with all of his previous injuries.

His two enemies beat on one another on the port side of the cabin. Ezekiel enjoyed the advantage of fighting a man belted into his seat, but Casey still managed a significant defense. Tanner looked over the consoles. The starboard side chair offered all the same controls as the port chair. He promptly got behind the virtual wheel.

The viewscreens revealed the city skyline all too closely. The lifeboat flew so low that it would have hit any number of towers by now were it not for the automated collision override. Tanner felt surprised Casey hadn't killed that function, too, but he probably had his hands full evading the swarm of police aircars zooming in around them.

"Computer! Navigation! Local map!" Tanner demanded, and added as he saw the screen come to life, "Point of origin!"

"Don't get any ideas!" warned Ezekiel. Casey planted another punch in Ezekiel's gut, putting a little more space between himself and the agent. Tanner turned and shoved Ezekiel forward onto Casey's side of the helm console with both hands. Ezekiel's elbow and face smacked into the panel as hard as Tanner hoped. Screens cracked and blinked out. The two men fought on. Helm control now fell entirely to the starboard console.

Tanner spotted Uriel Shipyards on the map. That gave him his bearings. He knew exactly where he needed to go from there. Only when he reached out and assumed manual control did he remember the one awful wrinkle in this plan: *Oh, right. I suck at this.*

The lifeboat lurched wildly once again, this time out of operator error. Ezekiel fell against Tanner's seat. A police aircar flashed into view as the lifeboat swung around in the sky. Tanner yelped, turned to avoid a crash and instead managed to clip the tall trees of some apartment tower's rooftop garden.

"What the fuck are you doing?" Casey all but shrieked.

Tanner ignored him. He glanced down at Ezekiel, saw the agent rising again, and brutally dropped his left elbow down on his enemy's face. Once more, the lifeboat jerked with the careless motions of its helmsman, which ultimately contributed more to Ezekiel's concussion than the elbow. The agent's head hit the deck hard, leaving him dazed on his back.

Casey tried to take over the helm. The lifeboat's computers objected. "Your console is damaged," said a voice. "Use starboard helm control."

He saw the focus on Tanner's face. The lifeboat flew lower than ever. "Pull up!" Casey demanded. "Are you fucking insane? Pull up!"

"I came all this way and committed three kinds of treason just to see you, and *now* you ask me if I'm crazy?" Tanner shot back.

More police aircars swarmed in. The chase through the skies caused no particular disruption to traffic on the ground, though pedestrians looked up in surprise as the parade of vehicles soared by.

The screen on Tanner's right showed the lifeboat closing in on their destination. In spite of himself, Tanner felt a grin on his face. Kelly might have been right. Perhaps he only needed a chance to do things for his own reasons. He glanced at Casey and saw his foe trying to find some sort of opportunity to take control of the situation again. Tanner's grin turned into a full smile. "Hey," he said, "you think all this is gonna hurt my university applications?"

"Aw, the hell with this," Casey decided. He had to take the gamble. As soon as he saw Tanner's eyes turn back to the controls, Casey unlatched his harness. He rose up to vanquish his enemy and take control of the helm once more.

Tanner turned the lifeboat into a steep descent. Casey felt his stomach lurch, half with gravity and half in fear as he realized Tanner fully meant to land the boat. The younger man glanced at him one last time. "Figure I'd better warn you: I'm a real shitty pilot."

Casey threw himself back into the seat, hooking his arms into the safety harness. "Struts!" he shouted. "Landing struts!"

"Oh, right!"

• • •

Occasionally, Usman missed working among the stars, but his new life on Uriel fulfilled far more of his needs. He could provide for his family here and look out for his people. If he'd stayed on Qal'at Khalil rather than fleeing to Archangel on that packet ship a few years ago, he would doubtlessly have been a victim of the civil war.

He naturally wanted to pitch in for the king and Prince Khalil. Other responsibilities took priority. His family needed him. So did many of his fellow refugees. He found work with a parts supplier outside the shipyards soon after arriving, where he could provide for his family and improve his English. Soon after settling on Uriel, Usman became something of a community leader.

The last few months offered him a chance to serve in the great conflict, however minor that role might seem. After his apparent death, Prince Khalil emerged alive once more to fight on. Archangel formally recognized him as the rightful head of state and gave him control of all of Hashem's shuttered embassies and consulates, including the one that lay only a few kilometers away from Usman's previous job. He signed on as a consulate guard without hesitation.

Only once did his work present actual danger. Only once, for a short stretch, did he have to deal with tense crowds and angry local authorities that had to be reminded of the rights and privileges of diplomatic missions.

It began when a lifeboat fell out of the sky and crashed through the main gates of the consulate, sliding to a halt in the middle of the courtyard.

The alarm wailed almost as an afterthought. Usman and his fellow guards surrounded the vessel with weapons drawn while others evacuated the area. He shouted commands in English and Arabic, using the small loudspeakers built into his epaulets to amplify his voice. "Power the vehicle down and come out with your hands up!" he instructed. "Do not make any sudden moves! We will shoot to kill!"

Local police aircars swarmed the area. A couple of them flew overhead into the compound, but quickly pulled back. One of Usman's subordinates asked what should be done about them. Usman shook his head. For all he knew, they might soon need the aid.

The lifeboat's engines spun down as Usman demanded. He and his guards waited until the hatch on Usman's side opened. They kept their weapons ready.

A pair of silhouettes staggered through the exit. As they emerged into the light of day, Usman saw blood and scrapes and other signs of terrible struggle. The first man, older than the other, collapsed in the dirt. The second raised his arms as instructed. In one hand, he held up a slightly crumpled, embossed envelope bearing golden script.

"My name is Tanner Malone," said the battered young man. "I need you to contact Prince Khalil right away."

Epilogue: Swagger

> *"Ezekiel's guys say they were supposed to round up the rest of the crew and wait for his orders, but they won't explain what sort of orders they expected. We can't help but notice they're all security agents. This is looking seriously dodgy even for a covert op. Somebody from on high better come down here, and I don't mean so they can make problems 'disappear,' you get me?"*
>
> --AGENT BREWER, INTERNAL MINISTRY COMMUNICATIONS, AUGUST 2279

"The first response to this is critical, Victor," Andrea pressed. She stood before the chief of staff with her arms out in exasperation. "I'm scheduled to go on in fifteen minutes. You know how bad it's gonna look if we cancel."

"We're not canceling," replied Victor.

"Then you have to let me into the room." Andrea pointed to the door to the president's office. "You can't send me out to block and dodge questions."

"We need someone to block and dodge."

"No, the president needs his press secretary out in front of this!"

"He can't send you out there looking like you're in the dark—"

"I *am* in the dark!"

"—and there's concern about how you could handle this."

"How I could—? Oh for the love of God, Victor, it was an on and off fling for a few months that ended three years ago! I haven't spoken to him since the Assembly. This is a crisis here! You think I give a damn about my personal life right now?" Again, she pointed to the door. "I gave up my Senate seat to get him elected. Do you seriously question my loyalty?"

The older man looked at the time on his holocom. They'd only been out in the entryway for a couple of minutes. "We only get one shot at a first response," said Victor. "There's no time to put you into the loop on every detail—not that we're going to do that regardless. This was all covert operation stuff. It should have *stayed* a covert operation."

"That's not something you can tell the public. They want answers."

"No! No, they don't," Victor snapped. "They don't *want* to know the things we do to keep them safe, Andrea. They want to have their cake and eat it, too, and so here we are. They only get upset when they see into the kitchen."

Andrea shook her head. "Fine. Here we are," she repeated back to him. "Let me in."

"You're really up for this?"

"When have I ever backed down from my responsibilities?"

"Okay," he relented. "We're still working on a response. We spent the whole first hour confirming everything that happened."

"Yeah, I know. Everything I've heard so far has been from the media and the statements released by the Hashemite consulate."

Releasing another frustrated breath, Victor opened the door to the president's office. Shouts and tension seemed to spill out of the room as he led her inside.

Andrea took careful note of everyone in the president's office as they entered. Aguirre stood behind his desk, looking as angry as she'd ever seen him. David Kiribati stood nearby with a couple of men in suits she guessed were part of his staff. She saw one of the general counsel's deputies—and not, Andrea considered, the general counsel herself. Defense Minister Robert Kilpatrick took up another spot near the desk. She did not see Theresa Cotton or the vice president, nor any other cabinet ministers, and most notably not anyone from the military.

Ascension Hall never lacked for officers. Even if no one of flag rank could be present, someone in uniform would at least be here to hold up an open holocom screen for one admiral or another. The absence said much about the situation.

"…we have clear legal standing to charge Malone for any of the deaths in this, even if it's Casey who pulled the trigger," explained the counsel deputy.

"What the hell good does that do us right now?" grunted Kilpatrick.

"I think Claire here is considering deflection," Aguirre replied with a patronizing glare to the defense minister. "It's useful to drag your accuser down with you in a situation like this, or so I've heard. I wouldn't know for sure, though. I've only been in professional politics all my life." He looked up as Victor and Andrea walked in, then held up his hand to silence further conversation. He waited until Victor nodded. "I'm glad to see you here, Andrea," he said.

"Yes, sir," Andrea replied. "We've got a press conference in less than fifteen minutes. Obviously it's going to look bad if we cancel. What's the plan?"

She watched the exchange of glances around the room: Aguirre and Kiribati, Aguirre and Victor, others. Kiribati cleared his throat.

"You understand, Andrea, we're still assessing the extent of all this," he explained warily. "We don't want to discuss any classified information that we don't absolutely have to address."

"The media already has video of Casey being brought into the Hashemite consulate, sir," pointed out Andrea. "They have a continuous line of action leading back to the shipyard. The consulate hasn't put out an official statement yet, but they will."

"Yeah, like that video isn't a statement itself," grumbled Kiribati.

"Then do I confirm that it's really Casey?" asked Andrea.

"It's him," said Aguirre, fuming. He shared another sharp glance with Kiribati. "He was a vital source of information. An intelligence asset, nothing more. We had him under lock and key all along." He looked around at the other faces in the room. "Obviously the story won't end there. We'll take that as it comes. This is where we start."

"Sir, the more I know, the better I can handle questions," explained Andrea with a cool, controlled voice. "If I deflect or deny something that later turns out to be true, whatever comes after that will sound less credible."

The defense minister snorted. "Oh, there'll be more." Kilpatrick scowled at Aguirre. "We can tell the media and the public whatever we want. They can buy it hook, line, and sinker. This still comes down to what Khalil and his people believe, and they're not going to care what Ascension Hall and the president say through a press conference. They'll get it straight from the horse's mouth."

"You might want to consider closing your own mouth, Robert," suggested Victor.

"That's what we tell the media," Aguirre spoke up again, silencing the other two. "Casey was held as a source of intel. The Ministry had him under guard the whole time."

"I've gotten questions about how Ta—how Malone got in there," she corrected. "I assume I can say we're still assessing that?" She looked to Kiribati. "Casualties, too?"

"There have been casualties," the spymaster confirmed. "Still assessing."

Andrea nodded. She didn't relay the other questions she'd gotten from the media—the truly unsettling ones that reached back to before the war. She knew enough now to do what was necessary. "I think I can take it from here. Best not to start late."

"We planned on putting Claire up on the podium," said Victor. "We could send you in together."

"No, I think it's best if I go alone," Andrea replied, looking to Claire. "If you send out lawyers right from the start, they'll smell blood." She saw reluctant nods all around the room.

No one seemed to notice her subtle shift in language. Before today, Andrea addressed every crisis and scandal in terms of "we."

"Emphasize Malone's crimes," said Claire. "He violently broke into a top secret Ministry site and disrupted an operation that he couldn't possibly have understood. He got people killed and hurt in all this."

"I understand," said Andrea. She looked at the time. "I should go."

"Good luck," said Aguirre. "And Andrea: thank you."

"Yes, sir," she replied as she left.

Andrea headed straight for Ascension Hall's well-appointed briefing room. Victor walked with her, saying something about delaying answers, the president waiting to speak directly with Prince Khalil, and perhaps a bit about extraditions. She mumbled her acknowledgment. Outside the briefing room, Andrea adjusted her small lapel pin microphone, tying it into her personal holocom and, from that, to the briefing room's speakers. Victor wished her luck and walked to the rear entrance of the briefing room to watch.

Exactly one hundred seats spread out in an arc around a small stage rising only one meter above the floor. The podium was more of a prop and a point of reference than a high-tech media device. It also created a small but psychologically significant anchor and shield for anyone who might need it in front of so many faces and cameras. That alone made it a vital implement for the briefing room. Not everyone up in front of the press was as self-assured and accustomed to public speaking as Andrea.

Given the task at hand, anyone could have understood if she stood behind the podium. She did not. Andrea felt far too angry to be afraid. She walked onto the stage a full two minutes before the scheduled start time and stood clear of the podium without a holo screen for notes or any last checks with her aides.

The briefing room held considerably more than a hundred guests that afternoon. A standing-room-only crowd awaited her, talking animatedly amongst themselves, listening to news over their earpieces, and watching screens from their holocoms. The questions began as soon as she appeared, and only intensified once she stood on the stage.

"Andrea, how does Ascension Hall explain the presence of Casey at—?"

"When will the president speak on what happened on Uriel this morning?"

"Has the president spoken with Prince Khalil?"

"Andrea, Hashem's consular has alleged that Casey carried out the pirate raid on Qal'at Khalil on behalf of the Ministry of Intelligence. What is Ascension Hall's response?" That one came through the din loud and clear, as if everyone quieted down for it on cue.

Andrea blinked. This was the second time she'd heard this today. The first time came in private exactly one minute before she demanded to see Victor outside the president's office. Either the Raphael Tribune was giving up on its potential for an exclusive, or someone else already had the same scoop.

"Andrea, did you know about this?" someone asked in the pause created by the last question.

"No, Eduardo, I did not," Andrea answered, grateful for the opening. "Ladies and gentlemen, I've come straight from the president's office." She paused only long enough to make sure she had everyone's attention—and their cameras. The questions ceased. "I came into a meeting about this matter between the president, his chief of staff, Deputy Counsel Claire Murphy, Defense Minister Robert Kilpatrick, and Intelligence Minister David Kiribati. No other cabinet ministers were present, nor any representative of the navy. It was my first discussion of any regard to these matters."

The reporters all listened attentively. No one interrupted. Andrea spotted Victor along with several other Ascension Hall staffers. None of them looked alarmed or surprised by her preamble. It made sense that she might start out this way, if only to get herself on solid ground. Presumably, this would be a long, rough press conference.

"There is not enough lipstick in the world for this pig. I hereby resign in protest and outrage. You can route any questions you have of me personally through my lawyer. I quit." Andrea pinched the lapel pin that held her mic, dropped it, and strode off the stage right through to the back of the room amid an even louder storm of questions.

Any other time, she'd have taken the side exit, which wouldn't have subjected her to crowds. Today, she wanted to be in the public eye as long as possible. If any reporters wanted to follow her all the way out to her car and then to her home, she felt perfectly fine with that. She might even call to have dinner delivered for them.

The cacophony of voices dimmed as she closed to within a meter of the shocked chief of staff at the back of the room. She glanced at Victor only once and said, "The difference between me and your boss is that I stab people from the front."

• • •

Matters spiraled further downward over the next eight hours. Kiribati watched one senator after another call for a full investigation on the senate floor and in the media. Most of them spoke of impeachment. All four of Archangel's planetary governors carefully evaded any opportunity to support the president. The navy naturally refused to comment, but no one could miss the cold shoulders from the officers on staff at Ascension Hall. Kiribati knew, without a doubt, that Admiral Yeoh spoke with them all personally.

Kiribati knew where this would all lead, too. Khalil had Casey, Malone, and Ezekiel in his consulate. Even if Malone had no records or evidence—even if Casey and Ezekiel both died in the consulate lobby—the trail had been uncovered. All anyone had to do was follow it back far enough. Plenty of interested parties would do whatever it took.

The Minister of Intelligence remained at Ascension Hall exactly long enough to demonstrate his loyalty and his resolve to his "co-conspirators" as Senator Castillo called them in a press conference on the steps of the Senate. He advised and commiserated. He helped devise contingency plans and assured the others of legal defenses and political deniability. Then, as time inevitably eroded the intensity of emotions and his allies accepted that this would not be settled in a single day, Kiribati found his opportunity to "head back to his office" and "shore up his own side of all this."

Ascension Hall provided several discreet exits. Kiribati knew them all well. He'd dismissed his aides hours earlier, but he wouldn't be leaving alone. Per standard protocols, the Minister never traveled anywhere without an armed escort. Kiribati took great care in the selection of his protection detail.

Unfortunately, as he left the president's offices, he didn't find his usual bodyguards. He knew only one of the faces that greeted him in the hallway outside. "Hello, Minister Kiribati," Vanessa Rios said with a broad smile.

"Agent Rios," Kiribati replied, frowning. He looked around at the others. "What are you doing here?"

"I'm the head of your protection detail. Temporarily," she added. "Your regular guys are unavailable. The evening shift got some sudden transfer to Gabriel, for what I don't know. Your swing shift guys both got suspended just today on an abuse of authority complaint—ugly stuff, really. Sounds like bullshit to me, but you know the regs. I'm sure it'll get cleared up in time.

"What's really crazy is Taylor and Mario," she continued, feigning a perplexed frown. "They both took a tumble down the stairs a little while ago. Right here in Ascension Hall. Taylor broke his ankle, and Mario, gosh, did you know he's allergic to most common painkillers? He's going to be out for weeks.

"On the bright side, I'm not on any assignments. I have all the time in the world to devote to this. And I got these nice gentlemen here from the Investigative Service and these other fine officers from Naval Intelligence to help out." Her polite smile faded as she added, "We'll make sure to keep you safe and get you *everywhere you're supposed to be.*"

• • •

"With this decision comes the ascension of Vice President Julio Escobedo to the presidency for the duration of President Aguirre's trial. He was sworn in directly after the impeachment vote in the Senate. Ministers Kiribati and Kilpatrick will likewise be replaced until a verdict is reached. Insiders and experts warn that it may be months before the first day of hearings.

"The vote to impeach President Aguirre and Ministers Kiribati and Kilpatrick comes as little surprise. What stood out this morning was the decision to hold Minister Kiribati in custody pending the outcome of the full trial by the Senate. Given the sensitive and diplomatically embarrassing nature of the charges—treason, acts of undeclared war, violation of treaties, evasion of Senate oversight, and the aid and abetting of interstellar piracy among them—many voices in the Senate caution that more closed-door hearings are likely on the horizon.

"On the interstellar front, an Assembly vote led by Quilombo and New Canaan quashed a motion by NorthStar to throw out recent legislation forcing NorthStar's transition to statehood. Quilombo's ambassador and others argued that revelations of President Aguirre's alleged misconduct and conspiracies do not mitigate NorthStar's own misdeeds.

"Regardless, this series of events has renewed calls for high court with jurisdiction over disputes between Union states and interstellar organizations."

--BOB NORRIS, RAPHAEL PUBLIC MEDIA, AUGUST 2279

"I believe when this is over, they will grant you some form of pardon or amnesty," said Prince Khalil. He stood with Tanner in the consulate's courtyard, looking over freshly-repaired concrete walkways and newly-replaced garden plots. The mess from Tanner's arrival took a couple of weeks to fix. "The fact that safe passage was expressly assured speaks to President Escobedo's eagerness to put all of this to rest."

"I hope so," said Tanner.

Khalil turned to look at him. He realized Tanner's eyes were on the skyline beyond the consulate's walls. The younger man wore casual, inconspicuous clothes. He stood next to a pair of bags—one full of personal effects stowed away before his day at the shipyards, the other a collection of clothes bought for him by the consulate staff. "I wish there was more that I could do," said the prince. "You have done so much for us."

Tanner blinked. "More you could do? Your Highness, I couldn't ask for more than you've done. Hell, I put you in an ugly bind. Your war isn't over, and you need allies."

"You gambled on my integrity, and the integrity of your senate," Khalil replied, shaking his head. "To continue on in alliance with Aguirre and his cabal after all they had done to my people would have been unthinkable. Besides, I have cemented other alliances since our day in the Assembly. My brothers have only three worlds left between them. We will win, with or without further aid from Archangel."

"You're not worried about what will happen if Aguirre wins the trial?"

"Not at all. I do not see how he could. Your Senate clearly understands the need to resolve all of this to come back into the Union's fold."

"Aguirre didn't put too much importance on our standing in the Union, Your Highness."

"In the short term, no. In the long term? Even he did not wish to make Archangel a pariah state."

"Huh. 'Pariah.' There's a word," Tanner thought out loud.

"I do not think that will be your fate."

"Hopefully not for long, anyway. But I can't stay here."

They spotted the incoming shuttle as it broke smoothly from the lanes of sparse air traffic along the city's skyline. Its size made it stand out from the airvans and other flyers, but the change in course confirmed its identity.

"I wish we could have provided a proper reward," said Khalil. "We gave only a fraction of what my father promised for Casey's head. Not that he'll meet the sort of fate my father intended anytime soon. He has more use for us as a live prisoner than as a dead man. For now, at least. Do not worry," Khalil added. "If he is pronounced dead again, it will be because I stood as witness."

"I believe it," said Tanner. "As for the reward, I didn't expect so much as it is. That'll cover travel, longevity treatments, my parents' debts, non-resident tuition… Hell, I might even manage to be a full-time student without needing a job to supplement."

Khalil chuckled. "I see your reward is well spent already."

Tanner shrugged and offered a grin in return. "Not like I can collect the money in my bank account. I can't access that while I've got charges pending, free passage or no."

The shuttle's engines filled their silence as it settled to the ground. The Union fleet seal stood out brightly along its grey hull. A large hatch on its side opened up to reveal a pair of fleet officers. One wore a major's insignia and the red shoulder braid of the Union fleet's diplomatic corps. The other, a marine lieutenant with a welcome and familiar face, smiled at Tanner in a small breach of military bearing.

He smiled back, then winced in sudden memory. "Aw, shit," he grumbled. "I gotta get a tuxedo, too. Keep forgetting that."

Khalil clapped him on the shoulder and shook his hand. "You will visit your parents when you are finished with the fleet interviews? And then on to university?"

"That's the plan," Tanner said as they started walking.

"And what then?" asked the prince.

"I don't know," said Tanner. "But I'm gonna be happy."

Acknowledgments

As usual, I owe thanks to many people for their help with this book. To all my "beta readers," thank you so much, especially Zach and Matt D. whose input went above and beyond the call of duty. It's not even fair to call it a duty; you were simply being good friends, and I'm so grateful.

Once again, I need to thank Lee Moyer and Venetia Charles for always making my books look so good and for being so patient with every transition and every question that took a while to answer.

A few points in this book had me nervous as I wrote them. Several times, I went to a closed filter of friends on Facebook to pitch the ideas and ask if I was crazy or nonsensical or silly. The support and reasoned input I found there was incredibly valuable.

And in case it wasn't clear from the dedication, I'm so grateful to Erica for all her support. Many times, I wandered out of my office to babble about something I was considering for this book. She almost always said the same thing, and was right every time: "Just write it and see how it looks when you're done." That's really the best advice I can pass on to anyone looking for guidance in their own writing.

About the Author

Like many Seattleites, Elliott Kay is a refugee from Los Angeles. He is a former Coast Guardsman with a Bachelor's in History. Elliott has survived a motorcycle crash, serious electric shocks, severe seasickness, summers in Phoenix and winters in Seattle.

He can be reached by email at elliottkaybooks@gmail.com or on Twitter @elliottkaybooks. He maintains a blog at elliottkay.com.

To cut to the chase: Hell yes, there will be another book in this series.

Printed in Poland
by Amazon Fulfillment
Poland Sp. z o.o., Wrocław